THE

KING'S SON

A CROWN, SO EASILY WON,
CAN BE LOST IN A HEARTBEAT

Darren Harris

JOUSTING KNIGHT PUBLISHING

ISBN-13: 978-1-7399696-0-8

This novel is entirely a work of fiction although some of the historical details and characters are factual. Persons named within the script are fictional and are the product of the author's imagination. Apart from those in the public domain, any similarity to persons past or living is coincidental. Representative of the era, the novel contains a small amount of strong language.

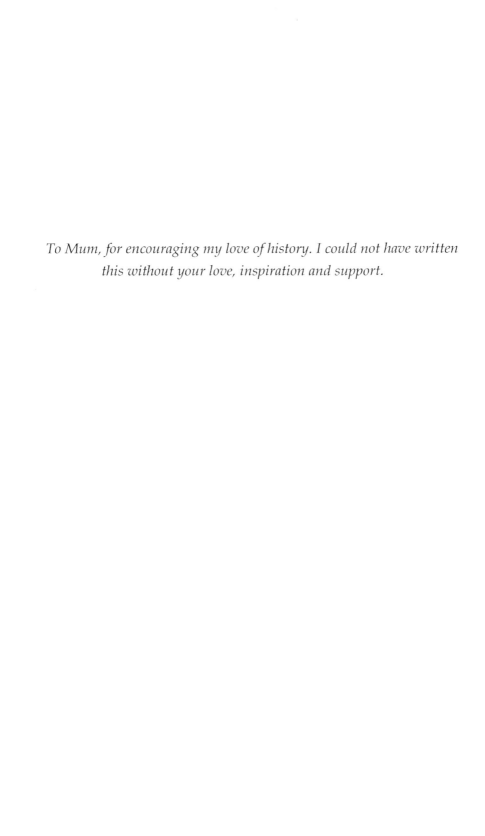

To Mum, for encouraging my love of history. I could not have written this without your love, inspiration and support.

Plantagenet. The most royal of names. A name borne by fourteen kings of England, no less. A name of status, power and wealth that was far too important to be found scrawled in oak gall ink upon the vellum leaves of a burial record in a tiny village in Kent. And yet there it was!

'Richard Plantagenet buried on the 22 day of December,
in the year of Our Lord 1550.'

He was not buried with the pomp and ceremony of a royal son, as befits one of his lineage. In accordance with his own wishes, he was buried in the churchyard of St Mary's in Eastwell, in a plot of land next to a lowly village priest, on a cold grey winter's day. It was a simple ceremony befitting a humble bricklayer; for that is how most people knew him, but I knew better. I knew the man and the truly remarkable life he had led, and I was not prepared to let that royal name or his story go unrecorded.

The priest looked at me with horror when I asked for the burial to be recorded under the name Plantagenet.

'It is treason!' he exclaimed.

But a gold sovereign soon soothed his fears and enabled his

quill hand to flow.

So now Richard Plantagenet lies beneath the shadow of St Mary's Church in a quiet corner of South East England, but his story must be told; a story of love, betrayal and a burning desire for revenge against the men who murdered his father and took his royal name.

*

Distant trees shimmered in the summer heat as the unflinching sun bore down harshly on the back of Richard's neck. The crude brimmed hat he had roughly fashioned out of straw that morning gave his neck little protection against the glaring mid-day sun. As he lay on the grass reading the book of hours Father Martin had lent him, Richard shifted irritably on his elbows, shuffling to a more comfortable reading position rather than moving to escape the glare of the sun. The contents of the precious book captivated him so much that he was almost oblivious to the heat. The ornate gold, red and black handwritten letters and elaborate pictures bursting from the pages in vibrant colours transfixed him. He soaked up every word, every sentence, the symbolism of every picture, pondering as he had done many times before the word of God. Richard had recited the Horae before him over and over many times but still he felt no closer to God. It worried him.

A shrill but distant scream broke Richard from his reverie. He sat bolt upright and scanned the landscape from the tower of St Mary's Church to the lake, and from the lake to the woods, but nothing caught his eye. He surveyed the scene for several minutes but nothing attracted his attention. Had he imagined it? He scanned the horizon carefully, studiously looking for any sign of movement or something that stood out, but saw nothing. He began to doubt himself and started to settle down to his book once more when he heard the distant shriek again. He raised his head, and then hearing the noise again, he quickly jumped to his feet and cast his gaze down the slope towards the woods on the other side of the lake. Through the trees, a brief movement caught his eye. Then flashes of colour flickered between the distant trees, dragging his gaze with them. Brown and black moving right to left, hardly discernible. Flashes of red, brown, white and green in pursuit. Someone was running through the woods and several others were chasing, closing in. Richard continued watching, trying to gauge what was happening. Was it a game? A muted but panicked scream suggested it was something more serious.

Richard cast his straw hat aside and ran down the slope as fast as his young legs would carry him. He sprinted towards the lake until his chest heaved with the exertion. Eventually he slowed to a walk, snatching quick shallow breaths as he approached the reeds at the edge of the dark forbidding waters. He cautiously made his way around the lake towards the woods, not sure what he would find or what he would do when he eventually got there. As he neared the edge of the woods his heart pounded in anticipation and nervous excitement. He found that, as his breathing gradually steadied, his hands were trembling involuntarily and his stomach became knotted with anxiety at the unknown prospect of what lay ahead. He walked through the trees, nervously pushing his way deeper and deeper into the woods, until he paused at the sound of laughter. Not the sound of fun and merriment, but a cruel, malicious laughter.

From behind the safety of an ancient, gnarled oak tree, Richard could see that a small boy of about ten or eleven was cornered by three older boys. The pink, oval-faced young boy, with a mop of thick black hair dangling over his eyes, had backed himself up against a tree. He panted, gasped, and stared wide eyed at the three boys who surrounded him, not sure whether to try to run again or just curl up and hope they would leave him alone.

'Let's throw him in the lake,' the smallest of the three predators hollered in delight.

'Be fun to watch him drown,' one of the others added.

'I didn't chase him halfway across Eastwell just to throw him in a lake,' the oldest boy said with grim determination.

As the boy spoke Richard recognised the voice and realised who the three boys were.

'Tie him to that tree. I need to test my throwing skills,' the oldest of the Kempe brothers sneered as he spat out the words.

The two younger brothers obediently grabbed the young boy as he cowered in fear. The Kempe brothers were sons of Thomas Kempe, Lord of the Manor of Ollantigh, a few miles from Eastwell. Their father owned most of the land in the area and they revelled in the power that gave them. A power they openly abused without fear of consequence or punishment.

Most children, and indeed most adults, would not wish to cross the path of the three Kempe brothers, Thomas, William and John, let alone upset them and incite the wrath of their father. Thomas Kempe the elder was a brutal man who fiercely protected his children regardless of what they did, whether right or wrong. A year ago he had a man hung by his wrists from a tree and flogged until his back was flayed of skin. The man was left hanging by his wrists for a day and a night as a warning to others and no one in the village dared to cut him down until Thomas Kempe allowed it. The man's crime? To push sixteen-year-old Thomas Kempe away from his son then wrap himself around his nine-year-old boy to prevent Thomas Kempe from beating him to a bloody pulp for staring at him in the marketplace. Richard of Eastwell's conscience, however, would not allow him to walk away leaving a young boy to be terrorised, despite the fear that now welled up inside him at the prospect of facing the Kempe brothers.

The young rosy-cheeked, dark-haired boy sobbed uncontrollably as William held him steady and John tethered his wrists behind his back with a leather thong. The siblings stood aside to leave their older brother a clear target. Thomas pulled a knife from the sheath at his waist. He steadily drew back his arm, readying himself to throw the knife at the sobbing boy. Thomas aimed to hit the tree trunk between the boy's legs, as close as possible to the genitals without actually hitting flesh. However, should the knife draw blood then so be it! It was all part of the game of chance, and this boy had been unlucky enough to be caught alone when the Kempe brothers were out looking for sport, so he was now part of their game.

Thomas chuckled to himself then focused on his target. He steadied his breathing and felt the blade's weight balanced between his fingers. He watched the boy squirm against the tree and derived immense pleasure from the futility of the boy's actions.

'You're likely to lose a bollock if you wriggle,' he mockingly advised the boy.

William and John giggled their agreement while the boy continued to sob hysterically.

'Simon, there you are!' Richard shouted across to the sobbing boy as he stepped out from behind a tree. 'Father Martin has been looking for you everywhere. He sent me to find you, now come along, we must hurry back.'

The Kempe brothers stood and stared in amazement. The boy stopped sobbing and looked at Richard in surprise. His name was not Simon and he did not know Richard, but he realised that here was a chance to escape the fate the Kempe brothers had planned for him. Richard strode over to him and without untying the boy's wrists, turned him by the shoulders and pushed him towards a clearing between the trees. The boy did not need a second chance. With his hands still tethered behind him he walked briskly, heading deeper into the woods, and away from the Kempe brothers to safety.

'What in God's name do you think you're doing?' bellowed Thomas Kempe, seething fury evident on his crimson face. Richard turned to face him and was aware that the other two Kempe brothers now stood either side of him, waiting on Thomas' word to spring into action.

'I said what in God's name do you think you're doing?' Thomas bellowed even louder, his face turning purple as spittle was forced from his mouth in unbridled rage.

Richard watched a gob of spit dribble from Thomas' lips onto his chin. The veins pulsed on Thomas' temples and his puce-coloured face looked like it was about to explode. The furious Thomas did not wait for Richard's answer. He swiftly drew back his knife hand and unleashed the weapon with deadly speed and accuracy. The knife whistled through the air towards Richard's chest. Richard reacted by throwing his hands up and tensing his body as he anticipated the piercing blow to his chest. But the fatal blow never arrived. Instead Richard felt a thud and recoiled as the knife struck the book of hours he'd been carrying, only subconsciously aware of its presence, but that he now held out defensively in front of himself. The blade buried itself into the leather cover, piercing deep into the sacred text.

All four boys stood motionless, in disbelief that Richard remained unharmed and that the knife hadn't found its mark. It was Richard who gathered himself and sprang into action first, leaping at the nearest of the brothers. He swung the book of hours, with the knife still lodged in it, in a sweeping arc that caught William Kempe flush on the nose. William's nose cracked on impact and a spray of scarlet blood danced through the air, coming to rest across Richard's shoulder and right cheek.

The momentum from Richard's effort spun him completely round so that he faced away from William, who emitted a pained gurgling noise as he doubled over clutching his broken nose. John lunged at Richard's back and Thomas shrieked in abject rage as he ran at the boy who had hurt his brother. Richard felt John thump into his back and he stumbled forward, off balance. He staggered, his left hand brushing the ground, almost dropping to one knee, then regained his footing and instinctively began to run. He ran knowing that his life depended on it. He heard Thomas and John shouting behind him and knew that they were in pursuit. Richard swerved in and out of trees, jumping over fallen trunks and branches, stumbling through nettles and sharp briars in a desperate attempt to escape the pursuing Kempe brothers. He ran in blind panic feeling thorns and briars ripping his clothes and tearing into his flesh. His face, arms and legs became more and more scratched, his lungs swelled to bursting point with his exertions and his muscles burned. Yet he ran and ran, never more than a stone's throw ahead of the chasing pack. They pursued him relentlessly, even blood-soaked William joining in the hunt, his rage and the chance of retribution driving him on.

The Kempes chased Richard through the woods, William directly behind and Thomas and John to either side, deliberately herding him and driving him forwards knowing that he would soon be forced to exit the woods and be penned in at the edge of Eastwell Lake. Richard tried to swerve left or right but each time he found himself heading towards Thomas or John and he was forced to turn and run forward again to escape them. The Kempes hooted and jeered as they drove their prey closer and closer to the edge of the wood where it met the lake. Richard, given no choice, kept on running, oblivious to the thorns and needle-sharp branches of shrubs and bushes that were ripping his skin as he stumbled and pushed his way through them.

Eventually the woods cleared and he ran out onto the open muddy bank of the lake. Before he had time to run along the shoreline of the lake, the three Kempe brothers emerged from the trees and walked towards him. Their faces seething with malevolent anger. Their teeth gritted and their fists clenched, they clearly intended to do him great harm. Richard, exhausted and still gasping for breath from his exertions, slowly backed through thick, lush reeds into the lake; terror welling up inside him and clawing at his entrails until he felt that his bowels were about to give way. He was fearful of drowning in the lake's deep dark waters but even more fearful of what the Kempe brothers were about to do to him. He clutched the book of hours to his chest, with Thomas Kempe's knife still lodged deep inside, and began to recite a prayer as he felt the water rise higher and higher up his legs and waist as he backed into the dark murky lake. The Kempes surrounded him at the water's edge but Richard kept backing in, deeper and deeper, until the water was up to his chest and he stood, temporarily out of their reach, with the book of hours held aloft above his head. Sunlight reflected off the water and although he could feel the heat of the August sun on his face, it was nothing compared to the cold chill of the lake that began seeping into his body and the icy fingers of fear that clutched at his stomach.

The brothers did not follow Richard into the water, and for the time being he was safe, although he could not remain in the lake indefinitely so he turned and began to wade across it in an attempt to escape them. As he slowly edged across the lake the water rose higher until it was up to his chin. Another step and he was on tip-toe now. Water splashed across his face and entered his mouth and nostrils. He choked and spluttered, momentarily contemplating returning to shore, but from the corner of his eye he saw William, blood-spattered, staring at him, eyes wide with fury, so he continued to wade across praying that the water would not get any deeper. His prayers were in vain, as with each step Richard realised that the slippery sediment beneath his feet sloped gently towards the centre of the lake, where it was probably deeper than his height. He was trapped, as the only way to reach the other side of the lake before the three brothers could run around it would be to cross through the deeper centre. Richard could not swim and the thought of drowning terrified him only slightly less than the thought of walking out of the lake into the hands of the Kempe brothers.

Richard shivered, whether from cold or fear he was not sure. What he was sure of was that he had to reach the opposite side of the lake before any of the Kempes. They were still gathered at the shore by the woods, certain that he would eventually give up and come out of the water. They jeered and teased him.

'Can't the priest's bastard son swim?' William mocked. 'Maybe he should have spawned you with a duck instead of getting a pig pregnant.'

All three howled with laughter. It was common knowledge

that Richard was Father Martin's bastard child, for Father Martin favoured him and gave him expensive books, like the book of hours he now held aloft in a vain attempt to keep it dry.

'Your precious book is ruined, little piglet,' Thomas yelled across the lake. 'Give me back my blade or I'll cut you with it. Maybe I'll slice some bacon off you and we can have it for supper.' With that, all three Kempes roared with laughter again.

Richard had known the rumours about Father Martin being his father. He had been teased by the other children in Eastwell about it for as long as he could remember. Once he even asked Father Martin if it was true, but Father Martin had said that his holy orders prevented him from having children. This was not in itself a denial so Richard had continued to press for an answer, but Father Martin would not concede. However, Richard found that he was not disappointed; he could have done far worse than having the kindly Father Martin as his father. He wished the priest was here now to help him out of this predicament.

Richard shivered as the coldness of the lake penetrated deep inside him and the dark water lapped over his face. He found himself bouncing on his tiptoes to try to keep his face out of the water but this churned up the sediment on the floor of the lake, releasing foul-smelling gases which rose to the surface in streams of bubbles to burst around him. His efforts were in vain as the green-brown water washed over his face and into his mouth and nose, making him cough and choke. But the more he bounced the more he was able to gasp in a mouthful of air every time his face bounced above the surface of the water and hold his breath every time his face sank back below the water again.

'Come on out, priest spawn, and I might let you live. I'll even tell you which whore is your real mother,' Thomas Kempe goaded.

Richard ignored the jeers and insults and began to bounce rhythmically – breathe in, bounce, breathe out. Breathe in, bounce, breathe out. Bouncing on the tip of his toes slowly but steadily along the bottom of the lake, able to just take in a mouthful of fetid air each time before his face sank below the water again. Occasionally he choked and spluttered but he gradually worked his way across towards the centre of the lake. Breathe, hold, bounce, release. Richard passed the midpoint and could see salvation in the green banks at the edge of the dark water. The Kempes began to sprint around the lake to head him off at the far side. So long as he could keep his footing on the greasy sediment at the bottom of the lake he would be out of the water and escape to safety before any of the brothers could reach him. As Richard crawled out of the water at the far side of the lake, still holding the book of hours above his head, he heard a boy call out.

'Down there!'

Richard looked up to see the oval-faced, dark-haired boy he had saved from the Kempes standing at the top of the slope overlooking the lake. The mop of thick black hair still dangled over his eyes. He pointed down at Richard by the water's edge. A group of mounted men, mail and armour gleaming in the sunlight with banners unfurled, watched from the top of the slope. As Richard stood and stared at them transfixed, he did not realise that his inactivity was costing him valuable time to escape. The Kempe brothers, unaware of the watching horsemen, finally caught up with him.

William was the first to strike, punching Richard in the side of the head, sending him sprawling back into the water. Pain jolted through Richard's temple and his ear throbbed where the blow landed. He staggered but before he could rise to his feet Thomas followed up with a vicious kick to his stomach and William followed this up with a kick to his ribs. Richard gasped and tried to suck in air but the wind had been knocked out of him and his lungs seemed unable to function. He retched violently, spewing lake water from his mouth. John joined in with the other two Kempes and all three repeatedly rained down savage blows and kicks onto Richard's head and body.

Richard was almost paralysed with shock and pain. The only reaction his battered body would allow as he knelt at the water's edge was to try to shield himself with the book of hours and his spare hand. His efforts were wasted as blow after blow landed and he tasted the ferrous saltiness of blood in his mouth, felt his lips split and bloat, and his face, head, back and ribs throb with a pulsating pain that seemed to emanate from, and into every part of his body.

He felt himself shoved forward and a weight pressed between his shoulder blades as one of the Kempe boys stood on his back and forced him under the water. He gulped for air but only swallowed water. Blind panic took over and he thrashed around furiously then desperately attempted to save himself by pushing his body upwards against the foot on his back. He did not have the strength to throw off the weight forcing him down and he felt the air gush from his mouth as he exerted himself. He tried to hold the last of his breath in, but it seeped away, bubble by bubble, and finally he felt the last of the precious bubbles trickle from the corner of his mouth. Even his imminent death did not give him the final bout of strength needed to fight against the weight pressing down on his back and force his head back above the surface of the water. And so, as he felt his life slowly ebb away until all was black, peace descended and Heaven finally beckoned.

he sun was setting as the king and his army approached the town of Leicester from the north. They crossed the River Soar over two narrow bridges situated downriver from the town. Animal bones, scraps of decaying sackcloth and remnants of broken clay vessels lay scattered or stuck out of the embankment of the river. A watermill clattered rhythmically in the distance to the west of the two bridges. On the small mud islands dotted along the river, reeds grew verdant and tall on soil made fertile by waste washed downriver from the town. Groups of pigs and dogs scavenged at the water's edge in the ever-decreasing daylight but they scattered at the noisy approach of men clad in leather and mail.

The king's army entered the northern suburb that sprawled beyond the town walls. Dyers and fullers occupied the land next to the river and the smell of stale urine used by the fullers in their trade permeated the warm August evening air. Men, women and children, seemingly oblivious to the pungent smell, lined the dusty road leading to the North Gate, many having left the narrow streets of the town to see their king close up. They jostled for position, while still keeping a respectful distance, wary of the armed men surrounding their sovereign.

A fiery orange glow warmed the western sky as King Richard, armoured and wearing a gold coronet, gave orders for his soldiers to set up camp in the fields outside the town walls. His captains repeated the orders and men began to spread out and set up tents and cooking fires in the fields surrounding the abbey to the northeast of the town. Women and children searched for firewood or went to buy food from the monks. Some inhabitants of the town ventured out towards the growing encampment, eager to sell their wares to the newly arrived soldiers and their camp followers.

The king stretched in his saddle to relieve the discomfort brought on by the day's ride from Nottingham. Amid the noise and bustle of soldiers encamping, hawkers selling their goods, and the general chatter of the people around them, King Richard spoke to his chamberlain, John Pilkington.

'Have my bed and chattels taken up to my room and have Lord Howard sent to me when he arrives.'

'Yes, Your Grace,' Pilkington replied before heading off to carry out the king's orders.

From his saddle, King Richard surveyed the busy scene around him in the fading light. His gaze moved from the campfires and tents that were being hastily erected in the adjoining fields, down along the crowd-lined narrow road towards the town gate where, he noticed, the walls on either side of the gate were in a ruinous state of repair and patched with mud and straw. Richard had originally intended to stay at Leicester Castle as he had done on his many previous visits to the town but he lamented, like the town walls, the castle had deteriorated in recent years and was now in need of much work to make it fit for a royal visit and able to accommodate the king's large retinue. John Pilkington had therefore arranged for the king to be lodged in the White Boar Inn, the largest of the town's inns and shrewdly named by its owner after the king's own heraldic device. Richard thought to himself that before his next visit to Leicester he would provide money for the upkeep of the town walls and also start repairs to his castle here. But for now, he had more pressing matters at hand.

As soon as he had received the news that Henry Tudor had landed with a group of English exiles and foreign mercenaries in Wales, he began preparations to meet the invasion. He sent messengers to Lord Stanley and Henry Percy, Earl of Northumberland, to meet him in Nottingham with as many supporters as they could rally. He would meet his eastern force, commanded by the Duke of Norfolk, and his southern force, commanded by Sir Robert Brackenbury, at Leicester.

Now at Leicester, and content that his army was encamped and preparations for feeding them were in hand, Richard patted his warhorse, White Surrey, gently on the neck and led his mounted retinue towards the town gate. People lined the route, cheering and waving their hats in the air as the king approached and rode past them. The North Gate to the town was a low and narrow entrance made even more cramped by the throng of townsfolk crowding either side of it. The people parted as Sir James Harrington, the king's standard bearer, led the way and ushered them aside. Even so, the North Gate was so narrow and so low that the horsemen could only enter the town in single file and each of the riders, including the king, had to duck his head as he passed through the gate.

Once inside the town walls the king rode through the cheering crowds gathered along the roadside. He went on past a large inn, timber-framed wattle and daub houses, past All Saint's Church, and past the Hospital of St John the Evangelist and St John the

Baptist. Crowds jostled for position along the High Street, filling every doorway and open space along the route, lining the road and standing in entrances to narrow alleyways between houses whose upper storeys jutted out into the street, blocking what little daylight remained. Children balanced high on adults' shoulders and to get a better view of their king, some men stood on the stone base of the High Cross where the High Street met Hot Gate, so called because it was where the town's common ovens were located. Lanterns and rushlights illuminated the scene. People hung out of every available window to get a glimpse of their king and cheered raucously as he acknowledged them with a casual wave of his hand or a kindly smile.

Before they reached the High Cross the king and his retinue turned at the wide timbered frontage of the White Boar Inn where they rode under the painted wooden sign and through the gatehouse entrance into the courtyard. Horses' hooves scattered dust from the dried, compacted earth of the courtyard and as they drew up alongside the inn's kitchen the armoured riders caught the smell of cooking fish and spices from the kitchen at the rear of the courtyard, mingled with the odour of horse dung from the nearby stable.

King Richard pulled White Surrey up outside the stable block and let out a small groan of discomfort as he swung his leg over the horse and slid off the padded wooden saddle to dismount. The group of nobles and knights accompanying him also dismounted and each handed the reins of his horse to a stable boy. There was a clatter of metal as squires helped the king and some of the nobles and knights to remove pieces of armour and carry away helmets and other items no longer needed by the men.

The mayor and aldermen of the town waited in the inn's

courtyard and greeted the king and nobles after they dismounted. The king spoke to each in turn as if they were old friends. He patted the mayor on the shoulder and thanked him for the welcome and for the hospitality of his town.

The innkeeper, a large pot-bellied man with a broad smile, rosy cheeks, and a mass of russet hair and beard that made his head look twice its actual size, hurried to meet the newly arrived guests. He removed his cap and bowed his head low as he approached the king.

'Welcome, Your Grace,' he said, finally looking up. 'May I show you to the hall where food and drink have been prepared for your arrival?'

The king smiled and nodded assent then followed the innkeeper to the spacious hall that was open to the wooden roof beams. The compacted mud floor was strewn thickly with freshly cut rushes that were interspersed with a scattering of herbs and flower petals to hide the smell of stale food, spilt ale, and urine from the innkeeper's dogs. Grey wood smoke spiralled from a newly lit fire burning in a central hearth, filling the space between the smoke-blackened beams before escaping out through a louvre in the roof. On this warm August evening a fire wasn't really necessary for warmth but the innkeeper had it lit as a sign of hospitality and to add extra light within the dim hall.

The king placed a gold coin between the innkeeper's sausage-like fingers. The rotund man nodded his thanks, barked orders to the waiting servants, bowed once more, and then excused himself, still beaming with an ear-to-ear grin as he left. The servants jolted into action and scurried about the hall, fetching wine or using the small fire in the central hearth to light reeds coated in animal fat, then using these to light tallow candles mounted in metal brackets around the hall. A ewerer poured water from a jug onto the king's hands. Another servant knelt with a bowl to catch the water as the king rinsed, while a third servant handed the king a cloth to dry his hands on. The servants then offered this service to each lord and knight in turn.

King Richard seated himself on a bench beside a large trestle and board table which ran down one side of the hall. The table had been covered in extremely fine embroidered white linen cloth especially for the royal visit. Richard's war council helped themselves to food and then seated themselves on benches around him; the Earl of Northumberland and the Earl of Lincoln to the king's right, Sir William Catesby and Sir Richard Ratcliffe to his left, and other nobles and knights facing the king with their backs to the hearth. Servants hurriedly poured small ale and wine for the assembled guests before withdrawing to the far edge of the hall, leaving the gathered dignitaries to eat, drink and talk.

Northumberland, dark haired and swarthy, his face dominated by a long pointed nose, reached out and took a slice of thickly cut bread off a platter. He took a knife from his belt and hooked himself a piece of smoked herring, placing it on his trencher. The church prohibited the eating of meat on Fridays but there was no shortage of fine food for the king's party. They started to fill their trenchers and feast on the supper provided. The king supped his ale. He did not eat but waited until all of his council were seated and eating before he spoke.

'Henry Tudor has gathered an army of around five thousand mercenaries in Wales. The Earl of Huntingdon's messengers tell me he has passed through Shrewsbury and is marching along Watling Street towards London.'

'And we will cut off his advance before he leaves the

Midlands,' Northumberland stated as a matter of fact, still chewing on a mouthful of food.

'We will march out to meet him when my lord Norfolk and Sir Robert Brackenbury arrive with their forces,' confirmed the king.

'And what news of them, Your Grace?' asked Sir William Catesby, one of the king's closest friends.

'Norfolk marches from East Anglia and Brackenbury from London. I expect both to be here tomorrow. All being well we shall leave Leicester on Sunday morning and ride out to meet Tudor before he bypasses us. I have already sent scouts out to survey the area between here and Tamworth and report back to me. We shall meet again tomorrow morning after mass to discuss strategy and where best to face Tudor's army.'

The king drained the last of his ale and stood to address his men.

'My lords, sirs, enjoy the hospitality of the White Boar, I shall retire now and leave you in peace.

'What of Lord Stanley's forces?' the Earl of Lincoln suddenly interjected.

The king grimaced at his nephew's question. 'I have heard from Lord Stanley that he has the sweating sickness and cannot join us.'

A murmur went up from the assembled council. Every man there knew that Lord Stanley, despite pledging his allegiance to King Richard, was married to Henry Tudor's mother, Lady Margaret Beaufort. His support for the king was at best questionable, especially as he and his brother, Sir William Stanley, had a history of swapping allegiance between the houses of York and Lancaster and refusing to commit their troops in battle.

'Stanley is a coward and will not support Your Grace through fear of upsetting his wife,' the Earl of Lincoln said. A ripple of laughter went round the hall.

Sir James Harrington was more forthright in his condemnation of Lord Stanley. 'Nay, Your Grace, Stanley is a traitor who designs the throne for his wife's son. Only death or imprisonment will prevent him from plotting against you.'

A vociferous argument broke out among Richard's council as to whether Lord Stanley was a traitor or merely a coward. Voices were raised and fingers waved angrily as the argument raged but the king calmly watched on.

'My lords!' Richard eventually shouted above the din. He banged his empty tankard forcefully on the table. The arguments receded and the men became quiet as they listened to what the king had to say.

'I have sent a messenger to Lord Stanley to remind him that the wellbeing of Lord Strange is dependent upon his continued support.'

The previous month Lord Stanley had requested permission from the king to visit his estates in Lancashire. Fearing that Stanley might be plotting to join up with Henry Tudor, King Richard had given him permission to travel and stay in Lancashire on the understanding that his eldest son, George, Lord Strange, stay with the king at Nottingham. The gathered men realised that the king was using Lord Stanley's son as leverage to ensure his loyalty and stop him joining forces with Henry Tudor.

'Forgive me, Your Grace, but even with this surety I still don't believe you can rely on Lord Stanley.'

It was Sir William Catesby who spoke. Richard smiled kindly at the blond, tousle-haired man who had been his friend since they were children.

'Nothing can be taken for granted in this world of ours,' the king said. 'I have done what I can and will trust the rest to God. If Lord Stanley is willing to forfeit the life of his son to join Tudor then only God can judge him for that. Now once again, my lords and sirs, I will bid you goodnight.'

Every man bowed his head as the king stood.

'Sir William, will you accompany me?' the king asked Catesby as he left.

'Of course, Your Grace,' William said, leaving the confines of the hall and stepping into the courtyard beside the king.

It was now dark outside and the firelight from the hall sent the two men's shadows flickering across the flattened earth of the courtyard.

'Have you word of Francis yet?' the king asked.

'Not yet but he should be on his way north by now. Do not fear, Richard, he will be here in time.' Catesby only ever called the king by his given name in private.

'I hope so, Will. I hope so.'

Concern showed on the king's narrow face which appeared pale, even in the reflected light from the hall.

'I regret not doing this sooner,' he said, almost in a whisper.

'I know.' Catesby smiled and placed a reassuring hand on the king's shoulder. 'All will be well in the end, Richard. It always is.'

'I have led many men and fought many battles and always acquitted myself well, Will, despite my infirmities.'

'I know, Your Grace, I was at your side many a time. And your infirmities mean naught as you are a better soldier and fighter than most able-bodied men.'

'Against old King Henry's men, against the Scots, even against my cousin Warwick,' the king continued, 'luck has always been on my side, but something feels different this time.'

'It was always more than luck, Your Grace. You are a great warrior, a good and respected leader and king.'

The king scoffed. 'If I was truly respected men wouldn't be flocking to Tudor's banner and Stanley wouldn't be wavering.'

'Men are hardly flocking to his banner! Tudor has less than five thousand men, most of whom are foreign mercenaries,' Catesby reassured him, 'and Stanley has always been a turncoat, siding with whoever he can profit from the most.'

'Who will he profit from the most this time? I have rewarded him with titles and estates, raised him to the Order of the Garter and made him High Constable of England. What more does he want of me that he will not commit to my cause?'

'You have his son so he cannot commit to Tudor, and even without Stanley we outnumber Tudor's forces three to one. You're a better leader and soldier than Tudor could ever be and you have the support of England, so have no fear, Richard, we will prevail.'

'Tudor leads his army in name only. John de Vere commands it and he is a man to be reckoned with on the battlefield. I remember how he beat Hastings' forces and nearly carried the day at Barnet. I am uneasy about this, Will. I need Francis to get here quickly so that I may put the final piece into place so that, come what may, I can be at peace.'

*

A lone rider thundered along the old Roman road at breakneck speed, only occasionally leaving the track to seek the safety of nearby woods or to hide behind thorn thickets at the roadside when Yorkist horsemen appeared on the horizon and rode by in small groups, scouting the landscape. The Yorkist scouts were already aware of Henry Tudor's army gathered at Tamworth and would be reporting this information back to their king.

The rider knew that Lord Stanley was playing a dangerous game. Stanley had already refused King Richard's summons to join him against Henry Tudor, claiming to be sick, but he had also refused Tudor's request to join his army in Wales. Stanley cited his son who was the king's captive, as his reason for not openly joining his stepson. However, Lord Stanley and his brother, Sir William Stanley, now brought their combined force of five thousand men south from North Wales and Cheshire, shadowing Tudor's army at a distance as it marched into the Midlands. The Stanleys held their cards close to their chest, not committing to one side or the other.

Now, sending a secret message to his stepson, Thomas, Lord Stanley was taking a huge risk. If his messenger was captured by King Richard's scouts Stanley could be executed for treason. But games of power are not played by the faint hearted. Stanley knew that his five thousand men could tip the balance of the forthcoming battle either way. If he could secretly meet with Tudor and agree a plan without Richard's knowledge, Stanley could become the greatest magnate in the land if the Welshman won, second only to the new king himself. If Henry Tudor lost and Stanley didn't commit himself then King Richard would still be none the wiser and Stanley would remain Constable of England, Steward of the Royal Household, and a prominent beneficiary of the Yorkist king. Either way he was a winner. All he had to do was keep stalling and hold off from committing himself to either man until he was sure who would win.

Adam Laybourn allowed himself a wry smile as he galloped

towards Henry Tudor's encampment at Tamworth. Lord Stanley was a cunning old dog, he thought to himself. Duplicity had its risks but it could also bring massive rewards, and by serving the duplicitous Lord Stanley he hoped to reap some of these rewards for himself.

Having evaded the king's scouts Laybourn rode into the market town and was immediately challenged by armed sentries. The soldiers surrounded him, swords and billhooks pointed menacingly at his face.

'State your business here,' a scrawny-looking soldier with lank grey hair and several days' growth of facial stubble demanded.

'I'm here to bring a message to the Earl of Richmond from Lord Stanley,' Laybourn said, using Tudor's formal title.

'Give me the message and I'll see 'is Lordship receives it,' the grey-haired man said, revealing a row of rotten brown teeth as he spoke.

'It is not written down and it's for the earl's ears only,' Laybourn insisted.

The scrawny grey-haired soldier grimaced, showing his rotten brown teeth again, then ordered Laybourn off his horse, making him hand over his sword and dagger. He escorted Laybourn through town streets busy with soldiers, to a large timber-framed building near the marketplace. Smoke from the fires of Tudor's army camped beyond the town walls drifted into the marketplace as the pair halted outside the three-storeyed timber building. Two formidable-looking soldiers armed with billhooks stood either side of the large oak door.

'Wait here,' the scrawny grey-haired man ordered before walking over to the two armed sentries guarding the door.

He spoke to the men then nodded in Laybourn's direction. One of the guards hammered his large fist on the heavy oak door without taking his eyes off Laybourn. Eventually the door creaked open. Laybourn could see the guard talking to someone inside the building but couldn't see who it was. The guard called Laybourn over as the door slammed shut again.

'Hands in the air,' he said, handing his billhook to the scrawny grey-haired soldier.

The guard who had spoken began to pat Laybourn's arms, back, chest and legs. He searched thoroughly until he was certain that Laybourn carried no concealed weapons then he gestured for him to go inside the building.

Laybourn pushed open the large oak door and stepped over the threshold, finding himself in the cross passageway of the house. The door slammed shut behind him and Laybourn blinked as his eyes grew accustomed to the dim interior. The doorways to his left and right led into different areas of the house but directly in front of him at the end of the passageway was a doorway that led into the garden. This doorway was open but it took Laybourn a moment to realise this as a giant of a man filled the entire space, blocking out the natural light.

'This way,' the giant man's deep voice echoed in the passageway.

It was only when the man ducked below the lintel and stepped out into the garden that the natural light came flooding back into the passageway. Laybourn followed the man out into the garden and once outside he realised how truly enormous this fellow was. He towered over Laybourn, who was by no means a small man, by at least a clear foot. The giant was broad and muscular. His chest was like a barrel, his neck was as thick as an ox's and his fists were like sides of ham. This could only be the legendary Sir John Cheyne, once Master of the Horse to King Edward IV but now rumoured to be the Earl of Richmond's personal bodyguard. *God help any man who should have to face this beast in a fight,* Laybourn thought to himself.

'So who do we 'ave 'ere then?' a voice called from the garden in a lilting accent that was a curious mix of Welsh and French.

Laybourn looked up to see a group of men striding towards him. Most were in their late forties or older, grim faced, clad in leather, mail or armour, but at their head was a tall, thin, delicate-looking man in his late twenties, with a wide smile, who looked strangely out of place among them. He was fashionably dressed in yellow woollen hose, square-toed leather shoes, a green velvet and gold brocade doublet with sleeves buttoned to the wrist, and a brown, fur-lined over-gown fastened across his chest with pairs of ribbon ties. A metal-framed purse covered in red patterned silk hung from his belt and on most of his fingers he wore heavy gold rings studded with gemstones. A black, brimless, velvet hat adorned with a gold and jewelled brooch sat atop light brown wavy hair that fell past his slender neck to his shoulders. His complexion was sallow. His face was long and thin, as was his aquiline nose, and his small blue eyes seemed to stare out from beneath thin eyebrows as though looking at slightly different points in the distance.

'A messenger from Lord Stanley,' Sir John Cheyne answered Tudor's question in his deep gravelly voice.

'And what news do you bring from my stepfather?' Tudor asked in his soft lilting accent.

'Lord Stanley requests that you meet him at Atherstone, my lord. His forces will withdraw from the town just after first light but Lord Stanley will stay behind to await your arrival.'

'Lord Stanley will not meet me openly and join our forces against the usurper?' Tudor questioned, clearly dismayed at

Laybourn's response.

'I cannot say what Lord Stanley's intentions are, my lord. I was merely charged with delivering—'

'Cannot or will not?' Tudor shouted in a sudden rage.

The soft lilting voice was replaced with a harshness and vehemence at odds with the amiable man Tudor had been moments before.

A man in his fifties wearing a white quilted arming doublet stepped forward from the crowd of men accompanying Henry Tudor. His face was brown and weathered in stark contrast to his cropped white hair and white goatee beard. Ornate gold rings on his fingers gave him away as a man of wealth and status. He placed a hand on Tudor's back and spoke with a Welsh accent in a calm, steady voice.

'Stanley is your relative, Henry. God knows he's in a difficult position with his son held hostage by the usurper. Meet him and hear what he has to say.'

Henry Tudor calmed as quickly as his emotions had bubbled to the surface. His eyes no longer bulged with anger and his fists unclenched as the tension seeped out of him.

'You're right, Uncle,' he said to Jasper Tudor before turning back towards Laybourn.

'Go tell your master that I will meet him at Atherstone.'

Tudor paused before adding, 'After his forces have withdrawn, of course.'

With that, Laybourn bowed then turned and walked past the giant frame of Sir John Cheyne. He walked through the cross passageway of the house and back into the marketplace looking for the grey, lank-haired soldier with brown teeth who would lead him back to his horse.

3

easants working in the fields briefly stopped to watch a group of knights riding into Eastwell, their horses kicking up a trail of dust behind them. None of the onlookers recognised the knights from their livery of a silver wolf mounted on a blue and yellow background but they knew they did not belong to the retinue of Sir Thomas Kempe or John Moyle, the two greatest landowners of the area. It was not uncommon to see the odd knight and his servant passing through the area but this was a war band of twelve knights, fully armoured, on warhorses with banners unfurled, and that was a sight not seen in these parts since the days of the royal cousin's war twenty-five years ago.

Father Martin was folding vestments in the sacristy of St. Mary's Church when he heard the shouting. He rushed through the church towards the source of the noise and was met at the doorway by a young dark-haired boy in floods of tears. The boy sobbed uncontrollably, gasping for breath and struggling to get his words out.

'Father… They have…'

The boy bent forward and rested his hands on his knees.

'It's alright, Peter,' Father Martin reassured him, 'take your time and get your breath back.'

'No, Father… No time… They're chasing the boy who lives here with you,' Peter blurted out. 'They're going to kill him.'

Father Martin knelt in front of the boy and clasped his shoulders.

'Who? Who is going to kill him?'

'The Kempe brothers,' Peter sobbed, rubbing the sore patch on his wrists where he'd broken free of the leather thong that had restrained him.

As Father Martin raised himself to his feet the war band of armoured knights rode down the lane and halted outside the church doorway in front of him and the distressed boy.

'Father Martin, good to see you. I've come for the boy. It is time…'

Father Martin interrupted the knight. 'Forgive me, lord, but we must go. I think Richard is in danger.'

He turned back towards the dark-haired boy.

'Where are they?' he asked Peter, the urgency clear in his voice.

The boy pointed then turned and ran towards the slope that led down to the lake. Father Martin and the knights followed him. They reached the top of the slope where Peter stopped and pointed down to the lake's edge. Richard was just emerging from the water holding a leather-bound book above his head with a knife jutting out of the cover. Richard saw them and paused, transfixed at the sight of mounted armoured knights.

Three boys ran around the edge of the lake and one of them punched Richard, knocking him down onto his knees in the water. All three boys furiously kicked and punched Richard as he held the book over his head trying to protect himself.

Father Martin shouted down the slope.

'Stop! Stop now! Stop that at once!' but he was too far away for his voice to carry.

The eldest boy stood on Richard's back and forced his face under the water.

One of the knights did not wait for a response to the priest's pleas. He spurred his horse and galloped down the slope towards the group of boys, pulling up alongside them and leaping from the saddle in one swift movement. Despite being fully armoured apart from his helmet, he leapt into the water and grabbed the boy standing on Richard's back by the scruff of the neck and swung him round in an arc so that he flew through the air and landed with a forceful splash in the lake.

Richard floated to the surface, face down and motionless. A leather-bound, gilt-edged book floated to the surface beside him. The knight hauled the lifeless body out of the water and began to carry it to the shore. Father Martin ran to him and tried to revive the pale, lifeless body that the knight laid on the ground, while Peter retrieved the book of hours from the water.

Thomas Kempe erupted to the surface of the lake in a fit of outrage at having been thrown into the water.

'Do you know what you've just done? Do you realise who I am?' he shouted furiously at the knight while wading back towards land. 'My father is Sir Thomas Kempe. He's going to have your guts for garters.'

The knight replied, 'I already have a garter, and I'll wager its value is more than any your father can muster. I am Francis, Viscount Lovell, Knight of the Garter, and you, boy, are nothing more than a murderer!'

Thomas Kempe's jaw dropped in shock as he was suddenly forced to contemplate the precarious situation he now found himself in. No longer the master of his own little realm and hunter of whatever quarry took his fancy, he was now facing a real-life viscount. And worse, he could be hung like a common criminal for murder. Thomas Kempe considered his own fate and was no longer sure that his father's status would save him. For the first time in his life he was truly scared. He began to blubber and sob, alternately protesting his innocence and begging Lord Lovell for mercy.

The sound of coughing and spluttering made Francis turn quickly; just in time to see the boy he had dragged from the lake roll onto his side and vomit grey-brown water all over Father Martin's feet.

'Thank the Lord!' Father Martin shouted joyously into the air. 'Praise be, Richard is alive.'

Richard coughed and groaned. He vomited again then continued to retch as his stomach emptied of lake water until there was no more fluid to bring up. Francis let out a sigh of relief. Even Thomas Kempe looked relieved that Richard was not dead.

William and John Kempe looked on with a mixture of relief and anxiety. The two Kempe brothers had tried to flee the scene as soon as Lord Lovell charged into their midst but they did not get far as his fellow knights rode down the slope to cut off their retreat. The boys were rounded up and brought back to the edge of the lake where they now shared their brother's sense of relief at not being held responsible for murder. However, they were not off the hook yet and were anxious at not knowing what was going to happen to them now.

Richard sat on the ground shuddering. Francis took a cloak from one of the knights and wrapped it around him.

'Take him back to the village,' Francis instructed the knight.

Father Martin tried to lift Richard up but struggled. The mounted knight took Richard by the arm and pulled him up onto the horse's back behind his own saddle, while Father Martin helped get him into position so that he sat firmly behind the knight and would not fall off. Richard weakly put his arms around the knight's midriff and held tight.

'Take him to my house next to the church if you will, sire,' Father Martin requested.

As the knight trotted away with Richard clinging on behind him, Peter handed Father Martin the soggy book of hours he had retrieved from the lake. A thin dagger protruded from the book's cover. It had impacted with such force that the blade had gone clean through the front cover and through the pages inside, pinning them to the back cover. Richard had come to within the width of a book cover of losing his life.

Father Martin ruffled the mop of black hair on Peter's head.

'You did well, Peter,' he told the boy. 'God has smiled on us today.'

The priest and Peter walked up the slope towards the church, following the knight and Richard. The remaining mounted knights arranged themselves around the three Kempe brothers, hemming them against the lake. Francis Lovell stood, hands on hips, and stared fiercely at the three boys. He was a good-looking man, around thirty years old with friendly eyes, but the gaze that bored into Thomas Kempe was in no way amicable. Thomas started to cry again, making an unintelligible mewing noise.

'Shut up, boy!' Lovell demanded.

The mewing noise stopped but Thomas Kempe continued to sniffle and cry. William and John Kempe stood by his side, trembling with fear, their heads hung in shame.

Lord Lovell addressed his knights without taking his eyes off the three boys.

'Take them back to their father and tell him that I caught them trying to murder a boy from Eastwell. They are to remain in their father's custody until they are indicted or lawfully acquitted. I expect them to be tried fairly and punished accordingly. Sir Thomas Kempe himself is to arrange this. I will provide an affidavit to testify what I have witnessed. Tell Sir Thomas that I will return within a month to see that he has arranged a trial and carried out any appropriate punishments.'

Lord Lovell raised his voice to make his final sentence very clear to the three trembling boys.

'I expect this to be carried out regardless that these are his sons.'

Thomas Kempe stared at Lord Lovell with an air of defiance.

'I expect that you will escape lightly if your father is willing to pay a fine for your actions,' Francis informed the boys.

Thomas was going to boast that his father would not punish them but he saw Lord Lovell glaring at him and thought better of it.

Francis watched as his knights escorted the three boys around the lake and off towards the nearby manor of Ollantigh. He imagined the shock Sir Thomas Kempe would get when this party of knights arrived with his sons in tow and informed him that he had to arrange a trial for them on the orders of the Lord Chamberlain, Viscount Lovell. Dare Sir Thomas disobey the orders? Francis did not think so but he could not be sure as he did not know the man. It was not customary for the local lord of the manor to arrange a trial for his own sons but this was a matter of expediency as Francis was urgently needed elsewhere and couldn't spare any of his men to see that an appropriate trial was arranged. He would have to trust Sir Thomas Kempe and check that this had been carried out once his other priorities were dealt with.

Several days ago Francis had been stationed in Southampton, defending the south coast from the expected landing of Henry Tudor's army. Tudor's fleet had eventually sailed past the south coast and landed in Wales. Francis should have brought his forces to join King Richard in the Midlands but he had received a message from the king telling him to make a detour to Eastwell to pick up the boy. His mission now was to get the boy safely to the king as soon as possible.

Francis took his horse's reins and walked the beast up the grassy slope towards the church. To one side of the large flint-built building was a small timber-framed cottage with a thatched roof. The knight that had brought Richard up to the priest's house sat on the grass in the shade of a large oak tree eating an apple. Francis tethered his horse next to the knight's, beside the church, then walked to the cottage. He knocked on the slatted wooden door before pushing it aside and entering. Inside, Father Martin sat on a wooden stool next to Richard, who lay on a straw-filled mattress that lay across wooden boards. He was covered with a coarse linen blanket and propped up in the bed with several stuffed bolsters and pillows.

'I think he'll be fine,' Father Martin told Francis as he entered. 'Thank you, Lord, you saved his life.'

Francis smiled kindly at the priest. 'It wouldn't do to let him die. Not when he is on the brink of such momentous change in his life.'

'What do you mean?' Richard asked through swollen lips.

Francis hadn't realised Richard was awake and listening. Richard's face was bruised and battered, his right eye so swollen that it was difficult to know if he could see out of it. Francis looked at the sixteen-year-old boy with pity.

'Get some sleep. We have to leave in the morning and now we'll already be a day later than I had hoped. I will explain everything when we set off tomorrow.'

'Where are we going?' Richard persisted.

'To save a kingdom,' was Francis Lovell's enigmatic reply.

4

n early morning mist drifted out from the River Soar across reeds and riverbanks to shroud the fields and soldiers' tents outside the town of Leicester. It reminded King Richard of his first battle as an eighteen-year-old at Barnet; he had fought alongside his brother, King Edward IV, on a fog-shrouded morning against the Lancastrian army led by their uncle, the Earl of Warwick. Warwick had died that morning amid the thick fog, and the victory, followed by another at Tewkesbury less than a month later, had ushered in fourteen years of peaceful Yorkist rule. Richard regarded the morning mist as a good omen.

By the time he returned from church the mist had evaporated in the sunlight and his army was decamped and ready to move out. John Howard, Duke of Norfolk, his son Thomas, Earl of Surrey, and Sir Robert Brackenbury had all brought their forces to Leicester the previous evening to swell the ranks of his army, and they now joined the king's war council in the Guildhall this morning to hear his plans for the forthcoming battle.

The king surveyed the nobles and knights gathered before him.

'Tudor's army has left Tamworth and he is heading towards London along the Roman road,' he told them. 'We must march out to meet him and cut off his advance. He will either have to turn and fight or risk being outflanked and destroyed. We have two or three times his number of foot soldiers and we also have more armoured knights and cannon. Provided Lord Stanley and his brother join us, or at least do not join Tudor, there should be only one outcome.'

'And where are the Stanleys now, Your Grace?' asked Northumberland.

'They are several miles east of Tudor; and if history tells me anything,' King Richard replied, 'they will probably position themselves between us and Tudor's army so that they will not give away which side they hope to join. I do not doubt for a moment that the Stanleys are in communication with Tudor but I also think they will stay out of the fray until the last moment, and indeed they may choose not to fight at all. They are hardly renowned for committing themselves,' the king added with a wry smile.

Laughter rippled around the Guildhall.

'The Stanleys should not be underestimated but they should also not be our primary concern. We will cut off Tudor's advance along the Roman road between Atherstone and Hinckley and defeat him before the Stanleys can have a say either way. I have identified an area where we will camp tonight, and in the morning we will take up position within reach of Tudor to force his hand. My lord Norfolk will take up the vanguard, myself the main battle, and Earl Northumberland the rear guard. Now, my lords, gather your men and let us head out to stop this mob of Welsh rebels and French mercenaries from bringing ruin upon our kingdom.'

The Duke of Norfolk, a man of about sixty years of age with a long narrow face, high cheekbones that belied his age, tight pursed lips, and a thin white moustache that drooped at the corners, stood and looked out over the gathered crowd.

'God save King Richard!' he shouted with gusto.

Every man in the hall followed his lead and let out a series of rousing cheers showing their support for the king. Gradually the cheering subsided as the king left the Guildhall. The assembled nobles and knights then began to disperse into the streets ready to gather up their men and accompany the king out of the town.

Outside the White Boar the mayor and aldermen had gathered, along with a large crowd of commoners, to watch the king depart. King Richard, in full armour, with a gold crown atop his helmet, mounted on a white courser draped in the quartered lions and lilies livery of the royal house of Plantagenet, was a marvellous sight to behold for all those who came to watch him ride out of Leicester at the head of his army. The king stood high in his stirrups so that everyone could see him as he spoke to the gathered mass of people. For a man of such slight build his voice carried powerfully above the crowd and quietened them in an instant.

'Good folk of Leicester, I thank you for your hospitality, your support, and your prayers for the trials ahead, but I know that with God's help we will prevail and put an end to the revolt of the traitorous Earl of Richmond and his kinsmen. When I return, I shall remember this town and repay the kindness and support you have given me.'

'God bless Your Grace,' someone shouted from the crowd.

'God bless King Richard,' many voices chorused together.

'Show the Welsh bastard some English steel,' another voice shouted, 'and those who support him the end of some English rope.'

'God bless you, King Richard,' a woman screeched in a high-pitched voice.

The townsfolk continued to shout their support as the king turned and began to ride away from the White Boar Inn towards the High Cross. The army slowly began to follow suit, crawling like a giant metal-bristled caterpillar, riders squeezing two abreast along the narrow streets that were made tighter by the thronging crowds of excited spectators. The colourful procession with the king at its head, banners and pennants hanging in the still air and armour gleaming in the morning sunlight, turned at the High Cross and continued along Hot Gate. The smell of freshly baked bread filled the air, overcoming the stench of horses, stale sweat, and the foul muck that was being churned up by so many feet and hooves passing by.

King Richard, attended by the Duke of Norfolk and Earl of Northumberland, led his army along Hot Gate, into Apple Gate and its surrounding orchards and out of the town of Leicester. They headed towards West Bridge which spanned the eastern arm of the River Soar and passed through the archway of the Chapel of Our Lady of the Bridge which was built over West Bridge's eastern arch. Crowds lined every step of the way cheering the king and his army on with shouts of 'God bless King Richard'.

The king and his leading entourage reached the two Bow Bridges leading over the western arm of the River Soar near the Augustinian friary. The magnificent armour-clad procession of mounted knights took the larger of the two bridges that carried the road towards the town of Hinckley. The thronged masses parted to let the king onto the narrow bridge which was only wide enough to allow the passage of two horses abreast. It had niches recessed into the stonework so that folk on the bridge could step aside to let horses and carts pass without getting trampled. In each niche were gathered excited men, women and children waiting to reach out and touch the red, blue and gold hanging livery or shiny armoured foot of the king as he passed them by. King Richard indulged them, even sticking his leg out a little so that a small girl could say she had touched the foot of the king on his way to the battlefield where he defeated the traitorous Earl of Richmond. Richard allowed himself a smile at the thought.

As he reached the last of the stone niches on the bridge King Richard saw through the slit of his visor a grim-faced old woman wrapped in a filthy brown shawl almost hidden in the recess. Her grey hair hung lank and greasy around her dirt-smeared face. Deep furrowed wrinkles gave her the impression of having lived an age only possible for an ancient from the bible, but despite her dirty, ragged appearance King Richard was drawn closer to her. He was not certain why he was drawn to her or what he wanted to say but he noticed that her eyes were a mesmerising bright hue of pale blue that seemed to shine out of the filth that covered her skin, captivating him. She shrank back further into the recess as the king approached, as though fearful of him.

The king halted his horse, lifted his visor and leaned over his saddle towards the old woman to speak to her. He involuntarily stuck out a foot to maintain his balance, and hit his spur on the stone parapet of the bridge as he did so.

'You have no reason to fear me, lady,' he said in a kindly, reassuring voice.

''Tis you who hath need to be fearful, Your Grace, for where your spur strikes on the way to battle, so your head shall strike on the way back,' the old woman prophesised.

'Cease your traitorous prattle, old hag!' shouted the Earl of Northumberland vehemently from behind the king.

'It's alright, Harry, she means no harm,' the king spoke calmly to Northumberland. 'I have heard many a prophecy over the years and few, if any, bear the test of time. Allow her a moment with her king to say what she will.'

'Then I will foretell this, Your Grace,' the old woman continued. 'Heed the moon for it will change twice on the morrow and you will surely lose your crown.'

'I thank you for your words of wisdom, lady,' King Richard continued to address the old woman respectfully, 'but I believe crowns are won and lost through leadership, bravery and good fortune, not prophecies. However, if your prophecies come true then I beg that you pray for my soul, although if I remain your king after the forthcoming battle then I shall pray for you.'

The king tossed a silver coin towards the old woman but instead of catching it she flinched and pulled away from it as though the coin were cursed. The coin spun and settled in the dirt between the old woman's bare feet. She crouched and stared at it intently as if she had never seen a silver coin before. King Richard shook his head and rode on with a pitying look, leaving the woman crouched in the stone recess mumbling to herself. The Duke of Norfolk stared straight ahead, ignoring the old woman as he rode by but the Earl of Northumberland made a point of glaring at her to show his intense disapproval that such a creature could be allowed to halt the king's progress and speak such nonsense in his presence.

As if in defiance of Northumberland, the old woman stood and fixed her eyes on his, not breaking her stare until he had finally ridden past and looked away. She then turned her gaze towards the king, who by now had reached the end of the narrow bridge. She shouted after him.

'Your garden has been blessed with four white roses, Your

Grace. Three survive, but two not much longer.'

King Richard halted, spun his horse round and glared at the old woman. His face had turned a sickly pallor of ashen grey, so that those watching feared he might fall from his horse as he appeared so suddenly unwell. He sat for a moment as though wanting to say something but then seemed to think better of it so instead pulled on the reins of White Surrey, turning the horse about again, and continued to ride away from the bridge and the old woman without saying another word.

Norfolk, Northumberland and Sir Robert Brackenbury all stared at each other trying to make sense of what they had just seen and heard. Sir Richard Ratcliffe and Sir William Catesby, two of King Richard's closest confidants, gave each other an enquiring glance before the jovial Catesby smiled, leaned over, and spoke in a hushed whisper.

'Coincidence, my friend, nothing more.'

The look on Ratcliffe's face showed that he was not convinced.

Muttering and murmurs spread through the crowd gathered at the far end of the bridge lining the road out of Leicester. Everyone who had heard the dialogue on the bridge speculated about what the meaning was and why the king had appeared so stunned by what the old woman had said. The marketplace, streets, inns, houses and alleyways of Leicester would be a hotbed of gossip for the rest of the day as rumours spread like wildfire through the town. The lords, knights and common soldiers marched on, loyally following their king to battle, and only their return, either in flight or with the king at their head in a day or so, would quell the rumours and gossip and settle the question of whether Richard Plantagenet would still be king.

*

Henry Tudor was nervous as he approached Atherstone. His scouts assured him that Lord Stanley's forces had vacated the town but even so, he found it difficult to fully trust his stepfather. He had been trying to negotiate with Lord Stanley and his brother for weeks but what should have proved a simple matter dragged on and on, and even though battle was now imminent the Stanleys would still not openly declare for him. There had been messengers with vague promises of meetings that were then later rearranged, and others with stories of how Lord Stanley's eldest son, George Lord Strange, had been handed over to King Richard as a surety, and therefore Stanley was unable to publicly declare himself for Tudor, but how did he know that the Stanleys weren't colluding with Richard and luring him into a trap? Lord Stanley might be married to Henry's mother but, after all, Richard had made Stanley Steward of the Royal Household, Lord High Constable of England, Knight of the Garter, and heaped titles and land upon him, so where did Stanley's true loyalty lie? Henry found himself despising the man and his brother for not declaring their support for him.

Henry's spies informed him that five days previously Lord Strange had tried to escape the confinement that Richard had placed him under but had failed. Was this just a connivance meant to add an apparent air of truth to Lord Stanley's story? Henry let out a loud sigh of exasperation, startling his Uncle Jasper, who jolted with a start in his saddle.

Both men sat armoured, astride their horses, along with John de Vere, Earl of Oxford, who was Henry's trusted military commander, and a contingent of mounted knights. The party straddled the Roman road that led to London cutting through the small market town of Atherstone ahead of them. They watched soldiers scurry from the road into houses and alleyways, checking for possible assassins, hidden troops or weapons. Henry watched anxiously as the soldiers swarmed like ants through the town leaving no stone unturned. Houses were ransacked and townsfolk turned out into the streets.

'You really don't trust him, do you?' Jasper Tudor stated as fact rather than asking a question.

'Neither of us would be alive now if I trusted every man who you put your faith in, Uncle,' came back Henry's terse reply. 'Was it not you who advised me to trust Pierre Landais before he betrayed us?'

Jasper Tudor could not argue with that statement, even though it was harshly spoken. Pierre Landais had been chief minister to Francis II, Duke of Brittany, and had arranged support from the duke for Henry and his followers while they were in exile in Brittany. Landais had provided Henry with a chateau, money, and later with ships with which he could launch an invasion of England. That invasion, two years ago, had failed and Henry had been forced to return to Brittany in defeat without even setting foot on English soil. Landais then secretly negotiated with King Richard to have Henry and all of his followers captured and extradited back to England. Landais assembled an armed force to march to Vannes, where Henry and his followers were residing. Henry was informed of the plot before Landais' soldiers arrived, and he and Jasper managed to flee across the border into Anjou, crossing only hours ahead of Landais' pursuing men.

Jasper put Henry's current irritability down to the strain his nephew was under as the time for battle fast approached. He replied to Henry's question anyway.

'Yes, I advised you to trust him Henry,' Jasper admitted before adding, 'although Landais had served us well until he finally betrayed us.'

'My point exactly, Uncle, trust no one, not even those that appear to serve you well. Mind you, Landais got his comeuppance as his own nobles hanged him in a meadow in Nantes after confessing his sins. They tortured the confession out of him, you know.'

Henry grinned to himself, visibly delighted with his tale of retribution, even though he'd told it in far more graphic detail to his uncle many times before. Jasper feigned interest but then nodded towards the town as something caught his eye. Henry was still caught up in his reverie and did not notice.

'My lord,' the Earl of Oxford interjected to catch Henry's attention.

Henry looked up see his captain waving the all-clear and beckoning them to ride onwards. He shook the reins in his hand and urged his horse forward, the other men with him followed suit. Their horses gently trotted along the Roman road and into the town. Henry's soldiers lined the town's street and directed the mounted party where to go. It was not long before they pulled their horses up beside a large timber-framed building that had been a leading merchant's house before it was requisitioned. Henry dismounted and handed his reins to a soldier who took them dutifully.

Two of Stanley's knights watched Henry's approaching soldiers scour the streets and houses of the town, and went outside to meet them to explain that Lord Stanley waited inside alone for the earl to arrive. Nevertheless, the soldiers came inside.

They addressed Lord Stanley reverently. They apologised for having to do so, but they still checked the house for men and weapons and removed his sword and dagger before leaving.

Now Lord Stanley sat by the main hearth rubbing his aching fingers as he waited for his stepson to arrive. He had recently turned fifty and looked and felt his age. He wore furs despite the August heat. His grey hair was cropped close to his scalp and an overgrown grey goatee beard that was a good foot in length trailed down onto his chest.

Outside the house Henry paused, cautiously waiting for Jasper and Oxford to enter first, even though he knew that his soldiers would have thoroughly checked it already. Jasper smiled at Henry's overcautiousness as he pushed the wooden door aside and entered before his nephew. As the door swung open, Lord Stanley stood ready to greet his stepson. He was mildly surprised that Jasper Tudor, the Earl of Oxford and half a dozen knights entered first and formed a protective guard around the room before Henry entered. When he did so, Henry Tudor seemed timid and shrew-like. His eyes darted around the room before settling on the figure of his stepfather who stood waiting with outstretched arms.

'My beloved son. At last, we meet again,' Lord Stanley gushed with obvious overenthusiasm.

He hugged Henry who was unsettled by the show of mock affection. Henry broke free of the embrace and quickly sat on a nearby wooden chair. Lord Stanley sat on the other chair leaving Jasper and Oxford standing. Once Henry was content that there was no danger, he gave a nod and the other knights filed out of the room leaving the four lords alone.

Henry tugged at his bevor as the piece of armour bit

uncomfortably into the skin on the back of his neck. He hated wearing armour at the best of times but in this August heat it was unbearable. Now sitting in a stuffy room, about to discuss how or indeed whether his stepfather would support him in his hour of need, it seemed the most inappropriate attire possible, until he noticed that his stepfather was wearing a thick fur-lined doublet. Henry wished he was wearing his own favourite doublet and hose but instead he settled for removing his gauntlets to give his hands some air and freedom. He placed the gauntlets on his lap then looked up with a piercing stare at Lord Stanley sitting opposite him.

'Would you sit in the presence of your future king without being asked, Lord Stanley?' Henry asked.

'I meant no disrespect, Your Grace,' Stanley replied in alarm as he quickly stood again.

'And now you give me a title I have yet to win. Sit, my lord, and let us discuss the future.'

Stanley looked ill at ease as he obediently sat back down and waited for Henry to speak.

'Can I count on your support, Thomas?' Henry asked, calling his stepfather by name for the first time.

'Of course,' came the unwavering reply. 'I am your loyal servant and my men, and those of my brother, are at your command, my dear son.'

'Then why has it taken you so long to declare this?' The anger was evident in Henry's raised voice.

'My lord, to declare so openly would have meant the death of my eldest son who is held captive by King Richard,' Stanley protested. 'I had no choice but that doesn't mean that I do not —'

'Enough lies!' Henry vehemently cut Stanley short.

'Henry, your father has pledged his support. Isn't that enough?' Jasper Tudor tried to soothe the situation, fearful that his nephew would alienate the strongest and potentially most important ally they had.

'Unfortunately, it has to be enough,' Henry replied grudgingly.

'You have my oath, my lord. On my honour and on my son's life you will have my support,' Stanley promised, anxiety and fear evident in his voice. 'I swear it to all those here in the presence of Almighty God.'

Henry smiled, stood, walked over to his stepfather and patted him on his fur-lined shoulder. 'So be it, dear father, so be it.'

The tension ebbed away from Stanley's face. Jasper and Oxford were also visibly relieved that Henry now appeared placated. They knew his was a vexatious soul, quick to temper, quick to calm, but never one to get on the wrong side of.

'Now to the matter of how you will support me, Father.'

Henry paused before he spoke again. He rubbed a long delicate finger against his temple as though in deep thought.

'Richard has left Leicester and will be camped within a few miles of us by nightfall. My lord Oxford thinks it better for my army to camp near here tonight and face Richard in the morning rather than march on and risk having him flank us and attack our rear. I am inclined to agree. My scouts tell me that just off the Roman road there is marshy ground to the north west of Stoke Golding. That is where my lord Oxford plans to make a stand. The marsh will protect our flanks and prevent Richard making use of his greater numbers. You, Thomas, will take your forces to Stoke Golding where there is a hill overlooking the fens. I want you to wait there until Richard has assembled his army opposite mine and then you are, very obviously and deliberately, to bring your forces off the hill and around the fens to join us. I want Richard to see his support melting away and coming to join the ranks of my army before his very eyes.'

Henry grinned to himself at the thought.

'Once Richard's men see you join us in force, Lord Stanley, they will be less inclined to fight and some may even desert him,' Oxford added. 'Such a deliberate show will strengthen our hand enormously.

'Do you understand the role I am asking of you Thomas?' Henry enquired.

'Yes, my lord, I understand perfectly,' Stanley replied as he shifted uncomfortably, stiff boned, on the hard chair.

'Then go and organise your forces ready for the morning. If you need to send word to me before then I shall be camped at Merevale Abbey.'

'Yes, my lord,' Stanley said with a grimace as his knees cracked when he straightened up ready to leave.

'God bless you and may He bring you a speedy victory on the morrow, dear son.'

'Thank you, Father,' Henry responded.

'Oh, Father,' Henry added as an afterthought, 'whatever happens, George will not be harmed.'

Henry referred to Stanley's captive son.

'God will see that right will triumph.' Henry smiled knowingly.

'I hope so, my son, I dearly hope so,' Stanley muttered, half to himself.

5

ight was creeping in around them as Francis Lord Lovell, a still battered and bruised Richard, and twelve armoured knights entered the town of Leicester and left again just as swiftly. They crossed the bridge that King Richard's army had crossed that very morning and headed out into the enveloping darkness in search of the king. The darker it got the slower the party travelled for fear that a horse would stumble and unseat a rider. Even so, Lord Lovell urged them on.

'An hour or so and we'll be there,' Francis reassured the boy.

Richard had ridden a horse many times before but never for so long, so fast, and with hardly a break. His thighs and buttocks felt sore and his back ached, partly from the long journey and partly from the beating the Kempes had given him. He longed to be able to get off this horse and climb onto a straw-filled mattress and sleep. This quest had initially seemed fun, an adventure, and an escape from the hateful Kempes, but now he found it tedious and tiring. Lord Lovell would tell him no more than that they were going to meet the king. Richard had asked why he, of all people, should be rescued by a passing lord and then taken to see the king. Francis explained that he was sent to collect Richard and deliver him to the king at Leicester but obviously the king had moved on, so now they had to find him.

'But why does the king want to see me?' Richard asked Francis for the dozenth time.

The answer was always the same. 'The king will explain everything when you meet him.'

Richard asked questions about what the king was like, how he should address him, should he bow, and what would happen if he said or did something wrong.

Francis laughed at Richard's constant questioning and worrying.

'You call him Your Grace and you speak to him the same as you have spoken to me. You no longer seem nervous or worried about how to speak to a viscount, do you Richard?' Francis chided him.

'I have spent days with you and you don't talk to me as though you're a viscount and I'm just a priest's son. I feel at ease with you and I like you,' Richard admitted.

He felt himself blush as the words slipped out and was glad that it was too dark for Lord Lovell to see his face suddenly redden.

'And you will feel equally at ease with the king when you meet him, I'm sure,' Francis said, smiling. 'King Richard is a good and kindly man. He treats all men with respect, even the son of a priest.

'King Richard has done much for the common man these past years,' Francis continued. 'He has introduced a system of bail so that no man, however rich or poor, has to languish in gaol awaiting trial for a crime he may not have committed. He has acted to safeguard men's property rights and he has done much to remove corrupt juries so that all men may have a fair and honest trial. He is not a high and haughty man as some of his forebears and peers are, Richard. Remember, he is the first king to take his coronation vows in the English tongue. This is the man whose laws are written in English, rather than Latin, so that all men can understand them. He is not like any previous king. He is a king who commands love and respect because of who he is, not because of what he is. You will like him, Richard, without a doubt.'

Richard hoped that he would like the king as much as he liked Lord Lovell and that he would find him just as friendly. Nevertheless, despite the picture that Lord Lovell painted, the prospect of meeting the king was a daunting one for a sixteen-year-old boy who lived in a small village, helped work the fields and spent most of his free time reading the scriptures in or around Father Martin's church.

The conversation tailed off as they concentrated on finding their way through narrow lanes and dirt tracks in the dark; traversing a landscape that gently rose and fell as they crossed pastureland, forest and smaller woods, and areas that had been cleared of woodland to provide land that could be farmed. Occasionally they passed through a small village or rode past isolated wattle and daub houses with thatched roofs. Richard wondered how many such houses he'd passed in the darkness without noticing.

Through the trees ahead, Richard was suddenly aware of dozens of twinkling lights as though stars had been sprinkled across the landscape.

'See that?' Francis asked him.

'What is it, my lord?' Richard enquired.

'That's the king's encampment. We're here at last, Richard.'

As they cleared the trees, they could see campfires spread across a hillside in front of them. A group of soldiers sat around a small campfire by the side of the dirt track. The soldiers, armed with swords and bill hooks, got to their feet and blocked the pathway as the horsemen approached. Francis could see by their liveries that they were the Duke of Norfolk's men. He leaned forward in his saddle so that the men could see his face and his own livery in the light cast out from the campfire.

The men stood aside as they recognised Lord Lovell's livery of a silver wolf mounted on a blue and yellow background.

'Good to have you with us, my lord,' one of the soldiers greeted Lord Lovell as he passed by.

Francis thanked him in response as he let his horse follow the dirt track up the hill towards the tents sprawled across its flat summit. He dismounted and Richard and the knights did the same. Francis handed his reins to a young man who then took the reins from Richard too. Francis led Richard through the encampment, past campfires and through the smoke-filled night air, past men sitting polishing swords or mail, or drinking and playing dice as they tried not to think about the morning ahead and the imminent bloody battle that it would bring. Many of them were veterans of the cousins' wars or the Scottish campaigns under King Richard when he was Duke of Gloucester, and they knew what horrors the forthcoming day held in store.

Through the darkness the tantalising smell of meat roasting over a nearby fire wafted into Richard's nostrils. Saliva filled his mouth and his stomach growled as he realised he hadn't eaten since that morning. Francis had other thoughts on his mind as he seemed oblivious to the delicious smell drifting on the August night air. He strode purposefully with Richard in tow, through the encampment. A man with tousled blond hair and a beaming smile came bounding out from between the tents and slapped Francis playfully on the back.

'Will, it's good to see you again,' Francis exclaimed.

'And you, my friend,' the man replied.

'Richard, this is Sir William Catesby,' Francis introduced the man to Richard.

'Call me Will,' the man beamed as he patted Richard on the shoulder and gave him a friendly wink.

Richard found himself instantly liking the man.

'The king will be so pleased you're finally here,' Will said. 'I'll take you to him.'

As they followed Will Catesby through the camp Francis noted the banners and livery of Northumberland, Norfolk, Surrey, Ratcliffe, Brackenbury, Ferrers, Zouche, Scrope, and many more of the leading dukes, lords, knights and gentry of England who had gathered en masse to support their king.

To Richard the banners meant nothing more than pageantry and colour. Instead, he was awestruck at the sheer size of the encampment he was being led through and the mass of men who were sprawled out on the grass between the colourful tents and banners, and around the campfires. Richard was still looking around in amazement when Will led him and Francis past several armed guards who nodded their assent, and towards a large blue and burgundy tent trimmed with gold, with the emblem of a large white boar stitched into the fabric. They paused under the canopy at the front of the tent and waited as a guard called out.

'Lord Lovell is here, Your Grace.'

The flap of the tent opened and a slim man in his mid-thirties came out with a glowing smile. He had straight, light brown, collar-length hair and was dressed in black and gold doublet and hose. He exuded happiness as he extended his arms and hugged Lord Lovell.

'I'm so happy to see you, Francis,' he said, unable to contain his joy at seeing his old friend again.

Then he turned to the boy and seeing the bruises on his face, exclaimed, 'Dear God! What happened to you?'

'I got into a fight with some boys in my village,' Richard replied innocently.

'Not his fault, Your Grace,' Francis interceded. 'He saved a young boy's life and was set upon for his trouble by three ruffians.'

The king looked him up and down with a broad smile.

'You're a brave lad. You have the heart of a lion, I see. You also have the look of your mother about you.'

Richard furrowed his brow in a look of puzzlement. He turned to Francis hoping for an explanation but none came.

'Richard, I have so much to tell you,' the king said. 'Please, come inside, all of you.'

He beckoned Francis, Will and Richard to follow him as he disappeared through the flap of the tent.

'Bring food and drink,' the king shouted to no one in particular as he directed Richard to sit on a bench draped with large plump cushions.

'Your Grace,' Francis said, 'I think it better if we leave you both alone to talk.'

The king paused momentarily then nodded in acquiescence.

'Aye, Francis, you are right, Richard and I do have much to talk about.'

Francis gave Richard a reassuring smile before bowing to the king and darting back through the flap of the tent. Will followed and lowered the flap as he parted to give the king and the boy some privacy.

King Richard sat astride the bench facing his namesake and briefly placed his hand on the boy's shoulder before letting it drop back into his lap. Richard noticed how blue the king's eyes were. The king seemed nervous as he tried to speak but then stopped, whatever he was about to say hanging precariously at the edge of his lips. Eventually the thought spilled over into words.

'Richard, there is no other way to say this. I am your father!'

There was silence as Richard absorbed the enormity of what King Richard had just said to him.

'You can't be!' was Richard's eventual reply.

King Richard smiled kindly at him.

'I know it's a lot to take in but let me explain. Your mother's name is Alice. She was a servant to my cousin the late Earl of Warwick. We grew up together at Middleham Castle, although in different circles. We—'

'No, Your Grace,' Richard interrupted, 'I meant I can't be your son because Father Martin of Eastwell is my father.'

The king sighed and looked up to the heavens for inspiration.

'I'm so sorry, Richard, but your mother died in childbirth and Warwick had the baby, YOU, sent away. I didn't know until recently that you were given into the care of the priest at Eastwell. I found out through my mother that money was sent to Eastwell to provide for you. Richard, I'm so sorry, I was told that you had died at birth otherwise I would never have let you be taken from me.'

A tear trickled down the king's cheek. Richard just sat there dumbstruck. His life and the events of the past few days were finally making sense.

'Your mother was beautiful, Richard. She had long black hair and eyes that sparkled like emeralds. Warwick used to call her the swan of Middleham because of her long slender neck, pale skin and the gracefulness with which she moved. She was sixteen, the same age as me, when we fell in love, and I was truly in love with her, Richard, I really was. Then she became pregnant. She hid it well for a while but then Warwick found out and had her sent away.'

'So she may still be alive?' Richard ventured with hope.

'I wish it were so, Richard, I really do, but Warwick sent me to see her when he learnt of her death, to prove to me that she really was gone. She looked so peaceful, laid out to rest, a smile still upon her face. They told me that she had given birth to a son two days before but the boy had died and that Alice had lost so much blood that she died too. I swear I did not know that you lived and been given to the priest to be brought up away from me. Warwick and my mother did not think it right that the sixteen-year-old son of a nobleman be left with a servant's child in his care. I suppose they were right but I would have resisted them taking you away if I'd known, honestly I would. Maybe that's why they didn't tell me. At least they paid for your care and upbringing. You have had a good upbringing?' the king asked.

'Yes,' Richard replied, 'Father Martin takes good care of me. He schooled me and taught me to read and write, in English and in Latin. He brought me up like a son… but now my world has been turned upon its head and I don't know what to make of it.'

'I don't know if you're angry with me, upset or…' King Richard left the sentence hanging as he did not know what else to say.

Richard found himself overcome with emotion and instinctively hugged his father. The king cradled the back of his son's head and whispered, 'I'm sorry.'

The king and his son finally ended their embrace, and as each pulled away, they could see that the other was crying. King

Richard wiped his tears away with his sleeve. Richard sniffed deeply then wiped his nose on the back of his hand. The king laughed, partly with relief, and handed Richard a square piece of linen cloth. Richard stared at it in confusion.

'To wipe your nose on, my son,' the king said by way of an explanation.

As Richard wiped his nose a servant entered bringing a large silver platter laden with food and drink. He placed it on a wooden table next to the king and paused. King Richard waved the servant away then picked up a ewer and extended it towards his son who attempted to take it thinking the king was offering him a drink. King Richard let out a chuckle.

'Hold out your hands,' he commanded his son.

Richard did so and the king poured water from the ewer over them.

'Rub your hands together,' the king instructed him.

After Richard had rinsed the dirt and grime from his hands and wiped them dry on a proffered linen cloth, the king poured him a drink and offered him food. Richard avidly attacked the succulent roast pork, bread and cheese, biting off large mouthfuls, before using the last of the bread to mop up the meat juices. He washed it all down with several gulps of wine, which made him cough as it was far stronger and more pungent than the wine he was used to drinking. King Richard, having washed his own hands, also sat and ate, although picking at the food in a far more refined manner than his son. As Richard licked the last of the meat juices off his fingers the king spoke to him again.

'The reason I wanted to meet you so urgently is because I am to go into battle and if all does not go well then this may be my last chance,' King Richard said solemnly. 'Tomorrow I fight for my crown and my kingdom, and I may not survive the day.'

'Lord Lovell says you have three times more soldiers than Henry Tudor,' Richard said, quickly trying to allay the king's fears.

'There is more to war than weight of numbers,' the king countered. 'If I win this battle, I will teach you, Richard. I will teach you the art of warfare, leadership and a myriad of other important things. But I fear a prophecy of betrayal, my death, and also that you might not survive the morrow.'

The king took Richard's hands in his own and began to tell him the tale of what had happened that morning.

'An old woman on the bridge out of Leicester caught my eye. She seemed familiar and reminded me of someone from my past, but even now I cannot say exactly who or where from. It is an eerie feeling I had then and still have now thinking about it. As I approached her my spur hit the parapet of the bridge and she prophesised that my head will strike the same spot when I return to the town. She also said that the moon would change twice on the morrow.'

'Just superstitious nonsense,' Richard assured his father. 'How can the moon change twice in one day? It is either a full moon or waxing or waning. It cannot change more than once each day.'

'I thought the same, but she made a further prophecy that rings true. She knows I have four children, Richard. Only a handful of my friends and relatives know that, so how could a poor old wretch from Leicester know of such things?'

'It could have been a guess or a coincidence,' Richard offered in reply.

'She said I had four children, one is dead and that two would not survive for much longer. I am worried, Richard, worried that I will die in battle and you and my other children will be hunted down and killed by the Welsh usurper.'

'Father, do not speak of such wicked things!' Richard exclaimed. 'Tell me of my siblings instead.'

The request caught King Richard off guard.

'Oh, of course, you do not know of your brothers and sister.'

'I know of Edward of Middleham, your son who passed away last year.' Richard regretted saying it as soon as the words had passed his lips.

The king stared mournfully at Richard, although his gaze seemed to pass straight through him.

'He was my heir, my one legitimate son, and he should have been king after me.' The king looked rueful. 'But I have three other children, bastards but loved no less for it. John, I have recently raised to be a Captain of Calais. He is strong, courageous, and forthright and will grow to be a fine soldier and leader. Katherine, my beautiful princess; demure, kind, caring, but with such a sharp mind. She is married to William Herbert, the Earl of Huntingdon… and then there is you, Richard. I have great plans and hopes for you, but first I must ensure your safety. Hold out your hand.'

The king removed an ornate jewelled ring from his right thumb and placed it in Richard's upturned palm. The ring was made of gold and set with a large red ruby, but as it caught the candlelight Richard could see what appeared to be a face inside the jewel. He held it up to the light cast from a nearby flame and looked closely at it. As Richard stared more intently at the jewel, he saw the white outline of a jester's face through the polished gemstone.

'A Hopper ring,' the king said as though this would explain everything.

'What's a Hopper ring?' Richard asked him.

'It is a ring that will ensure your safety.'

Richard looked at his father quizzically.

'It's the sign of a fellowship, a brotherhood sworn to support and help each other. I am a king now and have no great need for it anymore but you do. If you meet a fellow ring wearer they cannot kill, injure or do anything to your detriment. They must offer you whatever support is within their means, no matter how rich or poor they are. My friends and counsellors Lovell, Catesby and Ratcliffe are among the fellowship but there are others too.

'If I defeat Henry Tudor and his rebel army tomorrow, I will raise you up and give you land and titles but if I fail then you are to take that ring and go to Cheapside in London where you will find a goldsmith named Herricke. Show him the ring and he will know what to do. Do you understand?'

'Yes, Father, but—'

'There can be no buts, Richard, your life could depend upon this,' the king said gravely.

The king removed a black velvet purse hanging at his waist and handed it to the boy.

'There is enough coin there to get you to London and keep you fed and sheltered for a year or more.'

Richard opened the bag and stared with wide eyes and open mouth at the gleaming gold and silver coins. There was more money in that small purse than he could hope to see in a lifetime. He took out a gold noble and held it in the palm of his hand admiring its beauty.

'I don't know what to say, Father,' he said honestly. 'You have just made me rich beyond my wildest dreams.'

The king laughed out loud.

'It is but a handful of coins, Richard. A man learns to live within his means so it will not take you long to learn how to spend those coins quickly. I would urge caution though. Do not flaunt your new-found wealth. Spend your coins wisely on the necessities of life, not the luxuries, and they will last you longer, especially should you have need of them after I am passed from this Earth.'

Richard looked ruefully at his father as he spoke.

'I have known you but a short time, Father, but God willing, we will have many, many more days together and I will have no need of your ring or coins.'

King Richard smiled and patted his son on the shoulder.

'God willing, Richard, my son.'

The king stood and then paused in thought.

'I have arranged a tent for you to sleep in tonight but in the morning you're to stay here on this hilltop and watch the battle at a safe distance. I'll leave you in the safe care of Sir Thomas Montgomery. He is a good and trusted knight, if too old and infirm to fight on the morrow, although he would still if I allowed it.'

'Is he in the fellowship... the Hopper ring?' Richard asked the king.

'No, Richard. Very few men are. There are only thirty or so. They were originally all high born but some rings have been passed on to younger sons, friends or close relatives. My brother King Edward gave that ring to me after I led the vanguard of his army at Tewkesbury when I was eighteen. It had belonged to my father before he gave it to Edward.'

Richard held the ring in his hand and stared at it again.

'Why a jester's face?' he asked inquisitively.

'The wry sense of humour of old Master Herricke, the goldsmith who originally made the rings, or maybe a private joke of King Edward the third, our ancestor, who ordered them to be made? Who knows?' The king shrugged his shoulders. 'But if

Tudor carries the day tomorrow, I do know that you must get that ring to Master Herricke in Cheapside. It was his great-grandfather who made the original rings and he will help you if all my loyal lieutenants are perished.'

'It won't be necessary, Father,' Richard continued to try to allay the king's fear.

King Richard sighed deeply.

'It is late, son. I will get one of my men to show you to your tent.'

The king walked to the mouth of the tent to summon his guard, and it was then that Richard noticed for the first time that the king's gait was awkward. King Richard seemed to stoop slightly to one side as he walked.

'Father, what is wrong with your back?' Richard asked.

'An affliction that has been with me for many years now but causes me no bother or harm. I am fine but if I am to defend my kingdom I will need my sleep so it is time for you to go.'

Richard dutifully rose and walked over to the king. He embraced him tightly and King Richard returned the embrace with equal measure.

'Goodnight, Richard, I'll see you in the morning.'

'Goodnight, Father. I'm so happy that I've finally met you,' Richard replied before ducking through the tent flap and out into the warm night air.

Though for all of his joy at finding out that King Richard was his father, he couldn't help but feel a sense of trepidation knowing that a battle that would seal his father's, his own, and the kingdom's fate, lay just hours ahead.

6

The king endured a tortuous night. Richard lay in his tent listening to the king's pained cries, as whatever visions appeared to him in his nightmares came back and haunted him over and over. The king woke many times, eventually falling back to sleep, only to wake again screaming and wracked with fear. Richard went to him in the night but the king sent him back to bed, saying it was just a bad dream and there was nothing to worry about; but he had seen the king's sickly pallor and fevered brow and couldn't help but to be concerned.

The king was up before the first light of morning spread over the horizon. He looked tired and pale and refused food as Norfolk, Northumberland, Surrey, Lincoln and Brackenbury ate a breakfast of smoked herring and sop in wine as they discussed the last-minute preparations for battle with him.

King Richard played down the wretched evening that had tormented him, even though his men were well aware of it. He rallied his army on the brow of the hill upon which they had camped. He mounted White Surrey. Clad fully in armour that gleamed silver in the early morning light, with a gold coronet upon his helmet, and proudly displaying the Plantagenet livery of gold lions and fleur-de-lis against a background of red and blue, he stood high in the saddle so that all of his men could see him as he spoke to them.

'The hour is finally upon us and battle will soon be joined,' the king's voice carried across the hilltop. 'Trust in your lords and captains and heed their command. We are superior in numbers to the rebel forces and we have God and justice on our side. Gentlemen, you are fighting to save England from the hands of Welsh outlaws, French, Breton and Scots mercenaries, and English traitors. A cause every true Englishman should be proud to give his all for. When victory is ours, poets and balladeers will forever sing your praises and speak of your deeds of heroism.'

The king unsheathed his sword and held it high above his head by the blade so that the handle and hilt formed a cross above him.

'For God, St George and England, let's give them something to sing about.'

Almost as one his men repeated the battle cry.

'For God, St George and England,' as many marked themselves with the sign of the cross.

King Richard turned White Surrey and began to lead the army off the hill and down into the rolling fields of Leicestershire below. The king's scouts had already informed him that Tudor's army was on the move, leaving Atherstone and marching down the old Roman road. The question was, would Tudor turn and face him or would he try to march on to London? The king knew how wily Oxford was and suspected that he would advise Tudor to make a stand to prevent themselves being attacked from the rear. Tudor's best chance would be to leave the Roman road and set up a defensive position on the plain between Upton and Stoke Golding.

The king was already aware of Sir William Stanley's forces positioned near Stoke Golding on Garbrody's Hill, overlooking the lane that cut across the plain, and Lord Stanley's forces on the nearby slopes of Dadlington Hill. Were they waiting to support their king and pounce on Tudor's army as it crossed the plain or had they positioned themselves to protect Tudor's rear as he marched past them and on to London? King Richard could not take any chances so he had sent a messenger asking Lord Stanley to confirm his intentions and to remind him that his son's life was still dependent upon the Stanleys' loyal support.

King Richard was still waiting for Lord Stanley's reply when he heard his scouts shouting to draw his attention to the movement on the horizon. He looked up to see banners of red and gold appear on the skyline followed by knights, horses and soldiers wearing the same livery. King Richard recognised the Vere star of the Earl of Oxford and recalled how it had been mistaken in the fog at Barnet for King Edward's banner with a sun in splendour. As a result, Oxford's own allies had turned upon him thinking they were being attacked by the Yorkist army of King Edward, and the Lancastrians were routed as the separate factions fought among themselves. Such luck today would be most welcome, the king mused.

Oxford's forces spread either side of the narrow lane and marched across the plain towards the king's army. As the opposition army advanced, King Richard noted Henry Tudor's banners at the rear of Oxford's and scoffed at the cowardice of the man. He also noticed, without surprise, that the rebel army could muster fewer cannons than his own army. King Richard halted along the line of a meandering brook and gave orders for his artillery to be drawn up behind it for protection. He then deployed his men to the rear of his cannons in three main battles, with Norfolk to his right and Northumberland to his left, facing Oxford's small army of rebels across the plain while Henry Tudor still skulked at the rear of his forces.

Richard stood on the brow of the hill behind the king's army, with Sir Thomas Montgomery beside him. Both shaded their eyes from the morning sun, shining brightly from their left as they looked out across the plain below them. As the two opposing armies took up their positions the grey-haired old knight explained to Richard what was happening.

'The king has made use of his greater numbers by deploying his army in three battles and setting them side by side so that he can outflank and envelop Oxford's army when they come head to head. He is also using that brook as a defensive position from which he can launch a cannonade at Oxford's forces.'

Montgomery continued to observe as the Earl of Oxford moved his army into position. He then explained to Richard what he had noted.

'Oxford has amassed his force in a tight formation straddling the lane. He's probably using the marshy fenland in front of him as protection against a frontal attack by the king. See how the two armies aren't properly aligned facing each other because of how they're using the landscape for defence?'

Richard nodded as he saw what Montgomery was pointing out.

'If the king launches a frontal attack now, he'll have to use the narrow lane across the fens or risk getting his army bogged down in the marsh,' the old man continued, 'and that means his extra numbers will count for naught. That wily old fox Oxford couldn't have picked a better spot to make a stand.'

'So what will the king do?' asked Richard.

'He'll draw Oxford out and make him attack first. Make use of his greater numbers and bring them round to swallow Oxford's flanks and destroy him,' Montgomery explained, 'but he has to be careful of the Stanleys.'

Montgomery pointed to two distant hills on the far side of the fen lane.

'Lord Thomas and his brother Sir William Stanley have placed themselves over there, between the two armies. They are nominally the king's men but are notorious for keeping out of the fray until the last moment and then declaring for the victor. The king doesn't trust them, particularly as Lord Stanley is Henry Tudor's kinsman.'

'Does that mean the Stanleys will join Tudor?' Richard enquired worryingly.

Montgomery laughed.

'The king has Lord Stanley's son as his captive to prevent such a thing. Stanley won't dare risk his son's life, so will either join the king as the battle is won or stay out of the fight altogether. My guess is that he'll do what he normally does and join the king after it's already obvious the battle is won.'

Puffs of smoke rose from the ranks of the king's army on the plain below, heralding the start of the battle. Moments later Richard heard the loud bang of the cannons that had just discharged their lead shot. Smoke rose from Oxford's cannons in reply, and for several minutes the artillery of the two opposing forces exchanged fire and the two armies became shrouded in smoke. Ranks of archers and crossbowmen under the command of the Duke of Norfolk massed on the right flank of King Richard's army and fired volley after volley of arrows into the morning sky, watching them descend like sheet rain on the opposite side of the plain. Oxford's archers sent up a hail of arrows in return. Men started to fall on both sides as arrows found their mark, although neither contingent were really close enough for their arrow storm to work to its most devastating effect as most arrows fell short.

From the distance of Richard's vantage point up on the hill the scene below was deceptively peaceful, like watching a game of chess played out below him. However, Montgomery, an experienced warrior, understood the horror and carnage of the battle that was unfolding on the plain below.

'That may look like an entertaining affair from up here, boy, but those lead and stone balls can tear a man's head clean off. They can crush a man's armour and his chest with it, until they are as thin as a communion wafer. One of those arrows can pierce sheet armour and knock a man clear off his horse.'

Montgomery paused before adding, 'I don't know why the king has decided to leave you up here with me when we could both be down there by his side, but you should thank him for it later, boy, as the sights you'd be seeing down there would turn your stomach and make you retch for a week.'

Richard realised that Sir Thomas Montgomery had not been informed of his relationship to the king, but decided that the king had probably decided this was for the best until the battle was won. Sir Thomas probably thought that he was just a squire, or son of one of the knights in the king's army, who was left in his care. Richard tried to imagine the look on Sir Thomas' face when he found out the truth.

Amid the wreaths of smoke rising from the battlefield, cannon balls of varying sizes bounced and skidded across the plain in both directions. Most fell short of their target but some found their mark, ripping through the close ranks of men, felling them instantly or tearing into flesh and smashing bone, leaving men writhing and screaming on the blood-soaked grass. The greater firepower of the king's artillery and Norfolk's archers eventually started to take a toll on Oxford's army, forcing him to take decisive action.

*

Henry Tudor sat mounted on a grey charger in the middle of the lane, peering over the heads of his men through a mass of banners and billhooks, trying to make out what was happening ahead.

'Why is Oxford waiting?' Henry queried nervously.

'My lord Oxford knows what he's doing, Henry,' Jasper advised his nephew.

'The land slopes away and I can't see the right side of Richard's army. What if Northumberland is attacking us and we're just sitting here?' Henry asked, clearly anxious at not knowing what was happening.

'If we can't see him then he can't see us either,' Jasper said calmly. 'He's probably just as worried by what we're doing. Anyway, he can't attack us through the marsh. That's why Oxford chose this position. You are safe here, Henry, out of the reach of Richard's cannon and arrows. Also, Northumberland would have to pass the Stanleys, positioned on the hills between us, and expose his flank to them if he did try to attack us.'

'And what of my stepfather?' Henry snapped irritably. 'He and his brother have promised to support me and yet they ignore my messages instructing them to join us. All I get in response is that the time is not yet right! What sort of support is that? The lying bastard has deceived me with his false promises. I'll have his head when this battle is done, you mark my words, Jasper.'

'You don't know yet that he has deceived you. Your stepfather may yet hold to his word and come good. Even while he and his brother sit upon the high ground, they are not supporting Richard. They can only add to his worries because Richard can't send Northumberland against us whilst the Stanleys are a possible threat.'

'But they were supposed to make a visible show of joining us at the outset,' Henry thundered in a palpable rage. 'I made that perfectly clear to Lord Stanley, did I not?'

'Yes, you did, Henry,' Jasper agreed, before informing his nephew, 'Oxford is on the move.'

Henry stood in his stirrups to get a better view. The Earl of Oxford had turned his force to their left and was using the marsh to protect his right flank against attack while he manoeuvred. He marched his entire contingent north-west and then turned them eastwards around the marsh and brought them to face the right side of the Duke of Norfolk's battle at an angle.

It was a bold move. It brought Oxford's army out into the open where they were vulnerable to the greater numbers of Richard's army. However, it also meant that Norfolk had to swing the left side of his battle out to face Oxford's forces face on, but in doing so force the king's artillery to cease firing so that they didn't hit their own men.

The volley of arrows and small lead shot from hand artillery continued to pour into the massed ranks facing each other but as Oxford and Norfolk's forces each closed in on the other the archers, crossbowmen and harquebusiers retreated to the rear of their respective armies to leave the foot soldiers to battle it out hand to hand in bloody combat.

King Richard grudgingly admired Oxford's brilliant strategy from his vantage point at the centre of his army.

'In one fell swoop he's negated my artillery,' the king commented to Lovell and Catesby. 'I'd swing my whole army round to face him but that would leave the Stanleys at my rear and I do not trust them, even if I do hold Lord Stanley's son. And Oxford knows it too. The man is a brilliant strategist, I'll give him that. It's a shame he's fighting for Tudor and not for me.'

The king paused for thought then called over a messenger and commanded him to relay a message to the Earl of Northumberland.

'Tell my lord Northumberland to move his battle across the brook to face the Stanleys and then hold there until the Stanleys move or I give further orders.'

'What do you have in mind, Your Grace?' Catesby asked the king as the mounted messenger turned his horse and sped away.

The king explained his intentions.

'If Northumberland faces Lord Stanley that should prevent both the Stanleys joining the fray and leave me to swing the main battle round to support Norfolk's vanguard. Northumberland's presence should also keep Tudor skulking in the rear and prevent him bringing his horses up to support Oxford.'

No sooner had one messenger left then the mounted knights behind King Richard parted to let another messenger ride through.

'Your Grace,' the man called with a hint of panic in his voice as he approached. 'Your Grace, the Duke of Norfolk is dead. An arrow in his face. The Earl of Surrey has taken command of the vanguard but they are hard pressed. The Earl of Oxford's men are close to breaking them, Your Grace.'

'Go tell my lord Northumberland that he must cross the brook and face the Stanleys immediately.' King Richard raised his voice to convey the urgency of the matter. 'Tell him of my lord Norfolk's death and stress that he must do it with haste. Go now!'

'Yes, Your Grace,' the man shouted, already turning his horse towards Northumberland on the king's left wing.

'God's teeth, Francis,' King Richard uttered in frustration, 'if Northumberland doesn't act swiftly, I could lose my vanguard. It is time to act. Sound the advance and swing the main battle round and bring it up to support Surrey. I will have to rely on Northumberland keeping the Stanleys at bay long enough for us to crush Oxford.'

Trumpets sounded and captains barked orders. King Richard's main battle began to follow his orders. It took time to organise and execute such a manoeuvre but these foot soldiers, many of them veterans of the cousins' wars, were well drilled. They marched in line, dropping down into a slight valley through which the shallow brook meandered. Once in front of the artillery and across the brook, the right wing of the king's main battle halted and the left wing swung round so that the battle was aligned in ranks facing the rear of Surrey's beleaguered force. They then marched forward towards their comrades to add support and weight of numbers against the wedge formation that the Earl of Oxford was using to try to punch a hole through the Earl of Surrey's wavering lines.

On the land sloping gently down to the brook King Richard sat astride White Surrey watching his main battle move into place and gauging his next response. His hope was that as more men supported the Earl of Surrey's ranks, they would be able to envelop and outflank the Earl of Oxford's smaller force.

'That will shore up Surrey's ranks but Oxford will surely retreat back to protect his flank with the marsh if Surrey's greater numbers start to tell,' the king noted. 'Let us pray that Northumberland acts quickly so that we can press on and win this battle soon.'

7

he August morning was starting to heat up but the stifling mid-day heat of the past few days was not yet upon the battlefield. Despite this Henry Tudor was sweating profusely. He was so nervous that he began to tremble. His stomach churned and beads of perspiration trickled down his forehead. He tugged at the metal bevor that continued to dig into him and rub against his neck making the skin sore.

'That's another battle that has dropped down onto the plain where I can't see them. I don't like not being able to see what's happening. Jasper, send men to find out how Oxford is faring.'

'I already have, Henry, and you are being kept up to speed with everything that is happening. There's no need for panic. Norfolk is dead, Surrey is struggling to hold Oxford at bay, and half of Richard's army is immobile because of the threat of your stepfather and his brother. Hold fast, Henry, and the day will be ours.'

Tudor guided his horse along the fen lane, closer to the edge of the marsh and perched himself high in his stirrups trying to peer beyond and over the distant dip in the land. The sound of battle raged ahead and he could see sections of men fighting hand to hand in the far distance but the majority of the fighting was out of his view while he remained on the fen lane in the defensive position that Oxford had advised him to take up.

'A messenger returns,' Jasper shouted, pointing to the rider coming around the back of the marsh from the direction of the Stanleys.

Tudor sat back down on his saddle and reined his horse in to turn and face the incoming messenger. The mounted man rounded the marsh and then slowed as he approached the mass of Tudor's bodyguard. The dauntingly huge figure of Sir John Cheyne blocked his way.

'Let him through,' Tudor shouted. The giant armour-clad Cheyne turned his horse aside and let the man through.

'My lord,' the messenger addressed Tudor, 'Lord Stanley says the time is not yet right to join forces. He reminds you that his presence on the hill protects you from the Earl of Northumberland attacking your position.'

Tudor was apoplectic. 'Not yet right!' he raged at the messenger. 'Tell Lord Stanley I'll have his head if he and his brother don't bring their men round to support me and the Earl of Oxford right now.' The messenger obediently spun his horse around.

'Wait!' Tudor commanded. 'I'll tell him myself.'

'No, Henry!' Jasper cautioned. 'You are safer here. Oxford is doing well enough against Richard's men. Let the battle take its course.'

'Stanley made me an oath and I will hold him to it,' Tudor blustered.

'And risk everything?' Jasper challenged his nephew.

Tudor paused and considered his options before replying.

'It is no risk to put Lord Stanley in his place. If I stay here the battle could be lost as I do nothing.'

'Oxford will win the battle for you so long as you are safe. Richard will flee abroad and you can ride on to London to claim your rightful throne. If you leave here and expose yourself all of that could be lost. Don't take a needless risk, Henry,' Jasper implored him.

'That damn man has no right to refuse me!' Tudor thundered as he ignored Jasper's plea. He spurred his horse and galloped away towards the Stanleys, leaving his men no option but to follow him.

*

Neither side was gaining any advantage in the hand-to-hand fighting. The Earl of Surrey, reinforced by King Richard's main battle, had the greater number of men but the Earl of Oxford had made a tactical fighting retreat and brought his army back so that the edge of the marsh protected his right flank and prevented Surrey's forces from enveloping him. King Richard, watching the ensuing battle from the higher ground gently sloping away from the brook, realised that even though he couldn't outflank Oxford with his larger force, eventually the weight of numbers would tell in his favour. It would be a slow-fought gruesome affair but the course was now set as Oxford had nowhere else to go and had played out the only hand he had.

'Why hasn't Northumberland advanced yet?' the king enquired of Francis Lovell. 'The messengers must have reached him by now.'

'I'm not sure, Your Grace,' Francis replied. 'Shall I send another man?'

The king did not answer but stared out across to the far side of the plain.

'Your Grace, shall I send another man?' Francis repeated the question.

The king still did not answer and Francis followed his gaze across the plain to where he saw that Tudor's personal guard were on the move.

'Are they retreating, Your Grace?' Catesby asked the king.

'Maybe, but they don't seem to be heading back along the lane which would make sense if they are fleeing,' the king responded. 'I think Tudor is riding across to the Stanleys.'

'It doesn't make sense,' Francis commented. 'Why would he leave the safety of his position behind the marsh, to expose himself by riding across to the Stanleys?'

'Because he knows he's losing and this is his last gamble; to entreat the Stanleys to join him,' King Richard explained. 'Well, let's prevent that and cut him down before he gets there.'

King Richard beckoned a squire to bring him a lance. He raised it and rested the end on the edge of his saddle. He then guided White Surrey into a steady canter down the slope and across the brook as his household cavalry, all fully armoured and armed with lances did likewise. As the contingent of knights reached the opposite side of the brook they broke into a gallop. The armoured knights raced up the gently sloping ground towards the green and white banners with the red dragon that fluttered above Henry Tudor and his men. As they closed in, King Richard and his knights dropped their visors and lowered their lances in anticipation of the inevitable clash. Each of the king's men picked out an opposing knight and charged with lances pointing at their target.

Henry Tudor had left the fen lane and was rounding the marsh on his way towards the Stanleys when several of his contingent let out cries of alarm. The Welsh knights turned in panic towards the large group of horsemen that had suddenly appeared on the crest of the ridge just beyond the fen lane and were now thundering across the plain towards them with lances lowered. Tudor was caught in two minds whether to turn and fight or spur on, hoping to reach the Stanleys before the attacking horsemen reached him. He still lingered in indecision as King Richard was the first to reach his target.

White Surrey pounded across the soft turf driven on by his master, who aimed his lance at Henry Tudor's standard bearer. King Richard's lance caught William Brandon on the top of the chest. It shattered on the knight's breastplate and the lance's tip drove up, piercing the mail around Brandon's throat. Brandon keeled over sideways, falling out of the saddle and taking the green and white banner emblazoned with the red Tudor dragon with him to the ground, where it was trampled by frightened whinnying horses that jostled for space among the tightly packed mass of Tudor's mounted bodyguard. As his knights' lances each found their mark the king spurred White Surrey onwards, not even pausing or slowed by his first collision with William Brandon. King Richard could see Henry Tudor at the far side of his group of household knights and he furiously drove his horse on, with the broken lance still clutched in his gauntlet and held out in front of him, towards the man who desired his crown.

Tudor shied his horse away from immediate danger as his personal bodyguards closed in around him to protect their lord. The giant that was Sir John Cheyne placed himself directly between Henry Tudor and the melee of knights in front of him. Cheyne was a formidable man-mountain that towered above everyone he had ever met, but fully armoured and astride a giant warhorse with a large war mace in his hand he was the most formidable foe anyone would meet on the battlefield on that or any other day.

As lances splintered against breastplates and helmets, and the sound of swords clashing and beating against armour and mail filled the air around him, King Richard forged on, intent on reaching the Welsh upstart and ending this battle once and for all. He drove his shattered lance into the helmet of the giant armoured knight that barred his way to the pretender to the English crown. The sheer force of the blow unseated Sir John Cheyne and sent the mighty warrior tumbling to the ground where panicked horses kicked and buffeted his armour.

Shocked by the ease at which King Richard had felled his strongest and most feared knight, and seeing King Richard quickly closing in on him as his own supporters were hacked down one by one, Henry Tudor turned his horse and decided to make a run for it around the marsh and back towards the fen lane where he could flee westwards across the Midlands and towards the relative safety of Wales. The Earl of Oxford's forces were still locked in hand-to-hand combat with the Earls of Surrey and Lincoln's men, and hopefully this would give him and a small following of loyal supporters time to flee and prevent too many of Richard's men following and hunting them down.

'Treason! Treason!' The cry went up from the men fighting in front of the marsh.

'I have chanced my hand and failed,' Henry shouted across the din of battle to his uncle. 'It is time to flee and regroup our forces elsewhere.'

'Treason! Treason!' The calls continued to emanate from the

chaotic mass of armoured men.

Many were now fighting on foot after becoming unseated from their horses. Dying men writhed underfoot of the battling soldiers on the blood-soaked ground that was littered with dead men and horses.

'Wait!' Jasper Tudor shouted back at his nephew above the cacophony of battle.

Shouts and shrieks could be heard above the clash of metal on metal.

'Treason! A Stanley!'

'Treason!'

The calls became more panicked and urgent.

Jasper pointed beyond where King Richard was still trying to fight his way through to them. Gradually it dawned on Henry what was happening. King Richard and his knights continued to slash and hack their way through the bodyguard of Tudor's armoured knights towards Henry Tudor himself, but the men at the king's rear had turned to face the new foe that had descended upon them. Horsemen bearing the banners and livery showing the three stags and crescent moon of Sir William Stanley had charged down from the hill overlooking the fen road and had crashed into the rear of King Richard's knights. Stanley had joined him at last! Henry Tudor now realised that the tide had turned in his favour. Instead of fleeing he waved his men forward to keep King Richard's men pinned between his own force and that of Sir William Stanley.

'We have them, Jasper,' Henry shouted triumphantly.

Sir William Stanley's mounted men enveloped the rear and left flank of King Richard's embattled warriors and were soon joined by foot soldiers who had charged down the hill after them.

Tudor's men, who only minutes before were on the verge of fleeing, began fighting with renewed vigour. They joined the press of soldiers and knights that surrounded the king and his men and hemmed them in against the marsh that had previously protected Tudor's flank.

King Richard, tired and weary from hacking his way through Tudor's mounted bodyguard, reined in White Surrey and looked about him. He breathed deeply, gasping for breath and noticing the weight of his sword for the first time. The impetus of his charge was gone, his strength was sapped and his enemies closed in, hacking and slicing at his band of men who bravely tried to fend them off.

'We have to flee across the marsh, Your Grace,' implored Francis Lovell.

'Where in damnation is Northumberland?' King Richard shouted forlornly.

'He's not going to come. He's deserted us, otherwise Stanley wouldn't have got through, so let's leave the field and fight another day, Your Grace,' Francis repeated his plea. 'We can escape across the marsh.'

'Francis is right, Your Grace,' Catesby added.

King Richard didn't have a chance to reply because a group of Welsh foot soldiers broke through immediately in front of him. The king swung his sword down at a man who was about to lunge at him with a halberd. The sword sliced through the man's shoulder and he let out a piercing scream as the blade cut through leather, shattered bone and penetrated deep into the man's chest. An arc of crimson blood sprayed into the air as the dying man fell but another soldier immediately appeared in his place.

Sir James Harrington, carrying the royal standard beside the king, was bludgeoned from his horse by a man wielding a poleaxe. Sir Percival Thirwall grabbed at the standard and was able to retrieve it before Harrington was pinned to the ground by three Welsh foot soldiers and the leather straps holding his helmet in place were severed, the helmet pulled off exposing his head to the frenzied dagger thrusts of more Welsh soldiers who rushed forward to join in the butchery.

The sudden onslaught pushed King Richard and his remaining men further back until they felt themselves sinking in the marshy ground under the weight of their armour. The Welshmen and Stanley's soldiers continued to press, hacking and slicing at the ragged edges of the small band of the king's loyal followers, who jabbed out sword tips and slashed at any man who dared to step within their range. A burly bearded Welshman swung a billhook which sliced through the legs of Sir Percival Thirwall. He collapsed to his knees with no more than a grunt as his legs were hewn from under him. Blood pooled around his severed limbs but he bravely continued to clutch the royal standard which he'd planted in the marshy ground near the king, until the life finally drained out of him.

After that, Welsh soldiers took turns to step forward and swing halberds, billhooks and poleaxes in sweeping arcs to try to scythe the legs of knights or horses trapped in the marshy ground. Catesby's horse was brought down and it fell on top of him, crushing his armour and pinning him down so that he slowly sank into the marsh beneath its weight. King Richard wanted to go to help his friend but was unable as Welshmen prodded their weapons in his direction and goaded him. The screams of trapped and dying men echoed across the marsh while others shouted words of defiance as they were picked off one by one by the surrounding enemy.

Sir Richard Ratcliffe slashed down at one man who had stepped too close, trying to grab the reins of his horse to pull him from the safety of the king's band of warriors, but as his sword cut through the man's face, he was pulled from his horse by another leather-clad soldier. As several more Welshmen stepped in for the kill the king leapt from the stirrups of White Surrey, who was bogged down in the marsh, and jumped between the two assailants. He brought his sword down, cleaving the first attacker's head near clean off, then swung round and thrust his sword into the second man's belly. A group of knights on foot gathered round their king but in the boggy wet ground of the marsh their armour was as much a hindrance as it was protection.

More Welshmen and English soldiers wearing the stags and crescent moon livery of Sir William Stanley closed in. A soldier stabbed a sword upwards at the still-mounted Francis Lovell. The sword glanced off his breastplate as he smashed the edge of his own sword into the attacker's face releasing a welter of blood. Another man grabbed at his legs, trying to pull him off his horse so, as others ran forward to join in, Francis had no choice but to back his steed further into the marsh and away from the dwindling band of comrades and knight gathered around the royal standard at the edge of the boggy ground.

One of Stanley's men thrust a spear into the visor of Sir Richard Charlton who fought valiantly at the king's side. Lord Ferrers hacked the spearman down before he himself was brought down by a scything blow from a poleaxe. He regained his feet but only in time for one of Stanley's soldiers to thrust a dagger through his visor and deep into his eye socket. Ferrers let out a blood-curdling scream as the knife penetrated deep. Another man managed to hook a halberd behind the king's knee and pulled him off balance. King Richard staggered and fell onto one knee in the waterlogged ground. A Welshman seized the chance to rush forward and hack at the straps holding on the king's helmet and pull it off. As others splashed through the marsh to join the attack, King Richard grabbed the man's right arm and lunged upwards, yelling with pure rage as he pulled the Welshman hard onto his sword while thrusting it through the padded gambeson and deep into the man's midriff. A soldier wearing a mail hauberk hacked at the king's exposed head but Sir William Conyers parried the blow and stabbed the man through the neck releasing a torrent of blood that sprayed the king across the face, soaking his hair.

King Richard's lungs burned and his muscles ached but he continued to fight and shout words of defiance.

'I am your lawful king,' he shouted at the men surrounding him, 'and I would rather die than surrender my crown to a usurper.'

As if accepting the king's defiance as a challenge a soldier stepped forward and thrust a spear at the king's blood-smeared face. King Richard jerked his head back but the tip of the spear caught him on the cheek, drawing more blood to mingle with that already spattered across his face. King Richard hacked at the spear and his blade caught in the wooden spear shaft. He wrenched the weapon out of the grip of the spearman who tried to jump backwards out of reach of the king, but being bogged down up to his ankles in the waterlogged marsh he only fell onto his buttocks with a splash. The man let out a panicked high-pitched shriek and scurried backwards through the soft squelching marsh, fearful that the king would attack him. King Richard only watched with contempt as the unarmed man made his pathetically slow retreat.

By now, many of Tudor and Stanley's soldiers had ventured

out into the marsh to completely surround the king and the last of his few remaining loyal supporters. Francis Lovell and a handful of knights, cut off from the king and seeing that all was lost, managed to escape across the marsh on horseback and flee across the plain.

King Richard and his remaining supporters faced Welsh, French, Bretons, Scots and Englishmen who came forward in groups of three, four or five to attack each knight as a pack of hunting dogs attacks a stag. They probed, stabbed, slashed and hacked from all sides until a weak point was found and the quarry was brought down. Then the pack descended in force to finish off the hapless victim.

Two more soldiers stepped forward to attack the king. One swung a battle-axe and, as the king parried and thrust his sword at the assailant, the second soldier swung a sword from the side. The blade caught the king on the top of the head shaving his skull and slicing off a chunk of scalp, bone and hair. King Richard teetered forwards as the blow caught him. The man swung again and took another slice of scalp. The soldier with the battle-axe swung at the off-balance king and sliced off a third chunk of scalp with another glancing blow. King Richard yelled angrily as he lashed out in blind fury and smashed his gauntlet into the axeman's face. He regained his balance and composure and thrust his sword below the man's mail, slicing his thigh. The man yelped and stumbled backwards and then one of the king's comrades thrust a sword into the prone man's groin, removing it with a vicious twist. As the soldier with the sword raised it above the king's head for the killer blow another of King Richard's knights ran him clean through with a sword.

More men splashed into the blood-stained marsh so that for

every one killed by the king and his men two or three more replaced them. A large, brown-bearded Scotsman wearing a mail haubergeon over a padded jacket charged forward armed with a rondel dagger. He bounded and splashed through the marsh to confront the king. Without pausing he leapt at King Richard with the dagger and punched it forward at the king's face. The king swung his sword which cut through the attacker's arm but the square sectioned blade pierced the king's cheek below his eye and penetrated his jawbone. King Richard let out a cry of pain and hacked again and again at the man who had just stabbed him until finally the Scotsman lay in a pool of blood at his feet.

Another man stepped in and swung a mace at the king. The heavy ridged mace head smashed into the side of the king's armour, momentarily knocking him off balance. King Richard held out his sword to keep the attacker at arm's length but the man jumped to the king's left and swung another blow below the king's extended sword. The heavy ridged mace head crashed into the same spot again, smashing into King Richard's ribs and knocking the wind out of him. The king grunted as the blow struck. Another soldier swung a halberd which took the king's legs out from beneath him. King Richard landed on his back but quickly rolled over and pushed himself up onto all fours in an attempt to get up before the next attacker was upon him. His body throbbed, his lungs burned with the exertion, and he felt his strength drain from every aching muscle but the instinct to live drove him on as he pushed himself up into a kneeling position and again extended his sword out in front of himself in defence.

On a sandy ford by the marsh a group of horsemen watched as King Richard and the remnants of his company of knights fought on in vain.

'Not his face. I want that left unmarked,' Henry Tudor called to the men surrounding the king in the marsh.

Tudor needed the dead king to be easily identifiable so that all would know that he was the victor and no one could later claim that King Richard had survived the battle and rally an army in his name.

Almost all of King Richard's men were dead by now and the few that remained knew that their death was at hand. King Richard stood and wiped away the blood that was running down his forehead into his eyes, as he watched the mass of armoured and mail-clad soldiers closing in on him once more. He saw the livery of Sir William Stanley's men with its design of a crescent moon, and he had a sudden realisation; the old woman on the bridge was right. The moon had changed twice that day. It had passed through its usual phase in the sky but also Sir William Stanley with his crescent moon symbol had changed sides, betraying him and trapping him and his men in this marsh.

As the king stood in the blood-stained bog, sword extended out in front of him and still pondering his fate, a Welshman rushed from behind. The king turned too late and the Welshman thrust a square-edged rondel dagger into the top of his skull. King Richard toppled forward and knelt face down on all fours, no longer able to defend himself as the ring of soldiers surrounding him quickly closed in. A Welshman swung a halberd which sliced through the back of the prone king's skull, cleaving off a chunk of bone. A swordsman stabbed his weapon into the back of the king's head and then a pack of Welshmen dived in with daggers and swords hoping for the killing blow and immortal fame. Tudor called a halt to the butchery but the slaughter was already complete. King Richard lay dead, face down in the marsh among the bodies of the loyal supporters who had made the last fateful charge with him.

Tudor and Stanley's soldiers trudged through the marsh picking up weapons and anything of value that could be found on the bodies, which were then dragged through the reeds to the slightly higher dry ground where they were stripped of armour. Injured horses were butchered and stripped of harnesses and saddles. King Richard's gold coronet that had sat atop his helmet was recovered by a soldier from a spindly thorn bush at the edge of the marsh and handed to Sir William Stanley. The new kingmaker rubbed the gold coronet to remove some filth and smiled knowingly. He would be richly rewarded for his timely intervention and ensuring Henry Tudor's momentous victory. He would give the coronet to his brother, Lord Stanley, who he knew would make a big show of placing the coronet on the new king's head so that everyone, including Tudor himself, would be in no doubt that he owed this victory to the Stanleys.

As the victorious soldiers continued to scour the battlefield for anything of value a dead knight was pulled from beneath a horse, his armour crushed by the weight of the animal. Two Welshmen dragged the body out of the marsh then began to strip it of its armour. One of the Welshmen began to remove the dead man's helmet and jumped with surprise when the knight coughed and gasped for air. The knight's chest wheezed and rasped as the Welshman pulled out a dagger and grabbed his hair. The knight was weak, injured and unable to stop the Welshman from mercilessly slitting his throat.

'Stop!' Tudor shouted from the sandy ford at the edge of the marsh as the Welshman pressed his blade against the knight's throat. 'I want him alive.'

And so, William Catesby escaped the slaughter in the marsh.

ichard, Sir Thomas Montgomery and a few score of squires, pages and camp followers were watching the battle run its course from their vantage point on the hillside behind the king's army. They saw the fierce hand-to-hand combat between the Duke of Norfolk and the Earl of Oxford's forces, and the Earl of Surrey battle on against Oxford, after his father, the Duke of Norfolk's death. They watched as the Earl of Lincoln's reinforcements shored up Surrey's ranks and began to push Oxford back and then, inexplicably, they witnessed the Earl of Northumberland turn and lead his men off the battlefield leaving the rear of Surrey's vanguard, and the king's main battle, exposed to the Stanleys.

'Northumberland is a traitorous bastard,' Sir Thomas spat vehemently as he watched the earl retreat. 'I must warn the king.'

Before Montgomery had the chance, King Richard spotted Henry Tudor trying to reach the Stanleys and launched his fateful charge. Those watching from the hillside were powerless to prevent the king's charge or to stop Sir William Stanley's men from joining the battle on Tudor's side and enveloping and slaughtering the king and his loyal knights in the marsh.

News of the king's death spread quickly through the ranks of his army who began to disengage with Oxford's force. Men broke ranks, dropped their weapons and began to flee for their lives across the plain knowing that the battle was lost now that King Richard was dead. Oxford's soldiers pursued them mercilessly, hacking men down as they fled and giving no quarter to those that surrendered. Blood lust was upon them and they hunted down and slaughtered their enemies indiscriminately.

Richard was numb. He knew he should be sad, tearful, even angry at the death of his father, but inexplicably he felt nothing. He knew that he loved his father, however briefly they had known each other, and so he couldn't understand why he wasn't more upset; why a dark void existed inside him where he knew emotions should reside. As others on the hillside fled over the crest of the hill and down the other side to melt away into the fields and lanes of Leicestershire, Richard just stood staring numbly at the marsh on the far side of the plain to where the father he had known for no time at all lay dead.

'No time for gawping, boy,' Sir Thomas Montgomery cautioned him, 'we have to leave before Oxford's men find us.'

Richard just stared blankly into the distance.

'Now, boy!' Sir Thomas snapped.

Richard turned and looked at Sir Thomas but the morose expression on his face did not change. He began to walk back with the aged knight to where his horse was tethered on the hillside. A few people were scrabbling through the encampment gathering possessions before fleeing the inevitable arrival of Oxford's soldiers, but most had already fled without delaying to collect anything.

'Thieving bastards!' Sir Thomas suddenly bellowed, startling Richard. 'They've taken the horses. By God, I should have known this would happen.'

'Who took them?' Richard asked naively.

'Any bastard who had the sense to get out of here before we did,' Sir Thomas said angrily.

He began to unbuckle his armour.

'Help me out of this,' he ordered Richard.

'Won't you be better protected with it on?' Richard asked.

'I'll move faster on foot without it. Anyway, if they catch me in this I'll be slaughtered. The days are long gone when a knight would be held captive and ransomed back to his family. Our best chance is to travel light and keep moving. If we can evade Oxford's men until we get three or four miles away, we should be safe. Now help me get this bloody armour off before it's too late.'

Richard helped Sir Thomas, stripping and discarding the armour with haste, even using a knife to cut through leather laces rather than taking unnecessary time to untie them. Sir Thomas also removed his quilted jacket that was embroidered with exquisite silver thread before he and Richard began to run down the hill as fast as their legs would carry them. They could see fugitives from the battle fleeing across fields in the distance but as yet no sign of Oxford's men in pursuit.

'Over there.' Sir Thomas pointed to a copse of oak trees a short distance away.

As they ran Sir Thomas slowed and began to gasp for breath, clearly struggling with the exertion of running for cover. He stopped, stooped forward and placed his hands on his thighs to support himself as he breathed deeply, his chest heaving and rattling with every expelled breath.

'Go! Don't wait... for me,' he panted, before bursting into a fit of coughing that turned his face crimson.

Richard did not reply but stood waiting for Sir Thomas to stop coughing and catch his breath.

'I'm old, boy, and no longer fit enough to outrun the bastards. Go, save yourself. I'm not worth dying for.'

Richard smiled at that.

'Come on, old man. I can at least save one of the king's knights today,' he uttered with a new-found air of confidence.

Sir Thomas laughed. 'You're a presumptuous little horse fart but God love you, boy.'

He stood upright and patted Richard on the shoulder.

'We'd better get moving then,' he said before coughing to clear his chest and spitting out the resultant lump of phlegm.

Sir Thomas still wheezed as they trudged under the increasing heat of the August sun towards the cover of the oak trees.

'There!' Sir Thomas pointed to the right of the hill they had just run down. 'Horsemen!'

They began running again.

'They're Oxford's,' Sir Thomas said as he and Richard reached the safety of the thickly wooded copse.

They knelt and peered out from behind the cover of the oak trees. As they watched, more horsemen rounded the foot of the hill to join their comrades. About twenty knights in total briefly massed together before fanning out across the field looking for fugitives from the battle. They spread out in a wide line leaving about eight or nine feet of space between each horse. Each rider, with sword, battle-axe or mace in hand, guided their horse forward in line over the grass and scrubland. The horsemen edged ever closer towards the copse of oak trees from where Richard and Sir Thomas nervously watched them. The riders parted as they rounded thorn bushes or dense thickets of shrubs that were in their way but then immediately closed ranks into their original formation. Occasionally a rider stopped and prodded a sword into a bush or patch of undergrowth.

'What do we do?' Richard asked Sir Thomas.

'Pray,' was Sir Thomas' answer.

Richard and Sir Thomas instinctively began to move away from the edge of the copse towards its centre.

'We can hide in here,' Richard suggested. 'If we cover ourselves with leaves and branches and lay still, they won't see us.'

'Don't be a bloody fool,' Sir Thomas lambasted him. 'They'll search every inch and leave no stone or leaf unturned.'

'Then we can get out that way,' Richard said, pointing to the far side of the copse, 'and keep the trees between us and them until we've run far enough away.'

'Have you seen me run, boy?' Sir Thomas scoffed. 'Anyway, they're spread in such a wide line that they'd see us as soon as we're clear of the trees. It's hopeless.'

Richard ignored Sir Thomas' defeatism and worked his way through the tangle of scrub and branches to the far side of the copse to gauge the situation for himself. As he crouched at the edge of the treeline and looked out across the scrubland beyond, Richard heard the whinny of a horse and knew that Oxford's men were almost upon them. He could feel his heart pound with fear as he scanned the surrounding landscape looking for an escape route. The nearest trees were far too distant to sprint to and only grass and a few lone bushes and shrubs dotted the landscape between him and the nearest of them. As his gaze retreated from the distant trees towards the area in front of where he hid, Richard realised that he could hear the trickle of running water. He listened intently and for the first time noticed that the ground a short distance in front of him seemed to drop away to where a brook must be flowing below the level of the ground. Richard suspected that it must be a tributary or continuation of the brook that King Richard had positioned his artillery behind. He lay on his belly and, keeping as flat as he possibly could, he stealthily edged his way out from the trees towards where the sound of water was coming from. He reached an embankment, peered down and saw a narrow stream that meandered between beds of reeds and nettles.

Just then, as the first of Oxford's men reached the edge of the copse, a man broke cover from behind a briar bush and fled for his life away from the horsemen, several of whom whooped and shouted in delight as they began to give chase. The man ran in blind panic, heading directly towards Richard, who was now lying exposed on the embankment overlooking the brook.

Without giving it a thought, Richard rolled over the edge of the embankment and down into the brook. He rolled through a patch of nettles then slid into a reed bed where he sank into thick fetid mud. His skin itched as nettle rash blistered his arms, hands, face and neck. The foul smell of rotting vegetation invaded his nostrils as he lay on his back amid the reeds, half submerged in stinking mud. Despite the foul stench, the terrible itching that seemed to cover every inch of his exposed skin, and the nervous pounding of his heart that echoed through his chest and head, Richard lay totally still and silent, hoping and praying that he had not been seen.

He stared up at the pale blue sky that was streaked with thin wisps of white cloud and felt the heat of the sun on his face. He suddenly became aware that he was holding his breath, so nervous was he of giving himself away. He began to exhale slowly, trying not to make a sound. A man leapt over the brook directly above his head forcing Richard to let out a startled cry. He continued to lie still hoping no one had heard as he nervously bit his lower lip. A horse and rider leapt over the brook at the same spot as the fugitive had. Richard was relieved that the rider did not look down as he passed overhead. Seconds later Richard heard the swish of a blade and a grunt and realised that the fugitive had been chopped down in mid-flight. The rider whooped in triumph at his kill.

Richard listened for several minutes but other than the far-off cries of other riders and the constant babble of trickling water he could hear nothing. He stared up at the wisps of white cloud that hardly seemed to move in the August sky and wondered how long he would have to stay here. How long until a rider thought to look over the embankment and saw him lying there? He knew he couldn't outrun a man on a horse and certainly couldn't outfight one so he decided to play dead and hope that they would leave him. It was a feeble plan.

Out of the corner of his eye Richard caught movement but before he could react a dark shadow loomed above him and then came crashing down on top of him. He screamed and tried to punch and kick the weight that suddenly smothered him.

'Quiet, boy, or you'll get us both killed,' Sir Thomas hissed at him.

The panic subsided to be replaced with fear that they had been heard. Sir Thomas grabbed Richard by the scruff of the neck pulling him against the suction of the mud and then pushing Richard out in front of him.

'They're everywhere. Our only hope is to crawl along this bloody brook and get as far away from here as possible. Now go!'

Richard crawled on hands and knees, keeping low and moving as quickly but as quietly as he could. They stuck to the shallow water in the centre of the brook away from the thick glutinous mud that would hamper their movement or the beds of reeds that would rustle and give them away. It was difficult going as rocks and stones cut into their hands and knees making them yelp in pain but fear drove them ever onwards. After crawling for around fifteen minutes the water became deeper and faster flowing and the coldness of it began to chill them and bite into their bruised and torn hands and fingers. Eventually the stream flattened out into the landscape and they realised that if they went any further they would no longer have an embankment either side of the stream to shield them from any onlookers. Sir Thomas knelt up and carefully surveyed the landscape around them.

'All clear I think,' he said without any certainty.

Richard sat at the edge of the stream and scratched the nettle rash on his arms and neck.

'Dock leaf, boy,' Sir Thomas offered in advice. 'Here,' he said, proffering a leaf he had just plucked. 'Rub it all over. It will help ease the itching.'

Richard rubbed the leaf over his blistered hands and then helped himself to several more dock leaves from the land at the side of the stream which he rubbed on his arms, face, neck and ankles.

'It's not working,' he complained.

'Give it time, boy.'

Richard scratched at the nettle rash on his neck but then looked up startled as Sir Thomas let out an unexpected laugh.

'Look at the bloody state of us, boy. Battered, bruised and covered from head to toe in shit. Who'd have thought a knight of the realm could end up in such a state? God forbid!' he added.

Sir Thomas suddenly looked more serious. 'I'm presuming your master died on the field, yes?'

Richard didn't answer

'So, you'll be my squire when we return to my estates.' It was a statement not a question but Richard felt compelled to reply.

'Sire, I have no training as a squire. I was raised by a priest and all I know is the church and work in the fields.'

'Then what in God's name were you doing at a battlefield? And why did you arrive with Lord Lovell?' he added as an afterthought. 'It doesn't make sense.'

For a moment Richard considered telling Sir Thomas the truth but decided that it would sound too fanciful.

'Lord Lovell found me on the road leading to the camp and I begged him to let me come with him. I was curious and said I would work doing whatever was needed in the camp. I suppose he felt sorry for me.'

Sir Thomas looked dubious as he scratched his bristled chin. 'Then Lord Lovell should have had the sense to tell you to piss off!'

Richard laughed at that. His thoughts drifted to the friendly viscount who had rescued him and brought him to meet his father. Richard hoped that Francis Lovell still lived and wondered if he'd ever see him again if he were still alive.

'We need to keep moving,' Sir Thomas said as he stood and used a handful of grass in a vain attempt to wipe the filth off his clothing.

Richard grabbed a handful of grass and also tried to wipe the worst of the filth off. Both of them still looked dishevelled and filthy despite their efforts. Their clothes were torn and still wet from crawling through the stream and their hands and knees were bloody and bruised. They looked in a worse state than if they'd been actively involved in the battle that morning.

Sir Thomas walked up the shallow sloping ground into the meadow adjoining the stream.

'There,' he said, pointing to a distant church spire. 'We head in that direction.'

The pair trudged through the wild flowers and long grass of the meadow, walked around the edge of a small wood and continued until they came out on a narrow lane. Sir Thomas was still cautious and beckoned Richard to kneel in the long grass at the side of the packed earth track as he peered in both directions along the lane to make sure that there were no soldiers travelling along it.

'It's all clear, boy,' Sir Thomas said as he stood up.

'My name's Richard, not boy!' Richard said in exasperation.

'Remember who you're talking to, boy!' Sir Thomas growled back with menace. 'Don't forget your place or you'll feel the back of my hand lad.'

'I'm sorry,' Richard apologised as he emerged from the long grass onto the lane. 'It's just you've been calling me boy all day and never once asked my name.'

'Don't you...' Sir Thomas stopped abruptly in mid-sentence and stared beyond Richard.

'Get down!' he suddenly shouted as he dived back into the long grass.

Richard turned to see what had just startled the knight, then wished he had reacted quicker and just followed Sir Thomas into the cover of the grass. Instead, he was standing in the lane with a troop of mounted knights galloping straight towards him.

The long grass at the side of the lane shone in the summer sun as it parted and rustled. Richard realised that Sir Thomas was crawling through it to get as far away as possible. Richard assumed that the mounted knights hadn't seen Sir Thomas but it was obvious by now that they had seen him. It was too late for him to join Sir Thomas in hiding so Richard made the decision to walk quickly towards the approaching knights before they drew level with the spot where Sir Thomas was hiding.

The knights slowed to a canter as they approached him and Richard was suddenly acutely aware that he didn't know what to say to them. His mouth was dry and his stomach churned with nervous anticipation as the horses trotted towards him. If the knights asked him where he was from, he was not familiar with the area and didn't know the name of a single village or town nearby. At the very least he feared that he was probably about to be captured by Henry Tudor's men or possibly just cut down and left to die in that lane, but with great fortitude he continued to walk on towards the knights to give Sir Thomas time to escape.

The knights pulled up and surrounded him. They eyed him suspiciously.

'Where are you going?' one of them asked.

Richard struggled to find the words to extricate himself from the predicament he now found himself in.

'Well? Speak up, boy,' the knight demanded.

*

Adam Laybourn watched with dispassion as the dead king's naked body was slung over a horse in preparation for its journey back to Leicester. There the corpse would be publicly displayed for all to see, so that they would know Richard was truly dead and that Henry Tudor was now king. Sir Rhys Ap Thomas, the

Welsh magnate whose men had formed the backbone of Tudor's army and who, minutes before, had been knighted on the battlefield by a grateful King Henry, grabbed the dead former king's hair and lifted up his head to stare into the lifeless eyes.

'Richard Crookback's not so mighty now, is he boys?' Ap Thomas called aloud to his compatriots.

One man let out a snort of derision while several others voiced their agreement with Ap Thomas who, still smiling, unsheathed his dagger and walked around to the other side of the horse carrying the dead king's body. One of his men held the reins and stroked the horse's nose to calm the nervous beast. With unexpected and sudden ferocity Ap Thomas stabbed his dagger into the dead king's right buttock.

'Not so high and mighty with a pair of bollocks hanging out of his arse is he!' he joked.

Laughter rippled through the crowd of onlooking soldiers as they saw the handle of the ballock dagger, with its two oval swellings at the guard resembling a pair of testicles, sticking out of the dead king's buttock.

Laybourn turned away disgusted by the spectacle and led his horse back towards his master, Lord Stanley, who stood talking to King Henry, Jasper Tudor and Sir William Stanley.

Sir William Stanley had delivered the victory to Henry Tudor while Lord Stanley had kept his force in check as he sat impassively astride his horse watching the events unfold on the plain beneath him. Only when the battle was over and the outcome certain did Lord Stanley venture down from the hill to congratulate his stepson on his victory. One of Sir William Stanley's men had picked up the gold coronet that King Richard had worn atop his helmet and handed it to Sir William, who in turn had handed it to Lord Stanley. Holding the gold coronet and filled with self-importance, Lord Stanley had greeted Henry Tudor and suggested that the new king should be crowned immediately on the nearest hilltop for all his men to see.

On the crest of Garbrody's hill Lord Stanley made a great show of holding the gold coronet on high with both hands and turning full circle to show it to every man present before letting it descend to rest upon Tudor's head, declaring in a loud voice, 'King Henry! God save the king!' as cheers and shouts of acclamation echoed from the assembled throng of warriors. Not ten minutes later, King Henry VII stood laughing and talking with the men who had made him king.

A mounted messenger wearing the de Vere livery arrived, quickly dismounted and went down on bended knee in front of the group of men.

'What news from my lord Oxford?' King Henry asked.

The messenger raised his head.

'The Earl of Oxford has broken the king's...' he quickly corrected himself, 'the usurper's army, Your Grace.'

King Henry glared at the man.

'The earl is pursuing the fleeing army towards Dadlington, Your Grace,' the messenger added with haste.

'Tell my lord Oxford to finish the job and meet me in Leicester before nightfall.'

'Yes, Your Grace,' the man replied before remounting his horse and heading off again, relieved to have escaped the wrath of his new king.

'It's time to leave for Leicester. Have your men ready,' King Henry ordered the Stanleys. Then he turned and walked away while continuing a conversation with Jasper Tudor.

Lord Stanley waved a scroll of parchment in the air as he barked orders for his captains to ready the men to depart. He ceased shouting when he saw Adam Laybourn approaching and beckoned him over.

'I have a task for you, Adam,' Lord Stanley said. 'Take six men with you and ride to Leicester with haste. Find the mayor and aldermen and deliver this.' He handed Laybourn the scroll he had been brandishing. 'Tell them of our great victory, and that King Henry will be arriving in the town shortly. They are to make preparations to receive their sovereign lord.'

Laybourn acknowledged Lord Stanley and then took the scroll that had been scribbled in haste and bound with a leather thong. He turned and guided his horse back towards the mass of soldiers and knights that now bustled around the battlefield readying themselves to leave.

'Oh, Adam,' Lord Stanley called after him. 'Secure me lodgings at the best inn in the town.'

Lord Stanley flipped him a gold coin which Laybourn caught before turning and heading off to find the men to accompany him to Leicester. Minutes later the seven mounted men were galloping along the lane that cut across the fens towards Sutton Cheyney and beyond to the town of Leicester.

The lanes and fields were deserted as Laybourn expected them to be in the aftermath of such a great battle. No one would be foolish enough to be caught outside by Oxford's soldiers and mistaken for fugitives from the usurper's army. The seven knights hadn't seen any of Oxford's men themselves as those butchers were pursuing the remnants of the dead king's army towards Dadlington.

As his horse galloped along the hard baked earth of the fen

lane Laybourn felt the rush of air on his face; the first relief he had felt all day from the August sun. He licked his dry cracked lips and realised that he hadn't drunk anything for several hours. His mouth was parched and his throat coated with the dust kicked up by the horses from the dry road. More reason to spur his horse on and get into Leicester as soon as possible, he thought. As the vision of a welcoming jug of cold ale flickered across his mind Laybourn noticed a boy in the lane ahead. He slowed his horse and his fellow knights did the same. Laybourn wondered why a boy would be wandering the lane alone, far from the nearest hovel or cottage. Didn't he realise the danger he was in?

'Where are you going?' Laybourn asked the boy as the group of knights pulled their coursers up around him.

The boy was dirty and dishevelled and looked like he kept pigs and probably slept with them too. The boy looked up in stunned silence but did not reply.

'Well? Speak up, boy,' Laybourn demanded.

'That way,' Richard mumbled fearfully, pointing down the lane and hoping that the knight wouldn't ask him what village lay in that direction.

'You don't want to go that way,' Laybourn cautioned him. 'There's been a battle and the fugitives have fled towards Dadlington. If you get caught up in that you won't live long enough to see the day out.'

'Oh, I didn't know there'd been a battle.' Richard feigned ignorance of the day's events. 'Who was fighting, sire?'

'King Henry has defeated the usurper, Richard Plantagenet.'

'King Henry?' Richard enquired. 'But our king is King Richard.'

Laybourn had a message to deliver and didn't have the time or the inclination to have a conversation with the boy who was obviously a dullard but he also didn't want to leave the boy to the mercy of Oxford's men. Laybourn had seen enough slaughter for one day.

'Here, jump up and I'll drop you off in the next village,' Laybourn said as he proffered a hand ready to pull the boy up onto the rear of his horse.

'Where are you going, sire?' Richard asked, taking the knight's hand.

'Leicester,' Laybourn replied.

'My father's dying and I have an uncle in Leicester. I need to see him so I'd be ever so grateful if you could point me in the right direction.'

Richard looked at Laybourn imploringly. Laybourn let sympathy get the better of him.

'Get on,' he said as he pulled the boy up behind him. 'Hold tight, we're in a hurry,' he warned as he dug in his spurs, shook the reins, and forced his horse into a gallop.

The group of knights and the filthy boy sped off towards Leicester leaving Sir Thomas Montgomery lying in the long grass besides the fen lane. He let out a deep sigh as he released the grip on the dagger in his hand and thanked God that the boy hadn't given him away.

9

he town of Leicester buzzed with activity. People scurried into the streets, alleyways, and lined the bridges leading across the river into the town, jostling for position to see the new king when he finally arrived. News of King Henry's victory had reached the town before Laybourn and his comrades arrived. No doubt, Laybourn thought to himself, news of the usurper's defeat had been borne by those fleeing the battle and made his task of informing the mayor superfluous. Nevertheless, it was a task he was ordered to complete so he urged his horse on past the hovels and narrow strips of arable land that lay either side of the road into Leicester. As he approached the first of the narrow bridges that led into the town across the River Soar, Laybourn could see the Augustinian friary on the island in the middle of the river's tributary at the far end of the bridge. There black-robed figures went about their daily routine, oblivious to the excitement that crackled like wildfire beyond the walls of the friary.

As Laybourn and his comrades approached, a crowd surged forward eager for fresh news. The seven mounted men struggled to make headway against the tide of people that suddenly surrounded them.

'King Henry has defeated the usurper.' One of Laybourn's comrades called out the scrap of news to placate the crowd. 'We have news for the mayor so let us through,' he shouted when the crowd did not give way.

The crowd continued to press and cajole them for more information but the mounted men at arms pushed on, ignoring the questions and eventually making their way in single file over the bridge. At the far side a throng of people again crowded around them, barring their way and continually clamouring for news of the battle.

Again, one of the mounted men called to the crowd, 'King Henry has defeated the usurper. Let us through, we have news for the mayor.'

Laybourn wanted to let the boy down from the back of his horse but was unable to do so in the crush of bodies that pressed against him. He wished he'd dropped the stinking wretch off on the other side of the river or even better, in Sutton Cheyney when he'd had the chance. He let out a deep sigh as he instantly regretted the thought. It wasn't the boy's fault, Laybourn conceded to himself. The boy was just in the wrong place at the wrong time and he was just tired, irritable, and needed to get out of this relentless afternoon heat. A jug of cold ale beckoned as soon as he could fight his way through this crowd and speak to the mayor. The seven mounted men turned right after the bridge and slowly forced their way through the crowds, past the friary and then left onto the road that crossed the main bridge across the Soar and on into the town. Laybourn could see the mayor and aldermen waiting for his arrival, resplendent in their finest clothes and jewellery, as they stood on the bridge beneath the chapel built over its eastern arch.

Finally, he neared the group and set down the boy before he approached them.

'Go find your uncle,' he said as the boy melted into the crowd lining the bridge.

Looking up and forging on towards the men gathered to welcome him, it was obvious to Laybourn that the mayor and aldermen were nervous. He and his comrades were the first of King Henry's men they had seen and they would be conscious of the fact that they had welcomed the usurper and supplied his army on its way to do battle with them and the new king. It must be preying on these men's minds whether King Henry would forgive them or hold them accountable. Laybourn understood their fears as he approached them.

'Welcome, welcome,' the mayor bowed as he greeted the seven mounted men.

'We hear that the Earl of Richmond has won a great battle over the tyrant Richard Plantagenet. God be praised.'

'The Earl of Richmond is your sovereign lord and you will refer to him as King Henry,' Laybourn said with sternness in his voice, taking advantage of the man's fears as he scowled down from his horse at the mayor.

'Of course, sire,' the mayor grovelled for an apology. 'It is not in doubt. I meant nothing by my careless words.'

The mayor wouldn't defer to a mere emissary under normal circumstances but, for the moment at least, Laybourn revelled in the power Henry Tudor's victory had given him.

'Lord Stanley sends formal news of King Henry's victory and asks you to prepare for the king's arrival.'

Laybourn handed the mayor the scroll prepared by Lord Stanley. The mayor felt Laybourn's eyes boring into him as he opened and read it. He shifted uncomfortably beneath their stare before brushing away a wisp of white hair that had fallen over his eyes. After reading the message he looked up at Laybourn once more and smiled broadly.

'Consider it done, sire,' he replied with false sincerity. 'We would be delighted to entertain His Grace when he arrives,' the mayor said, gesturing towards the nervous-looking aldermen who stood behind him. 'Leicester offers King Henry and his men its hospitality with open arms.'

'Then please direct me towards a suitable inn,' Laybourn said, the irritability clear in his voice.

The mayor summoned a squire who led the seven mounted men through the town to the High Street where several inns were located. Laybourn smiled when he saw the sign of a blue boar hanging from the gable of one inn. The paint was still wet and had been smeared in the landlord's haste to repaint the white boar sign, a symbol of the deceased king, Richard. Did the landlord know that the blue boar was the sign of the Earl of Oxford, one of King Henry's chief supporters, or did he just have it painted any colour he could lay his hands on in his panic to get the white boar covered before King Henry and his men arrived? Laybourn supposed it didn't matter but wondered how many of King Henry's supporters would also notice. He didn't envy the landlord if they did. No doubt there would be many a drunken soldier in Leicester that night and it wouldn't take much of a reason to spark a fight.

Laybourn ignored the Blue Boar Inn and decided to arrange lodgings for himself and the leading members of Lord Stanley's retinue in a slightly smaller inn on the opposite side of the High Street.

'The Cross Keys will do us fine, lad,' he called to the squire as he looked up at the wooden sign painted with two gold keys crossing each other that hung over the inn's doorway.

As the squire led his horse into the courtyard of the inn Laybourn licked his dry cracked lips and the thought of a jug of cold ale again crossed his mind. It would be fun to sit and drink cold ale in the late afternoon sun whilst watching the landlord over the road shit himself in fear when Tudor or Oxford's men noticed his hastily painted Blue Boar sign.

*

Richard left the seven knights behind on the bridge and pushed through the crowd that had gathered to see the arrival of Henry Tudor. He fought his way under the archway that spanned one end of the bridge, pushing against the tide of expectant onlookers, until he was inside the town walls. There the crowds finally relented and he felt able to breathe again amid the usual coming and goings of a market town. Instinctively he placed his hand at his side and felt the pouch of gold and silver coins his father had given him the night before. The pouch and the money were there, safe. Richard reminded himself that he must not flaunt his wealth or he would be questioned and would probably be accused of stealing the money, but it did give him some immediate options. He could afford to stay at an inn for the night or he could purchase a horse and head back down south to Eastwell. However, neither choice filled him with inspiration. The more that he considered it the more he realised that his options weren't that favourable. He feared sleeping in an inn with soldiers and strangers who might steal his money or question him about who he was and why he was there, and to pay for a room to himself or buy a horse would arouse suspicion. After all, why would a filthy dishevelled boy have a purse full of gold and silver coins?

Whilst he pondered what to do Richard walked through the butchers' shambles and past the meat sellers who traded in the streets around Saint Nicholas' Church. The smell reminded him that he had not eaten since breaking fast with rye bread and ale at first light that morning. His stomach rumbled as he wandered aimlessly, following the streets wherever they led him. He walked past the open areas where the sheep market and swine market were held, and on towards the site of the Saturday market in the south-east quarter of the town. Eventually he paused and looked around him. A young boy rolled a wooden hoop along the street, guiding and speeding it up with a stick. A group of children ran behind him laughing, giggling, and urging him to go faster. Two women stood gossiping on a doorstep. A steady stream of people walked up and down the street and Richard watched with amusement as one elderly man struggled to control a goat which stubbornly kept stopping and refusing to travel in the direction the old man was trying to pull it in.

When he was sure no one was watching Richard turned into a narrow alleyway between a timber-framed house and a large hall belonging to the Guild of Saint George. There, under the eaves of the two buildings and shielded from public scrutiny, he loosened the leather pouch from his belt and tipped the coins into his hand to count them. A small fortune in silver and gold filled his cupped palm, way more than a simple priest's son would normally see in a lifetime. The wealth that lay in his hands made Richard nervous. He took out a few small coins, enough to pay for food and drink, and put the rest back in the leather pouch which he secured onto his belt, tying several knots and pulling them as tight as his strength would allow. He headed back out into the street trying to look casual and unassuming. Even then he found it difficult not to let his hand nervously keep falling to his waist every few minutes to check that the pouch was still there.

Richard bought some bread, cheese and small ale with the coins he had kept in his hand. After he had sated his hunger and thirst, he wandered around the town exploring its streets and alleys, until time overtook him and he realised that he would finally have to make a decision about where his future lay. He did not want to remain in the town at nightfall so decided to follow the decaying Roman town wall until he came to the next gate. He would follow the road away from the town, wherever that led him, and when far enough away he would buy a horse somewhere where he would attract less attention.

To Richard's dismay the crowds by the town gate had grown throughout the afternoon. He fought through the mass of people, squeezing between fat merchants, past filthy labourers and every other class of citizen that the town held, until he found himself under the same archway that the knight had dropped him off at several hours before. He pushed onwards through the crowd, over the bridge and along the side of the Augustinian friary, battling against the tide of people every step of the way. Eventually he was within sight of the two Bow Bridges that crossed the western arm of the River Soar and led away from the town, but that was as far as he could go. The mayor, aldermen and leading dignitaries of the town had now gathered on the far side of the larger of the Bow Bridges ahead of the crowd to await the arrival of their new king. Armed men blocked the path onto the bridge and kept the swelling crowd at a distance. They also prevented Richard and others from leaving the town in that direction. Exasperated, Richard let out a deep sigh and turned back the way he had come knowing that he would have to fight his way back through the crowd into the town to get out through one of the other three gates.

Behind him a fanfare of trumpets sounded and heralds' voices echoed across the river as they announced the arrival of the new king. Richard turned and craned his neck to see above the heads of the people in front of him. As he stood on his tiptoes, he was almost knocked off his feet and was then suddenly carried away on an ebullient tide of people as they surged forward to see the arrival of Henry Tudor. Richard was pushed along, unable to stand still let alone walk in the opposite direction, until the momentum of the onrushing crowd threw him forcibly against the line of armed men stationed to prevent anyone getting on to the bridge. A brutish bearded man armed with a thick wooden staff bellowed at him and used the staff to push him back into the press of shouting men, women and children.

Richard struggled to stay on his feet as the crowd behind him continued to drive forward and the line of armed men aggressively pushed them back. He fought for breath as he was trapped between the two groups and pushed back and forth as neither party would yield to the other. Tempers flared. A flurry of punches was thrown by a man who had been hit in the face with the butt of a sword to keep him back. As he tried to get revenge upon his assailant another armed man beat him down with a wooden staff until he disappeared beneath the feet of the pressing crowd. A woman screeched and cursed the armed men for their violent reaction and then tried to claw at the face of one of them before being pushed back herself.

Beyond the squabbling crowd, horns and trumpets blew as the vanguard of Henry Tudor's triumphal procession reached the mayor and alderman on the far side of the bridge. The party of dignitaries greeted them and then the procession moved on with hardly a pause. As King Henry himself mounted the bridge on horseback at the head of his army with a gold coronet upon his head, the anger of the crowd dissipated and they parted to let the king and his men pass by. The armed men who moments before had been pushing them back now merged into the crowd and Richard found himself standing alone by the stone pillar that marked the end of the parapet of the bridge.

As King Henry approached Richard felt hatred and resentment well up inside him. His hand drifted to his belt feeling for his knife. He would gladly give his own life for the chance to plunge a steel blade into the man responsible for the murder of his father. He was now within touching distance of King Henry and filled with enough violent hate and anger to take down the king and ten of his men with a blade but his hand fell on nothing more than the purse tied to his belt. He looked down to his waist and forlornly ran his hands around the length of his belt already realising that he did not have his knife with him. His fists clenched and he was tempted to snatch a sword or knife from the sheath of a passing soldier but knew he would be cut down before he could draw it and get to the king. The moment was past and Richard realised that he could do nothing but watch futilely as the man responsible for his father's death rode by.

Jasper Tudor and the Earl of Oxford rode behind King Henry followed two abreast by the king's retinue and army as they rode over the bridge and on into the town. The watching crowd, with the earlier flash of violence seemingly forgotten, cheered raucously, waving arms, hats, strips of cloth or anything else to hand to welcome their new monarch. Richard watched, the hatred still seething and boiling within him, as horses and soldiers marched, clinked and rattled their way past in an ostentatious procession of colour. He noted that every battered and bruised soldier was patted on the back by someone in the crowd and welcomed as a returning hero; ironically cheered and greeted by those same people who only the day before had cheered his father's army as it rode out to meet these rebels in battle. The thought sickened him and he realised that he couldn't wait to leave this foul nest of hypocritical vipers. As soon as the procession of knights and men at arms had passed, he would be over the bridge to find somewhere to buy a horse and make his way south.

Then, amid the line of men and horses that crossed the bridge, he saw a naked body slung over a horse. It was spattered in mud and blood and the hands and feet were tied with lengths of cord. The man's right buttock bore a deep gash and his hair was matted thickly with dried blood, though a gaping hole at the base of the skull exposed the man's brain matter in a sickening display for all to see.

'No!' Richard let out an involuntary cry as he pushed past several mounted men in an attempt to get to his father's body.

'Stand back, bachgen,' a gruff dark-skinned Welshman hollered at Richard as he blocked the path to the dead king. 'You don't want to be taken for a Yorkist sympathiser or you'll end up the same way as that there usurper.'

Blinded by tears and rage Richard pushed on, oblivious to the Welshman's words. The Welshman again shouted for him to get back but Richard tried to force his way past to reach his father's blood-stained body. Richard attempted to grab the horse's reins, spooking the horse and making it shy to the side. As it did so the dead king's already shattered skull thudded against the stone parapet of the bow bridge. Several people in the crowd let out gasps of shock as it happened and a grizzled old woman with lank grey hair and bright blue eyes stared at Richard from the end of the bridge and smiled wryly before she slid back into the depths of the tempestuous crowd of townsfolk.

The Welshman grabbed hold of Richard, wrapped his arms around him and pushed him back into one of the niches that was recessed into the stonework of the bridge. There he held Richard firmly, despite the boy's struggling and protestations, as the dead king's body was carried onwards on its journey into Leicester. The other Welshmen that accompanied the dead king's body across the bridge laughed and jeered at Richard as they passed by, eager to provoke a reaction.

'The boy thinks King Dick is still fit to rule!' one man scoffed as his comrades laughed in appreciation of his humour.

'Throw the Yorkist brat off the bridge and be done with it,' another taunted.

'Whatever your grief, it's not worth dying for,' the Welshman advised Richard with genuine compassion. 'Ignore them and be on your way.'

He squeezed something into Richard's palm and then closed his hands around Richard's before backing away. As the Welshman turned and trotted after his compatriots Richard sank to the ground in utter dejection. He sat in the stone niche sobbing as Henry Tudor's army continued to file past him with barely a second glance. As fast as he wiped away the tears more appeared; an endless flow that reddened and stung his eyes before falling and soaking into the dusty ground where he sat. His throat was dry and he felt throbbing, the first sign of a headache beginning at his temples. He opened his hand and saw that the Welshman had pressed a small coin into his palm. In disgust he stood and tossed the sympathy money over the parapet into the bickering waters of the River Soar below.

When he turned back towards the centre of the bridge an unexpected sight greeted him and filled him with delight and trepidation in equal measure. He wiped his tear-blurred eyes on his sleeve trying to clear them enough to take in the scene in front of him and make sure he wasn't imagining it. Half a dozen prisoners from the battle, stripped of all armour and valuables and with hands bound in front of them, were being herded across the bridge. To Richard's surprise, among their number was Sir William Catesby. Despite the broken nose, missing teeth and bruised face Richard instantly recognised the jovial, blond, tousle-haired friend of his father.

Catesby caught sight of Richard at the same time but instantly turned away, pretending not to recognise the boy. Richard hesitated, wanting to speak to him but realising the danger of doing so. Catesby, fearing the boy would give himself away, subtly shook his head and gestured with his eyes for Richard to leave. A soldier pushed Catesby in the back forcing him onwards. Catesby sent out a silent prayer as the soldier's action sent him staggering past Richard who thankfully hadn't said a word. Richard watched with puffy red eyes as Catesby and the other prisoners were led onwards across the bridge and through the turbulent crowd who jeered, insulted, cursed, poked, and threw clods of soil and grass at them, torn up from the banks of the River Soar.

Despite his dislike of the townsfolk Richard knew then that he could not leave Leicester until he had spoken to William Catesby.

Catesby was one of the few remaining men who knew his real identity and could tell him what to do and where his destiny lay. The problem was, how could he get close to Catesby without arousing suspicion?

10

Sunset stained the evening sky blood red following King Henry's arrival into Leicester. Some townsfolk took it as a good omen, some as a bad one. Few doubted that Henry Tudor was their rightful king; dead King Richard's head striking the stone parapet of Bow Bridge as the old wizened seer had prophesised was proof of that, but would Henry be a good king? Was the blood-red sky a portent of what was to come or God's epitaph of a bloody battle now fought?

Richard sat in the corner of the inn at the end of the long trestle table silently listening to townsfolk argue for and against King Richard and King Henry. Shadows cast by the sparse light of tallow candles danced across the inn's walls, as a plume of smoke mingled in the warm air with the stale odours of ale, sweat and dog urine.

A talbot, the inn's guard dog, came sniffing around Richard, seeking out the remnants of a bread trencher that was still soggy with gravy from his evening meal. Richard pulled off a hunk of the stale gravy-soaked bread and threw it on the ground where the dog avidly gulped it down then pressed against him, nuzzling his hand in the hope of being fed more. Richard pulled off more pieces of the stale bread and fed the animal one at a time as he continued to listen to the conversations going on around him.

'Old King Dick wasn't that bad,' one man asserted. 'He did good by us common folk and wasn't as haughty as most lords. Did you hear his speech as he left town to go to battle? He promised to come back and reward the citizens of Leicester. Can you imagine Henry Tudor doing that? The only reward we got from him was bloody Welshmen stealing our food and taking our home for the night with not so much as a thank you,' he said bitterly.

'But did you see King Dick's crooked back?' a rather portly fellow interjected. 'A crooked body can only be a sign of God's displeasure. It's proof that he was evil and should not have been king, which was obviously why God granted Tudor the victory.'

'Obviously, my fat hairy arse!' The portly fellow bellowed. 'Don't talk such tripe, man. King Richard was like it from birth, so if God was displeased with him, He wouldn't have let him become king in the first place, would He?'

'Then why would God afflict him so?' A ruddy-faced man with a bushy white beard questioned.

'God afflicted you with a face that looks like a sheep's arse,' another man retorted, 'but we don't take that as a sign that you're evil.'

The gathered party burst into laughter and the man with the bushy white beard gave his tormentor a friendly shove in the chest.

'Are you going to see King Dick and pay your respects?' the portly fellow asked.

'Aren't they taking his body to bury in London?' white beard asked.

'No, the king has decreed that King Dick's body is to be displayed in the church in the New Work for a few days. He wants everyone to see it and spread the word that crippled King

Dick is well and truly dead.'

'Bloody hell!' exclaimed white beard. 'His torn body will stink to high heaven in this summer heat after a few days.'

'That's why I'm going first thing in the morning,' the fat man chuckled.

Richard had heard enough. He tossed the last of his bread trencher on the floor for the talbot to gobble down and squeezed past the party of men who were still discussing the state of the deceased King's remains. Richard made his way out through the inn's doorway into the courtyard at the rear. The smell of the nearby cess pit assaulted his nostrils so he pulled his shirt over his nose and took a deep breath which he held until he had mounted the wooden steps of the staircase that led to an external gallery, then on to the dormitory where he would reside for the evening. For a few pence he'd purchased an evening meal and a space for the night in the shared bedchamber. Even in such an unsavoury establishment as this Richard had been forced to pay in advance as the innkeeper initially refused to let him in, claiming he looked like a vagrant and would not be able to pay.

Once inside the dormitory he squinted in the flickering half-light cast out from two fat-soaked rushlights burning at the far end of the long bedchamber. The space was filled with wooden bedframes, strung with rope, with straw mattresses encased in hemp covers placed on top. Two, three or sometimes four people would sleep in each bed so that the innkeeper could maximise his profits. Richard made his way through the tightly spaced empty beds until he found himself a space to sleep at the far end of the dormitory beneath one of the rushlights. There, far from the doorway where, he suspected, drunken revellers would later stagger in search of a bed, he hoped to lay undisturbed for the night. He took off his boots, curled up on the thin straw mattress and adjusted his purse which, still heavy with coins, dug into his side. He made sure that it was still tied securely to his belt, then took off his grubby, mud-stained tunic, folded it and placed it beneath his head.

As he lay on his side staring down the length of the dormitory into the darkness, he mused over the events of the previous few days. As memories of his father came flooding back, he recalled the ring the king had given to him. He pulled a leather cord that hung around his neck and fished the ring out from deep within his shirt. He examined it in the flickering rushlight. The ring gleamed, shining gold as the light caught it. The jester's face stared up at him through the bright red gemstone, taunting him with its cruel smile. He was a king's son with a king's pouch of gold at his waist and a king's ring in his hand. Yet he found himself alone on a hard thin mattress in a rough town inn, noisy revellers below him, mud and filth staining his clothes and skin, and the foul odour of the inn's cesspit clinging to his nostrils. He fought back the tears welling up in his eyes but was unable to prevent them bursting forth and cascading down his cheeks.

'What's the matter with you?' a husky voice called from the darkness, startling him.

Richard sat bolt upright and stared into the dark void of the bedchamber trying to gauge where the voice had come from.

'Cat got your tongue?' the voice rasped.

The man the voice belonged to started coughing; a hacking cough that came from deep within his chest. As the man sat up and spat phlegm into a piece of coarse cloth he held, Richard could see him in the guttering light lying on a bed in the far corner of the room. He hadn't noticed the man when he first entered the dormitory but now, even in the meagre light cast out from the fat-dipped rushes, he could see that the man was old, pale and extremely thin with grey stubble covering the lower half of his gaunt face.

'Nothing's the matter with me,' Richard eventually responded. 'I've just had a long day and I'm tired.'

The old man coughed fitfully.

'Are you alright?' Richard enquired.

The old man got up and shambled across the dormitory, feeling his way as he went until he arrived at the bed next to Richard and sat down.

'Nay, lad, I'm dying. I have an illness that is eating me up from the inside,' he said before breaking into a bout of coughing again. 'I've either got the chills or I'm sweating. The weight's just falling off of me and now I'm naught but a bag of bones. And this bloody cough…' he said as he started another bout of hacking coughing.

'Can I do anything to help?' Richard asked almost apologetically.

The old man grinned showing a row of worn yellow teeth.

'That's a pretty bauble you have hidden in your shirt. Steal it, did you?'

'No!' Richard exclaimed. 'It was my father's before he died.' Richard clutched the ring defensively.

'A poor boy like you doesn't have a father who could afford such a pretty trinket. I'm guessing you've struck lucky and stolen it off of one of the noblemen in town with Henry Tudor's army?' He stared enquiringly at Richard waiting for an answer. Moments ticked by awkwardly but no answer was forthcoming.

'Well good luck to you, I say.'

The old man laughed changing the mood.

'I would have fought for King Richard against the rebels if I'd been well enough. A bloody Welshman as king of England! Who would ever have thought it possible? You can go out there and rob all the Welsh bastards blind for all I care.'

With that he started coughing again before spitting more phlegm into his cloth.

'You really would have fought for King Richard?'

'Aye, that I would. He was a good king. As good as they get.'

'And would you help one of his men if you could, even now the king is dead?' Richard looked dubiously at the old man, not sure whether to trust any answer he gave.

'Ah! The ring belongs to one of King Richard's men. Given in return for a pledge of support from your master, I'll wager?'

Again, Richard said nothing as the old man waited expectantly for an answer.

'Cat really has got your tongue, ain't it, my lad?'

The old man hacked up a lump of phlegm into his coarse cloth before continuing.

'Let me guess. You have a Yorkist soldier, knight, noble or whatever he is, hidden, and now the town is swarming with Tudor's rebels you can't get him out. Am I right?'

'Not exactly,' Richard replied enigmatically.

'Bloody hell, lad, you're hard work. Do you think you can spit it out before I'm dead and buried?'

Richard smiled wistfully at the old man.

'Henry Tudor's men have captured my master. I just need to know where they're likely to be keeping him.'

'They wouldn't keep him captive unless he's important or wealthy, but I know the answer to that from the trinket you're clutching. I should think he's probably in the gaol at the far end of this street between St John's Hospital and the Shire Hall but I wouldn't go down there if I was you, lad. They'll just as soon hang you as look at you if they know you've a Yorkist master.'

'But if I needed to speak to him, how could I do it?'

'Is it a death wish you have, my lad?' The old man shook his head, his wide grin exposing empty voids and the odd stump of grey-black amid his worn yellow teeth.

'The only way is to go in the dead of night. You'd have to turn right down the second street along, St John's Lane it's called, before you reached the gaol. Then go around the back of St John's Hospital, through the garden and over its wall to get to the back of the gaol. It's risky mind. The night watchman will be patrolling and if anyone in the hospital, gaol or nearby inns or houses sees you and raises the hue and cry you'll be hung as a thief for creeping about out there at night. It's not worth it lad. It really ain't.'

The old man patted Richard on the shoulder then rose and made his way back to his own bed in the flickering rushlight.

'Good night, lad. Get some sleep and we'll think on it on the morrow.'

*

Richard woke with a start. He had intended to stay awake until all the drunken revellers had staggered into bed and fallen asleep. Instead, he had been the one to fall asleep. He didn't even hear anyone else come into the dormitory he'd been so soundly asleep. He had no idea how long he'd been asleep, although both of the rushlights had burned themselves out. He squinted into the dark void trying to tell if the beds next to him contained sleeping bodies. A snore and grunt from somewhere near the centre of the room told him that they did, even before his eyes began to make out their shape. He put his hand to his chest and felt the lump where he'd hidden the ring. Then he felt for the purse at his waist and was relieved to find that that was still there too. He sat up and picked up the crumpled tunic that had supported his head and pulled it on over his shirt. Then he felt around under the bed until he found his boots.

As he stood, holding a leather boot in each hand, the bed creaked loudly and Richard gritted his teeth fearing someone would wake and ask what he was doing. Instead, a loud fart echoed through the dormitory. Richard supressed a giggle as he crept slowly across the room towards the doorway, sidling his way between the rows of beds. The floorboards creaked and to Richard the noise seemed to overwhelm the gentle sound of breathing or the odd cough or snore that emanated from the room. When the door was within reach, he banged his shin against a wooden bed frame and let out a strangled grunt of pain.

'Good luck and don't get caught,' a voice whispered, startling Richard.

'Thank you. I'll try not to,' Richard whispered in reply to the old man as he rubbed his aching shin.

Then he was out onto the wooden gallery and down the stairs leading to the inn's courtyard. The night air was warm and thick clouds covered the sky, obscuring the moon. Richard made his way to the gateway that separated the courtyard from the street. It was bolted shut. As he began to ease the bolt open it grated against the metal socket. The inn's talbot started barking at the noise and in his panic, Richard left the gate and dived into the shadows at the side of the inn's stable. The talbot, attached by a leash to its kennel, ran into the courtyard and growled and barked at the shadows. It snarled and strained at the maximum length of the leash, its claws tearing at the packed earth of the courtyard in its frenzied attempt to reach the intruder hidden in the shadows.

Richard chose not to hang around until the innkeeper came out to investigate the commotion. He placed one foot upon an empty barrel at the side of the stable and hoisted himself up and over the stone wall marking the boundary of the inn. He dropped down into a narrow lane that ran between the side of the inn and St. Peter's Church. As the barking continued from the courtyard behind him Richard quickly crossed the lane and moved on to another lane leading to the church. He entered the churchyard and tentatively made his way forward in the dark until he pressed his hand flat against the rough-hewn exterior stone wall of the church. He used the stonework to guide and steady himself in the darkness as he traversed the uneven mounds and divots until he reached the far side of the churchyard. From there he was able to make his way onto another lane and find the junction with the High Street.

Despite his roundabout journey he had come onto the High Street just a few hundred yards from the gate of the inn he had originally intended to leave by. He paused, looking up and down the street, squinting in vain as he tried to make out any discernible shapes, before stepping out and walking away from the direction of the inn, where he could still hear the barking talbot and also a man's voice berating the noisy hound.

The High Street was black as pitch with not even a glimmer of candlelight escaping from any building to illuminate his way. Richard stole down the street, clinging to the edge beneath the eaves of the overhanging houses and inns. He crept silently through the enveloping darkness, his heart pounding so loudly he feared someone would hear it. He arrived at St John's Hospital, which stood on the corner of the High Street and a lane that disappeared past gardens and orchards and on into the never-ending night. The poor and destitute who resided in the hospital slept fast as Richard edged his way into the stygian depths of the lane.

Clouds parted to reveal an almost full moon. Silver-grey moonlight bathed the end of the imposing timber-framed building exposing the entrance to a walled garden. The gate was bolted shut from the inside but Richard scaled the wall with ease, crossing the garden, climbing the wall on the other side and dropping into the open area at the rear of the gaol as the old man had told him it was possible to do. He crouched, expecting someone to cry out at any moment but the only sounds he heard were the distant screech of some night creature and the thumping of his own heart, threatening to burst out of his chest and give him away.

Occasionally moonlight found its way between the massed ranks of thick clouds which trapped the heat of the day underneath them to make the evening warm and humid, even at this late hour. Richard knew it was well past midnight but could not be sure how long it was to sunrise. His back and armpits were drenched in sweat; whether through the humidity, his exertions or nerves he was not sure.

He scanned the back of the gaol in the fleeting moonlight, observing a heavy wooden door and a row of shuttered windows on the ground floor. He kept himself low to the ground and shuffled his way across the open space to the rear of the building. He crouched beneath one of the shuttered windows not knowing if Catesby was held there or in another room in the gaol. Coming here was a mistake, he decided. He could quietly call through each shutter in an attempt to locate Catesby but he'd probably wake prisoners and guards alike. Richard wavered as he tried to decide whether to stay or go. Then tentatively he tapped on the shutter. After a minute he realised he was holding his breath in anticipation. He let out a deep breath and tapped again slightly harder. He found that his hand was shaking uncontrollably as he went to tap a third time so instead, he put his mouth to the shutter and made a noise.

'Pssssst.'

He repeated it several times. 'Pssssst. Pssssst.'

Eventually he heard shuffling from behind the shutters.

'Who's there?' a voice whispered.

Richard paused trying to decide how to respond and whether to give his name.

'Richard,' he nervously replied.

'What do you want? Why are you waking us at this ungodly hour?' the voice whispered again.

'I need to talk to William Catesby,' Richard replied in hushed tones.

'Who are you again?' the voice asked.

Before he could reply the shutter opened to reveal a face pressed against the tiny opening trying to peer out.

'I don't know you,' the man said.

'Err, is Sir William there?' Richard asked, as a sickening feeling started to spread through his stomach and he could feel himself trembling with nerves.

The man at the window was pushed aside and Catesby's face appeared in his place.

'Bloody hell, Richard! What in God's name are you doing here?' Catesby asked.

'I had to see you. There's no one else left.' Richard's voice quivered with emotion. 'My father's dead, Sir Francis has fled…'

'Francis is alive?' Catesby asked with a quizzical expression on his face.

'Yes,' Richard confirmed. 'I saw him flee the battlefield on horse with several others after…' He felt a sudden wave of emotion overcome him. 'After King Richard died,' he finally added with a lump in his throat.

'I'm sorry about your father, Richard, but no one must know about you. Do you understand? No one! It is for your own safety.'

'I understand,' Richard said forlornly.

'You have to get away from here,' Catesby warned him. 'There is a man in London who can help you. His name is Master Herricke. He resides on Cheapside. If you tell him I sent you, he will make arrangements for your welfare and safekeeping. I would give you my ring as a surety to show him but I have been stripped of all jewellery.'

'It's alright. I already know of Master Herricke. My father told me everything, including about this.'

Richard pulled out his father's ring and held it in front of the small opening that Catesby peered through.

'Good. Then you understand that you must seek out Herricke,' Catesby smiled. 'If Francis is alive, he will probably have sought sanctuary in St John's Abbey in Colchester. It was where we agreed we'd all meet if ever routed in battle. It is, and has long been, a loyal Yorkist place of sanctuary. Ask Master Herricke to get a message to Francis there to let him know you are safe and well.'

'I will,' Richard replied, 'but first I want to go and see my father's body and pay my respects. He's in a church in the new work so I'll go this morning. What will happen to you?'

Catesby shook his head. 'I expect myself and my friends here will be told to kneel and swear fealty to King Henry. We'll probably have our lands confiscated and our titles attainted, reducing us to the ranks of common men. It's not the end of the world, Richard. Attainted men have found favour again. Whether I would be willing to swear fealty to a man who has no right to wear King Richard's crown is another matter though.'

'And if you don't?' Richard asked.

'Well, imprisonment, banishment, maybe even execution depending how merciful our new sovereign lord is feeling.'

'No! That can't happen. Just swear fealty Sir William, please,' Richard begged him.

The jovial smile returned to Catesby's face and then his tousled blond hair bobbed up and down as he laughed out loud.

'Shhhhh,' a voice whispered behind him. 'You'll wake the bloody guard and have him in here!'

Catesby put his hand over his mouth in mock alarm.

'He's right. I should be quieter,' he said with a cheeky grin before winking at Richard.

Then his face turned more sombre.

'Go see the king's body and pay your respects but don't do anything that will draw attention to yourself. When you've done that, get the hell out of here and seek out Master Herricke in London as soon as you can. Before you set out go to one of the friaries here in Leicester. There are black, white and grey friars in the town. All of them often travel south on pilgrimage, so find some who are and go with them, Richard. You'll be a lot safer and they will ensure you're fed and looked after. You could offer them a few coins in return if you have them.'

'I do,' Richard confirmed.

'Good. The sun's starting to rise,' Catesby observed and nodded behind Richard, who turned to see the first blue hint of morning twilight at the foot of the night sky.

Catesby offered a hand through the narrow opening and Richard grasped it.

'I'm sorry about your father but you can still make great things of your life,' Catesby said with a genial smile.

'And you will rise to greatness again, Sir William, I have no doubt about that,' Richard replied.

They both released their grasp and Richard returned the smile before skulking off into the remnants of the night.

 ing Henry smiled as he reflected how the murky clouds of the past fourteen years of exile in Brittany had parted and the sun now shone brightly upon the fortunes of the house of Tudor. He rose at first light and dressed in a white shirt with fine gathers and fancy stitching that was gathered about the neck by a ribbon. Upon this was a stomacher, of the most gorgeous patterned gold thread, laced together at the back by a servant. This reached to Henry's waist where it met long hose of finest scarlet. On his feet were shoes of blue velvet, beautifully worked with slashes of white silk. A fine brown petti-cote with hanging sleeves and a small brown felt cap with a narrow rolled-up brim, and a peacock feather finished off his outfit. Henry looked and felt like the king he now was.

Resplendent in his finery he met his leading supporters at the Guildhall of Corpus Christi in Leicester where he again asserted his right to kingship by right of conquest, not from the day of the battle but from the day previous to the battle. Henry allowed himself a wry smile at his own cunning. This declaration meant that anyone who had fought for Richard against him was guilty of treason and thus, Henry could legally confiscate their lands and property. He would be magnanimous to some of his enemies, he decided, but first he would purge those who were closest to the former king. He would seize their land and property then reward his most loyal supporters while keeping the choicest estates and manors for himself. He also resolved not to address his lords or summon parliament until after his coronation so that he had time to consolidate and make his own position strong. He would be crowned in Westminster Abbey as the rightful and unquestionable king of England. Then, and only then, would he honour his pledge to marry Elizabeth of York, daughter of the former king Edward IV, to unite the warring houses of Lancaster and York, and finally bring peace to the realm after thirty long years of warfare.

Henry was already considering precautions to prevent any rebellions against his reign. He looked out over his supporters gathered in the Guildhall to hear him speak.

'Robert Willoughby,' he said, 'you are to ride to Sheriff Hutton in Yorkshire where you are to apprehend and arrest the boy, Edward, Earl of Warwick, and escort him to the Tower of London.'

'Yes, Your Grace.' Willoughby stood and acknowledged his king.

Warwick was the son of George, Duke of Clarence, and a nephew to the previous kings Edward IV and Richard III. Henry knew that he presented a rallying point for Yorkist dissidents and a threat to Henry for the crown of England, so he decided to negate that risk immediately. The boy could be locked up indefinitely or made to disappear should Henry so wish.

'Go immediately,' he commanded Willoughby, who bowed and left the hall to set off on the task he had been given.

'Robert Broughton, you are to travel to Calais and inform John of Gloucester, the bastard son of the usurper, that he has been removed from the position of Captain of Calais. You are to escort him back to London. The Treasurer, Thomas Thwaytes, is to assume temporary command until I send instructions otherwise. Is that clear?'

'Yes, Your Grace,' Broughton responded before bowing and taking his leave.

'Before making arrangements for my travel and entry into London there is one small matter that needs taking care of.' King Henry addressed the men packed into the Guildhall with obvious glee in his voice.

'The traitor William Catesby shall be executed.'

Several voices called out their agreement but many more remained pensively silent. Only Sir William Stanley spoke out.

'With respect, Your Grace, shouldn't he be tried by a jury of his peers first?'

'Do you doubt his guilt, Sir William?' The king's stare bore right through Stanley, making him feel ill at ease.

'I'm sure… I don't… I don't doubt that William Catesby is a traitor,' he finally conceded, 'but surely that is for his peers to decide?'

The king continued to glare at him.

'Are you not all peers of William Catesby?' King Henry said with a sweep of his arm gesturing to all those present. 'Are there any here who would deny that William Catesby is a traitor?'

The packed Guildhall was silent except for the muted sound of shuffling feet.

'There you have it, Sir William. Catesby has been found guilty by his peers. You will make the arrangements for his execution.'

The king smiled smugly, clearly enjoying asserting his new-found royal authority and putting Sir William Stanley in his place.

Stanley calmly nodded his acquiescence, while inside he quietly seethed at the humiliation that had just been forced upon him by the man he had won the throne for, only the day before. He briefly grimaced as he swore to himself that he would not forget or forgive this slight.

*

Richard leaned against the wall leading up to the grand stone archway marking the entrance to the Church of the Annunciation of the Blessed Virgin Mary. The sun had cleared the horizon and swept away the last traces of the morning haze and dew, yet still there was no true brightness to the day. A blanket of cloud had drifted over the town, obscuring the sun and preventing it from filling the air with the stifling August heat of the previous few weeks. Twenty or so individuals had arrived before Richard and stood patiently in line from the wooden gates beneath the stone archway to where Richard now stood. Townsfolk gradually began to gather behind Richard and as the minutes passed the crowd swelled until it trailed back through the South gate of the town. Despite the size of the crowd, a sombreness darkened their mood and idle chatter did not flow easily between them.

Eventually the gate of the New Work, or 'Newark' as Richard had heard the locals call it, creaked open and two solemn-looking monks gestured the townsfolk into the precinct. They led the way across an open space facing the hospital and chantry houses, to the church on the south side of a walled quadrangle. There they paused before the taller of the two monks addressed the crowd that had obediently followed them in silent procession towards the church.

'Good folk of Leicester, please show respect for your former sovereign lord and spare some silver for the church into whose care he has been delivered. Any alms would be gratefully appreciated.'

As if from out of thin air both monks produced wooden alms bowls and held them out as they stood partially blocking the church doorway. Clouds parted and a shaft of light shone down from the dull morning sky to illuminate the giant oak door that towered above the two monks. They squinted into the invading light and proffered their alms bowls as one by one the procession of both mourners and the curious filed past, dropping coins into the bowls as they entered the gloomy interior of the church to see the body of their former king.

Richard so desperately wanted to see his father again but the prospect of seeing his mortal remains, battered and hacked, on public display filled him with dread. This was Henry Tudor's way of getting a message out to the populace; King Richard III was dead and *he*, Henry Tudor, was the new and rightful king. The message would be spread far and wide by those who had actually seen the cold pallid corpse of the king lying almost naked in the church. Like everyone else there to see the body of the former king, Richard understood the message quite clearly, but for him this was also a personal pilgrimage. It was the end to a chapter of his life that it seemed had only just begun. For a fleeting moment in time he had been a king's son and his destiny had seemed so assured. Now all that remained was the chance to pay his respects to the king and father that had been so cruelly snatched away from him. So, despite his misgivings about witnessing whatever battlefield wounds and atrocities had been inflicted upon his father's body, Richard steadied himself and walked on stoically.

He dropped a silver coin into the monk's wooden alms bowl and stepped over the threshold into the church.

The sheer vastness of the building impressed him. It was longer and taller than the parish church at Eastwell. Candles guttered in mounts along its walls, lending an eerie light to the inside of the giant stone building. Soldiers wearing the green and white livery of the new Tudor king were interspersed throughout the church, some standing rigidly with hands clasped in front of them or placed warily upon scabbards, while others leant against grey-white stone pillars, clearly unimpressed that they had been woken so early to be tasked with keeping order and with preventing mourners from getting too close to the deceased former monarch whilst their comrades enjoyed a day of respite after the previous day's battle.

The crowd shuffled through the church, drawing ever closer to where the dead king's body was displayed. Richard looked nervously away from the spot and his gaze came to rest upon the magnificent brightly painted alabaster tombs in the chantry chapel built by the Dukes of Lancaster. Effigies of Constance, Duchess of Lancaster and wife of John of Gaunt, and Mary de Bohun, first wife of King Henry IV lay recumbent in flowing gowns, with hands clasped in prayer upon their chests, as light from the chantry windows highlighted their angelic and pristine faces. In stark contrast the still-mud-streaked and blood-spattered, pale, limp body of the erstwhile king looked so pitiful, wrapped only in a loin cloth to cover his privy parts. The body, thin and twisted, was deliberately propped on its side to exaggerate the deformed spine. The rope that had secured his body to the horse for its final journey back into Leicester still remained tied about his wrists, which were bound right over left in front of him.

Mourners crossed themselves as they approached the body which was laid out on a white linen cloth. Many struggled to fight back a tear while a few openly wept. Soldiers hurried them on after a moment's pause so that as many people as possible could witness the spectacle; a procession of witnesses who would go out into the community and spread the word. Yes! King Richard was truly dead, the Plantagenet dynasty was really over. A steady stream of people would witness the dead king's twisted and misshapen body so that everyone would hear that King Richard had been a deformed beast cursed by God Almighty and that Henry Tudor had done England a great service in defeating the crook-backed tyrant. Richard fought back a tear at the thought of his father's name so besmirched and sullied because of his physical appearance. None of the townsfolk who came to see the king would have really known him, understood what an honourable man he was, or have known the kind and gentle father that Richard had met two nights ago. All they would see would be a defeated monster, touched by God's curse; and that is how the kingdom would remember him because, Richard realised, history is written by the victors.

As the crowd shuffled past the dead king, Richard finally approached his father and crossed himself. King Richard's body seemed untouched by the trauma of battle, except for his face which was framed by hair thickly matted with blood and tilted to face the onlookers in the church as they filed by. A small but deep piercing wound to the right cheek below his eye was the only obvious evidence Richard could see of the assault that had ended his father's life, although he guessed from the blood-matted hair that his father had also received a savage blow or two to the back of his head.

Sunlight momentarily broke into the church through the large stained-glass window behind the altar, casting bright colours along the stoned flagged floor of the church and across the body of the king. Richard, like many others present, shed a tear as he stared at his father's serene face bathed in God's colourful light.

'Move on,' a soldier with close-cropped grey hair and a bristled chin to match, uttered unsympathetically as he placed a hand on Richard's shoulder and pushed him forwards to keep the procession moving.

Richard turned for one last look at his father and from this angle could see the deep gash to the back of the king's head that must have ended his life.

'Thank you and God preserve your soul,' he whispered into the still air of the church for his deceased father to hear, before turning and following the line of mourners along the far side of the church and out past those still queuing to get in.

Once outside Richard took a deep breath and wiped away the tears that were now streaming uncontrollably down his cheeks. Emotions bubbled and swirled inside him and Richard struggled not to let them overwhelm him. He coughed to try to clear a lump in his throat. Townsfolk milled about in the open space besides the church. Some wept, overcome with grief and emotion, but most were avidly chatting amongst themselves about the twisted and deformed king's body they had seen, or excitedly informing friends and neighbours in the queue, or indeed anyone who would listen, of the spectacle that awaited them inside the church.

Richard gathered himself and wiped away his tears. For reassurance he placed his hand on the purse hanging from his belt that his father had given him, and he remembered his father's words to him on the night they had met.

'If I defeat Henry Tudor and his rebel army tomorrow, I will raise you up and give you land and titles but if I fail then you are to take that ring and go to Cheapside in London where you will find a goldsmith named Herricke. Show him the ring and he will know what to do.'

Richard pulled out the gold ring hanging on a leather thong about his neck. He briefly glanced at it before tucking it back inside his shirt and steeling himself for the next step he would take. He would use his father's money, buy a horse and make his way to London to seek out Master Herricke and find out where fate would lead him.

Leaving the crowd behind in the church compound Richard walked past the snaking line of mourners and through the South Gate back into the town. He hadn't eaten since the previous evening and his stomach began to grumble in complaint. He decided to head to the marketplace to buy some food and drink for the journey south before trying to purchase a horse.

Despite the large queue trailing out of the town to the church in the New Work, the town itself was still filled with artisans, merchants, soldiers and a throng of townsfolk. The numbers were swelled by a steady stream of people coming into the town from outlying villages to view the body of their former king. Richard was shoved and buffeted every step of the way as he slowly fought his way against the crowds and through the narrow streets until he finally reached the marketplace. There was a frenzy of activity as traders shouted to be heard above each other and above the general hubbub of the bustling crowds of people.

As Richard pushed his way apologetically between two gossiping women a herald's trumpet blared out a series of notes. Everybody in the marketplace turned sharply to see what was happening.

'Make way, make way!' a herald shouted at the top of his voice as soldiers forced the crowd to part and then shepherded them towards the outer edges of the marketplace.

As the crowds were pushed back the soldiers stood with swords and billhooks at the ready in a circle facing outwards from the centre of the now empty marketplace. Several traders meekly protested at having their custom interrupted but they were quickly quietened upon seeing a drawn sword or a mailed hand held up to their face in warning.

A further flurry of notes from the herald announced the arrival of more armed men who, with Sir William Stanley at their head, marched a shackled man into the centre of the ring of soldiers and then threw him unceremoniously to the ground. Two men carried a large block of wood and set it down in front of the prostrate prisoner.

The man pressed his forearms against the ground and tried to raise himself up onto his knees. As he did so he looked past the soldiers with their backs turned towards him and fixed his gaze directly upon Richard standing amidst the crowd. Richard recognised the man, and Catesby, staring back at him shook his head in warning for Richard not to do anything rash.

'William Catesby has been found guilty of treason by a trial of his peers and, by order of His Sovereign Grace King Henry VII, is to be executed forthwith,' the herald formally declared.

A collective gasp of shock went up from the crowd. Richard tried to push his way into the open space where Catesby was being pulled into an upright kneeling position in front of the heavy wooden block. Catesby stared at him with imploring eyes, willing Richard to stay silent and retreat back into the crowd.

Instead, Richard pushed on until he stood directly facing Catesby, his path barred by crossed billhooks held by the soldiers deployed to keep the crowd at bay.

As Catesby was forced down onto the rough wooden block, he twisted his head to look at Sir William Stanley then called out for all to hear.

'Sir William, help and pray for my soul, as you have not for my body. I trusted in you yet you broke your promise to me and to your sovereign lord King Richard.'

Stanley grimaced at Catesby's accusation even though he recognised the truth of it. He subtly shook his head at Catesby who acquiesced gracefully, closed his eyes and spread his arms as wide as his shackles would allow, baring his neck to the mercy of the axeman's blade. With a nod from Stanley the executioner arced the heavy wooden shaft of his axe through the air, expertly bringing the blade down on the back of Catesby's neck and cleaving his head clean away from the body in a single blow. Half of the assembled crowd let out a horrified gasp as the rest whooped in delight at the unexpected spectacle.

Richard screamed in anger and tried to push past the crossed billhooks barring his way. The soldiers stood firm, so he stooped quickly to dodge between them and below the billhooks, but one of the soldiers reacted first, slamming the hard wooden shaft of his weapon into Richard's face rather than let the boy get past him. Richard felt his nose crack with the impact of the sickening blow. A wave of dizziness and nausea swept over him as he tried to cling onto consciousness. He momentarily reached out hoping to grasp something to steady himself but instead blackness overtook him and he collapsed to the ground.

12

he brutality and cruelty of the world never ceased to amaze Friar Leo. God's plan was mysterious indeed! The soldiers had departed the marketplace, dragging the headless corpse behind them and leaving a long crimson smear of blood to show the direction in which they had left. The wooden block had been carried off along with Catesby's head, which no doubt would be tarred and placed above one of the town gates as a warning to other would-be traitors. Only a pool of blackening treacle-like blood at the end of the crimson smear and a single unconscious boy lying in the marketplace with several people stooping over him, gave any clue to the horrifying spectacle that had just taken place. Friar Leo stood in stunned silence as townsfolk resumed their business and the people who he thought were helping the boy walked away leaving him face down in the dung and filth of the marketplace. Friar Leo could not ignore a soul in need so he made his way over to the boy as townsfolk continued to pass by and even step over the prostrate figure. He rolled the boy over onto his back then knelt next to him, placing a hand under the boy's neck to raise him into a sitting position.

As the world came into focus, pain registered in Richard's nose and cheekbones with a pounding ferocity. He groaned and placed his fingers against the bridge of his nose. He stared at the sticky blood on his fingertips before realising that someone knelt beside him. Even groggy as he was, Richard recognised the grey habit and cowl of a Franciscan friar.

'Let me help you, friend,' the friar said as his thin face broke into a wide smile that seemed to extend fully from ear to ear.

'I'm fine,' Richard responded as he rose unsteadily to his feet then wobbled and reached out to the friar for support.

'You're clearly not fine,' Friar Leo said, supporting Richard's weight on his bony arms. 'Come, let me take you to the infirmary where we can get a salve for your wounds.'

Richard felt too weak to argue so he nodded in agreement and let the friar lead him away from the marketplace. Gradually the strength came back to his legs and his senses fully returned. On impulse he reached for the ring on the leather thong around his neck and was relieved upon feeling it beneath his tunic. His hand slid down to his waist and he felt for the purse of money hanging from his belt. It was not there so in panic he pulled away from the friar and ran both hands around his waist searching for the precious pouch in vain. He turned and scoured the ground back the few steps to where he had been lain on the ground and then the reality dawned on him. He'd lost the pouch of gold and silver coins his father had given him, or more likely he'd been robbed as he lay unconscious in the dirt.

Anger seethed within him, coursing through his blood until it boiled over in a tumultuous display of violence.

'Bastards!' he yelled at the top of his voice as he unleashed a flurry of punches into the side timbers of a building at the edge of the marketplace.

He kicked and punched the sturdy beams until he was

exhausted, his anger was spent and his hands were bloody.

'The thieving bastards have stolen all my money,' he sobbed. 'I have nothing left, no money, nothing.'

'Money is not everything. I survive without money,' Friar Leo consoled him.

'This is the end,' Richard sobbed. 'I was going to London. Now I have nothing. I can't afford a horse or even food and lodgings on the journey.'

'This is not the end,' Friar Leo said calmly. 'Where one journey ends, another begins. With money or not, with God's grace different paths will make themselves known to you,' he said with a knowing smile. 'With God's help you will find the right path to follow.'

Friar Leo's words were strangely calming. Perhaps it was because the father Richard had grown up knowing was a priest. Friar Leo also had the same calm demeanour, yet with the authority of knowledge in his voice that Father Martin had. As his anger subsided the pain in his hands began to register. Richard stared down at his bloody knuckles and was shocked at the sight of them, and upset that he had let his emotions erupt with such unprecedented fury.

'I'm sorry. I don't know why I reacted like that. It's just… my father died and then my money's been stolen and I have no home, and I don't know how —'

'It's alright.' Friar Leo cut him off mid-sentence as he tore a strip of material from the bottom of his already ragged habit and wrapped it around Richard's bloody right hand.

Then he bandaged the left hand and placed a comforting arm around Richard's shoulder.

'Everything can be sorted out but first we need to get you to the infirmary before you do any more damage to yourself.'

'I must get to London to see Master Herricke,' Richard blurted out.

'All in good time,' Friar Leo said kindly as he smiled with the widest smile Richard had ever seen.

'A day's rest, some food inside you, and a salve for your hands and face first methinks. My name is Friar Leo. And you are?'

'Richard,' he replied, proffering a blood-stained bandaged hand which Friar Leo declined.

Instead, the friar took Richard by the elbow, turned and led him firmly towards the direction of the Franciscan infirmary.

*

The Guildhall was empty now except for King Henry and his uncle, Jasper Tudor. The king, still in his gold-threaded finery and brown felt cap topped with a peacock feather, sat on a square wooden chair set upon a dais. In contrast, his uncle stood wearing a simple woollen shirt and leather jerkin as he ran a hand through his close-cropped white hair.

Henry let out a deep sigh.

'They still don't have faith in me. Even after this, they still doubt my right to be king.'

'Your right is by conquest and no one can doubt that, Your Grace.'

'But they do! They doubt and mock my bloodline and they will be looking to rally behind the first Yorkist pretender to raise his head.'

'What Yorkist pretender?' Jasper looked to the rafters in exasperation. 'We have already spoken about this. Richard is slain and his son is already dead. Warwick is to be arrested, you have already ordered that, and the only other Yorkist heir is the Lady Elizabeth who you are betrothed to marry. You, Henry, are the heir to the house of Lancaster, king by right of conquest, and you will soon unite the houses of Lancaster and York so there can be no more dispute, even from the staunchest of Yorkist supporters.'

The king pursed his thin lips and nodded.

'I want a proclamation issued,' he announced. 'Let it be known that Norfolk, and the usurper's henchmen Catesby, Lovell, and Ratcliffe are all dead and that Warwick is my prisoner.'

'Yes, Your Grace,' Jasper said dutifully.

'I also want Northumberland and Lincoln arrested. All knights and ordinary soldiers who supported the Yorkists are to be pardoned.'

The king paused, momentarily caught in a thought.

'There is one more… shall we say, delicate matter that needs resolving.'

'Your Grace?'

'We have all heard the stories, even as far afield as Brittany, that Richard has disposed of his nephews. But what if they are not dead? What if they are still imprisoned in the Tower, or worse still, spirited off somewhere?'

Jasper stroked his white goatee beard. 'A delicate matter indeed!'

'So?' the king asked.

'Your Grace has no need to worry about such matters nor must you have any direct involvement in such trivial details. I will see to it that this delicate matter is resolved to your benefit.'

'Thank you, Jasper.' Henry clasped his uncle's shoulder. 'Just one more thing.'

'Your Grace?'

'I do not want to know the outcome or indeed hear of this matter ever again. Is that understood?'

'Yes, of course, Your Grace.'

The king's mood lightened instantly.

'Uncle, we have dallied in Leicester too long. Dismiss the foreign mercenaries and gather the rest of our forces. Find fifty of the best archers to escort me on our journey. They will be my personal guard. Ready yourself and the men, Jasper. We are marching to London.'

*

The journey south was a torrid affair. The friendly chatter of Friar Leo, interspersed with his anecdotes and morality tales, had not lifted Richard's dark mood. Eventually the jovial friar gave up trying to lift Richard's spirits and they settled into a truce of silence as they trudged along the ancient Roman road that led to the capital. The intense summer heat did not help Richard's mood and even the hardened Friar Leo found the going tough as the sun beat down mercilessly onto his bald pate. It was a relief to sleep out in the open that night, even though it was on a bed of bracken at the side of the road.

On the second day the skies clouded over and a slight breeze broke through the heat, making their journey more tolerable, but as the day wore on, menacing purple-grey clouds moved in to cast long dark shadows over the rolling Northamptonshire landscape. The threat of a storm hung over them like the sword of Damocles as the warm summer air met cooler air drifting in from the north. Later in the day the rumble of thunder could be heard in the far distance but still the pair trudged on, maintaining their heavy silence.

In the late afternoon, as they reached a rise in the Roman road near the village of Weedon Bec the heavens finally opened. Friar Leo and Richard sought shelter in the local inn but, with no money between them to pay for a drink or a bed for the night, the landlord unsympathetically turfed them back out into the downpour. Three quarters of an hour later, drenched through to the skin, the bedraggled pair arrived at the church of St Michael in Stowe-Nine-Churches where the priest, who clearly recognised Friar Leo, took them in, gave them blankets, built a fire in the hearth of his lodgings and made them hot broth.

'Tell me of the battle,' the priest begged Friar Leo eagerly. 'I hear from travellers heading south that King Richard is dead and we have a new lord, a Welshman no less.'

'It is true. I heard that the king was unhorsed but fought on valiantly until surrounded by Welshmen and was...' He trailed off when he noticed Richard's dour face.

'The boy has had a hard time of it, Father. He needs some hot broth inside him.'

'Of course,' the priest said and then began to stir the broth he had placed over the fire, still waiting for it to heat up.

As the three of them sat round the crackling log fire Friar Leo broke the long silence that had lasted between him and Richard.

'You know why they call this village Stowe-Nine-Churches?'

Richard just stared into the flames ignoring the question. Friar Leo carried on regardless.

'When builders first decided to build a church here, they dug the foundations and started to put up the walls. But after weeks of work, they returned one morning to find that the walls had been razed to the ground. Like the good Christians they were, they began to rebuild the church but once again returned one morning to find that the very same thing had happened. Angry and frustrated, they nonetheless didn't give in and vowed to build a church in the village whatever it took to complete the job. They posted a sentry to watch over the church at night and began to build the church once more. However, the night watchman fell asleep and when he awoke the next morning, to his horror the building work had been demolished again.

'Seven times the villagers began to build the church and each time they posted a different, supposedly more reliable watchman, but seven times the night watchman fell asleep and the villagers returned to find the building work in ruins. The eighth time the local shepherd boy took up the vigil and attempted to stay up all night to keep watch over the church. When the villagers returned in the morning the church masonry was once again strewn over the site and the foundations churned up and backfilled.

'However, this time the shepherd boy had managed to remain awake all night and had seen what had happened. He explained to the villagers that the Devil had turned up after midnight and began to dance around the half-built church, cackling with glee, pushing the walls inwards and tossing chunks of rock over his shoulder with apparent ease. He had used his trident to shovel mounds of rock and earth into the foundation trenches, and then he had danced off into the night singing that no church shall ever be built on that unholy ground.

'The villagers took heed of the shepherd boy's tale and decided that they would attempt to rebuild the church a ninth time but this time they would find a new site for the holy building. It was built where the church of St Michael's is now and since that day this village has been known as Stowe-Nine-Churches.'

'I always tell my parishioners that it was the local priest who kept the final vigil,' the priest said as he stirred the pot of broth that was starting to bubble over the fire.

'Typical churchman taking all the credit!' Friar Leo said in a deadpan voice.

Richard couldn't help but let out a chuckle at the irony, and then the priest started laughing followed by Friar Leo, and eventually the three of them were guffawing raucously, tears streaming down their crimson-cheeked faces. As the laughter subsided Friar Leo wiped his nose on the sleeve of his habit. Richard smiled at him and spoke.

'I'm sorry I've been so bad tempered and miserable. You've done a lot for me and I've been so ungrateful.'

'That's alright, lad,' Friar Leo smiled sympathetically and patted Richard on the shoulder. 'You've been through a lot, what with your master executed and losing all your money.'

'He wasn't my master,' Richard instantly replied, referring to Catesby, 'he was my friend.'

Friar Leo looked at him quizzically.

'Why would a wealthy gentleman befriend a boy like you? Did he touch you, lad? Did he hurt you? The bastard deserved what he got if he did.'

'No! Oh no, nothing like that.' Richard's face flushed. 'He was a friend of my father's and looked after me when my father died.' Richard could feel his face redden further as he lied.

'And who was your father?' the priest pressed for more information.

Richard hesitated, not wanting to name King Richard as his real father but also not knowing what else to say. The truth teetered on the edge of his lips as his cheeks smouldered uncomfortably.

'He was a nobleman,' Richard eventually blurted out.

Friar Leo and the priest gave each other a look laden with disbelief.

'I'm not saying I'm a lord's son… Well, I am… but not like that.' Richard stumbled over his own words as he tried to dig himself out of the hole he had created.

'What I mean is… well… that I'm the bastard son of a nobleman, that's all… I just…' He could feel himself sinking deeper and deeper into the mire.

'I started to be trained as a priest,' he added, knowing that illegitimate and younger sons of the nobility were often sent into the priesthood, and hoping that this would be a smokescreen to cover his untruth.

'Et quæ est patris tui?' the priest asked in Latin, trying to catch Richard out.

'Francis Lovell,' Richard replied to the priest's question without hesitation, immediately wishing he could take back the words as soon as they'd passed his lips.

'Francis, Viscount Lovell is your father?' the priest asked incredulously.

'Yes.' The word was said in a hushed voice barely audible over the crackling of the fire, and yet it carried such weight.

'You expect us to believe that Lord Lovell is your father?'

Richard could hear the mocking tone in the priest's voice. He turned to Friar Leo for support but was only met by a look of reproach.

'I can prove it,' Richard said as he took hold of the leather cord around his neck and pulled the Hopper ring out from beneath his grubby grey stained shirt.

The priest's eyes widened and he gasped audibly as he saw the precious gold ring glinting in the firelight.

'Let me see.'

His excitement was palpable as he grasped at the ring. Richard leaned away, fearful that the priest was going to steal it.

'May I?' Friar Leo asked calmly, extending the palm of his hand for Richard to place the ring upon.

Richard leaned forward and held the ring towards the friar but still attached to his neck by the cord. Friar Leo knelt on the floor, leaning right into Richard so he could inspect the ring closely.

'It's gold and studded with a large ruby,' he informed the priest who also leant in close to get a better look.

'Very intricate work and worth a fortune I'd wager.'

'What's that?' The priest pointed to something on the inner surface of the ring.

'Lettering,' Friar Leo replied as he twisted the ring in the flickering light trying to discern what it said.

'The letter E and three stars.'

'Edward III?' The priest questioned.

'Undoubtedly a royal ring,' Friar Leo confirmed. 'I believe he is telling the truth.'

The priest let out a whistle. 'Well, I'll be... I'm sorry I doubted you.'

He paused then asked, 'Where is your father now?'

'I don't know,' Richard replied as he tucked the ring back inside his shirt. 'I think he survived the battle after the king died but I don't know where he fled.'

'So, what are you going to do now?' the priest enquired.

'I'm going to go to London with Friar Leo and then I have a... a friend on Cheapside that I shall visit.'

'We had better get some sleep, Richard,' Friar Leo said. 'We have an early start. Thank you, Father, for your hospitality.'

'You're welcome. I'll fetch more blankets and a bolster for your head. You can both sleep by the fire. Now help yourself to some broth and I'll be back shortly.'

He handed them a wooden bowl each and then disappeared into the adjoining room to fetch the blankets from a large wooden chest.

'I've known him for almost fifteen years,' Friar Leo said, ladling broth into a bowl and passing it to Richard. 'He's a good man but I'd still keep that bauble of yours hidden if I were you. Not all men of the cloth find the temptation of wealth easy to resist.'

'I will,' Richard confirmed, and that night he slept with the ring in his enclosed fist, tucked firmly beneath the bandages that still covered his swollen right hand.

*

The small army marched south past alder, ash, oak and rowan trees that swayed rhythmically in the breeze alongside the old Roman road. The downpour of the previous night had left the furrowed, uneven road covered in mud but the mid-day sun was now starting to dry it out. Henry Tudor thought it ironic that he was now joining the Roman road just a few miles south of where he had left it days ago to face the might of King Richard's army. Only now he was riding to London as king, flanked by fifty archers he called his Yeoman of the Guard.

The minor panic of the previous day had passed and in reflection Jasper was right, he had nothing to worry about. His delicate problem would be sorted out one way or another and the Yorkist threat to his throne was gone, save for a few stray rebels who had no figurehead to rally around. Henry resolved to hang those that still opposed him and be magnanimous towards the rest.

He smiled as the sun cast its warmth across his face. It was the end of August and summer would soon be ebbing away but this was the dawning of a new age, a new reign; the start of a Tudor dynasty that would unite the warring factions of Lancaster and York and extend long into the annals of time. King Henry watched three standards borne by his Yeoman of the Guard flutter in the light breeze. The standards of St George, the Red Dragon of Cadwallader, and the Dun Cow that had been carried from Brittany, across Wales and England, and under which he had fought Richard at Redemoor. His thoughts drifted back to that battle and how close he had come to losing his life.

'Your Grace! Your Grace!'

The Earl of Oxford's call snapped King Henry from his reverie. He turned to the earl, who was pointing beyond the fluttering banners to a messenger galloping along the Roman road towards them. As the messenger approached and slowed several Yeoman of the Guard stepped in front of him with weapons drawn.

'Let him pass,' King Henry commanded.

The rider dismounted from his horse and approached with his head bowed. The king steadied his own horse as the messenger stood beside him waiting for permission to speak.

'Your news?' the king enquired.

'Your Grace, I have a message for Reginald Bray.'

The king turned in his saddle to face the entourage behind him.

'Master Bray, please explain yourself,' the king demanded.

A man with dark hair, greying at the temples, in his mid-forties, handsome with deep-set dark eyes, rode confidently forward until his horse was level with the king's.

'Forgive me, Your Grace, but I took the liberty of sending men after those that fled the battlefield and placing men nearby who could keep an eye on any potential rebels or traitors.'

The king laughed out loud.

'Good man! Someone with intelligence and initiative. You will go far, Master Bray.' The king slapped Bray on the shoulder. 'So, what have you learnt?'

Bray nodded at the messenger.

'Speak.'

The messenger's eyes flicked between the king and Bray.

'Your Grace, Master Bray, your loyal servant sends his greetings and bids me to inform you that the traitors Lord Lovell, and Sir Humphrey and Thomas Stafford have sought sanctuary at St John's Abbey in Colchester.'

'Lovell is alive?' exclaimed the king. 'I was told he'd perished on the field of battle.'

'No, Your Grace.' The messenger looked nervously from the king to Bray and back again, then averted his eyes and stared at the ground.

'And by what means do you come by this information?'

'We have been watching the abbey and have also intercepted a letter written by Thomas Stafford to his wife,' the messenger said, handing the letter to the king who ignored it.

Reginald Bray took the letter from the messenger, read it and summarised for the king.

'All the usual tidings to his wife and children, then he goes on to say that he and his brother survived the battle and have fled to the sanctuary with Lord Lovell to wait upon further news of the king's clemency, or otherwise, towards those who supported King Richard. He asks his wife to send a messenger with news and money for their welfare. He prays for her safekeeping, and that's all, Your Grace.'

'And you will continue to monitor the situation and bring me any further news?' the king asked Bray.

'It goes without saying, Your Grace.'

The king nodded appreciably.

'I may have much use for you, Reginald Bray,' he uttered, as much to himself as to Bray.

13

 hen Richard awoke he instinctively felt under his shirt and around his neck for the gold Hopper ring his father had given him. The panic was only momentary until he realised he'd hidden it inside the bandage around his right hand. He removed the bandage to find that his hand had healed well. The swelling had gone down and the cuts had scabbed over. He looked at the ring in detail for the first time. He hadn't noticed the E and three stars inscribed inside the ring before Friar Leo had found it last night. He also realised that the jester's face that he had first noticed behind the large ruby was only apparent when the ring was held at certain angles to the light. Richard wiggled the ring so that the face appeared and disappeared as the morning light breaking through the shuttered window glanced off it.

'Put it away before Father Gilbert sees it and tries to convince you to donate it to the church,' Friar Leo warned him.

'Oh, good morning Friar Leo,' Richard replied, quickly tying the ring onto the leather cord around his neck and tucking it inside his shirt.

Richard realised that this was the first time he had heard the Father Gilbert's name mentioned.

'I've already packed some bread and hard cheese into a sackcloth for our journey,' Friar Leo informed him. 'We'll join Father Gilbert in the church to say Lauds then we'll be on our way. We can break fast as we journey on.'

Richard was relieved when prayers were over and they were heading off down the Roman road again, leaving Father Gilbert to his work. It took three more days of walking before they reached London. Two nights were spent sleeping in monastery hospitals, grateful for the pottage and hard bread they were given by the monks. Finally, on the morning of the third day they saw the tall pointed spire of St Paul's Cathedral on the horizon. As they neared it other church spires came into view, as eventually did the walls of the city.

The only other time Richard had been to London was when he briefly passed through with Lord Lovell on the way to meet his father. The sheer size of the place left him in awe. Richard could only guess at the tens of thousands of people who lived here. There were narrow lanes with houses three, four and even five storeys tall that blocked out the light; there were markets, shops, guild halls, theatres, inns, prisons, monasteries and more churches than Richard had believed could exist anywhere in the world. The noises and smells of the city assaulted his senses: from the shouts of hatters and cordwainers selling their wares to the odour of spilled offal, animal dung and urine on the cobbled streets.

They approached the gateway of a Franciscan Friary. Friar Leo was reluctant to let Richard go without him first coming in to eat and drink. Richard politely refused the offer saying he needed to see Master Herricke on Cheapside as soon as possible, so they bid each other farewell with a hug and Richard carried on his way.

Cheapside ran east-west between the great water conduit at the foot of Old Jewry to the little conduit by St. Paul's churchyard. It was a wide street lined with shops, whose fronts were open to the light and set out with displays of every luxury good available, from fine furs and velvet to herbs, spices, honey and sweetmeats. Traders called out their wares as the smell of cooked food and spices permeated the air. Cheapside was the site of a great Eleanor Cross, painted, and gilded in fading gold, three storeys high. A food market, along with the Mercer's Hall and Saddler's Hall, were located there. It was the centre of London's wealth, not least because of the goldsmiths' shops and the wealthy merchants who chose to reside in the area.

Richard didn't know which shop or house belonged to Master Herricke but he found Goldsmiths' Row which was on the south side of Cheapside, by the Eleanor Cross. The narrow alley contained ten houses and fourteen shops which displayed their golden rings, spoons, chalices, plate, and assorted jewellery on wooden shelves and trestle tables inside the shops, lit by the daylight that reached the rooms through small lead-paned windows. The shops in the alley were guarded by two burly men who eyed Richard suspiciously. The nearest man looked menacing as he beat a wooden cudgel against the palm of his hand and stared unblinkingly at Richard who decided to avoid him by turning into the first shop he came to.

Inside an elderly man sat picking his nose. He looked up and wiped his fingers on his brown velvet doublet as Richard entered.

'Excuse me sir,' Richard asked nervously, 'do you know Master Herricke?'

'Two doors down, on your left,' the man replied gruffly as he continued to search inside his nostril with his little finger.

Richard nodded his thanks and left the shop only to find the two burly guards stood outside the door as if waiting for him. He walked past them without saying a word but he could feel their gaze burning into the back of his neck as he turned into the doorway two shops down on his left.

Even though it was a warm day the shop smelled of wood smoke. A man pulled a curtain aside and peered from the room behind to see who had just entered his shop.

'Greetings young fellow, are you lost?' the man's voice whistled past his two remaining yellow teeth.

He looked as old as the hills. His skin was brown and leathery and a few wisps of white hair still clung to his scalp.

'Are you Master Herricke?' Richard asked hesitantly.

'I am William Herricke,' the man replied.

He stood staring at Richard waiting for some sort of explanation but instead of speaking Richard pulled the leather cord out from beneath his shirt to reveal the gold ring. He held it out to show the old man.

'How did you come by this ring?' Herricke asked before even examining it.

'It was my father's.'

'May I take a closer look at it?'

Richard removed the cord from around his neck and handed the ring to the old man. Herricke picked up a glass lens from a table and used it to look closely at the ring as he held it up to the light of the window at the front of the shop.

'Come,' he said, beckoning Richard into the room behind the curtain.

'Sit,' he said, gesturing towards a wooden stool.

Richard sat as instructed. Herricke walked behind him. Before he could turn his head to see where the old man was going Richard felt the sharp point of a knife pressed against the side of his neck. Herricke held the knife against Richard's jugular vein and pulled the back of his collar downwards at the same time to forcibly keep him on the stool.

'Tell me why I shouldn't call in those two brutes from outside to dash in your brains with their cudgels,' the old man demanded.

'Because my father gave me that ring and told me to come to Cheapside to speak to you.'

'Who are you, and who is your father?'

Richard knew there was no point in lying.

'My name is Richard and my father is… was… King Richard,' he admitted.

Herricke smirked.

'It's the king's ring alright but how do I know you didn't find this on the battlefield after he died or steal it from his finger after he was slain?'

'How would I know to bring it here?'

'It's Goldsmith's Row. Where else could you sell it for a fair price?' Herricke asked, still doubting that this boy could be King Richard's son.

'But how did I know your name was Herricke?'

'Because anyone around here could tell you that,' Herricke answered matter-of-factly.

'Oh!' Richard felt his heart sink. 'But how did I know to bring it specifically to you and not any goldsmith?' he persisted.

Herricke didn't answer but instead pressed the knife firmly against Richard's neck.

'But I know of the fellowship; Lord Lovell, Catesby and others. My father told me, sir. In God's name it's the truth.'

He felt the hand loosen its grip on his collar.

'You know what this is?' Herricke held the ring in front of Richard's face but continued to press the knife against his neck.

'Yes. It's a Hopper ring,' explained Richard. 'My father said that while I own this ring, any other member of the fellowship must offer me whatever support is within their means, no matter how rich or poor they are.'

'God in High Heaven!' Herricke exclaimed. 'Are you really the king's son?'

'Yes,' Richard confirmed.

'And King Richard is truly dead?'

'Yes,' Richard said gravely.

'God rest his soul.' Herricke crossed himself. 'Then we need to get you to safety, lad.'

'Oh, it's alright. I'm not in any danger! I just came to you because my father said that's what I should do. I haven't really thought things through. I suppose I should go back to my village and —'

'Hush now, lad! Your father sent you to me for a reason. He knows that if your true identity is revealed then your life will be in danger. The Welsh king won't tolerate any threat to his new crown.'

'I'm not a threat!' Richard exclaimed.

'Anyone with Plantagenet blood in their veins is a threat. Remember that! You'll lay low, stay low, and you'll live if you have any sense. I can give you a new identity and a new life. I have a friend who is a master mason in the city. I'm sure he will take you on as an apprentice. You can learn a trade and earn your lodgings and keep. How does that sound?'

Before Richard could answer they heard shouting and

screaming as a scuffle broke out in the alleyway outside the shop. A voice bellowed, 'Richard! Richard! Richard!'

Herricke reacted by pushing Richard behind him and holding the knife out in defence against anyone who would come through the door.

'It's alright, I know him,' Richard said as he pushed past Herricke and ran out through the shop doorway to find Friar Leo lying in the alleyway with Herricke's two henchmen stood over him, cudgels in hand.

'Stop!' Richard exclaimed and Herricke nodded at the two men to follow the boy's command.

'He came running down the alley screaming like a mad man. He wouldn't slow down when we asked and he tried to push past us so I gave him one.' The henchman held up his cudgel to Herricke in explanation.

'He's my friend. You had no right to hurt him,' Richard screamed at Herricke's men.

Friar Leo sat up groggily, a large egg-sized lump already apparent on his forehead.

'Help him inside, Walbrook,' Herricke instructed the man.

Walbrook and his companion lifted the frail friar and carried him inside the shop where they laid him on the reed-covered stone floor.

Richard knelt by Friar Leo's side and took his hand while the three men stood by waiting for the friar to regain his senses.

Friar Leo groaned as Richard eventually helped him to sit up. He rubbed the still swelling lump on his head and stared round the room as if trying to recall where he was.

'Soldiers!' he suddenly and loudly exclaimed, startling everyone else in the room. 'Soldiers!' he exclaimed again, remembering why he had so urgently charged down Goldsmith's Row in search of Richard, before being beaten over the head.

He looked at the two large men still holding cudgels and cowered.

'They won't hurt you,' Richard told him. 'It was a misunderstanding. They were just protecting the goldsmiths' shops.'

Friar Leo nodded his understanding.

'Soldiers are coming for you, Richard.' He spoke calmly and quietly. 'Father Gilbert told them who you are and they're searching the streets and houses for you. They know you've come to London; to Cheapside.'

'Walbrook, help the good friar. See that he gets whatever help he needs. Take him to an apothecary or, even better, the friary hospital. Tell them he tripped and bumped his head.'

'Thank you,' Friar Leo said weakly.

Herricke continued. 'Swyft, we're going to the river. Go back into the alley and if any soldiers appear, misdirect them or at least delay them.'

'Yes Master Herricke,' Swyft acknowledged obediently before heading back into the alley.

After the others had left, Herricke locked up the shop and beckoned Richard to follow him. They walked down the cobbled alley past Swyft and out into the streets of London. They walked quickly, following the lie of the land downhill, past the church of All Hallows, past Finimore Lane, Pissing Alley and the church of St. Nicholas Olave, along Bread Street and down to the bustling harbour at Queenshithe; each step marked by the fear that accompanies a hunted man. Herricke was out of breath by the time they got to the harbour. He glanced furtively around to make sure there were no soldiers nearby before stopping and putting his hands on his knees to gather himself and catch his breath.

'We'll go downriver where we can collect horses and make our way to Essex,' Herricke explained once his breathing had steadied. 'If any of the fellowship have escaped the battle and need sanctuary they will have fled to the abbey at Colchester. But don't forget, the fellowship of the Hopper ring extends beyond the loyalty of the House of York; if Lord Lovell, Ratcliffe or Catesby have fled to Colchester their enemies will be aware of it too.'

'William Catesby is dead,' Richard said glumly. 'Murdered after the battle, in Leicester.'

'I'm sorry to hear that, Richard, but maybe others have survived.'

Herricke suddenly grabbed Richard's shoulder and pulled him around a corner.

'Soldiers! Keep walking.'

They both looked at the ground as they walked briskly up the slope away from the river, back the way they had come.

'There's another mooring at Trig Lane. We'll head there,' Herricke said as he held Richard's arm and dragged him onwards.

'Oi you!' a soldier shouted. 'Stop there.'

Herricke and Richard ignored the order and began sprinting. They heard shouting behind them, the padding of leather boots on cobbles, and the jangle of swords as the soldiers set off in pursuit. Herricke turned into Thames Street and ran as fast as his old legs and weary lungs would carry him. He and Richard supported and urged each other on in turn but the soldiers were closing in quickly upon them. As they passed the church of St. Mary Somerset, Swyft appeared out of the adjoining lane to join them.

'Go! I'll hold the bastards off,' he shouted as he waved them on.

He walked calmly towards the soldiers and as the first soldier went to run past him Swyft pulled a pair of cudgels from the back of his belt and hammered one into the man's stomach without warning. The soldier crumpled, devoid of breath. Richard saw four more soldiers halt their chase to surround Swyft who quickly lunged at the first man, taking him down with a swipe to his neck. For a big man he was quick and Richard hoped he could hold the soldiers off long enough for them to escape.

Herricke and Richard turned left into Castle Alley and then right into Trig Lane, which in turn led to a set of stone steps descending to the river. The lane was crowded with sailors, porters and prostitutes plying their trade. The pair pushed past them and made their way down the steps to the water's edge where merchant vessels queued for access to the landing point. Herricke yelled at the captain of the first vessel.

'We need passage immediately.'

As the captain was about to protest Herricke jumped on board and thrust a purse full of silver coins into the man's hand.

'Now if you please, skipper?'

The man looked inside the purse and decided that the fistful of silver was more than enough recompense for his trouble. He smiled broadly.

'Welcome aboard, my friends.'

'Downriver, as quickly as possible!' Herricke demanded.

The captain shouted orders at the crewmen who quickly responded, untying the river barge from its mooring at the quayside and pushing it away from the wharf with long wooden poles. The barge slowly made its way through the crowded harbour but before it made clear water, soldiers began to push through the crowd to the river's edge. They stood on the quayside hurling insults at the occupants of the barge as it cleared the other vessels, until finally it made clear water and was able to turn and follow the current downstream and out of earshot of the soldiers.

'I'm sorry for the trouble I've caused,' Richard said apologetically.

'It's not your fault,' Herricke told him. 'There's bigger events at play here.'

Herricke stared downriver at the dark clouds building on the horizon.

'We'd better get you to safety, Richard Plantagenet, there's a storm brewing.'

*

Rain lashed down in sheets against the grey stone walls of St John's Abbey, finally breaking the intolerable summer heat. Francis Lovell strolled up and down the length of the south aisle mulling over his recent bad fortune as the rain beat a constant rhythm against the leaded roof above him. His plans were in tatters and the Yorkist cause as dead as the vermin being washed out of Colchester's filthy alleys into the River Colne by the deluge. At least he was safe in the pro-Yorkist abbey which had been granted special rights of sanctuary way back in the reign of the first King Henry.

Francis recalled that the abbey had sheltered John Howard, Duke of Norfolk, during the brief restoration of Henry VI fifteen years earlier. His thoughts drifted back to the recent battle and the news that Norfolk had been killed by an arrow. How things could have been different if Norfolk had broken Oxford's ranks and scattered Tudor's army, rather than falling so early in the fray.

As he mused an abbot came scurrying over and broke Francis from his thoughts.

'My lords,' he addressed Francis and the two Stafford brothers who had fled into hiding with him. 'Emissaries from King Henry are at the abbey gatehouse and wish to speak with you.'

The three fugitives looked at each other, startled. Of course the new king would have had word that they had fled into the sanctuary of the abbey, but had he sent his men to make peace with them or to demand that they leave the abbey to face justice?

'How many of them are there?' Thomas Stafford, a wiry man with pale grey eyes that looked on the edge of crying, worryingly enquired of the abbot.

'Twenty, perhaps twenty-five,' the abbot replied.

'Have they said what they wish to talk to us about?' Thomas asked nervously.

'No, sire. Just that they wished to speak directly with Lord Lovell on behalf of the king.'

As the most senior in rank of the three men it was not unusual that the king's emissary would want to speak directly with Viscount Lovell rather than the Stafford brothers.

'Maybe they'll offer us a reprieve,' Thomas said expectantly.

'More likely the end of a rope,' Francis added.

'Perhaps they'll offer us safe passage abroad in return for our agreement to stay in exile,' Sir Humphrey Stafford, Thomas' stout fair-haired older brother, offered more in hope than expectation.

'Let us find out,' Francis said, turning towards the white-haired, tonsured abbot waiting to carry their reply back to the mounted men at the gatehouse.

'Abbot Stanstead, please invite them to the abbey door.'

The three fugitives stood in the abbey doorway watching

Abbot Stanstead scurry through the teeming rain to speak to the emissary at the impressive twin-turreted abbey gatehouse. He then turned and led the party of mounted men through the gatehouse archway and along the avenue leading to the entrance to the abbey itself, as the rain lashed incessantly down upon them. Upon reaching the doorway the bedraggled abbot begged his leave and slipped past Francis and the Stafford brothers and back into the confines of the abbey to dry off. The emissaries of the king were not so lucky, as they sat astride their horses with cloaks pulled tight to keep out the slanting rain that beat against them.

'I am Sir John Risely, here on the king's business,' the lead rider shouted to be heard above the noise of the rain. 'His Majesty, King Henry, demands your presence at court, Lord Lovell. He has matters of importance that he wishes to discuss with you,' he informed Francis.

'His Majesty now, is it?' Lovell scoffed. 'Well, you can tell your master that I am unable to leave this sanctuary without a formal pardon, for fear of reprisal for fighting against him.'

'That is understandable,' agreed Risely, 'but the king has asked me to convey to you that he intends you no harm if you give yourself up and return to court. In fact, he has promised that your lands shall not be forfeit and prays that you will accept the honour of carrying the royal sceptre before the queen at her coronation.'

'High honour indeed but I am still unwilling to leave until I have a written pardon signed and sealed by the king himself.'

'It can be arranged,' Risely said matter-of-factly as the rain dripped off the end of his nose.

'And my comrades?' Lovell asked, gesturing to the two Stafford brothers standing beside him.

A flash of lightning lit up the grey sky and several of the horses reared up in fear before their riders brought them under control again.

'I have no authority to discuss any more than I already have,' Risely responded as the rumble of thunder could be heard above the rain.

'Then there is nothing more for us to discuss, Sir John. I bid you farewell and a safe journey back to your king in these treacherous conditions,' Francis said, smiling warmly at Risely. 'However, should your master wish to offer a full, signed and sealed pardon for all three of us, then I would be delighted to come to court and to carry the royal sceptre before the queen at her coronation.'

Risely smirked, acknowledging the derision in Francis' voice. 'I will convey your request to the king,' he replied nonetheless.

With that he nodded farewell, turned his horse about and trotted towards the gatehouse with his party in tow. Humphrey slammed the large oak door shut against the wind and rain before turning to Francis and Thomas.

'Do you think Tudor will grant us a full pardon?' he asked, refusing to acknowledge the Welshman's title of king.

'I doubt it very much,' Francis replied. 'He'll probably try to keep us here while he sends emissaries back and forth with hints of offers and false promises. That will give him time to quell any lingering support for the House of York while we're holed up here.'

'Support for what House of York?' Thomas asked scathingly. 'The House of York died with King Richard. All we can hope for now is to escape with our lives!'

'The House of York lives yet!' Francis declared vehemently. 'The Earl of Lincoln was named heir by King Richard himself.'

'If he hasn't already been killed in the battle or arrested afterwards,' scoffed Thomas.

'Face it. Most are dead, captured or fleeing. Anyone of name who opposed Henry Tudor and survived has been attainted, their lands and titles forfeit, including us!'

'More reason for them to join us then,' Francis argued.

'Join us to do what?' Thomas spat back.

'Put a Yorkist king back on the throne in place of this Welsh upstart! The cause is not dead, Thomas. Together we can rally those that are left. We can raise an army. If needs be, we can flee to Flanders and raise support there. King Richard's sister Margaret would offer us her support. Her stepdaughter, the duchess of Burgundy, could provide soldiers to our cause. Would she not want to see her stepmother's kin back on the throne of England, and once more gain a valuable ally against France?'

'What kin, Francis? What if Lincoln is dead? What sons of York are left then to reclaim the throne?'

'Clarence's son, the young Earl of Warwick,' Humphrey interjected.

'But he was attainted after his father was found guilty of treason against King Edward. He no longer has a claim to the throne,' Thomas stated.

His pale grey eyes flicked from Francis to Humphrey and back again trying to gauge their reaction as each weighed up their thoughts. Thunder echoed outside the abbey breaking the momentary silence, then Francis spoke again, calmly and assuredly.

'Better an attainted son of York than a Welsh rebel who claims his right to be king through Beaufort bastards, barred by King Henry IV himself, and by Act of Parliament, from any claim to the throne.'

'Aye,' Humphrey agreed, rubbing a hand over his paunch while nodding vociferously.

'Then it is decided. We proclaim Warwick as king?' Francis asked, looking at Thomas for his consent. 'We leave sanctuary and go to raise support for our cause?'

'Yes,' Humphrey said firmly.

Thomas nodded his tacit approval.

'We must be unwavering in this, Thomas,' Francis admonished the younger Stafford. 'Are you whole-heartedly with us?'

'Yes Francis, I am,' Thomas retorted, annoyed that Francis could suggest that he may not be fully committed to the cause.

'Then I'll head north to Yorkshire and rally support among our heartlands,' Francis continued. 'You both head back to your estates in the Midlands and south west and rally support there. Bring your troops north to meet me at York. Between us we can raise enough men to topple Henry Tudor from his usurped throne.'

'Then it is finally time for us to leave the confines of this sanctuary,' Humphrey said with a smile of relief.

As thunder cracked overhead and rain continued to hammer down in sheets on the lead roof, the three fugitives tightened their cloaks and went in search of Abbot Stanstead to retrieve the swords and knives they had surrendered upon entering the sanctuary of the abbey.

14

I t seemed to King Henry that his triumphal entry into London had been the highpoint of a so far short but dismal reign. Trumpeters had sounded their welcome as the lord mayor, accompanied by fifty swordsmen of the mayor's bodyguard met him at Shoreditch, along with aldermen and sheriffs, guarded by armed servants in gowns of tawny. Over four hundred liverymen from the city's seventy companies, dressed in gowns of scarlet and bright mulberry lined the route to the city and shouted their welcome and well wishes to their new sovereign.

Henry had revelled in the moment as each and every one of them had stooped and kissed his hand before he was escorted into the city, through cheering crowds shouting their acclamation, past the pageants and joyous celebrations in the main thoroughfares, and on to St. Paul's Cathedral. There he offered up the three banners beneath which he had given battle: the red cross of St George, the Red Dragon of Cadwallader, and the Dun Cow. A great mass of thanksgiving for his God-given victory was said and the Te Deum sang. Henry reflected on that most wondrous, yet seemingly distant, moment of his life.

Now, months later, the lord mayor and many of those who

greeted him were dead, and many others were dying from the sweating sickness that his foreign mercenaries had brought with them into London. His coronation had been delayed until late October and, although it eventually passed without incident, rumours were rife that this new sickness, which could see a man wake healthily at sunrise and be dead by sunset, was the king's fault: a curse from God for usurping the Plantagenet line. Henry seethed at the thought of the word usurper. A word that he had used to describe Richard, the hunchback king whose unjust rule he had ended; and now that word was being used to describe him, Henry VII, the true and rightful king of England.

However, even now that right was still being questioned as Yorkist rebels were stirring up trouble in the north of his realm and fomenting rebellion. Small-scale riots had been put down but the ringleaders, using assumed names like Tom a' Linn and Jack Straw had dispersed with the wind before they could be arrested. Word had reached Henry that they were colluding with the Scots and that he may soon face an invasion from the north.

To make matters worse, two hundred men from the garrison at Calais under their captain Thomas David, and the garrison at Jersey under Governor Richard Harleston, had deserted their posts and marched to Mechelen in the Low Countries. There they joined the growing number of Yorkist dissidents at the court of Richard III's sister, the dowager Duchess of Burgundy, from where they too could threaten an invasion. Nothing in life, Henry realised, would be easy; so it was a relief that William Parron had arrived at court to foretell his future and advise him on what to do next.

King Henry turned from the window of the bishop's palace, from where he had been staring out into the cold grey sky, and looked at the five men patiently waiting for his response. He lowered the linen cloth that he had been holding to his mouth to prevent breathing in the noxious miasmas of the city that spread the sweating sickness.

'I will not make my decision until I have consulted my astrologer,' the king announced.

'But Your Grace, you place yourself in great danger if you remain in London. Yorkist sympathisers continue to stir up trouble in the land and if nothing is done, they may rally behind a pretender or raise enough support to march on London itself. A royal progress to the north would assuage the people and assert your royal authority in the former Yorkist heartlands,' Sir Giles Daubeney pleaded with the king.

'It would also remove you far from the sweating sickness that plagues the capital, Your Grace,' Jasper Tudor added hoping this would sway the king.

'My Duke of Bedford,' Henry responded using Jasper Tudor's newly conferred title, 'I have already stated that I will make my decision after consulting with Master Parron. I must know what the stars foretell before I decide whether or not to make a royal progress into the north.'

'Yes, Your Grace,' Jasper conceded as he and Daubeney bowed in assent, the disappointment obvious on their faces.

The king waved away the five members of his council, who diligently turned and walked out past the roaring fire in the great hearth.

'Sir Reginald, please stay,' the king said, changing his mind. 'There is something I wish to ask you.'

Sir Reginald Bray paused while Daubeney, the Duke of Bedford, and Bishops Morton and Foxe slid through the great oak door at the far end of the great hall. As the door closed behind them, he turned and walked back towards the king who was gazing out of the window, the linen cloth again held up to his mouth.

'Your Grace?' Bray waited patiently for a response as the king seemed to mull something over in his mind.

After a minute the king lowered the cloth and spoke but did not turn away from the window to face him.

'The boy, do you trust the priest that it was Lovell's son?'

'We have no reason not to believe him, Your Grace.'

'Has he been found yet?' the king enquired.

'Not yet, Your Grace, but my lord Oxford's soldiers are looking for him and I have men keeping a close watch on several places where he may turn up.'

'Do you think he may try to get to his father in Colchester Abbey?'

'It is a possibility, Your Grace.'

'I would like him found quickly. He will prove valuable leverage in bringing Lovell to heel.'

'Yes, Your Grace.'

'Also,' the king added as an afterthought, 'I want the guard doubled on the Tower. It would not do to have the young Earl of Warwick escape to be made a figurehead for any Yorkist rising.'

'I will see to it immediately, Your Grace,' Bray confirmed.

'And tell Master Parron that I will see him now.'

With that final order Bray bowed and left the room.

*

It was nightfall before Richard and Herricke reached Colchester. Richard was cold and tired but he forced himself onwards.

'Not far now,' Herricke reassured him.

They approached St. John's Abbey from the south, avoiding the town itself and the busier roads leading to it. They had left the horses Herricke had purchased in Tilbury, at an inn in a village on the outskirts of Colchester, paying the innkeeper a shilling for his silence and telling him that if they didn't return in two days, he could keep them. Richard was grateful that they had at least eaten at the inn before moving on.

Now, in the dark, they approached the abbey on foot along a narrow track that was thick with wet mud that clung to their boots like potter's clay and sucked them into the ground, hindering their progress at every step. The heavy rain and storm of the previous day had abated but a light wind still drove a fine drizzle into their faces, soaking them through to the skin. Richard admired the fortitude of Herricke who, despite looking as old as Methuselah and as frail as a dry autumn leaf in a tempest, never once complained about the hardship.

'Are you in the fellowship of the Hopper ring?' Richard asked Herricke as he pulled his sodden cloak tight around his head.

'No but those that are reward me handsomely for my services so I have no complaints about that.'

'I'm grateful for your help Master Herricke. I really —'

Richard stopped talking because Herricke put a hand over his mouth, then crouched low to the ground pulling him down with him.

'There's two lookouts sitting atop the abbey wall, one at each end,' Herricke whispered as he removed his hand from Richard's mouth. 'I don't think they're out in this weather for the fun of it.'

'Are they looking for us?' Richard asked.

'Either that or they're keeping an eye on the abbey's comings and goings. I hope Lord Lovell is leading them a merry dance,' he chuckled.

'What shall we do?' Richard asked with some concern.

'We cannot get to the abbey from this direction so we are going to have to risk coming from the town side and hope we are not spotted,' Herricke explained. 'That means we have to skirt round in a wide arc to avoid the lookouts and then approach the wall at the northern end near St Giles' Church. At least the weather should keep folk indoors so we are not going to have awkward questions about why we're skulking about in the fields instead of using the road.'

They trudged through the mud, heavy footstep by heavy footstep, until they reached the wall at the northern end of the abbey. After Herricke had scouted the area to ensure there were no lookouts posted there, they used the wall to scrape as much mud off their boots as they possibly could. They then followed the line of the abbey wall keeping low until they were opposite St Giles' Church. Herricke left Richard crouching against the wall behind a Hawthorn bush as he again scouted the area to ensure it was clear before they went any further. After a few minutes Herricke returned.

'It seems they're only watching the main gate. They must be there to let the king know if Lord Lovell leaves sanctuary.'

Herricke shook his cloak to remove some of the water.

'Did you know that sanctuary only lasts for forty days? After that the king has the right to remove any refugees. Mind you, after the furore when King Edward had the Duke of Somerset and other prominent Lancastrians dragged out of sanctuary at Tewkesbury, I doubt any king will ever do that again. Risking excommunication by the pope would be a step too far, even for Henry Tudor methinks.'

'But he could have Lord Lovell arrested once the forty days have passed?' Richard had assumed that sanctuary was permanent until the person left the confines of the church they were sheltering in.

'Don't worry, it definitely won't happen.' Herricke seemed genuinely unconcerned but Richard could not help but feel worried.

'Right,' Herricke suddenly said with determination, 'we are going to stand up and walk to the door of that church like we're meant to be there. Stand up straight and walk quickly and purposefully. When we get there leave all the talking to me. Understand?'

He was up and striding towards the church at a brisk pace before Richard even had a chance to respond. Richard swept his wet hair out of his face and followed, trying to keep up with Herricke who arrived at the church door and immediately banged against it with his fist. There was no response after a minute so Herricke banged on the door again. Within moments they heard a bolt sliding out of its latch, then a man with a very serious look on his face peered around the door.

'Yes?' he snapped, glancing them up and down.

'Forgive me,' Herricke said, 'but I need a favour; for which I'm willing to pay.'

He held out the palm of his hand where several silver coins lay. The man's face softened.

'What sort of favour?' the verger asked.

'My young friend and I need to borrow two monks' habits and need entry through the church and into the abbey grounds at the rear.'

The verger shook his head. 'I will not be party to any mischief, sir. I'm sorry but the answer is no.'

He pushed the door shut but Herricke quickly placed his foot to stop the door closing completely.

'There is no mischief at play here, my friend. Would you not show favour to the House of York?'

'I hold no political allegiance and as I've already said, I will not be a party to any mischief.'

He tried to push the door shut again but Herricke persisted, pushing the door back with his shoulder.

'We merely need to speak in person to Lord Lovell, who has sought sanctuary in the abbey, but there are men watching the front gate who we would prefer to avoid.'

The verger peered around the half open door and glared at Herricke.

'Sounds like mischief to me. Now if you'll please remove your foot before I call —'

'Would this help ease your conscience?' Herricke interrupted.

The gold coin glistening in Herricke's palm was too much for the verger to resist. He opened the door and beckoned Herricke and Richard inside, eagerly snatching the gold angel from Herricke's outstretched fingers as he passed. The verger examined the gold coin closely before tucking it into a purse hanging from his belt. The gold angel, worth six shillings and eight pence, was more money than he would normally earn in a month. He drew the purse strings tight with a hint of a smile, then placed his finger to his lips indicating that they should be quiet, before he turned and walked with haste through the shimmering puddles of candlelight that illuminated the inside of the church. Herricke and Richard followed him into the vestry where he shut the door behind them.

'There are no monks' habits but you may take whatever clothes you find in this chest. They are mainly the priest's vestments but you may find other clothes in there too. When you are ready there is a door in the south of the church that will lead you out into the abbey grounds. I am going to unlock it now and then leave as I do not intend to be blamed for this if you are caught. As far as anyone else is concerned, I did not let you into this church and I have never seen you before. You can hang a noose around your own necks, but not mine. Is that clear?'

'Perfectly,' Herricke stated, with a grin of disdain.

The verger left with a sour look on his face that belied the fact that he was now a gold angel richer.

'Do you trust him?' Richard asked. 'What if he fetches the night watchman from the town?'

'No, I don't trust him but he won't alert anyone because he'd risk losing that gold angel if we told how he let us in.'

Herricke removed his damp cloak, placing it on a nearby table. He opened the large wooden chest and rummaged through its contents. There were scant pickings. He took out a priest's black cassock and put it on. The large garment hung off his frail frame and trailed on to the stone-flagged floor. Herricke hitched up the lower half, securing the loose material with a sash knotted tightly at his waist.

Richard found a long grey woollen shirt, leather belt, clean white hose, and a black surcoat in the wooden chest. He dressed quickly. His boots were still wet but he had no choice but to put them back on.

'Not as I had hoped but we can pass for a priest and...' Herricke chuckled to himself. 'I'm not sure what you can pass for but it will have to do. Let's go,' he said as he grasped Richard on the shoulder and gave him a friendly pat on the back.

They paused at the unlocked door at the southern side of the church. Herricke opened it and cautiously peered out into the darkness.

'I can't see a bloody thing!' he exclaimed. 'Ah well, we'll get there. Stay close, we're going straight to the abbey. Walk normally and stay silent.'

It was easier said than done. The rain had ceased some time ago but the grass was still slick and greasy underfoot as they made their way past molehills and divots, under a blanket of cloud that obscured the moon and made their journey more treacherous in the pitch-black night. Out in the open there was no wall to feel their way along, so step by step they walked with hands out in front of them feeling nothing but the cold, still, dark night air. Richard let out a grunt as his foot caught in a divot and he stumbled and then slipped as his back foot went out from underneath him on the wet surface. He went to ground with his legs splayed in opposite directions. Before he could shout out in pain Herricke was crouching over him with a hand held forcefully over his mouth to silence him.

'Don't make a sound!' he warned Richard in a stern whisper. 'Stay where you are and don't move or speak.'

Herricke scanned around and listened intently to detect if anyone had been alerted by the commotion. After a few minutes he was satisfied and helped Richard to his feet.

'Are you alright?'

'I've pulled a muscle in my groin but I'll be fine. I can still walk,' Richard whispered as he began to make his way gingerly through the darkness.

Eventually they arrived at a door on the northern side of the abbey. Herricke turned the handle and pushed but the door would not open. He rapped softly on the wood to beckon those inside but no one came.

'I can't tap any louder or it will alert the sentries on the wall. I'll have to lift you up to a window so you can get someone's attention,' he said in a shallow voice.

They skirted along the northern side of the building until they stood below a narrow window. Herricke interlocked his fingers and held out his cupped hands into which Richard placed a foot. Richard grimaced at the pain in his groin muscle as Herricke hoisted him up to the narrow slit of a window. He pulled himself level with the opening then pushed aside a thin sheet of oiled hide that had been preventing a draft getting through, and peered inside. The room was dark and empty but Richard made a noise anyway in the hope of catching the attention of someone inside the abbey.

'Psssst. Psssst. Psssst.' Nothing.

Richard persisted. 'Psssst. Psssst. Psssst.'

'What in God's name are you doing?' a voice boomed out beneath him, scaring him half to death. Herricke too jumped in fright and released his cupped hands from beneath Richard's foot so that the youth came tumbling down on top of him. Abbot Stanstead looked down sternly upon the pair.

'What are you doing here?' he said again in a raised voice.

'Pray be quiet, friar! Please, we are here to see Lord Lovell,' Herricke pleaded in a hushed tone.

'Why?' Abbot Stanstead asked warily.

'Because we are friends of the House of York,' Richard said, pulling the leather thong about his neck until the Hopper ring revealed itself. 'Did you see Lord Lovell with a ring the same as this?'

'I cannot see in the dark! Come inside and keep your heads bowed until we are there,' the abbot instructed them.

He walked to the main doorway on the south side of the abbey overlooked by the sentries. As they neared the entrance porch, he again raised his voice so that anyone surreptitiously watching would hear.

'I have warned you both before about picking mushrooms at night. Yes, they come out after rain but they will still be there in the morning, now get inside, you fools! You will both do penance for this,' and with that he shoved them both through the oak door and slammed it behind him.

Once inside Abbot Stanstead gave the ring a cursory look then he glared at Herricke. 'Couldn't you find a way of getting a message to me without making such a scene?'

'I'm sorry friar but…'

'I'm the abbot,' he snapped angrily at Herricke. 'Abbot Stanstead. Now, what did you want with Lord Lovell?'

'I apologise, Father Abbot. What we have to say can only be said to Lord Lovell in person.'

'Then you are out of luck, I'm afraid. Lord Lovell left here two nights ago.'

Richard sighed deeply and Herricke looked up towards the vaulted ceiling for inspiration.

'Do you know where he went?' Richard asked desperately.

'I was not made privy to that information.'

'Do you have any idea at all?' Herricke pleaded.

'My guess would be to the coast, to escape to Flanders via Harwich or Clacton maybe? Other than that, I cannot help you.'

'Thank you, Abbot Stanstead. We appreciate your help.' Herricke shrugged and looked at Richard sympathetically. 'We can try to find him but failing that all I can do is find you work as a stonemason's apprentice.'

Even in the dim light of the abbey, it was clear that Richard was not enthralled with the notion. He toyed with the idea of going back to Eastwell to see Father Martin but he knew deep down that Eastwell held nothing for him other than a life of toil in the fields whilst constantly looking over his shoulder, in fear of reprisal by the Kempe brothers or being discovered by the king's men.

'Let's go find Lord Lovell,' he instructed Herricke.

*

The king paced anxiously across the room as William Parron examined the vellum manuscripts and scrolls laid out on the table. Parron stroked his beard, pulling it to a fine point at the tip of his chin. After several minutes he looked up and spoke; his Piacenzan accent still noticeable despite many years in England in the service of the new king's mother.

'The stars have revealed their secrets to me, Majesty.'

'And what do they tell you?' the king enquired.

'That the red dragon shall be triumphant over the white rose.'

'It already has, Master Parron,' the king smirked.

'Ah Majesty, but there are still rebels who would carry on the lost cause and hope to find a new white rose to sit on your throne.'

'Pah! I shall crush these rebels and destroy every sprig of that damned white rose that dares to show its head above ground,' King Henry spat vehemently. Then he paused in thought for a moment. 'The Yorkist line is virtually extinct anyway. What do I have to fear from a few errant rebels?'

Parron smiled. 'The stars foretell that Your Majesty will rule for many years, and your children, grandchildren, and many generations of Tudors after them. Fear not, Majesty, the bear shall remain in chains and all of your enemies will soon die.'

King Henry smiled at that. The bear Parron referred to was the bear and ragged staff: the heraldic symbol of the ten-year-old Earl of Warwick; nephew to both Yorkist kings Edward IV and Richard III, and one of the last potential claimants to Henry's crown. Henry had held Warwick captive in the Tower of London since he had become king. It pleased him to know that the bear would remain there.

'The stars and alignment of the planets foretell that the mighty house of Tudor will flourish. I am pleased to reveal that the marriage of Your Majesty and the Lady Elizabeth will result in many male heirs.'

'And her current pregnancy will go well?'

'The stars foretell that the Queen shall be delivered of a healthy baby boy in the autumn.'

'Then I shall name him Arthur, after the great king of Britain. It is a name that will resonate among the English and Welsh.'

'He will be a great ruler like his father and even greater than the previous king Arthur,' Parron declared. 'It is written in the stars for all to see, Majesty.'

'That is good to know, Master Parron.' The king stared at Parron's charts laid out across the table. 'Tell me what the stars say about a royal progress to the north?'

'They say the timing for a royal progress to the north is perfect, Majesty. You are newly crowned, married to the daughter of the House of York, and the birth of your first heir is imminent. Your Majesty has concluded your first parliament and you have no need to stay in London any longer. The people need to see their king, Majesty. The stars foretell that many will flock to see the royal progress and that the people will rejoice in your coming. Nevertheless, beware, Majesty, for there are those at large who will spread malicious rumours and try to incite rebellion against you.'

'What malicious rumours?' Concern suddenly showed on the king's furrowed brow.

'That you are not the rightful king,' Parron added hesitantly.

King Henry's face began to turn puce with anger.

Seeing the king's reaction Parron quickly added, 'But of course, this is untrue and the stars also foretell that those people born under bad stars will die before infecting the country.'

'Then so be it,' the king said with grim determination. 'Tell me one more thing though.'

'What is it, Majesty?'

The king walked past Parron and began to peruse the manuscripts on the table. He unrolled a scroll but could not make sense of the lines and symbols that adorned it. He continued to look at the scroll he had unfurled as he asked Parron a question.

'Despite our union and my wife's pregnancy I am still not sure…' Henry paused, unable to find the right words. 'I detect a coldness… What I am trying to ask, Master Parron, is will my wife ever truly love me?'

The question caught Parron off guard. He was surprised that the king, usually such a secretive man, should lay his cards so openly upon the table. Parron stroked his beard and then unrolled a manuscript, placing four heavy carved wooden blocks at each corner to hold it flat. He perused the manuscript's strange lines and markings, trying to gather his thoughts before answering. He stroked his beard to a point once more then looked up at the king.

'The Lady Elizabeth has been a political pawn for most of her life, Majesty, and only now is she able to settle. It may take a little time, but yes, she will come to truly love you.'

'Thank you, Master Parron.' King Henry smiled and patted him on the shoulder. 'You have put my mind at ease and set me on the path I must take.'

'Not I, Majesty, the stars. I am merely the interpreter.'

'Then you must interpret the stars again upon my return from the royal progress.'

15

I t was in the cold grey half-light before sunrise that the Stafford brothers left Kidderminster with two hundred and twenty-four men at their backs. They had done well recruiting from their estates and nearby towns and villages, in and around Worcestershire. At first men questioned whether Humphrey and his brother Thomas had the right to raise troops, as they were attainted traitors outlawed by the king. However, Humphrey swore that the king himself had pardoned them and he even produced letters patent proving that an Act of Parliament had reversed the attainders. That forgery of letters patent cost Humphrey half an angel; twice the weekly wage of a skilled workman and enough to buy a pound of cloves in Worcester market. It was worth it though, Humphrey thought, especially after what had happened at Bromsgrove when he and Thomas faced the stiffest challenge to their authority.

Sir Humphrey had stood on the base of the High Cross, facing the marketplace. He surveyed the crowd gathering in front of him. Although he had Thomas by his side and half a dozen of his own men with him, he was wary of the members of the local militia who watched on from the outskirts of the marketplace. They could arrest him and end the uprising before it even began.

The crowd were hostile from the outset, pushing forward, closing in around the High Cross in a seething volatile mass of bodies, jeering and calling Sir Humphrey and his brother traitors. They shouted over him, refusing to listen to anything he said. The militiamen watched carefully, poised, ready to pounce if things got out of hand and haul the troublemakers off to the town gaol. It was a nervy situation but Humphrey ignored the shouts and insults and instead revealed the letters patent, holding them high with the king's seal attached for all to see. The townsfolk closest confirmed to those standing behind them that these were indeed letters patent, bearing the king's seal and confirming that the Staffords' attainders had been reversed.

The news spread through the crowd with a ripple of excitement, smothering the air of hostility until the jeers died away and the people stood, shamed into silence; finally prepared to hear what Sir Humphrey Stafford had to say. He spoke calmly but with authority, still holding the letters patent out for the townsfolk to see. A skilled orator and former Member of Parliament, he knew now that they would listen, that he could win them over.

'I need men, brave men, fearless men, men who know how to ride and how to handle a sword; men who can follow orders and who wish to serve their country and earn silver into the bargain. I will pay any man who offers me his service four pence per day or five pence per day if he has his own horse. Who here will follow me?' Humphrey bellowed over the heads of the townsfolk crowded around the foot of the High Cross as he delved a hand into his purse and held up a fist full of silver coins for all to see.

The militiamen kept their distance as Humphrey spun his oratory and persuaded men to join him. They surged forward, clamouring to sign up and earn Stafford silver. A woman pushed her reluctant husband forward and scolded him for his hesitancy to earn such easy money. Women and children around him laughed as he shuffled forward, cowed and constantly berated by his wife until he finally reached the sergeant-at-arms, made his mark on the scroll, and took the four pence in pay. Humphrey patted the fellow on the back and whispered into his ear.

'At least you'll get some respite for a while and a good wage to take home to keep her quiet a bit longer.'

The man smiled as an invisible weight lifted from him and he suddenly grew in stature. He joined the other mercenaries who laughed, clapped him on the shoulders and welcomed him into the fold.

Humphrey left Bromsgrove that morning with a hefty sigh of relief and another eighteen men willing to offer their services in return for the Stafford brother's silver.

That morning John Stafford, the bastard son of Sir Humphrey, took a raiding party to the king's stables at Upton on Severn and rode away with seventy-two horses to join up with his father and the growing band of rebels now gathering at Kidderminster. Richard Oseney, summoned by Sir Humphrey, arrived in Kidderminster that evening bringing more men, horses, weapons, mail and armour, swelling the rebel numbers to two hundred and twenty-six men. Now they were ready to begin the rebellion to bring down Henry Tudor and replace him with the Earl of Warwick, the nephew of King Richard III.

It was a gamble leaving Kidderminster before sunrise. Horses could stumble on the uneven road surface in the dark and wreak havoc amid the tightly packed ranks of riders, snapping horses' legs like straw and breaking the necks of both man and mount. It was a gamble Humphrey Stafford was prepared to take as it was imperative that they reach Worcester just after the sun rose and the gates opened, but before the city had sprung to life and the walls could be quickly fortified if the alarm was raised. Humphrey explained to his brother and son, to Richard Oseney, and to his captains, that the capture of Worcester was to be, as far as possible, a bloodless affair. They needed the people of Worcester to join them, not turn against them. If Humphrey's plan was successful, the men they had recruited would follow their captains' lead, and Worcester would soon be under his control. From there the rebellion would spread and more men would join him. Lovell was raising an army in the north and together the two forces would join to depose Henry Tudor and restore a Yorkist king to the throne of England.

Birds chattered and squawked in the first light of morning as the riders cleared the woodland to the north of Worcester, the sandstone walls of the city appearing ahead of them. Crofters' cottages lined the road that led southwards to the twin circular towers of the gatehouse that protected the Foregate into the city. A thirty-foot-wide, water-filled ditch surrounded the walls so that the only way into the city was through the imposing Foregate. Humphrey knew the perils of riding into the city with an armed force. If they were spotted, the alarm would be raised. The giant wrought-iron portcullis would be dropped and the gates slammed shut to bar their way. Arrows and crossbow bolts would rain down from the walls and gatehouse arrow slits, making it impossible for them to assault the impenetrable barrier before them. Humphrey's best chance of success relied on good timing, speed and lots of luck.

Humphrey said a prayer to the Virgin Mary and crossed himself as he lowered his visor and spurred his horse into a gallop. The sun had already cleared the horizon to their left as all two hundred and twenty-six riders charged at full gallop along the dirt road, between the crofters' cottages, towards the city gates. His heart pounded with fear and excitement but to his immense relief Humphrey could see that the gates were open and there seemed no movement on the city walls, no peal of church bells or panicked shouts to announce the impending arrival of several hundred armed men.

Humphrey looked up through the slit in his visor at the top of the city walls and the gatehouse arrow slits, expecting to see a crossbowman or archer aiming at him, but even as he cleared the last crofter's cottage, he saw no sign of resistance.

'A Warwick! A Warwick!' Humphrey shouted with only yards before he reached the open gate.

He wondered if his muffled shout could be heard through his helmet but the cry was immediately taken up by his captains and his men.

'A Warwick! A Warwick!' the riders cried as they funnelled through the gateway and poured into the open streets of the city.

It was too easy, Humphrey thought to himself, but he knew better than to complain that the Virgin Mary had smiled upon him and granted him this victory.

'A Warwick! A Warwick!' the riders continued to raise the cry as they swarmed through the streets and alleyways of Worcester.

The experienced captains ignored the startled onlookers who jumped out of their way as they rode on to find the targets they had been allocated by Humphrey the previous night. They spread out, some on horseback and some dismounting and going on foot, sword or daggers in hand, along the High Street, Broad Street, and Gaol Lane. Some headed for the port area, some for the

Cathedral Close, and others to the civic buildings and houses of the high-status and important men of the city. They spread like swarming ants, securing the gates, walls and key areas of the city. The bailiffs, bishop, leaders of the militia and other officials were rounded up and herded into the Cathedral Close where Humphrey Stafford, with his brother Thomas alongside him, waited patiently to address them. Richard Oseney finally nodded to Sir Humphrey to indicate that all of the men they had targeted were now present.

'Fear not,' Humphrey assuaged the worried faces assembled before him. 'We are not here to harm you. We are here to bring you joyous news!'

'Then why have you taken the city by force and herded us together like common criminals?' a red-faced man with bushy grey eyebrows demanded to know.

Humphrey looked at the man, dressed in a simple nightgown with a woollen cap pulled tight over his head, and at once recognised him as John Alcock, Bishop of Worcester. He smiled kindly at the bishop as he explained.

'Forgive me, my lord Bishop, but the usurper Henry Tudor has been captured in Yorkshire by Lord Lovell.'

A murmur rippled through the Cathedral Close as the assembled personages turned to each other with looks of disbelief.

'The Earl of Warwick has been freed from captivity and is riding north to join Lord Lovell, where he will be proclaimed king at York. I am commanded to secure Worcester in the name of our new sovereign lord, King Edward VI, and to raise a force in the West Midlands to join him and Lord Lovell on their march to London. God save King Edward!' Humphrey shouted.

'God save King Edward!' a few of the stunned people in the

Cathedral Close called back dutifully.

Humphrey stared directly at Bishop Alcock, knowing that the man had been one of the few churchmen to openly propose that Henry Tudor should marry Elizabeth of York, and that the new king had recently appointed him Lord Chancellor.

'Does any person assembled here oppose King Edward VI's right to his uncle's throne?' He challenged everyone assembled while still maintaining eye contact with Bishop Alcock.

No one spoke.

'Does any person here wish to leave Worcester to rally troops against your new sovereign lord?'

Again, there was silence, this time accompanied by a few shaking heads.

'Then go, my friends. Go and spread the good news that Henry Tudor has been overthrown and that the House of York rules over us once more. Tell everyone that the Earl of Warwick is now King Edward VI and that we should assemble a force to join him and escort him back to London. Go now! Go!'

The crowd began to wander off with startled looks upon their faces as they digested the news. Humphrey waved away the last few congregations of chattering people as his soldiers helped to shepherd and disperse them away from the Cathedral Close. Humphrey knew that gossip and rumour would quickly spread far and wide. He had lit the touch-paper that would spread the news of Henry Tudor's demise, and the rise of a new Yorkist monarchy. Men would flock to the banner of the Staffords in support of their Yorkist king, Edward VI. A great army was about to gather and ride north to meet Lord Lovell. Then their combined forces would face Henry Tudor and the real battle for the throne of England would begin.

*

The fire crackled and hissed as Henry extended his stockinged feet towards the flames to soak up their warmth. He idly scratched through his woven woollen hose at a fleabite on his knee. He knew that he would reek of wood smoke but at least that would drive out the fleas that had been feasting upon his legs for the past few days. The royal progress north wearied him, and days of travelling through the damp English countryside, bitten by fleas and midges, accompanied by intermittent periods of sunshine that brought out the people to see him and then the intolerable drizzle of rain which permeated through his clothes and seemed to seep deep, into his very bones, left him exhausted. Now he wanted nothing more than to stretch out in front of the fire like a contented hound and sleep, but his royal duties prevented him from doing this.

'Tomorrow Your Grace will wash the feet of the poor of Lincoln in the cathedral for the Easter ceremony, as Our Lord Jesus Christ did almost fifteen hundred years ago. There will be twenty-nine of the poor destitute creatures; one to represent each year of Your Grace's age,' Bishop Foxe informed the king.

Henry sighed and rolled his eyes. He revelled in the adulation he received at every village, town and city on the progress; the fairs held in his honour, the gifts given to him, and the cheering populace who lined the route to shout their support, but the endless travelling in poor weather and the interminable ceremonies were getting him down. He knew that washing the feet of the twenty-nine poor was seen as an act of humility and that it had been arranged by his advisor Bishop Foxe along with

John Russell, Bishop of Lincoln, to portray him to the public as a humble monarch, and yet Henry still found it an onerous chore.

Bishop Foxe saw the king roll his eyes and reminded him of Matthew's words from the bible, 'he who exalts himself will be humbled and he who humbles himself will be exalted'.

King Henry sighed again. 'I know this, Bishop, and I shall do the duty I have been brought up and trained for, but I long to be back in London with my wife.'

'It is important that the people see you, Your Grace. They must learn to adore you and respect you. They cannot do that if you are cooped up in a royal palace in London,' the bishop chastised him.

Before Henry could respond, a chunk of charred wood in the fire crackled and collapsed into the flames sending a shower of orange sparks into the air. Henry jumped to his feet as one of the sparks landed on his leg and sizzled through his woollen hose, causing him to beat at it with the palm of his hand.

'These were a gift from the mayor of Cambridge,' Henry yelled in frustration as he picked at the charred edges of the hole burned into his purple woollen hose.

'Never mind, Your Grace. I believe the abbot of Waltham gave you an identical pair,' Bishop Foxe noted with some amusement.

'That he did.' Henry nodded in agreement as he sat back down and once again extended his legs towards the fire.

There was a knock on the door, which creaked open to reveal a Yeoman of the Guard, resplendent in his black and scarlet uniform. Henry looked enquiringly at the man.

'Reginald Bray requests an audience with Your Grace,' the Yeoman informed the king.

Henry looked questioningly at Bishop Foxe who shook his head in uncertainty.

'Then show him in,' Henry instructed the bodyguard after a short pause.

Bray entered the chamber and went down on one knee with bowed head, waiting for the king to give him permission to rise.

'What brings you here at this hour, Sir Reginald?'

Bray stood and addressed the king. 'You Grace, there is news that Lord Lovell, Sir Humphrey Stafford of Grafton, and his brother Thomas have left sanctuary at Colchester and are at large in the kingdom. They may be trying to raise a rebellion against you.'

'Who brought you this news?' King Henry demanded. 'Who?'

'Hugh Conway, Your Grace.' Bray could see the colour flushing into the king's face.

'Bring him to me,' the king commanded.

Bray turned to execute the king's order but was quickly halted in his tracks.

'Not you, Sir Reginald,' King Henry ordered. 'You wait here.' He nodded at his bodyguard who quickly turned and scurried off through the doorway to find Hugh Conway.

There was a long awkward silence as King Henry paced back and forth across the worn wooden floor, pausing occasionally to scratch at the fleabite on his knee. Bishop Foxe and Bray stood side by side, neither of them speaking, until eventually, the silence was broken when Hugh Conway was escorted into the room by the Yeoman of the Guard. King Henry turned to look at him.

'How do you know Lovell and the Staffords have left the abbey at Colchester?' he asked Conway.

'I have an informant, Your Grace. He reliably informs me that the fugitives left the abbey almost a week ago.'

'I too have informants, Master Conway, and they have not brought me such news,' the king replied. 'Are you telling me that your informants are better than mine?'

'I am just telling you the truth, Your Grace. I trust my man to bring me accurate news and wish to pass this on to you.' Conway nervously cleared his throat.

'Who is your informant?' the king demanded of him.

'I cannot say, Your Grace. I always promise my informants total anonymity. Without it they would not work for me. Then I would have no information for Sir Reginald to pass on to Your Grace.' Conway's nervousness was apparent as a bead of sweat trickled off his forehead and into his eye.

'I asked who your informant is,' the king demanded again.

'Please Your Grace, I can't.' Conway blinked as the sweat stung his eye.

Henry broiled with anger. 'Would you tell me if I were to have you drawn apart by wild horses?'

'Your Grace. Please! I fought for you against the usurper Richard Plantagenet. I am a loyal servant. I only wish to bring you news and loyally serve you as I have always done,' Conway pleaded.

'He speaks the truth, Your Grace,' Bishop Foxe interjected, placing a calming hand on the king's shoulder.

'Bah!' Henry exclaimed, waving Conway away. 'The man is just a self-seeking rascal trying to earn my royal favour with his lies.'

Conway bowed and scurried backwards out of the chamber, never once raising his head to look in the king's direction. Bray wavered, not sure whether to follow Conway out of the door or remain in the king's presence. His indecision did not last long.

'Bishop Foxe, please leave us. I have matters of importance to discuss with Sir Reginald.'

Bishop Foxe bowed and left the room. The Yeoman of the Guard closed the door behind him leaving only King Henry and Sir Reginald Bray in the chamber.

'Have you any news on the boy that escaped from London? Lovell's son,' the king enquired.

'Not yet, Your Grace. I know that the man who died holding off the soldiers who tried to arrest the boy, was a lowlife of the city who plied his trade fighting for prize money and guarding some of the shops in Goldsmith's Row. I have had his family, and the shopkeepers and their guards interrogated but nobody will admit to knowing anything about the boy or the old man who was with him. I have posted spies but I doubt the boy will return there. I have also interrogated the boat master and his crew who ferried them away but they all say they were offered a bag of silver to transport the boy and old man downriver but hadn't seen either of them before that.'

'Then maybe you should use less subtle ways of interrogating these people that will yield the answers we need,' the king suggested to Bray.

'Yes, Your Grace,' Bray conceded, being left in no doubt what the king expected but not liking the idea of torturing innocent people.

'I am going to appoint Sir Richard Edgcombe and Sir William Tyler to apprehend Francis Lovell and bring him to me,' the king explained. 'I will draft the necessary letters of authority. You will take the letters and advise them that I want Lovell captured as a matter of utmost urgency. They are to gather men and block all ports and means of escape, and they must hunt him down to whichever stone he may be hiding beneath. Is that understood?'

'Yes, Your Grace,' Bray responded.

'At the end of this holy week I will leave Lincoln and ride to York, and you are to meet me there. I have further use for you and your spies. I do not care how you come by your information and I will ask no more questions of your informants, so long as their information proves accurate. I shall weave a sticky web and you, Sir Reginald, shall be the spider in the centre of my web.' The king grinned mischievously before adding, 'I have many flies to catch.'

16

'Are you going to join Lord Lovell's army?' asked the man with the strange hollow-shaped dent in his forehead, as he lugged a large sack of grain through the doorway of the watermill.

Seconds later he reappeared through the doorway and looked expectantly at Richard and Herricke for an answer.

'No, we are just travelling to the market at York looking to buy wool,' Herricke told him.

'I'd steer clear of York if I were you,' the miller advised them. He scratched the odd-shaped hollow in his head with his large weathered hands. 'King Henry is in York and Lord Lovell is gathering an army in the surrounding areas. Robin of Redesdale has joined Lord Lovell too. Together they've roused the whole of the north against King Henry and they intend to put good King Richard's nephew, the boy Warwick, on the throne. Good luck to them I say but one way or t'other York will be a bloodbath. Unless you plan to join them, I'd steer well clear of that place, my friends.'

Richard and Herricke had heard many such stories over the past few days. No one could say for certain where Lord Lovell was but it was clear that many people in the north were leaving their towns and villages to go and join him in a pro-Yorkist rebellion against King Henry.

'Aren't you going to join Lord Lovell's army?' Richard asked the miller, who seemed content to just stand in the doorway of the watermill and stare at the two riders who had turned up asking to buy food.

'My fighting days are over,' he laughed heartily to himself as he pointed to the large indentation in his forehead. 'I got this fighting at Towton for King Edward when I was a lad. My helmet was battered into my skull with a mace. I was unconscious for days. I'm blind in my left eye you know, never been right since. I still get headaches from it,' he added matter-of-factly.

'I fought like a wild beast that day. Charging with the snow blizzard at my back, into the enemies' ranks, chopping and hacking with all my might. I must have killed ten men that day before they caved my head in.' He stared through Richard into the distant past as he spoke, reliving the events in his head of that wintery Palm Sunday at Towton.

'Lancastrian bastards!' he suddenly spat out with rancour, startling Richard. Then he smiled and the mild mannered, softly spoken miller returned to the present once more.

'Where did you say you were going?' he asked.

'To York to buy wool,' Herricke told him again.

'Oh, I wouldn't go there, it's going to be a bloodbath!' the miller repeated. 'Robin of Redesdale has stirred up the north. He's joined Lord Lovell and they're—'

'Thank you for the food,' Herricke said, ignoring the miller's ramblings. 'We must be on our way.'

Richard took heed of Herricke's cue and mounted his horse.

'Thank you,' he said to the miller, as he and Herricke spurred on their horses and rode away from the watermill, leaving the man still muttering to himself in the doorway.

'Who is Robin of Redesdale?' Richard asked as they trotted along the overgrown track that followed the path of the river. 'I've heard his name mentioned by folk several times now.'

'A ghost from the past. He may be real. He may be myth. Some say he died at the Battle of Edgecote. Some say he still lives,' Herricke replied enigmatically.

He looked across to see Richard's questioning expression and realised that he needed to elaborate on his answer.

'About sixteen or seventeen years ago Robin of Redesdale started a rebellion in the north against King Edward because the king elevated his own wife's family, the Woodvilles, to positions of power. The Woodvilles were commoners but King Edward arranged beneficial marriages for them and gifted them earldoms and other titles, which only served to infuriate the old nobility. Probably most galling was the marriage of the nineteen-year-old John Woodville to the sixty-five-year-old Dowager Duchess of Norfolk, which was a blatant and vulgar grab for money and land. It scandalised the country and turned many against the Woodville family and King Edward.

'Robin of Redesdale rallied support in the north and, at Edgecote, defeated King Edward's army. The Earl of Warwick opposed the Woodvilles, and with the king's army defeated, was able to take the king captive at Nottingham. Some folk say Robin of Redesdale died fighting at Edgecote yet he came out in support of Warwick and the Duke of Clarence again the following year.

'Although King Edward ultimately defeated Warwick and brought his brother Clarence to heel, once again Robin of Redesdale is rallying the people of the north and joining Lord Lovell in open rebellion against a reigning king? He was successful before, so the people of Yorkshire will know that and come out to support him. Alive or not, Lord Lovell has hatched a cunning plan in evoking the name of Robin of Redesdale and linking it to his cause to crown the Earl of Warwick king.'

'How do you know Lord Lovell has deliberately done that?'

'Because he'd be a fool not to,' Herricke smiled. 'I bet King Henry is quaking in his boots.'

'Are we still going to York?' Richard asked with a worried look on his face.

'We can't, Richard, King Henry and his men are there. We're fugitives so need to keep off the beaten track. We will stick to the river and keep heading north. Eventually somebody will know where Lord Lovell is. He can't remain hidden for long with an army gathered around him, can he?'

'Is there really going to be a battle?'

'It seems inevitable,' Herricke replied. 'You can avoid it though. It is not too late to return south to the village where you grew up.'

Richard vetoed the idea immediately. 'Now that we know Lord Lovell hasn't fled abroad, I need to find him. Whatever my future holds I'm certain it lies with him.'

'Very well,' Herricke conceded, 'I will do my best but I can't help you look for him forever as I have business to attend to elsewhere. It will not be easy relocating my goldsmith's business away from London, especially under the noses of the king's spies.'

Richard noticed how Herricke had aged in the months since they escaped London. He looked ancient when they first met but now the goldsmith looked thin and drawn. The wrinkles under his eyes had turned purple and his once leathery brown skin had turned sallow and thin so that all the veins could be seen through it. The few tufts of white hair that had clung to his head were gone so that he was now completely bald.

'Do not feel obliged to do anything more for me. I cannot thank you enough for what you have already done, Master Herricke. I owe you everything.'

'I will try to see my task through to the end if you please, young Richard. Your father gave me more than enough recompense in his lifetime. It is the very least I can do in his memory. I have served the House of York throughout my life and been well rewarded for it, so the least I can do is try to return one of its sons home.'

'I don't feel like a son of York.'

'God in high heaven! You are the son of King Richard III, Nephew of King Edward IV, and cousin to both Edward V and the Earl of Warwick who may soon be king. You have Royal blood coursing through every vein in your body and were it not for the circumstances of your birth you too may have one day been king.'

'That is a burden I am relieved not to have to carry,' Richard admitted.

'Nevertheless, you are a royal son of the House of York, if not a royal prince. If Lord Lovell and your cousin can win the forthcoming battle then you will be acknowledged and rewarded as a royal cousin to the king.'

'And if that is the case Master Herricke, then I will reward you in turn for your services to the House of York.'

Richard and Herricke both laughed at that as they continued to ride on. They followed the meandering river through the Yorkshire countryside until a few miles to the north of the watermill they dismounted, tied their horses to a grey willow tree that arched its branches out over the water, and they sat in the sun eating the bread, cheese and hard-boiled eggs that the miller had sold them.

Two swans drifted lazily past them on the river and a blue damselfly danced from reed to reed exploring the water's edge. Richard wondered how God could create such a beautiful and tranquil land and then allow it to be marred by the ravages of war. His gaze wandered past the swans and down the river, as his mind flirted with the hope that King Henry would relinquish the crown and flee abroad rather than face the combined army of Lord Lovell and Robin of Redesdale. It may be a vain hope but Richard prayed that whatever the outcome in the days ahead, Francis Lovell would live and that he would see him again.

'Good morning,' a man in a leather jerkin hailed them as he emerged through the tall reeds shading the path besides the river, in the opposite direction to which Richard had been staring.

Two companions emerged along the path behind him and it was soon apparent to Richard and Herricke that the men were well-armed warriors despite their lack of armour, mail or helmets.

'I don't know if they're Lovell or the king's men so don't say anything careless,' Herricke warned Richard in a whisper, as he stood to face the approaching men.

Richard stood beside him, a half peeled hard-boiled egg still in his hand.

'A lovely morning it is too,' Herricke called back in reply to the first man.

'Where are you headed?' the man asked as he and his two companions stopped in front of Herricke and Richard, resting their hands on their sword hilts.

'To York market to buy wool,' Herricke told him.

The warrior laughed and his two companions smiled and shook their heads in mock disbelief.

'You can go to York if you like but it is about to become a

battleground. A great army in support of the Earl of Warwick is about to descend on the city. Henry Tudor is there with the entourage of his great northern progress. There's maybe a thousand lightly armed men to defend him against a well-armed army of ten or fifteen thousand men under the command of Lord Lovell. I know which side I'm joining!' He laughed again.

Herricke feigned shock at the news. 'Do they need more men?'

The warrior grinned. 'I don't think they'll have much use for you, old man, but the boy and your horses would be a handy addition. I'm sure they'll pay you a bob or two for them.'

'Where is Lord Lovell's army?'

'They're at Middleham Castle but they will be marching to Ripon any time now to join up with Robin of Redesdale before the assault on York. We're heading to Ripon so you're welcome to join us. We wouldn't mind a share of your food though, if you can spare some?'

Herricke opened the cloth bag and let the warriors delve inside for some bread, cheese and eggs.

'My name is William,' Herricke introduced himself to the three men, 'and this is my grandson, Richard.'

'John Skelton, but everyone calls me Jack,' the man in the leather jerkin said, 'and these are my brothers James and Robbie.'

The five men shook hands then munched on the shared food, as they set off on their journey to meet up with Lord Lovell's army.

*

The narrow lanes, yards and cobbled streets of York buzzed with frantic movement. Stalls and tents erected for the fair to celebrate King Henry's triumphal procession into the city were being hastily dismantled. Goods were taken indoors, bags packed, chests and coffers emptied, and house and shop shutters quickly battened down, before folk fled the city. The previous day, at Micklegate Bar, King Henry, accompanied by the mayor and aldermen in scarlet gowns, and the town clerk, councillors, chamberlains and citizens in equally colourful garb, had entered the city to the joyous cries of children shouting the king's praise. Now, through the same gate, there was a steady stream of sombre, ashen-faced refugees leaving the city with whatever possessions they could take with them.

There was a haste bordering on panic as people ran through the streets calling out the news to anyone who had not yet heard that Lord Lovell and Robin of Redesdale were marching on the city with an army. Some folk said the rebel army was ten thousand strong, some said twenty thousand, some said more. The figure grew with each telling of the story but what was certain was that the rebel army would soon arrive at the gates of York. If the mayor and aldermen refused to hand the king over to them, the rebel army would besiege York and if they broke through the city gates, there would be carnage and slaughter on an unprecedented scale. All of those trapped inside would be at the mercy of the marauding soldiers; shops and houses pillaged, men killed, and their wives and daughters raped. The news spread through the city streets like fire through thatch. It was no surprise that York was emptying faster than an inn that had run out of ale.

King Henry heard the news from Sir Reginald Bray and it filled him with absolute terror. He felt queasy and his hand trembled as he reached for a goblet of Malmsey wine to steady his nerves before he addressed the hastily assembled council. Henry would not allow the men of his council to think of him as fearful or weak so he took a deep breath, closed his eyes, and steadied himself before exhaling and walking into the adjoining chamber to face them. Everyone bowed as the king entered, looking resplendent in a gown of cloth of gold, trimmed with ermine. He sat on the purple velvet-covered chair that had been specially prepared for his visit to York. Everyone else stood.

Henry scanned the faces of the men gathered before him in the Archbishop's Palace: Thomas Rotherham the Archbishop of York, Bishops Morton and Foxe, the earls of Northumberland, Lincoln, Westmorland, Wiltshire and Rivers, and Sir Reginald Bray.

'Gentlemen, it seems that we are faced with a predicament.'

Henry coughed to clear his throat and to steady the discernible tremble in his voice before continuing.

'A rebel army is gathered near Ripon and is marching towards York.'

None of the assembled party showed surprise at the news as it had reached their ears long before the king summoned them. Every member of the council now stared at King Henry with anticipation and trepidation, eager to find out what he planned to do.

'Francis Lovell and someone under the guise of Robin of Redesdale claim to lead the rebels.' Henry knew full well the significance of the name Robin of Redesdale but chose to play it down.

'These rebels aim to overthrow me and put the boy Warwick on the throne. As far as I see it, there are three choices: we assemble our troops and ride out to face the rebels; we send for reinforcements to my lords Bedford and Oxford, fortify the city walls and hold out here until they arrive; or we flee to London and raise an army there. So what, my lords, should I do?'

Henry rubbed his temple with a trembling hand, failing to keep his nervousness in check. The Earl of Northumberland shook his head in disbelief. He had served under the previous King's Richard and Edward; strong decisive leaders who would have roused men to follow them, not tremble and ask advice about whether to flee.

'What is the strength of Lord Lovell's force?' Northumberland asked.

'You will not call that man lord!' the king shouted in a fit of pique. 'He was attainted by parliament as the traitor he again shows himself to be. He is not a lord!'

'Forgive me, Your Grace.' Northumberland's face reddened beneath his fringe of dark hair as he dipped his head in acquiescence.

'How many men do the rebels have, Your Grace?' Earl Rivers rephrased the question.

The king, still agitated and puce faced, looked enquiringly at Sir Reginald Bray.

'Anywhere between four and eight thousand,' Bray informed him.

'Can't you be more specific than that, Sir Reginald?' the king, regaining his composure, asked.

'I'm sorry, Your Grace, but the rebels are amassing at various rendezvous points and their numbers are growing as men join them from all over Yorkshire, so it is difficult to put a final tally on their numbers,' Bray explained.

King Henry let out a deep sigh as he considered who could lead his forces if he chose to oppose the rebels. He dare not risk his own life riding out to face a rebel army with so few men behind him. The three churchmen could not fight, let alone lead an army, Earl Rivers had no military experience and the Earl of

Wiltshire had barely turned sixteen. Northumberland and Lincoln were experienced soldiers who had commanded men on the field of battle before, but both had also been supporters of King Richard and had been in the army opposing Henry when he won the crown. Although they had come to heel, Henry did not trust either of them enough to give them command of his troops. They were just as likely to ride out and join the rebels, as they were to fight against them.

Ralph Neville, Earl of Westmorland, was also of dubious loyalty having served King Richard in putting down the rebellion of 1483 that had been Henry's first abortive attempt to take the English crown. In return for his services, Richard rewarded Westmorland with land that had formerly belonged to Henry's mother. Henry forced Westmorland to enter into a bond of £400 and 400 marks as a surety for his loyalty. As part of the arrangement, Westmorland also gave custody and the approval of the marriage of his eldest son and heir to the king, but even so, it was a different matter for Henry to trust him with troops to lead out against the Yorkist rebels. No! Of all the men present Sir Reginald Bray was the only one he trusted to lead his men, but he could not give such an important role to a commoner only recently raised to the rank of knight, when there were five earls present. Henry closed his eyes and pinched the bridge of his nose as he tried to think.

He lamented that his best generals were absent when he needed them most. If only he had not dispatched his Uncle Jasper to Wales to put down an insurrection there, then he would be here to lead troops against the rebels; and the Earl of Oxford, his greatest commander, was at home on his estates in Essex unaware of the threat to the king. Of course, Henry had sent for them the moment he had heard of the rising against him, but it could be days or weeks before they arrived and that would be too late. He needed to make a decision now. Yet still he wavered, unable to decide upon the best course of action.

'Your Grace, may I make a suggestion?' Bray asked.

'Yes, please do, Sir Reginald,' the king replied, rubbing his left temple to try to ease the dull ache that had appeared there.

'We need to spread fear and dissent among the enemy ranks,' Bray explained. 'We have barely a thousand men, and few swords or armour, but the enemy don't know that. If you send heralds out into the villages and towns of Yorkshire declaring that all the great lords and their retinues are descending upon York in support of their king and that Your Grace will give all rebels who lay down their arms a full pardon, then we may break their nerve. With some luck and God's will we may weaken their ranks enough that we can face them in battle on more even terms.'

'But I will not pardon the traitorous leaders of this rebellion,' Henry added stubbornly. 'The bastards will hang for this.'

'Rightly so,' a gruff Welsh voice said at the back of the room.

Everyone present turned to look at the doorway to find the Duke of Bedford standing there, clad in a scarlet doublet and hose, a stern face amid a head of white hair and a beard of white stubble that stood out starkly against his sun-browned skin.

'Uncle! You're here at last,' the king shrieked in delight.

A smile broke out on Jasper's weathered face as he strode through the doorway and across the chamber towards the king. Henry met him half way and the two men embraced.

'I assume all is well in Wales, my lord Bedford?' the king asked.

Jasper laughed. 'There was no uprising, or if there was it had petered out by the time I got there. I have left reliable men and a garrison at Pembroke just in case anything does happen though. I was on my way back to join the royal progress when I heard that there is a rising in the north so I rode to get here as fast as I could.'

'Thank God you did,' Henry blurted out. 'Francis Lovell and some other Yorkist upstart calling himself Robin of Redesdale have amassed an army and they are marching towards us.'

'How many men do we have?' Jasper asked calmly.

'Less than a thousand all told, and they are not armoured.'

'Yeoman of the Guard?' Jasper enquired.

'Sixty-six,' Bray answered.

'So at least we have good Welsh bowmen in our ranks,' Jasper grinned. 'We can buy or commandeer padded jacks and leather jerkins from the locals, and weapons too. Despite the numbers fleeing York, there are men coming into the city who have heard that you are in danger and wish to offer their support. It may be a small and rag-tag army but I believe we will nevertheless have an army to ride out with, to face whatever force Lovell has.'

The king turned back to face the members of his council.

'I shall send out heralds to declare that we have a great host made up of all the magnates and knights of the land, led by the Duke of Bedford, who are heavily armed and ready to ride out to quash this traitorous rebellion. However, in my clemency I will offer a pardon to any rebel, apart from the leaders, who willingly lays down his arms and returns home,' Henry declared with great gusto as though the idea had just come to him.

Jasper winked knowingly at Bray. 'We'd better get moving then or Lovell's army will be upon us before we know it.'

'We do have another advantage, Your Grace,' Bray added.

'Pray tell us then, Sir Reginald,' Henry beseeched him.

'It is impossible for the Yorkist rebels to have their so-called king crowned as you still have the Earl of Warwick in custody in the Tower of London. Perhaps your heralds could proclaim that as well?'

King Henry laughed out loudly. 'My heralds will do their work, Sir Reginald.' Henry looked extremely pleased with himself.

'My lord Bedford,' Henry addressed his Uncle Jasper, 'gather your forces and muster whatever horses, weapons, and padded jacks that you need and ride out and scatter this gathering of Yorkist rebels to the four winds.'

Jasper bowed his head respectfully towards the king then strode purposefully towards the door. He was about to depart when Sir Robert Willoughby almost collided with him in the doorway. Willoughby acknowledged the duke then walked past him and knelt before the king. He spoke with great anxiety in his voice as the king bid him rise.

'Your Grace, I bring grave news. Sir Humphrey Stafford and his brother Thomas have captured the city of Worcester. The rebellion has already spread throughout Worcestershire, Herefordshire and Warwickshire. Worcester capitulated without a fight.'

'What in God's name is happening?' was all the response King Henry could muster.

His heart sank and the forbidding sense of doom and terror that had taken hold of him when he first heard of the rebellion in York now returned. He now had the threat of two rebellions and two rebel Yorkist armies to face. He looked at Jasper standing in the doorway, and then back to Sir Reginald Bray for answers, but neither of them said a word. Henry pondered how the crown he had coveted for so long could so easily be snatched away now that it was finally his. He closed his eyes and rubbed both his temples with trembling hands, as the dull ache very quickly intensified into a rhythmic throbbing that pounded behind his eyes.

'Let's face one problem at a time, Your Grace,' Jasper finally offered in advice. 'We will deal with the rebels in Yorkshire first and then take stock of the situation and decide what to do next.'

'Fear not, Your Grace,' Bishop Morton consoled the king, 'you are king by the grace of Almighty God and He will not desert you in your time of need. Let us pray for salvation in this desperate hour.'

Jasper sneaked out of the doorway unnoticed, to go to prepare his men for battle as the three churchmen crossed themselves and everyone else, including the king, bowed their heads and clasped their hands together in prayer.

Just after first light the following morning, Jasper Tudor led a thousand men through the gates of York. Most were clad in leather jerkins and poorly armed with sickles, old billhooks and rusted swords. Jasper knew that despite the fifty mounted men and sixty-six Welsh longbowmen in his ranks, he had fewer than four hundred trained soldiers overall. For all his bravado to the king, Jasper knew that it was unlikely that this ramshackle force could contend with the army that Francis Lovell was amassing. At best, all he could hope for was to hold them at bay and provide valuable time for the Earl of Oxford and other nobles to arrive with reinforcements to support the king against the rebel army. He looked up at the pale blue sky and sighed to himself as he realised that this could be his final day on this earth. Nevertheless, the matter was now in God's hands. He would do his duty and ride out to confront the rebels somewhere on the road between York and Ripon.

17

 dozen plumes of ash-grey smoke drifted lazily above the treeline until caught by the breeze and dispersed into the distance so that they were no longer distinguishable from the grey-white clouds.

'It could be the campfires of Lord Lovell's army,' Jack Skelton said hopefully.

Richard and Herricke had found Jack and his brothers affable company over the previous day as they bypassed York and followed the River Ure to a crossing at Boroughbridge. They had slept in a barn on the banks of the river and now, a few hours after sunrise, Ripon lay ahead just beyond the treeline.

'I hope you're right,' Robbie said.

'I need to rest, my arse is killing me,' Herricke informed them.

'Not again,' Jack complained. 'You'd have us rest every ten minutes if it was up to you.'

'It is up to me,' Herricke told him. 'I'm the only one with some food left.'

Richard, James and Robbie all chuckled as Herricke waved the bag of food at Jack.

'Alright old man, you've made your point,' Jack retorted, taking a piece of bread from Herricke's proffered hand and smiling. 'We're almost there anyway. Ripon is no more than half a mile ahead.'

'Sorry lads, I can't take any more of this saddle. My arse is red-raw, my bones are old, and my back and legs aren't as strong as they used to be.'

'It's no bother,' Richard said. 'Why don't you dismount and we'll walk the rest of the way? The horses need to rest anyway.'

Richard and Herricke dismounted and the five men sauntered along the path leading the horses behind them.

'I'm certain we've found Lord Lovell's army,' Robbie said as they rounded the trees and the town came into sight in the distance, 'I can smell the campfires.'

'Why don't you three go ahead and find some food for us in the town and we'll catch you up shortly?' Herricke said to the three brothers.

'If you insist, old man, but I can't guarantee we won't have eaten it all by the time you get there,' Jack chuckled.

The three brothers walked off at a brisk pace leaving Herricke and Richard to follow slowly behind with the two horses.

'I'm sorry,' Herricke apologised again.

'It really isn't a problem,' Richard replied. 'It's a lovely day, we're in no hurry and we'll be there soon enough, so just take your time.'

As they ambled slowly towards Ripon, Richard's thoughts turned to meeting Francis Lovell again. Would he be there having joined up with Robin of Redesdale's forces or would he still be at Middleham with his own army? Richard hoped for the former. It was strange, but following the death of his father and Will Catesby, he felt alone in the world except for the companionship of William Herricke, who was actually old enough to be his grandfather, and Francis Lovell, a lord well above his own station in life, and a man who he had spent barely a week with. And yet he felt drawn to Francis Lovell and saw him as a friend, despite being almost twenty years younger than him. Richard wondered if Francis felt the same or just saw him as a boy who happened to be the son of his deceased friend. Richard felt his cheeks flush at the thought.

'Ooh my bloody arse,' Herricke grumbled.

Richard could not help but laugh.

'It's not funny. I'm in bloody agony,' Herricke remonstrated with him.

'Then sit down and rest a while.'

Herricke did not need a second invitation. He handed his horse's reins to Richard and sat down at the side of the path beneath the shade of a rowan tree.

*

Captain Tollington scratched at his bristly chin as he stood outside the Unicorn Inn and watched three men enter Ripon's market square.

'They are all armed, my lord,' he said to the man standing beside him. 'Shall we disarm them and send them on their way?'

'The king's heralds have warned people of the consequences of taking up arms against the king so they have had plenty of time to heed these warnings,' Jasper Tudor replied to the captain. 'I think it is time to make an example of them so that any more would-be rebels think twice before picking up a sword.'

'Yes, my lord,' the captain agreed as he signalled the sergeant-at-arms with a discreet nod towards the Skelton brothers.

Within moments, eight soldiers surrounded the brothers, pointing swords and billhooks at them.

'Lay down your weapons,' the sergeant-at-arms demanded.

James and Robbie looked to Jack Skelton for guidance on what to do next.

'What's this all about? We ain't done nothing, sir. We're just ordinary folk going about our business, that's all,' said Jack, holding out his open palms to show that he meant no harm.

'Lay down your weapons!' the sergeant-at-arms bellowed at them as the surrounding soldiers threateningly took another step closer.

'Lay down your swords, lads,' Jack told his brothers as he unbuckled his belt and crouched to lay his sword and dagger onto the cobbles of the marketplace.

His brothers did likewise and as soon as their weapons were on the ground, the soldiers pounced upon the three men and hauled them unceremoniously in front of the captain and the Duke of Bedford at the opposite end of the marketplace, where they were forced to their knees.

Jasper Tudor cast his eyes over the three men kneeling before him.

'Hang them,' he said calmly and without emotion.

All three brothers let out an exclamation of shock that matched the look of horror on their faces. They rose from their kneeling positions and vociferously protested their innocence but Jasper Tudor was already walking away, ignoring their pleas. While his brothers continued to shout after the haughty nobleman who was so easily ready to toss their lives away, Jack Skelton felt righteous anger swell up inside of him. He yelled in abject fury as he launched himself at one of the soldiers holding him and headbutted the man full in the face so that he collapsed, knocked clean out with a broken and bloody nose splattered across his face. Jack momentarily broke free of the other man's grasp but two more soldiers quickly jumped on him and hauled him to the ground, trying to pin him down as he lay on his back kicking and thrashing, resisting them with his utmost might. With the casual ease of a trained man, Captain Tollington brought the butt end of a staff brutally down into Jack's solar plexus, instantly knocking the wind out of him and allowing the men grappling him on the ground to get a better hold. A blade held to each brother's throat swiftly ended any lingering resistance.

'Take them to the trees on Kirkgate and hang them there,' Tollington ordered.

The order was still resonating in Jack Skelton's ears as the soldiers dragged him, still gasping for the air to return to his lungs, through the marketplace and between the shops and houses that lined Kirkgate with a knife held to his throat. The soldiers dragged the three brothers into the oak-lined avenue that formed the end of Kirkgate and led into the open area facing the cathedral. Jack watched helplessly as three nooses were quickly prepared from rope and placed over his own and his brothers' heads and tightened around their necks. Then the soldiers cast the ropes over the thick branches of several sturdy oak trees that lined the route from the marketplace to the cathedral. The three brothers were swiftly hoisted into the air by their throats and left to dangle so that their own body weight forced the noose to close tighter around their throat and slowly choked them to death.

His legs kicked out, his Adam's apple was slowly crushed, his eyes bulged out of their sockets, his tongue turned purple, swelling to fill his mouth, and the final gurgled breaths were strangled out of him, but perversely a final thought niggled at the back of Jack's mind; where did the soldiers find rope so quickly?

*

The twin towers of Ripon cathedral loomed high on the skyline as Richard and Herricke led their horses into the marketplace. The grey plumes of smoke they had noticed earlier still drifted lazily to merge with the clouds behind the cathedral.

'I thought the campfires were nearer,' Richard commented.

'The army are probably camped in the fields on the northern side of the town,' Herricke replied.

As he spoke, he noticed several people turn and glare in his direction. Herricke watched them for a moment trying to work out why they had reacted in such a way. He had a sudden realisation that there was not the usual hustle and bustle he would expect of a market town. The atmosphere was very subdued. The townsfolk quickly went about their business and a few milled about the stalls set out in the marketplace, but hardly anyone spoke with a raised voice and many kept their eyes on the floor as they walked. The obvious exception was a white bearded man of status, dressed in a fine red doublet and hose with gold rings adorning his fingers, who stood at the far end of the marketplace observing everyone who walked by. Next to him stood a grizzled old soldier who repeatedly scratched at the stubble on his chin, creating a sore patch beneath his bristles. The pair eyed Herricke and Richard suspiciously as they made their way through the marketplace with their horses.

'Something's not right,' Herricke whispered. 'Just keep your head down, keep walking, and don't speak.'

Richard could not help but look around, trying to work out what had spooked Herricke.

'Do as the man says,' a leper wrapped in rags said to Richard in a hushed voice as he emerged from an alleyway adjoining the marketplace to walk alongside him.

'Alms for a poor leper, sir,' he croaked in a loud voice as he stretched out a palm towards Herricke.

Herricke dug into his purse and placed a ha'penny into the man's hand.

'Follow me. Your life depends on it,' the leper whispered to him.

Herricke and Richard looked at each other, bemused, as the leper walked on ahead of them, but they were heading in the same direction anyway, so they followed him across the marketplace.

'Alms for a poor leper, sir,' he said again as he drew level with Jasper Tudor and Captain Tollington.

'Piss off!' Tollington hissed as he shooed the leper away from the duke.

Herricke and Richard both dipped their heads as they passed the scarlet-clad duke. Jasper Tudor just smiled to himself and stared past them into the marketplace, satisfied with his morning's work. The pair led their horses past the Unicorn Inn and into Kirkgate with its rows of half-timbered houses and shops with overhanging jetties that prevented the light from reaching the street below. A hundred yards on, the leper paused to wait for them. The man, wrapped in strips of rag so that the skin of his hands and face were barely showing, waved them on, urging them to hurry.

'Do not shout out, do not cry, and do not make any sound,' he warned them as they caught up. 'Just keep your head down and walk on until we are clear of the soldiers. It is a harsh truth and I'm sorry to tell you this but your colleagues are dead. You cannot change that so please follow me and it will save your lives. I will explain further when we are free and clear of this place,' he spoke quickly, conveying a sense of urgency.

'What do you mean our colleagues are dead?' Richard asked as the gravity of what the leper said sank in.

'Hung as rebels and traitors as soon as they entered the marketplace. Do not join them! Just do as I say and keep your head down and follow me.'

With that the leper turned and walked off along Kirkgate.

'Just do as he says. We'll get to the bottom of this shortly,' Herricke advised Richard as he set off in pursuit of the leper.

Kirkgate opened out from a dark, narrow lane into a wider, tree-lined avenue that led to the open space in front of the cathedral. Richard could see a group of soldiers standing chatting between two oak trees. Above them, three bodies hung limp and lifeless from ropes cast over the oak's thick branches. The leper paused at the group of soldiers and extended a bandaged hand.

'Alms for a poor leper, sir,' he begged, moving from soldier to soldier until one finally dropped a coin into his palm.

Herricke led his horse past the group without looking at the soldiers or letting his eyes rest upon any of the bodies swaying from the oak trees. Richard, however, stared intently at each swollen, bloated, purple face of his former comrades as he passed them by. Anger stirred within him, growing in intensity like wildfire as it nourished an all-consuming hatred of the soldiers in front of him and of the Tudor regime itself, for all the deaths it had caused to those close to him. Richard swore to himself that he would seek vengeance for the death of his father, William Catesby, the Skelton brothers, and all those who had died in the Yorkist cause. He placed a hand on his chest, touching the Hopper ring beneath his shirt, and swore that he would make it his life's aim.

'What you staring at, boy? Ain't you seen a dead traitor before?' a soldier taunted him.

The other soldiers all laughed and Richard swelled with animosity, wanting desperately to hurt each one of them. He clenched his teeth and his fists and felt the anger start to erupt inside him at the sound of their taunting laughter. Herricke halted and astutely turned his horse to place himself between Richard and the soldiers.

'Come on, son,' he said with a knowing look at Richard and placing a comforting hand on his shoulder. 'We have important business elsewhere.'

He coaxed Richard into moving on with a pat on the back. Richard turned and led his horse away but the anger inside him burned fiercely even as the soldiers' laughter died away. Herricke led Richard past the cathedral and on towards the open land on the northern side of the town.

'You have a lot to learn, lad,' the leper said as he caught up with them. 'If it wasn't for your friend here, you'd be strung up next to the other three by now.'

'Who the hell are you?' Richard bawled at the leper.

The leper unwrapped his bandages to reveal the face of a young man in his twenties, unblemished by disease. He continued to unravel the bandages from his hands as he spoke.

'I am Thomas Conyers and I have been entrusted with finding you and Master Herricke and delivering you safely to my master, Lord Lovell.'

'Where is he?' Richard cried eagerly, his anger dissipating instantly upon hearing Lovell's name.

Herricke stared out across the fields to where campfires still smouldered.

'And where is his army?'

'They were here, and coming in from all the towns, villages and districts around, but Henry Tudor's heralds brought news of a great army marching out from York under the command of the Duke of Bedford, and the heralds promised pardons to all those who laid down their arms. The majority just melted away. Those that remained turned tail and fled when they heard that Bedford's army was almost upon them. As it turned out this great army was less than a thousand strong,' he sighed deeply. 'But it is too late now, the damage is done, and my lord's army has dispersed. He has returned to Middleham Castle but he will be moving on from there very shortly. If he dallies too long, he will no doubt be surrounded and besieged so he must flee to safety soon where he can rally his forces to fight another day.'

'How did you know where we were?' Herricke asked.

Conyers laughed. 'Lord Lovell has his spies, just as the king and every other noble have theirs. He lost track of you for a long time but then received word that you had bought food at an inn in Boroughbridge. He sent me out to find you but then Henry Tudor's heralds came and—'

'Why was he looking for us?' Richard interrupted.

'I am not privy to that information, young man.' Conyers smiled, not put off by Richard's brusqueness. 'All I know is that I must deliver you both safely to him.'

'Where?' Herricke asked.

'A secret location I cannot divulge. You must trust me, Master Herricke.'

Herricke shook his head in exasperation. 'I'm too bloody old for this. I need to go home.'

18

York now bore a semblance of normality. The refugees that had fled the city in droves two days ago had, on the whole, returned to pick up their lives where they had left off. Raucous noise from taverns spilled out onto the streets as the fiery red glow of the dying sun lit the underside of dark clouds and illuminated them against a backdrop of deep purple sky tinged with violet and pink. Only the increased number of guards that ringed the city walls and patrolled its streets gave any indication of the fear and panic that had prevailed just days before.

A lone traveller walked quickly through the barbican and Micklegate Bar as the city gates were closed and locked behind him for the evening.

'Thank you, my friend. I wasn't sure I'd make it on time,' he beamed cheerily at the rotund gatekeeper.

The traveller was about to walk off into the city when the gatekeeper called after him.

'Wait there. You have to be searched first. It's on King 'Enry's orders I'm afraid,' the gatekeeper added apologetically.

The traveller paused and held his arms aloft as a guard stepped out from the shadows and patted down his clothing.

'What's in the bag?' the guard enquired.

'Wine. For my master,' the traveller said, holding open his bag for the guard to peer inside.

The guard parted the straw that was stuffed into the bag to reveal two bulbous, translucent green glass bottles with thin necks bunged and capped with lead seals. He pulled out a bottle to hold it up to a flaming torch so that he could see the rich deep red coloured liquid inside. He whistled into the evening air.

'That must have cost a pretty penny. I ain't never seen wine in a glass bottle before. I didn't even know they made bottles like this for wine.'

'Careful with it please,' the traveller said nervously. 'It has managed to arrive here safely from Romagna so it would be a shame to break it on my master's doorstep.'

'Aye that it would, that it would,' the guard agreed while he and the gatekeeper gazed longingly at the bottle's expensive contents.

'I've never even heard of Romagna,' the gatekeeper said.

The guard just shrugged.

'So, who is your master that can afford to have wine brought to him from abroad in glass bottles rather than in a wooden barrel like normal people?' the guard asked.

The traveller gingerly took the bottle back from the guard's grasp and placed it carefully back into his bag, re-covering it with straw.

'They are a gift for the king from the Duke of Ferrara and Modena.'

'Ah, that would explain it,' the gatekeeper said as the guard nodded in agreement.

'What I'd give for one sip of that fine wine.' The yearning was evident in the guard's voice.

'A taste too rich for any of our kind I'm afraid. I bid you goodnight, gentlemen,' the traveller said as he smiled, turned and departed into the cobbled streets of York, with the guard and the gatekeeper staring longingly after him.

That was too close for comfort, the traveller thought to himself as the surge of adrenaline at being searched began to subside. He felt his hands trembling. He took a deep breath and forged on past Holy Trinity Priory, over the Ouse and Foss bridges and the shops and houses that lined them, until he reached his destination on Walmgate. He paused and looked up at the imposing two-storey, wide-timbered house with leaded glass windows, and gabled roof with roof tiles that shone red-brown in the moonlight. It was nestled in among similar houses, each displaying the wealth and status of their owners by their size and the materials used to build them. He knew that the Earl of Northumberland owned a house a little further down Walmgate and would probably be staying there this very night, but his business lay elsewhere.

He looked furtively around, making sure he was not watched, then strode purposefully across the street to stand before the door of the house. Moonlight bathed the cobbled street and the flicker of firelight from the townhouse windows added to the illumination, so that the traveller felt very conspicuous in the warm yellow glow as he rapped several times on the wooden door. His heart pounded. God forbid that a night watchman or a patrolling soldier should appear now, he thought.

After what seemed like an eternity he rapped again, this time a little louder. He nervously looked up and down the street, and at the windows of the other houses, praying that no one was watching him. The door finally creaked open and a face peered at him questioningly through the crack.

'Yes?' the servant enquired with a furrowed brow.

'I must speak to Lord Lincoln.'

'It is late,' the servant said as though that was enough to send the man on his way.

'It is a matter of urgency,' the traveller pleaded.

The servant rolled his eyes and let out a deep sigh. 'Who shall I say is calling?' he relented.

'A servant of Lord Lovell,' the traveller said.

The door immediately swung wide open and John de la Pole, Earl of Lincoln, stood there in plain shirt and braes. He eyed the traveller up and down then beckoned him into the house. Once inside the smoky room Lincoln firmly shut the door behind them.

'Leave us,' Lincoln instructed his servant, as he flung a fur-lined cloak about his shoulders.

He waited until the servant was out of earshot before speaking to the traveller.

'Why does Lord Lovell send you to me?'

The traveller crouched and placed a hand in the top of his boot. Lincoln reacted swiftly, dropping a hand to his waist to reach for his dagger, before realising in horror that he was partially undressed and unarmed.

The traveller, seeing the look of horror on the earl's face, stood and slowly held out his hand.

'Forgive me, my lord. I never meant to startle you. I was just reaching for this,' he said as he handed Lincoln a folded piece of vellum.

Lincoln smiled nervously as he took the small parcel of dried calfskin from the man's hand. He unfolded it while keeping his eyes firmly fixed on the man. When it was open, he glanced down. The writing was difficult to read so he took the letter and crouched in front of the hearth so that the orange glow illuminated the tiny letters on the scrap of vellum. Eventually he rose, stared at the man opposite him and let out a deep sigh of resignation.

'Tell Lord Lovell that I cannot join him. The time is not right. When he had an army about to march on York and had King Henry trapped, I could and would willingly have brought men to the cause, but what cause is left now? Lord Lovell knows that I am York through and through. God knows I am the nephew of King Richard and was named his heir, but I cannot reveal my hand now and risk all for naught. Tell your master to flee to my aunt, Countess Margaret of Burgundy. There he can raise an army again, and in time I will join him but, I am sorry, now is not the time.'

The traveller looked up into Lincoln's despairing brown eyes. 'All is not lost yet, my lord. There is one more roll of the dice and you can yet play your part. Tomorrow, if all goes to plan, King Henry is to die in front of the assembled lords and if, in the chaos that will inevitably ensue, you can rally the lords to stand firm behind you and the House of York, the crown will be yours.'

Lincoln looked sceptical. 'Lovell has this plan in place?'

'Yes, my lord,' the traveller replied, subconsciously patting the straw-filled bag. 'You do not need to mire yourself in the details, my lord. Just be ready when it happens. King Henry is an only child with no heir. He is the last of a withered line. When that line dies be ready to spring into action.'

*

King Henry was to make his devotions at York Minster watched by all the great lords of the land who had either flocked to the city in defence of their monarch or had been summoned following the failed Yorkist rebellion. The Minster, awash with colour and noise, was crammed with lords, knights, bishops, abbots, esquires, the mayor and aldermen of the city, and merchants and craftsmen of the guilds. Hundreds more, townsfolk and peasants alike, gathered outside eager to get a sight of their king.

Henry arrived at the Minster on horseback, dressed in finest robes of scarlet trimmed with ermine. Behind him was the giant knight, Sir John Cheyne; unhorsed by King Richard in the battle at Redemoor but unhurt and now proud champion of the new king. Accompanying them was a body of heralds clad in tabards displaying the royal arms, King Henry's arms, for all to see. Forty Yeomen of the Guard, each dressed in a scarlet doublet, breeches and stockings, with black buckled shoes adorned with rosettes, marched behind in lines of four with six-foot halberds resting on their shoulders. At their head was their captain, the Earl of Oxford. Banners bearing Henry's royal arms fluttered overhead and trumpeters heralded the king's arrival to the joyous delight of the awaiting crowd.

Henry knew that he needed the loyalty of York as much as the city needed his royal patronage and goodwill. Once the northern capital's loyalty had been guaranteed he could then expect the other towns and cities of the north to follow York's lead. He had therefore waived the customary gifts and monies given by the city to their king. He had also chosen to hold a chapter of the Order of the Garter in the archbishop's great hall and to hold a feast there. It was unprecedented that the Garter ceremony and feast should be held anywhere but at Windsor Castle, but today, St George's Day, King Henry would bestow that privilege and honour on the city of York.

He had already sent out heralds to make a proclamation in every major town and marketplace that the northern rebellion had been defeated and an army would soon march to the West Midlands to crush the rebellion there. The heralds would ride to the heart of the rebellion in Warwickshire, Worcestershire and Herefordshire to announce that their magnanimous king, in his clemency, would grant a pardon to all those who lay down their arms and returned home, with the exception of the ringleaders of course. Henry hoped that this would have the same impact upon the southern rebels as it did upon the ones in Yorkshire. However, he would still send his uncle, the Duke of Bedford, south at the head of an army to crush whatever rebellion remained. This time, Henry thought to himself, there would be no doubt about the outcome. But first he would remind the people of York and the peers of the realm that he was king by right and by God's grace. He intended to put on a spectacle they would not forget.

The Earl of Lincoln watched King Henry enter the Minster as proud and confident as he had seen him since the king's coronation day six months earlier. Trumpets sounded and the chapel choir sang Te Deum Laudamus so that the heavenly notes echoed around the Minster. The king walked between the crowd and along the centre of the nave, towards the dais where Archbishop Rotherham waited with a gold crown before the altar.

Lincoln looked nervously around the Minster, scanning the faces about him. Would Lovell really be audacious enough to have the king assassinated here in the Minster? Every sharp movement around him caught his eye and he half expected to see the sudden flash of steel or hear the cries of 'treason' as a blade was plunged into the king's back. When it happened would he have the nerve to spring into action as Lovell's messenger had advised him? He dared to think so, yet he found the tension of not knowing when or where it would happen unbearable.

His throat was dry and he felt stifled by the crowd around him. Lincoln could feel the beads of sweat forming on his forehead. He knew many of the faces he could see around the Minster. Some were of questionable loyalty but none, Lincoln decided, would go so far as to murder the king, and definitely not risk an eternity in the depths of hell by doing it in a house of God. And then his eyes came to rest on Lord Scrope of Bolton, a prominent former diehard supporter of King Richard, who stood at the edge of the crowd by the dais staring intently at the king as he made his way up the central aisle towards him. Lincoln could see the hatred in Scrope's eyes as the king approached him. As King Henry drew level Scrope placed a hand inside his unbuttoned doublet.

Dear God, this is it! Lincoln thought as his stomach knotted with tension. All of the words he had planned for this moment left him as his mind wrestled with his emotions. Should he stand over the dead king's body and call for the nobles to support his claim to be king or should he stand on the dais where he would be raised above the crowd and could be better seen? What if the Yeomen of the Guard assigned to protect the king killed him as soon as he tried to assert his right to the throne? His thoughts were a blur inside his head, but time had rendered them useless as the king passed Lord Scrope and climbed onto the dais. As Lord Scrope put his hand down by his side, having scratched the flea bite on his chest, Lincoln's face flushed pink with embarrassment. He tried to appear nonchalant as he looked over at Lord Scrope again but when he saw Scrope staring back at him his face burned even brighter.

To Lincoln the tension was still palpable as the crowd fell silent so that they could listen to the words of Archbishop Rotherham praising God and the king. Lincoln fixed his stare directly ahead at King Henry as the king turned on the dais to face his subjects. The moment would surely still come, Lincoln thought, but next time he would have to be better prepared. His stomach quailed and Lincoln realised that before too long he would need to empty his bowels.

King Henry stood before the great and the good in the Minster of his northern capital. As all assembled were exhorted by Archbishop Rotherham to sing Gloria in Excelsis, the king gazed out on the faces of the earls of Derby, Northumberland, Oxford, Lincoln, Rivers, Shrewsbury, and Wiltshire; and he knew then, that in time he would begin to promote able men from outside the ranks of the peerage to support him, and in turn weaken the power of the nobility to strengthen his own position as king. It would not be popular among the peerage but he would isolate them one by one, cripple them with high taxes and fines, and disable them with new laws, for he could not risk further chance of insurrection. There could only be one ruler in this land and Henry would ensure that it was him.

'It is very mete and just, right and salutary,' Archbishop Rotherham declared to the gathered onlookers after the liturgy of the word had concluded.

King Henry saw his uncle, the Duke of Bedford, smile and wink at him. He ignored this sign of affection and maintained his dignified pose as Archbishop Rotherham recited the liturgy of the Eucharist and the crowd responded to each line with the Latin words that they had all learnt since childhood.

'Dignum et iustum est,' the people responded to the final line in unison.

The Sanctus was sung, acclamation and consecration made, and the concluding doxology read with a resounding 'Amen' from the gathered host before Archbishop Rotherham made the sign of peace and King Henry knelt to receive the consecrated bread and wine.

As he sat on the specially prepared throne and Archbishop Rotherham lowered the gold crown laden with jewels onto his head in the showpiece of the ceremony, it dawned on Henry that he was no longer the young man, lacking in confidence, who had wrested the throne from King Richard. He had found a new vigour, a new confidence, a new strength. He was now the sole, unquestionable king of England, chosen by, and accountable only to Almighty God.

He rose, crowned and resplendent in his ermine robes, and directly addressed all assembled before him.

'I am Henry, the seventh of that name, king of England, Wales, Ireland, and France, your sovereign lord and king. My right was earned in battle, before the sight of Almighty God. That heavenly right has been upheld despite discord and rebellion in my kingdom. That rebellion is ended and the houses of Lancaster and York are now united as one.'

Henry's stern countenance changed and a broad smile spread across his face. 'My wife, Queen Elizabeth, is pregnant and I am to have the first of many heirs. A Tudor dynasty is begun.'

It was at that moment that John de la Pole, Earl of Lincoln, shit his braes.

19

Sir Humphrey Stafford leaned out over the top of Worcester's great sandstone walls, narrowing his eyes to focus his failing eyesight on the banners fluttering above the camp in the fields beyond. Three thousand men were gathered under his leadership, to support the Earl of Warwick's claim to the throne. They were sharpening swords and billhooks, fletching arrows, exercising their sword arms and playing cards and dice as they waited for further reinforcements from Herefordshire and Gloucestershire.

'It is a pleasing sight, is it not?' Thomas Stafford said as he joined his brother on the wall. 'Who would have thought a few months ago when we were in hiding in Colchester Abbey that we would now be leading an army to put a Yorkist king back on the throne?'

'They're getting restless, and so am I,' Humphrey stated gruffly. 'I'm tired of dealing with petty arguments over whores, or settling arguments and fights over gambling debts. I've banned the damn lot of them from coming into the city because so many are getting drunk in the taverns and starting fights with each other or the locals. And the thieving bastards can't keep their hands to themselves. I had to hang one stupid whoreson this morning for stealing a milkmaid's purse.'

'You've been busy while I've been gone,' Thomas said sarcastically. He smiled at his brother who did not return the gesture, so he added, 'They're common soldiers, Humphrey, what do you expect?'

'I expect them to follow orders or swing from the gallows! I'll give it three more days for the men of Hereford and Gloucester to join us before I lead this rabble north to Yorkshire to link up with Francis and his army. I can't wait any longer.'

Humphrey rubbed his eyes with the thumb and forefinger of one hand before finally breaking into a semblance of a smile.

'I'm sorry, Thomas, I'm just tired, that's all. How did you get on?'

'The Mayor of London would not meet with me, nor could I gain access to speak to anyone of importance at the Tower. However, I met with the sheriff, John Tate, at his brewhouse in St. Benet Fink and although he would not promise to help us…'

'God's teeth! What was the point of me sending you to London if you cannot garner the support we need?' Humphrey snapped once more.

'But brother, Master Tate has provided me with valuable information.'

'It is not information we need, Thomas, it is fighting men!' Humphrey fumed.

He massaged his forehead and let out a long gasp of air between his teeth.

'What information?' he asked with furrowed brow as he calmed down.

'The Earl of Warwick is still held captive in the Tower but King Henry is planning to parade him around the city when he returns from the royal progress to the north.'

Thomas grinned from ear to ear as though he had imparted something wonderful.

'We already know that the boy is held captive in the Tower,' Humphrey stated, 'and the king won't be returning from the north, unless it's in chains, because we are going to defeat him.'

'Yes, but I have dispatched men around London to spread the news that Lord Lovell has captured King Henry and that we have risen in the south-west to support him.'

'That is the story I told to the Bishop of Worcester when I captured this city. I don't suppose it will do any harm circulating around London though,' Humphrey mused.

'Better than that,' Thomas enthused. 'Pro-Warwick sentiment is growing in London. The taverns are abuzz with it. The people there have always been pro-Yorkist and they hate that a Welshman now rules over them. With a little stirring I believe they will rise and march on the Tower, as they did in Jack Cade's day, less than thirty years ago, and they will demand the release of the Earl of Warwick. With the Constable of the Tower in the north of England with King Henry, who is going to refuse the mob?'

'Pro-Warwick sentiment and raising a mob are two entirely different things,' Humphrey argued.

'Aye, Humphrey, that is why I have paid men to rally at Westminster and march to Highbury beneath Warwick's banner of the Bear and Ragged Staff. I am confident of the groundswell of opinion supporting Warwick's right to be king. If I am right and enough men join them, they will march to the Tower and demand the release of Warwick. Once he is released my men will bring our new king to join us in the north.'

Humphrey's face broke out into a wide smile.

'It is a brilliant plan, well done Thomas, but it is important that

Warwick stays in London. He is to be king so needs to be seen by the people of London. They need to acclaim him. The decision now is, do we march to London to safeguard the new king or do we ride north to join Francis in defeating Henry Tudor? You have left me with a devil of a decision to make, Thomas.'

*

Lincoln left the cheering masses in the Minster and endured a fifteen-minute walk with soiled braes, to his lodgings in Walmgate before he could get cleaned up. It had been the most embarrassing hour of his life. He told his servant that the mishap must have been caused by eating rotten meat the night before. Whether he believed Lincoln or not, Gardener did not complain at having to clean up his master and wash his clothes. He lit a fire and heated water so that Lincoln could bathe, and he used some of the hot water to boil the soiled braes and shirt Lincoln had been wearing. It was a full three hours before Lincoln returned to the Minster by which time John de Vere, Earl of Oxford, and the giant Sir John Cheyne had been invested into the Order of the Garter. The Garter Knights had heard Evensong and the Requiem for departed Knights, and were now seated for the Garter feast.

Each Knight of the Garter, including the king, was dressed in full ceremonial robes of dark blue velvet with a badge on the mantle's left shoulder displaying the cross of St George, circumscribed by a blue garter with its motto *Honi soit qui mal y pense* emblazoned upon it in gold letters. Beneath the blue velvet mantle, with a slit on the right side to free the sword arm, they wore a white silk embroidered doublet, breeches, full hose, white doeskin shoes, and a blue velvet garter about their left calf. All wore sword and scabbard, a black bonnet, a collar chain of gold with twenty-six pairs of red and white enamelled roses surrounded by enamelled blue garters, each interspersed with twenty-six gold knots, joined together by gold links, and with a gold pendant representing St George slaying the dragon hanging from it. King Henry had spared no expense for his first Garter feast.

While the Garter Knights took pride of place on the tables beside the king, the remaining space in the Archbishop's Hall was filled with trestle tables where further lords and dignitaries joined in the feasting and merriment. Amid the noise, excited chatter, and drinking, few of them seemed to notice as Lincoln arrived late and was shown by the Marshall to his seat at a trestle table draped in white linen. He would have liked to sit at the back, out of the way, but his status as an earl meant that he was seated with the other earls and barons behind the Garter Knights but still towards the front of the hall near the king.

Lincoln was sullen and withdrawn. He was not in the mood for feasting and yet he was drawn back to the Garter feast by the knowledge that something momentous might still happen there, and that he had to be a part of it. He had feared that it might already have happened while he was absent from the Minster, but when the sounds of merriment filled his ears as the guards opened the door to let him enter the Archbishop's Hall, he knew he was not too late.

A ewerer brought rose-scented water in a silver bowl and a clean white linen cloth as soon as Lincoln was seated so that he could rinse and dry his hands, while another servant filled a cup with wine. Lincoln dried his hands then picked up the cup of wine but did not drink. He twirled the cup in his fingers absentmindedly as he looked around the great hall to see who was present. Lord Scrope of Bolton, dressed in his Garter robes and sitting at the head table near the king, immediately caught his eye. Lincoln felt none of the embarrassment of earlier. He saw Scrope's Garter badge and allowed himself a little smile as he considered the irony of its motto *Honi soit qui mal y pense* – 'shame on him who thinks evil of it.' Scrope saw him smiling and smiled back, giving a little nod of recognition. Lincoln's sullen mood lifted a little and he took a sip of wine.

Servants wearing the royal tabard of lions and lilies began to bring out the first course of food, starting from the king's table and then, only when that table was full, delivering platters table by table, until lastly they would reach the back of the hall where the lesser dignitaries sat and the less fancy food would be served.

The centrepiece of the king's table was a swan which had been gutted then redressed in its feathered skin so that it looked the same as it did when alive, other than its feet and beak were gilded with several thin layers of gold. Next to the gilded swan was a huge marchepane made with sugar, almonds, and rosewater, and strikingly decorated with beautiful artwork and gold leaf so that the royal coat of arms and the badge of the Order of the Garter stood out from its surface in amazing colour and glittering gold, and seemed almost too perfect to eat.

Lincoln had decided that he wasn't going to eat but the smell of the cooked meat brought to the king's table was tantalising. Servants brought out a quarter of stag which had spent a day in salt before being boiled in water, drained, then boiled again in red wine. They also brought out half a dozen chickens stuffed with minced veal, a civet of hare, a loin of veal covered with a German sauce made with butter and egg yolk, and gilt sugar-plums on a platter sprinkled with pomegranate seeds. At each end of the table they placed an enormous pie, topped with smaller pies to give it the appearance of a crown. The crust of every pie was silvered around the edges and gilt on the lid. Each of the two huge pies contained a whole roe-deer, eight pigeons, six chickens, four capons, two goslings, a pair of leverets, a rabbit, and twenty-six hard-boiled eggs; one to represent each of the Garter Knights. Each of the pies was dusted with saffron and flavoured with several pounds of white fat, minced veal and cloves.

'The king has excelled himself,' the Earl of Devon leaned over and shouted loudly into Lincoln's ear as the first platters arrived at their table.

Lincoln grimaced and nodded back. Not wishing to ignore the earl but not wishing to engage in conversation either. He continued to scan the face of each guest, looking for some tell-tale sign that would give away the would-be assassin.

'Dig in,' Devon said loudly, nudging Lincoln in the arm before taking his knife and slicing off a piece of a loin of veal. He tipped his head back, dropped the meat into his mouth and licked the German sauce from his fingers.

'Mmmm, delicious,' he gushed, looking at Lincoln, but the earl's attention was focused on a man crossing the hall between the rows of tables.

Giles Lamar felt the Earl of Lincoln's eyes boring into him but he resisted the urge to glance directly at the earl.

Look away, you fool, Lamar thought, hoping that Lincoln's gaze would not bring unwanted attention.

'Are you alright?' the Earl of Devon asked Lincoln.

'Er, yes I'm fine,' Lincoln replied, smiling, averting his eyes only momentarily from the servant of Lord Lovell who had visited him in his lodgings the previous night. The man was now dressed in a livery of gold, red and blue with fleur-de-lis, a double-headed black eagle, the papal crown and keys, all surmounted by a white eagle on a blue background. It was not a livery Lincoln recognised but he certainly knew that it was not English.

'You seem a little... distracted.'

'No, I'm fine thank you,' Lincoln replied as he made a show of taking his knife from his belt, wiping it on the tablecloth and carving himself several slices of chicken. 'I have a few matters on my mind, that's all. Just some trivial issues with my estate. Mmmm, you are right that the king has excelled himself, this truly is delicious,' he said with a false grin on his face as he tasted the meat.

His eyes continued to flick between Lovell's man and the Earl of Devon, who was now chattering away like a songbird. Whatever Devon was talking about bypassed Lincoln as he again firmly fixed his eyes on Lovell's servant, watching as the man edged between the tables, getting ever closer to where the king sat.

Giles Lamar carefully cradled a bulbous, translucent green glass bottle with a thin tapered neck as though it were a newborn child. Lincoln's heart pounded in nervous anticipation of the event that was about to unfold. He clasped his cup of wine tightly as Devon chattered on, oblivious that the king was about to die. Lamar halted in front of the king's table, held out the glass bottle and bowed his head.

'Your Grace, a gift from Ercole d'Este, Duke of Ferrara, Modena and Reggio.'

The Earl of Northumberland leaned in close and whispered into the king's ear. The king's face lit up as he feigned recognition.

'Ah, the duke was installed as a Garter Knight by my wife's father. I am sorry he could not be here with us today but I thank him for his gift.'

Lamar nodded his gratitude.

'What is in the bottle?' the king asked him.

'Wine, Your Grace. Sangiovese, known as the blood of Jupiter, the finest red wine from Romagna.'

'It has been decanted into this bottle just now?' the king asked.

'No, Your Grace, it has travelled from Romagna in this bottle, ` carefully packed in straw.'

'I never heard of such a thing!' The king was clearly astounded. 'And the wine does not spoil travelling all that distance?'

'It has been stoppered with tapered glass, sealed with wax and capped with lead to keep it in place and to stop it being tampered with, Your Grace.'

'How extraordinary!' the king exclaimed. 'I can't believe it hasn't spoiled.'

'Percy, have a taste,' the king urged the Earl of Northumberland.

'It is for Your Grace to savour first. My lord, the Duke of Ferrara, Modena and Reggio, was quite insistent on that,' Lamar smiled nervously.

'Nonsense,' said the king. 'Percy, you try it.'

Lincoln watched the exchange with horrid fascination. He put down his cup as his heart pounded faster and he feared that his trembling hands would spill his wine. Yet despite his emotions, he was ready. He knew that in a moment he would stand at the head table with the Garter Knights and proudly proclaim the end of the short-lived Tudor dynasty and the rise of a new Yorkist dynasty, with himself as king.

'I must insist, Your Grace,' Lamar croaked, tension breaking in his voice.

He raised a hand to his mouth to cough and clear his throat. At the same time the Earl of Northumberland reached over to take the wine from Lamar's other hand but only succeeded in wrenching it away, then inadvertently letting go of the bottle. Lincoln watched as the bulbous green bottle seemed to spin in the air in slow motion and then spiral to the floor where it landed and bounced, the thin tapered glass neck snapping off and spilling the rich, ruby red contents onto the floor, where two of the king's hounds immediately started lapping at the liquid as it spread out across the reed-covered floor.

Northumberland looked at the king in horror.

'I'm sorry, Your Grace! I will pay whatever it is worth and more. It was an accident. I am truly sorry.' He could not apologise enough as he feared the king's wrath was about to be unleashed.

Instead, the king took a step back and stood, arms spread wide, looking down, examining his clothing to see if any of the red wine had stained his expensive blue velvet robes or white undergarments.

Lincoln stood and silently pleaded for Lamar to react. *Stab him! Please have a knife. Stab him!* Lincoln imagined himself in Lamar's place, holding a knife and lunging at King Henry and plunging the blade over and over again into the king's stomach and abdomen.

One of the hounds licking the wine from the floor paused to cough up a fur ball, the sound breaking Lincoln from his reverie of violence. The hall fell silent and all eyes focused on the king, Lamar, and the hapless Earl of Northumberland, until one of the dogs began to quiver and jerk. Then it keeled over and lay motionless in the dark pool of wine. The second dog vomited but then also began to quiver and jerk as it retched. The king looked at Lamar in disbelief.

'You would poison me!' he bellowed, incredulous that the man could attempt such a thing. 'You would poison the king?' he shouted at the petrified figure. 'Seize him!'

Lamar turned to run but was immediately surrounded by onlookers and several Yeomen of the Guard. He attempted to push through the dignitaries surrounding him but was punched in the face and wrestled to the ground without much of a struggle.

'Seal the kitchen and have everyone searched,' the king demanded. 'I want everyone involved in this conspiracy arrested.'

The king stared down at Lamar who had been kicked and beaten and then dragged and forced to kneel before him. The left side of Lamar's face was already swollen and coloured with a bloom of fresh bruising.

'Why does the Duke of Ferrara wish me dead?' King Henry demanded of the trembling man.

In spite of his fear Lamar looked the king directly in the eye. 'It is not the Duke of Ferrara who would have you killed. It is Lord Francis Lovell, so that the true heir of the House of York can be returned to his rightful throne.'

The king's face twisted with raw hatred and anger. 'Hang him! Take this traitorous bastard outside and hang him… and anyone else found to be conspiring with him.'

Lamar was yanked to his feet and, though surrounded by Yeomen of the Guard who grasped and held his arms, he began to struggle furiously for his life. He kicked out until a hand clasped tightly around his windpipe and the point of a blade was pressed under his eye, defusing any lingering resistance.

As the Yeomen of the Guard finally dragged Lamar away to his fate, the king looked around to survey the shocked faces in the hall around him. The Earl of Lincoln stood beside the king, knife in hand, just the width of a wine-spattered trestle table between them. His face was ghostly white.

'It is alright, my lord Lincoln,' the king said to him, smiling, 'there is no need to fear, I am safe now.'

*

Conyers led Richard and Herricke to a white-plastered, two-storeyed jettied house in the countryside far from Ripon. They tied their horses to a post by a pond and let the horses drink as Conyers led them inside. As the large oak door swung open Richard saw an old man and woman standing waiting to greet them.

'My parents, William and Joan,' Conyers introduced the pair.

'Welcome,' the elderly couple chorused in unison.

'Please come in,' William beckoned them.

Richard and Herricke entered the room, and Richard started with fright as he realised somebody was standing to his left staring out of one of the casement windows. The man turned and Richard shrieked with joy.

'Francis!'

'Richard! You're safe,' Francis called out joyously.

The two hugged for an age as Herricke and the others watched on smiling.

'We've been trying to find you. Master Herricke has helped me. We've been to London, to Colchester and Ripon.'

'Slow down.' Francis tried to calm the excitable young man. 'Here, sit.' He gestured to a wooden bench.

Richard sat and beamed with joy at Francis. Herricke slid in alongside him on the bench.

'Thank you Master Herricke for keeping him safe. I trust he showed you his ring and explained his story?'

'That he did,' Herricke confirmed before adding, 'It is my duty and my pleasure to serve the Fellowship of the Hopper Ring, my lord. And a greater pleasure to serve the friends and kin of King Richard, God bless his soul.'

Francis patted Herricke on the shoulder in gratitude.

'I have a lot to update you both about. Events are moving fast and plans are constantly changing. Let me tell you what has happened.'

20

Six teams of men pulled heavy cannon; each with thick wooden wheels bound in strips of cloth to dull the noise of their passage through the soot black night. Across moor and around woods the six teams toiled, hauling their loads in uncomplaining silence. Scouts were sent out in front of the teams to spot and clear obstacles in their path or else report back if an obstacle was too big or impossible to pass. Whinnying horses had long been left behind and human muscle and sinew was all that Jasper Tudor would allow to complete the task so that the weapons arrived at their destination unnoticed and unheard.

The men bit down on strips of leather as they hauled, knowing that the slightest word, grunt or vocal expression would be rewarded with a lash of Captain Tollington's whip when the night was over. Sixty-two men carried the equipment needed to operate the cannons: kegs of gunpowder, lead shot – some the size of pebbles and some as large as a man's fist, rammers, sponges, priming irons, wad-screws, ladles, botefeux to hold the length of wound match, flints and iron strikers, wooden wedges, and wads of hay. More men carried bundles of swords, clubs and axes wrapped in swathes of material to keep them from rattling and the noise from carrying through the night air to the men they were about to attack. Altogether a hundred and twenty-one men accompanied the Duke of Bedford and his six artillery pieces as they crept across the Yorkshire countryside in the dark hours before the sun rose.

A scout returned and Jasper Tudor whispered to Captain Tollington to hold position until he had spoken to the man. Tollington in turn trotted over to each team sergeant and slapped him on the shoulder until all six teams had halted. The men breathed deeply as they removed the leather from between their teeth and wiped sweat from their brows with their sleeves, but still they made hardly a sound.

'The house is about five hundred yards over there,' Jasper whispered.

Captain Tollington squinted into the blackness in the direction the duke pointed but he could not discern any shape there.

Jasper continued to whisper, repeating what his scout had just told him. 'It is flat land between us and the house with no obstacles to hinder the guns. There is a pond and a small enclosure for animals at the back of the house. Lovell and his entourage are inside, most probably sleeping, nevertheless we must still be silent.'

Tollington nodded his understanding as he scratched at the raw patch of flaky skin that ran from the stubbly beard on his chin down to his throat.

'Where do you want the guns setting up?' he asked in a hushed voice.

'Set them in a semi-circle facing the front of the house. Thirty men are to wait behind the enclosure at the back of the house in case Lovell or any of the others try to flee. It is imperative that no one escapes. Do you understand? I would prefer Lovell captured alive but it is better that he dies than evade us once more. Remind the men of that; and that there is a reward of one hundred marks if Lovell is brought to me dead or alive.'

'They know that, Your Grace. The sum is already etched into every man's mind,' Tollington told the duke.

'Remind them again, Captain, then set them to their tasks in absolute silence,' Jasper commanded.

'Aye, Your Grace. That I will,' Tollington confirmed as he shuffled off to prepare the men for the assault on the house.

In less than an hour the artillery had been silently hauled up to the front of the house and every soldier was in place waiting for the first chink of sunlight on the horizon that would herald the start of the attack. Jasper Tudor stood, eying the amorphous mass of the house set into the darkness before him, while Captain Tollington nervously shifted his weight from one foot to the other as he scratched at his chin and throat again.

'Patience, Captain, it is nearly time,' Jasper cautioned him.

Eventually the grey outline of the house began to appear in the first half-light of morning as the sun edged ever closer to making its imminent appearance on the horizon. Every man stood or crouched, coiled like a wound spring, waiting for the order that would unleash a torrent of flame and lead shot at the house that gradually grew in shape out of the darkness before them. The fine twin brick chimneys became clearly defined first, then the thatch of the steeply pitched roof, before the frame of the house itself appeared. Darkness still cloaked the men surrounding the house, but the early hours were now dull grey rather than soot black. Gradually in this half-light the features of the house began to appear; wooden beams that ran both horizontally and vertically along the length of the two-storey jettied building, six casement windows with small rectangles of polished horn in a latticework of lead, a door made of oak planks at the front of the house, and the white plaster that covered the wattle and daub walls.

As he saw the emerging whiteness of the plaster covering the house Jasper Tudor knew that it was time.

'Light the matches,' he ordered in a whisper.

Captain Tollington repeated the order in hushed tones to his men. Shielded from view of the house by several comrades, a soldier used a striking iron and flint to create sparks and elicit a flame from a handful of hay. Six slow matches made from twists of rope soaked in a solution of saltpetre were lit from the resultant fire and then carried in botefeux – wooden poles with a split to hold the wound match, to stand beside each piece of artillery.

Each gun was packed with black powder, followed by a wad of hay, and then a lead ball or a handful of lead shot loaded into the end of the barrel. After this was all firmly rammed down, the cannon was aligned with the front of the house, its elevation set using a quadrant and a plummet, before wooden wedges were fixed under the wheels to keep the gun in place as it fired. A matross used a priming iron to clear the touch hole of old gunpowder or dirt. He then used the pointed metal tip to pierce the bag of primer and tip the gunpowder into the touch hole. Finally, the matross stepped back to allow the gunner forward with the botefeux holding the smouldering slow match.

As the first hint of true sunlight broke over the horizon Jasper Tudor nodded to Captain Tollington who broke the eerie silence by screaming at the top of his voice.

'Fire!'

Each cannon spat flame and belched smoke as it violently ejected the contents of its barrel in a thunderous roar.

Thomas Conyers awoke in sheer terror as balls of lead with

cores of stone and iron, ripped through the wattle and daub of his house, splintering timbers or passing through the walls leaving gaping holes to mark their passage. Fear, confusion and uncertainty gripped him as he struggled to understand what was happening. He rolled out of bed and lay flat on the floor. A great cheer went up outside his house as though a hundred men were greeting the annual crowning of the May Queen, but Thomas realised that something more sinister and deadly was taking place. He reached for his sword and unsheathed the blade from its scabbard before crawling across the floor to the partition that separated his room from the next.

Thomas peered into his parents' bedroom to see the wall shattered and the casement window completely missing. His mother lay slumped in the bed, mouth agape, eyes wide open and staring at him, propped up on a bolster with her chest a mass of crimson where a lead ball had torn straight through her. Thomas' father lay face down on the floor next to the bed, a pool of crimson blood spreading from beneath his head. Thomas grasped his father's shoulder and turned him onto his back. A large splinter of wood protruded from deep inside his father's eye socket. Thomas cried out in grief and held the limp, lifeless body as tears welled up in his eyes then cascaded down his cheeks.

A clatter resounded below as soldiers kicked aside the shattered oak panels that had once been Thomas' front door. They poured through the breech intent on capturing anyone that was still left alive inside the house. With reddened eyes, a heart deluged with anger and intent only on vengeance, Thomas clambered down the ladder from the second storey and jumped into the kitchen below. As the door burst open and the first soldier charged through, Thomas let out an unintelligible sound of anger as he lunged, piercing the man's throat with the tip of his blade. The man slumped to his knees, clutching the gash in his throat and gurgling blood. Two more soldiers closely following on the stricken man's heels, stumbled and fell over him leaving Thomas the easy task of stabbing his sword down into their prone bodies. He screamed in fury as more men pushed into the kitchen, some stumbling on the three bodies in the doorway.

Thomas stabbed and slashed as they came, bringing down two more men in the confined space before turning to face a soldier who had leapt over the bodies, falling past him into the kitchen. The soldier, regaining his balance, turned and swung his sword at Thomas' neck. Thomas parried the blade and sliced through the soldier's wrist in one well practiced movement before thrusting his sword into the soft flesh of the man's stomach and slicing sideways. As Thomas pulled his sword free the man stared wide eyed and clutched at the pink-purple ribbon of intestines that began to spill out. Thomas spun to face the soldiers coming into the kitchen behind him. He held his sword out in front of him and then, as a warm tingling sensation spread through his chest, he realised that a sword had pierced his heart. He felt the blood drain from him in a matter of seconds and a dizziness overtake him. He was dead before he hit the floor.

'Check every room; every nook and cranny,' Captain Tollington ordered his men.

They spread throughout the house smashing and overturning furniture as they went.

'Two more dead up here,' a voice called from the top of the ladder that led to the second floor. 'An old man and a woman. No sign of Lovell I'm afraid, Captain.'

'Hell and damnation!' Tollington cursed.

Jasper Tudor appeared in the kitchen doorway and glowered at him.

'I want him found!' Jasper shouted. 'Double the reward to two hundred marks, dead or alive.'

*

'Come on, Richard, they'll be after us if we don't move quickly.' The worry was clear in Francis' voice.

Richard released Herricke from a long hug, his eyes red with tears.

'Thank you,' he said with a hoarse voice. 'I'll miss you so much. Thank you for all you've done for me.'

'I'll miss you too, Richard, but I'm sure our paths will cross again soon enough.' Herricke thought for a moment and then added, 'I intend to move my business to the Midlands, to buy a smithy in the centre of the country and trade from there. It will be safer for me than in London, considering what has happened. I will get a message to Lord Lovell once I am settled so that you will know where to find me.'

He smiled and Richard's eyes welled up again. Overcome with emotion he hugged Herricke once more.

'Come on, before Tudor's men are upon us,' Francis said impatiently.

As Richard and Herricke parted again Francis stepped forward. He clasped Herricke's hand and pulled the man towards him.

'Thank you. You are truly a good friend of the House of York. I am indebted to you William.'

'No, my lord,' Herricke replied, 'the House of York has made me a rich man, and you and King Edward and King Richard have always been good friends to me. I am proud to serve you and to have reunited you with this young man.'

He turned to Richard. 'Remember Richard, you are a Plantagenet. You are the son of a king. Be proud of that.'

'I am,' Richard replied, trying unsuccessfully to fight back the tears.

Francis took the reins, put his foot into a stirrup and hoisted himself into place on his saddle. Richard mounted his own horse and began to follow Francis who had set off along the path riding towards the sunset.

'Goodbye Master Herricke,' Richard called behind him as he waved then sped up to catch Francis.

'Are you sure you still want to come with me?' Francis asked as Richard drew alongside.

'Of course,' Richard replied without hesitation.

'Despite that I'm a fugitive, my army is dispersed and my allies are few?' Francis asked. 'I don't even know what the future holds for me.'

'My father is dead, I have no home, and I don't know what the future holds for me either, so what have I got to lose?' Richard retorted.

'I am a hunted man with a price on my head,' Francis warned him. 'If you are caught with me, it will be a death sentence.'

'Then let's not get caught,' Richard said as he suddenly spurred his horse into a canter.

Francis rode after him.

'Whoa! Whoa!' he shouted as he caught hold of Richard's reins and slowed the horses to a halt. 'This is a serious matter. We will be hunted high and low, and they will not show us any mercy.

There is a high chance that we will get captured. They will probably torture you if you survive and then they will kill you anyway. It will not be a pleasant death. It would still be sensible to go with Master Herricke and take him up on his offer of an apprenticeship with a mason and a chance to build a normal life.'

'Am I not the son of a king, as Master Herricke just reminded me?'

'Yes, you are, Richard Plantagenet,' Francis said, looking at him with pride.

'So, I will fight like a king's son; like my father's son; like a true Plantagenet! Francis, we are comrades together,' Richard said, holding out his Hopper ring on its leather cord. 'It works both ways. We help each other.'

'Yes Richard, it does,' Francis said, seeing the Hopper ring in Richard's palm; gleaming bright even in the fading light of the sunset. He looked at the Hopper ring on his own finger, remembering the time when King Richard had given it to him as a gift. 'Then our best hope is to ride across the Pennines to the Broughtons or Huddlestons of Lancashire who will hide us. Maybe if we're lucky we can catch a ship to Ireland; the Irish lords have long been supporters of the House of York.'

The two men travelled slowly as night descended, so that their horses did not stumble or lame themselves on the dark tracks. They kept away from the main roads where they had a greater chance of being captured by Tudor soldiers or anyone hoping to collect the reward on Lovell's head. They skirted villages and kept close to the edge of woods wherever possible. Few travellers dared to venture out into the thick of night, so whenever they did see anyone they were very wary and headed for the shelter of a wood or else lay the horses down in the long grass and heather until the danger had passed.

Before daybreak they crossed the Pennines and were deep inside Lancashire. Richard was tired and fighting a losing battle to keep his eyes open. At first the motion of the horse jerked him awake every time that he started to fall asleep, but eventually he slumped forward in the saddle, oblivious to the bouncing gait of the horse as exhaustion finally overcame him and he slipped into deep unconsciousness. Francis took hold of his reins and led the horse on, slowly winding his way through the countryside towards the Lancashire coast.

With daylight wiping out the last orange and purple tinges of sunrise, they arrived on Furness Fells, where a large peel tower made of local stone loomed over the surrounding area. It was broad and square, with crenellated walls and narrow arrow slits, built to defend against Scottish raids. To one side of it was a huddle of huts from which people were emerging. Francis led the horses towards the tower and, as they approached, he leaned over and shook Richard awake.

Richard sat up, his back stiff from slumbering in the saddle. He stretched as much as his saddle would allow him to, and rubbed his eyes.

'How long was I asleep?'

'Long enough for us to get here,' Francis said as they pulled up before the giant stone keep.

'Where are we?' Richard enquired.

'Sir Thomas Broughton's peel tower on Furness Fells. It will be a safe place to hide until we can catch a ship to Ireland,' Francis explained.

'What brings you here?' a voice called down from the top of the tower.

'Tell Sir Thomas that Lord Lovell bids him good morning.'

The man scurried off leaving several others peering down from the walls. Francis knew that they would have crossbows cranked and bolts loaded, ready to shoot at the first sign of trouble or with a command from Sir Thomas. He shifted irritably in his saddle as he waited.

'Francis! Is that really you?' Sir Thomas called down.

'Good morning Thomas,' Francis called in reply as he looked up to show his face to the man now peering down from the battlements.

'Welcome,' Sir Thomas greeted him before shouting at his men, 'let them in.'

The iron portcullis of the tower was cranked up and then the iron studded oak door swung outwards to reveal an opening in the wall, about eight feet above the level of the ground. One of the men who had come out from the huts took the reins of their horses as Francis and Richard dismounted. Men inside the tower pushed a ladder out through the opening in the wall, allowing the two visitors to climb up. Sir Thomas greeted them at the entrance.

'Welcome to my humble home,' he said, beckoning them inside. 'I was informed that you were dead, Francis. Twice in fact! First at the battle fighting beside King Richard, then at the failed rising near York.'

'The Welsh usurper has not buried me yet, Thomas.'

Sir Thomas laughed. 'So I see.'

He led them up a narrow staircase that wound to the right; a design that allowed soldiers to use their sword arms to defend against attackers coming up the stairwell but prevented attackers from effectively swinging a sword in their right hand against them. They arrived in a room with tapestries hanging on the walls, straw strewn thickly upon the floor, and a fire ablaze in the broad hearth to keep the cold and damp at bay. They sat and Sir Thomas was about to say something but Francis spoke first.

'This is Richard Plantagenet,' he said without further embellishment.

The confusion was clear on Sir Thomas' face.

'King Edward's second son?' he eventually ventured.

'King Richard's eldest son,' Francis confirmed.

Sir Thomas was a broad, stocky man with a head as square as his own peel tower, but in that moment he seemed to shrink under the weight of the information Francis had just given him. He looked at Richard then his expression changed as he tried to fathom the meaning of what he had just heard.

'What does this mean for the House of York?' he asked with a perplexed look on his face.

'I honestly don't know yet. I haven't discussed it with him,' Francis said, turning to Richard.

'Discussed what with me?' Richard's eyes flicked from man to man seeking an answer.

'Discussed what with me?' he asked more assertively across the silence as Francis and Thomas stared uncomfortably at each other.

Francis eventually cracked under Richard's withering glare and ceded the information.

'Richard, at this moment it is not clear who is heir to the House of York and the crown of England. You have Plantagenet blood in your veins and you are the son of the previous —'

'What? I am not a king!' Richard shrieked, half in shock, half in laughter.

'Listen to me please, Richard,' Francis implored. 'Let me explain fully.'

Richard nodded, allowing Francis to go on.

'There are several who can lay claim to the throne. All are descended through the York line from King Edward III. It is not known if the two sons of Edward IV still live. The elder was named Edward V but never crowned as he and his brother were debarred from the throne by Act of Parliament when it was discovered that their father had been previously married.'

'Because they are bastards like me?' Richard interrupted.

'In essence, yes,' Francis conceded.

'Then how can I be considered for—'

'Hear me out,' Francis cut him short. 'In all likelihood the princes are dead. They were resident in the Tower of London but they have not been seen since your father's reign.'

'Wait! Are you saying my father had them killed?' Richard asked incredulously.

'No! Not at all. I was close to your father and I know he could never do such a thing. It is possible, however, that others may have spirited them out of the Tower after your father died. But in my opinion, it is most likely that Henry Tudor found them in the Tower and had them disposed of as they are too great a challenge to his tenuous claim to the throne.'

'So that leaves Edward, Earl of Warwick?' Sir Thomas interjected.

'Possibly,' Francis replied enigmatically before going on to clarify things for Richard.

'Warwick is the son of George, Duke of Clarence, who was brother to King Edward and King Richard. Warwick would be next in line except that his father was executed and attainted as a traitor, meaning that his lands and titles are forfeit and he is also barred from the throne; not that that stopped Henry Tudor whose ancestors were also attainted and debarred,' he added bitterly.

'So, who does that leave? And don't say me!' Richard quickly added.

'John de la Pole, Earl of Lincoln is a candidate. He married your aunt, Elizabeth, King Richard's sister, and was declared heir by your father after...' Francis paused and looked apologetic. 'After your brother, Prince Edward of Middleham died,' he concluded the sentence.

'All this talk of princes and earls related to me is making my head spin,' Richard declared. 'So who are you saying should be the rightful king?'

'It is complicated. Whichever line is traced there are problems,' Francis explained. 'The Princes are most probably dead; Warwick is captive in the Tower and debarred from the throne, although parliament could reverse his father's attainder if they were so persuaded; and Lincoln is part of King Henry's court, too scared or unwilling to step forward and claim his right. Unlikely as it sounds, you may be our best hope, Richard.'

Richard was about to speak but Francis put his hand up in front of his face, halting him.

'The difference between you and the others is that you are here. You are free. You are with us, and we have the ability to raise an army.'

Sir Thomas Broughton nodded in agreement.

'We can go to Ireland and raise an army there,' Francis pleaded with Richard.

'I am bastard born. Until last August I was a lowly orphan brought up by a priest in a village in Kent. I have no right to be king, nor do I want to be. I only want to bring Henry Tudor down. I want revenge on the man who murdered my father; nothing more, nothing less.'

Francis was ready to argue but was interrupted when a servant knocked and immediately entered the room. The man spoke without waiting to be asked.

'My lords, armed men are approaching.'

'How many?' Sir Thomas asked, rising to his feet in concern.

'Around forty; armoured and on horseback, approaching from the south-east, my lord.'

'Are they wearing livery or flying banners?' Francis questioned the servant.

'They are too far away to make it out my lord. Perhaps if we wait...'

'There is no time,' Francis snapped as he headed for the door. 'Richard, we must leave now.'

As they rushed down the narrow space of the stairwell Sir Thomas barked orders to the servants to open the entrance to the tower. The portcullis was slowly raised, the door opened and the ladder lowered for Francis and Richard to climb down. The servant who had brought news of the approaching riders shouted down from the battlements at the top of the tower for the men below to ready the horses. There was a delay as saddles, straps and harnesses were fastened.

'Hurry!' Francis shouted impatiently at the men who wrestled with the straps and buckles.

Individuals on horses could now be made out in the distance.

The servants stood back to let Francis and Richard mount, and then they were off, galloping west towards the coast.

'It's Jasper Tudor's men,' Sir Thomas Broughton shouted after them, 'I can see the livery now.'

That was all the encouragement they needed to spur their horses on and try to keep ahead of the chasing pack.

oger Pershore feared for his life. A shiver ran down his spine even though the sun was warm on his face. King Henry had entered Worcester and ridden straight to the Bishop's Hall, ignoring the fawning and grovelling civic officials who could not do enough to please their king. Pershore was a proud man and would not stoop so low; besides, the king would, he was sure, see right through such obvious obsequiousness. Instead, he was resigned to face his fate with calm serenity. As custodian of the keys for the city's Sidbury Gate that guarded the bridge over the Frog Brook leading to the London road, Pershore knew that he would be held responsible, along with all the other gatekeepers, for allowing the rebels to enter Worcester. It may not be fair that his was not the gate by which the rebels had actually entered the city but nonetheless it was a collective responsibility to keep the city safe so he would be as much to blame.

Pershore knew it was a bad omen when King Henry had refused to watch the civic pageant that had been especially prepared for him by the city's hierarchy in their appeal for clemency. The civic officials and townspeople of Worcester wanted to show the king that they were loyal and faithful subjects in the wake of the rebellion, and had chosen the theme of British History as the subject of their pageant, with the king's half-uncle, the last Lancaster king and saintly Henry VI, as the lead character and principal spokesman of the play. However, the king was not impressed and the city's bailiffs, gatekeepers, and other officials were now all under indictment for treason for allowing the rebels to capture Worcester and allegedly supporting them in their cause. Of all the senior figures of the city, only Bishop Alcock had escaped indictment.

The king rode into Worcester in a furious mood. News had reached him just days before that a great crowd had gathered at Westminster and walked to Highbury beneath the banner of the bear and ragged staff, protesting in favour of the Earl of Warwick and demanding that the boy be let out of the Tower. His mood was not tempered by hearing that this protest was violently stamped out by his deputies, and the Londoners dispersed back to wherever they came from. No ringleaders were discovered and no one punished but King Henry now knew that London was a hotbed of sedition and dissent. He was in no mood to watch a pageant laid on by people that had, whether wilfully or negligently, let rebels take over their city.

A soldier escorted Pershore from the sunlit yard into the hall where the earls of Oxford, Derby and Lincoln presided over the court commissioned by the king to look into the uprising at Worcester. Perspiration gathered on his forehead and Pershore felt his stomach knot as he stood before the three seated lords. He knew that they had already ordered twenty men to be hung in the towns of Warwick and Birmingham for treason, and he suspected that he would fare no better. He had considered fleeing the city as soon as he heard that men were being arrested but had decided that it was better to face the inquisition with the truth than to live the life of an outlaw, skulking around the forests and woods of Worcestershire constantly in fear of being captured by the king's men.

Lord Stanley, Earl of Derby, stroked his long greying beard and looked at the man standing with head bowed before him.

'You are Roger Pershore, gatekeeper of the Sidbury gate in the southeast of the city?'

Pershore raised his head, stood up straight and confirmed that he was the man just named. He maintained eye contact with Lord Stanley as he was questioned further.

'Were you at your post the morning that the rebels arrived?'

'Yes, my lord, but the first I knew of it was when they approached me from within the city. There were a dozen of them and all armed; I could do naught by then, my lord.'

'And then what happened?'

'They were shouting "A Warwick, a Warwick!" They threatened me with swords and took me captive. Some of the rebels manned the gates and walls and three others took me to the Cathedral Close where the rebels had brought the bishop, the bailiffs and other important men of the city.'

'Did they cause you or any others harm?'

'No, my lord.'

'Why do you think that was?' Stanley probed.

'They had no cause to, my lord. They were well armed and had caught us all by surprise. We weren't in a position to put up any resistance. They'd have killed anyone who did, there and then, I'm sure.'

'Didn't Bishop Alcock speak out against them?'

'He did, my lord, but surely no man would risk the wrath of God by harming a bishop?'

Stanley nodded.

'Where did the rebels enter the city?' Stanley changed the direction of his questioning.

'I did not see it myself but I have been told that they entered by the Foregate just after first light.'

'Who let them in?'

'I honestly don't know, my lord. I understand that they charged the Foregate from the nearby woods, just after it had been opened.'

The Earl of Oxford clasped his hands together and leaned forward before speaking. 'Who is responsible for seeing that the area surrounding the city is clear so that approaching danger may be spotted in good time for the gates to be closed?'

'I'm not sure, my lord; maybe the bailiffs Richard Howton and John Brook?'

Pershore felt a bead of sweat trickle down his forehead as the three earls confided with each other in a huddle of whispers. He quickly wiped it away, hoping the action had not been perceived as a sign of guilt.

'When did the rebels leave the city?' Stanley continued to question him.

'Three days ago, my lord, when news arrived that the rebellion in Yorkshire had been crushed by His Grace the Duke of Bedford.'

'And the rebels just abandoned the city and fled?'

'When they heard that King Henry's army was on its way, yes they did, my lord,' Pershore confirmed.

'And what of their leaders, Sir Humphrey and Thomas Stafford?' The Earl of Lincoln spoke for the first time.

I would not know of such things, my lord; I am just a gatekeeper.'

'But you must have heard rumours?' Lincoln persisted.

'I have heard it said that they have fled to the woods near Bewdley, but this is just hearsay, my lord. I wouldn't stake my life on it.'

Pershore regretted the last seven words as soon as they had left his lips.

Lincoln smiled at him. 'You may go, Master Pershore.'

Pershore looked perplexed. 'I may leave?' he asked, looking at the three earls for confirmation that he understood correctly.

'The king is magnanimous and has granted clemency to all except the leaders of the uprising, so yes, you may leave,' Stanley said, waving away the dumbfounded gatekeeper.

He huffed in exasperation after Pershore had left the hall.

'We are still no nearer to finding these Stafford scoundrels.'

'That they fled to woods near Bewdley is the same rumour confirmed by half a dozen men now. There has to be some truth in it,' Oxford suggested.

'I have sent Thomas Cokesey with four hundred men to scour the area and flush them out if they are in hiding there,' Oxford informed the other earls.

*

Shitting in the woods and wiping his arse with grass and leaves like a peasant was not the lifestyle Sir Humphrey Stafford had in mind when he set out to take Worcester in the name of the Earl of Warwick. He had not felt a soft piece of linen or wool on his arse for over a week and it irritated him. Faced with the news that Lovell's rising in Yorkshire had collapsed and that King Henry was marching on Worcester, he and his brother had fled without second thought for the daily luxuries of life. Now he was reduced to sleeping rough with no canvas as shelter, cleaning his teeth with a twig instead of a pebble wrapped in cloth, poaching rabbits like an outlaw, eating wild mushrooms, while still shitting in the woods and wiping his arse with grass and leaves!

'What on God's Earth are we going to do about getting some cloth?' he called to his brother as he walked away from the area they had been using as a latrine, whilst still lacing up his breeches.

'Shush!' Thomas hissed back at him.

'What's the matter?' Humphrey asked before realising that someone must be approaching as Thomas was heaping soil onto the campfire to smother it.

He crouched down beside his younger brother and stared intently through the trees to where Thomas indicated, but he saw nothing.

'I heard a horse whinny,' Thomas explained.

'Are you sure?' Humphrey asked.

The horse whinnied again before Thomas could answer.

'There!' he exclaimed.

'I heard it,' Humphrey confirmed.

'We need to muzzle the horses and walk them as quietly as possible, as deep into the woods as we can get.'

Thomas nodded in agreement. The two men crept silently back to the horses and, removing simple leather muzzles from their saddlebags, they affixed these to the horses to keep them from whinnying. They led the horses further into the woods, cringing every time that a stick or branch cracked under foot or hoof. They paused as startled birds flew from the undergrowth, squawking loudly to expose their presence. Every noise and sound was amplified by the trees and seemed destined to betray them to whoever was nearby. They nervously scanned the woods looking for any sign that they were being followed. The deeper into the woods they travelled the tougher the going got. Foxgloves, nettles, pignut and carpets of bluebells and red campion gave way to fallen moss-covered tree trunks and the twisted roots of trees that grew over large boulders barring their way.

Sir Richard Burdett knelt by the extinguished campfire, removed his leather glove and placed his hand over the pile of ash and soil, feeling the extant but dwindling heat.

'They were here moments ago,' he informed his men. 'Spread out and find them.'

The ten men walked into the woods spreading away from each other until they were far enough apart that each man could just see the next. They moved quickly through the trees, not caring about any noise that they made, ducking beneath branches and pushing through thicket as they forged ever deeper into the woods. Several birds flew past, startled from where they had been nesting.

'Over there,' Burdett called to his men, pointing in the direction that the birds had flown from.

The ragged line of men closed in on the spot, involuntarily forming an arc as those in the centre were slowed by bramble bushes and fallen tree trunks. The two men on the left of the arc were the first to reach an outcrop of rock that rose upwards from the floor of the woods.

Thomas Stafford crouched low behind the outcrop of cold grey rock that jutted from the earth like a series of giant fingers. He closed his eyes and let his heart slow. His breathing became shallower as he focused on nothing but the sounds around him. Humphrey sat next to him, breathing heavily and clutching at the pain in his side caused from the exertion of fleeing.

'I'm sorry Tom,' he whispered.

'Hush now, they're almost upon us.'

Thomas prayed that the pursuers would walk past the rocks but steeled himself to take action if they were discovered. He gripped a knife tightly in his left hand and had his sword lying ready at his right side. Humphrey too, readied himself. He tried to ignore the pain in his side as he gripped the hilt of his sword and steadied his breathing. Both men listened intently as the pursuers drew closer to the rocks.

'Wait!' one of them instructed.

'I'll climb up here and see if I can get a better view.'

Thomas readied himself to pounce as he heard the pursuer scramble up the rocks. A hand appeared on the edge of the rock in front of Thomas' face as the man hauled himself up.

Thomas prepared to lunge with his knife the moment the man's head appeared. What happened after that would be in God's hands.

'Don't do that, Thomas!' a voice called loudly from beneath them on the same side of the outcrop rocks as they were crouching on. 'He's one of my men.'

Thomas and Humphrey stared down at Sir Richard Burdett as more of his men gathered around him.

'God's teeth! You terrified the life out of me, you whoreson,' Humphrey bellowed.

'And nearly lost a few men for your trouble,' Thomas added as he sheathed his knife and sword.

'I'm sorry, but I had to bring you warning,' Burdett explained. 'Thomas Cokesey has been sent with four hundred men to search for you. He knows you're hiding here. You must flee.'

'Flee where?' Humphrey asked. 'The abbey at Colchester is too far. Tudor's men are everywhere.'

'Culham Abbey in Oxfordshire,' Burdett offered an answer. 'The abbot is a friend of the House of York. You can claim sanctuary there. It is within two days' ride.'

*

Angry grey-black clouds were closing in as Francis and Richard neared the coast, though that was the least of their worries. For nearly ten miles Jasper Tudor and his men had been close on their heels as they raced along dirt tracks, past villages and lone crofters' cottages, up and down slopes, along narrow lanes and across open heath. Their horses were close to exhaustion, even though at times they had been travelling at little more than a canter until they caught sight of their pursuers and sped up again. Francis looked over his shoulder and could see the group of chasing horsemen on the horizon, between the two hills that they had passed only fifteen minutes ago. Tudor was gaining on them again.

They could smell the tang of salt in the air before they saw the sea but the dark blue-grey water eventually came into view as they cleared a shallow rise on the narrow track. Heath and grassland dotted with yellow flowers lay on either side of them, with two fishermen's cottages standing prominent against the shifting white-capped waves at the bottom of the sloping ground ahead of them. Francis and Richard cantered on until they reached the end of the narrow track but instead of a port or a fishing village, the track just faded away to merge with grass and sand which opened onto a windswept, desolate beach that stretch as far as the eye could see in both directions. Tudor's men were now out of sight on the low ground behind them, somewhere in front of the two hills in the distance, but Francis knew they were only minutes away from catching up. There was nowhere to hide and only two choices left to Francis and Richard: whether to ride north or south.

Francis knew that they could ride north towards Carlisle and even on to Scotland if they chose, but their best bet was still to sail to Ireland, so he chose to ride south in search of a port where he and Richard could get passage to safety with their horses. It was doubtful that Jasper Tudor would risk following them across the sea to Ireland, he thought.

Rain began to fall in a soft drizzle as they rode south along the sand where it met the tide. It was tough going and the horses were already exhausted but what choice did they have? Jasper Tudor would reach the sea and see where hoof prints turned south along the beach, and he would follow them as quickly as he could, therefore they had to push onwards. Fortunately for Francis and Richard, Tudor's horses were just as exhausted as their own.

The whole sky filled with broiling slate grey clouds and the wind began to whip up rain so that it stung their faces as they rode. Francis glanced back again and could see the dark menacing shape of Tudor's hunting pack in the distance as they galloped along the sand between the ocean spume and the ridge of higher ground, determined to catch up with their quarry. After another half mile or so, Francis and Richard left the soft sand to ride along the higher ground beside the beach, trying to extend the distance between them and Tudor. It was to no avail as, no matter how hard they pushed the horses, the distance remained constant. Eventually the land began to curve inwards into an estuary and away eastwards into the far distance. The tide was high and the estuary was swollen with sea water. Francis' heart sank. It was a barrier impassable to man and horse. They could see land on the other side of the estuary but without a ship or boat they could not reach it.

Rain hammered down in sheets as they wearily rode their exhausted horses back inland, following the tidal river in the hope of finding a way to cross the estuary before Jasper Tudor finally caught up with them. They followed a track which took them across the high ground overlooking the estuary and then sloped down to where a river broke from the land, spreading out into separate fingers of water that cut five twisting gulleys across a wide expanse of golden sand before emptying into the estuary. Each of the five smaller rivulets was widening and threatening to join into one as the rain fell heavier and washed down in torrents off the land.

'Quickly, before we get trapped,' Francis yelled at Richard through the downpour as he led his horse across the first of the babbling rivulets. His horse began to sink into the wet sand and mud of the estuary with the weight of him on its back.

'Dismount and walk across,' he shouted to Richard.

But Richard was not listening. He sat motionless in his saddle, wet hair plastered to his face and water dripping from the end of his nose, with one arm extended and a finger pointing towards the mouth of the river. Up on the bank was an upturned fishing boat that they had almost ridden past. Francis handed Richard his horse's reins and made his way to the boat. It was small and not in the best condition but it may get them across the estuary in one piece. He heaved with all his might to turn the boat over and then began to haul it down the wet sandy embankment to the water. It floated and seemed watertight so he pushed it out along one of the babbling rivulets into the muddy estuary.

'Leave the horses but bring the saddles and harness,' he shouted to Richard.

Richard led the horses out as far as he could into the thick mud of the estuary before he began to unbuckle the harness and saddle of one of them.

'There!' Captain Tollington shouted from the top of the embankment.

A dozen horsemen lined the ridge and at their centre was Jasper Tudor, wrapped in leather and oilcloth to protect his armour from the rain.

'Leave it, Richard. Just get in the boat!' Francis shouted, with fear and urgency in his voice.

Richard ignored him and continued to undo the buckles, not realising that some of Tudor's men had made their way down to the beach and were now running along the sand towards the water's edge.

'Richard!' Francis screamed. 'Leave it. Just get in the boat.'

Richard threw the harness over his shoulder and heaved the saddle off of Francis' horse. He carried it towards the boat, each painfully slow step by painfully slow step, through the thick sucking mud that pulled at his feet preventing him from lifting them. Francis dare not leave the boat as it would be washed into the estuary in the growing torrent of water, but he also could not leave Richard to the mercy of Tudor's men who were running through the water, swords drawn, towards him. Francis kept one hand on the stern of the boat and dragged it against the current back towards Richard who was floundering in the mud. Tudor's men, at first sprinting through the shallow water, were now being slowed by the estuary mud too. Francis reached Richard, took the saddle off him and heaved it into the boat. He tried to pull Richard towards him but the suction of the mud held Richard fast.

The first of Tudor's men was only feet away now. The large bearded man with long straggly hair bawled threats and obscenities at Richard as he tried to work his way nearer but realised that he too was just as stuck as the boy.

'I'll have your fucking gizzards for my dog, you little turd. And the whoreson behind you too,' he shouted through the pouring rain as he managed to pull a foot free from the mud, temporarily losing his balance as he did so.

He placed his sword point down in the mud and leaned on it to steady himself but the blade just sliced down through the gloopy mud and he fell sideways as his weight shifted. He disappeared under the thick unctuous estuary mud but then came to the surface like a fearsome sea monster, all hair, stinking slime and vitriol.

'Fucking whoreson bastards!' he screamed as he thrashed about in the mud.

He threw his sword in pure anger and frustration. Richard ducked but the hilt end of the sword caught Francis on the shoulder, knocking him back and almost into the boat. More of Tudor's men were wading through the mud and gradually getting closer to them, but Richard and Francis were going nowhere fast as they battled with the sucking mud.

'Give me the end of the harness,' Francis ordered.

Richard took the harness still slung over his shoulder and, holding on to one end, tossed the other end to Francis. Francis turned and began to push the boat back towards the faster flowing water. With its streamlined shape and weight evenly spread, it slid effortlessly through the water-sheened mud. Francis pulled on the harness as he went. At first Richard struggled to move, but eventually he worked a foot free of the glutinous mud. As Francis tugged on the harness Richard was pulled horizontally across the surface of the mud until his second leg was freed too. He allowed his weight to spread and Francis to pull him. Francis pushed the boat with his left hand and tugged on the harness with his right until they were clear of the mud and into the waist-deep waters of the estuary, leaving Tudor's men stranded in the thick deep mud behind them.

'I can't swim!' Richard yelled in a panic as he realised the water was getting deeper.

'Neither can I!' Francis replied, finally heaving Richard out of the water and into the boat.

Richard pulled himself over the side and then extended a hand to help Francis, who took it and hauled himself over the gunwale to sit exhausted on a wooden thwart that acted as a seat spanning the width of the boat. The rotten wood immediately split under his weight and collapsed, spilling him onto the burden boards on the floor of the boat.

'Bloody hell! Let's hope the rest of this boat is in better shape or we're dead men,' Francis exclaimed.

He sat up and saw Jasper Tudor still mounted on his horse on the ridge above them. Several of Tudor's men had dismounted and fetched bows from their horses. They knocked arrows and aimed into the driving rain before loosing their shafts.

'We're not out of this yet. Paddle!' Francis shouted.

They had no oar or method of propulsion other than their hands so they both leaned over the gunwale and scooped furiously at the water, trying to drive the small vessel forwards. Two arrows dropped into the estuary mud about eight feet behind them.

'Faster, before they find their range,' Francis shouted.

Richard was paddling furiously and could not put any more effort into it but still they seemed to be bobbing about on the water but not actually going forward. An arrow cut through the water a few feet behind the boat, then another just to the left of it.

'Lie down in the back of the boat with my saddle over you,' Francis ordered.

'What for? Why?' Richard questioned.

'Just do it!' Francis barked.

He then jumped off the bow of the boat back into the water. He grabbed the boat's breasthook and waded out into the estuary pulling the boat along as he went. The water was already up to his armpits. Richard curled up in the stern of the boat with his back against the transom and a saddle on top of him. Arrows continued to hit the water, getting every closer to the boat. As the water became deeper and faster flowing, Francis fought his fear of drowning and began to kick his legs, holding onto the breasthook at the front of the boat to keep himself afloat. It was cumbersome and ungainly but by holding onto the boat and kicking his legs he gradually managed to guide it through the water away from the coastline. Rain and waves lashed against his face and arrows sliced through the water just yards away. He inhaled sea water and choked yet he could not stop until he'd got the boat into deeper water and out of range of Tudor's archers.

'They've stopped loosing arrows at us,' Richard announced as he eventually came out from beneath the saddle at the back of the boat. He grabbed Francis' arm and tried to haul him out of the water. Francis winced as he struggled to haul himself over the gunwale.

'Are we out of range now?' Richard asked as Francis finally tumbled over the side, coughing and spluttering before slumping into a seating position against the strakes of the boat.

He stared through the driving rain at the men on the ridge.

'No, we'd still be in range if it was a dry day. Fortunately for us the rain has ruined their bowstrings so that they can't get the range or accuracy. It seems they either haven't remembered to bring spare ones or they have already used them. Thank God for this rain!'

He lay back in the boat and suddenly clutched his left shoulder as a bolt of pain shot through it.

'What's wrong?' Richard asked as he saw Francis grimace.

'It's nothing much. Just a bit painful where that sword thumped into me. Lucky it wasn't the blade end.'

He let out a chuckle as the boat, caught by the faster flowing water, was washed out of the estuary into the open sea.

22

Sixty men wearing white hoods, the livery of Sir John Savage, marched across Culham Bridge in the dead of night. They carried blazing torches to light their way and were armed with swords, halberds, maces, axes, knives and cudgels. Savage was a veteran soldier who had commanded the left wing of King Henry's army when he had defeated King Richard, and he was in no mood to be outwitted by two Yorkist sympathisers who stirred up trouble and then retreated to an abbey to claim sanctuary when they failed in their quest. He would put an end to this matter once and for all.

The white-hooded men followed Sir John Savage along a well-trodden path which ran parallel with the banks of the Thames, past ancient poplar and willow trees until it diverged from the river towards the stone walls marking the abbey's boundary. Savage ignored the bell on the gatehouse and pushed open its gate, walking beneath the low archway and right up to the abbey's main entrance. He relentlessly pounded on the thick oak panels of the door with his fist. Within minutes a great cacophony of sound and confusion ensued within the building. Candles were lit and feet scampered about on the stone-flagged floor of the abbey until eventually the door partially opened and a bleary-eyed monk stood there, peering through the gap with a candle in his hand and a gaggle of fellow monks peering over his shoulder.

'What do you want at this hour? It had better be something important,' the tonsured monk bemoaned.

'I have come from the king to take Sir Humphrey and Thomas Stafford to face trial for treason,' Savage declared.

'At this hour? Besides, they have been given right of sanctuary,' the monk informed him. 'Who are you anyway?'

The question infuriated Savage who pushed the monk and tried to pull the door fully open to gain entry into the abbey.

The gaggle of monks tried to pull the door shut on the angry knight but this action only infuriated him more and he bellowed loudly as he wrenched the door from their grasp so that it crashed open against the stonework.

'If you wait by the gate outside the abbey walls I will—' the lead monk said feebly before Savage grabbed him by the throat and slammed him up against a wall.

'Where are they?' Savage roared into the terrified monk's face.

'Stop! In God's holy name I beseech you sir to stop,' the abbot pleaded with Savage, as he appeared from the darkness at the end of the nave. 'This is sacred ground and it should not be defiled by such base actions. Whatever you want, we can discuss it like reasonable men.'

'In the name of King Henry, I am here for Sir Humphrey and Thomas Stafford. They are to be tried for treason,' Savage called out in a voice loud enough to be heard throughout the abbey.

'That cannot happen. They have claimed the holy right of sanctuary,' the abbot calmly explained.

Savage let the monk he was holding by the throat go. The man slid down the wall and slumped in a cowering heap on the floor.

'Search the building and find them,' Savage called to his men, ignoring the abbot.

'No! This is sacrilege. You will burn in the eternal fires of Hell's damnation if you do this,' the abbot warned the white-hooded men as they poured into the abbey.

As they searched, the irate abbot moved from man to man personally pleading with them to stop, so as to save their souls from the tortuous flames that awaited them if they persisted, but not one man listened to him. The white-hooded figures forged on, checking the church, cloister, chapter house, infirmary and dormitories until several men emerged back into the nave with the hapless Stafford brothers held at knifepoint.

'This is an outrage!' the abbot exclaimed furiously.

'You are breaking the law,' Humphrey stated bluntly as he was marched towards the abbey doorway.

'The king is the law,' Savage retorted.

'No man is above the law of the Church and God!' the abbot said as he bravely stood between Savage, the Stafford brothers and the open doorway.

Savage walked up to the abbot, placed his hand on the man's chin and with one almighty thrust, launched him up into the air. The abbot landed with a thump on the flagstone floor, knocking the breath clean out of him. The gaggle of monks swarmed around the winded abbot whose eyes bulged as he gasped for breath. Savage walked past them and out of the abbey with his white-hooded followers and the sullen faced Stafford brothers in tow.

'The pope shall hear of this,' one of the monks attending the stricken abbot threatened as the last white-hooded soldier departed the abbey into the darkness of the night.

*

Summer reigned in all its gold and green splendour as crowds lined the banks of the Thames to watch King Henry's triumphal entry into London on a barge from Sheen. He had completed his royal progress to the North, flexing his military muscles and putting down rebellions in Yorkshire and the West Midlands on the way. Hereford, Gloucester and Bristol had welcomed the king like a returning hero and now London too was about to pay its tribute.

The king disembarked at Westminster Bridge where he was welcomed by the mayor, sheriff, aldermen, masters of the guilds and other principal residents bedecked in their finest costumes, clothing and jewels. The mayor carried the mace and the sheriff the rod, as they escorted the king to the Palace of Westminster amid a procession of the friars and churchmen of the city. Henry laughed inwardly at the irony of being escorted by monks and clerics as he knew full well that Abbot Sant of Abingdon, under whose jurisdiction Culham fell, had written to Pope Innocent VIII to complain about his breaking the rights of sanctuary when he had the Stafford brothers hauled from the church. Henry had sent his own ambassadors to Rome to argue his case but had no qualms about putting the Staffords on trial while he awaited the papal decision.

Such matters aside, Henry basked in the adulation he received on the short procession from Westminster Bridge to the royal palace. One roughly made banner waved above the heads of the crowd even portrayed a red and white rose symbolising the union of the two great houses of Lancaster and York through his marriage to Elizabeth of York. It reminded Henry that he was about to see his wife again and pleased him greatly. He wondered how much her belly had swollen since he last saw her, and how she would fare with the task of carrying his firstborn child and heir. But first he had more important matters to attend to; he must meet with William Parron.

Once inside the Palace of Westminster he dismissed the Yeomen of the Guard who had escorted him in the procession from the river, and sent a servant to summon Master Parron. He went to his royal apartment and seated himself on a plush velvet window seat, staring out across the Thames as he waited. As he watched the ships and boats sail up and down the great river and the people returning to their daily business, there was a knock upon his door. It was too soon to be his astrologer.

'Yes?' he called, suddenly wishing he had not dismissed the guard.

The door opened and Jasper Tudor's sun-browned, white-bearded face appeared.

'Uncle, come in,' Henry beckoned.

Jasper, wearing a magnificent blue, fur-lined coat with yellow satin trim, stood beside the king and removed his hat.

'Do you have good tidings for me, Uncle?' Henry asked.

'Unfortunately not, Your Grace.' Jasper looked downcast. 'I'm afraid that Lovell and the boy escaped. Their boat has been discovered near Fleetwood on the Lancashire coast. My informants tell me that they tried to find a ship that would take them to Ireland but were not successful. Even the Lancashire fishermen turned down Lovell's gold, refusing to make the perilous journey in their small boats. It appears that Lovell and the boy then bought horses and have ridden inland. The latest report I have is that they are hiding out in the fens around Ely. I have dispatched men and raised the reward to five hundred marks for their capture, dead or alive.'

'It is but a trifle,' Henry remarked casually. 'Thanks to you, Jasper, the rebellions are ended. Humphrey Stafford and his brother are to be tried for treason and no doubt Lovell will soon be joining them. I will make an example of the ringleaders and offer clemency to all others. It is a policy that has served me well and brought the populace over to my side. All is good, except...'

Henry stood and faced his uncle, his tone becoming more serious. 'There are a few diehards in the north; men such as Sir Thomas Broughton and Sir John Huddleston, who would seek to place a crown on the Earl of Warwick's head. They hide behind the jurisdiction of the Duchy of Lancaster but I am about to end that and bring them to heel. I will issue a proclamation charging them all with grave and treasonable offences against my most royal person and of inciting rebellion, hiding in secret places and ignoring royal commands to attend court. They shall have to present themselves before me within forty days to take an oath of allegiance or be declared traitors and forfeit their lives and their lands. I have had enough of these rebels, Jasper. They will submit to me or I will take an army north and crush them once and for all.'

'They will submit, Your Grace, I have no doubt about that,' Jasper said, smiling. 'But what of Warwick? What do you intend to do with him?'

Henry sat down on the plush velvet window seat again and plucked at his lower lip as he thought for a moment.

'I think it best to have him paraded around London so the people can see that he is my prisoner.'

'You don't think it best to have him smothered in the night or dropped from the Tower walls? You could say he died trying to escape,' Jasper added callously.

'No, that would just lead to rumours and they in turn could incite further rebellion. It is important that the people know that Warwick is both alive and my prisoner, so that they understand he is not with Lovell or Robin of Redesdale or any other would-be Yorkist kingmaker. It is decided, I will have him paraded through the streets of London.'

Another knock on the door of the royal apartment prompted Jasper to bow and take his leave.

'Before you go,' the king said to him, 'please check that my wife is alright and inform her that I will visit her in her apartment shortly.'

'Of course, Your Grace,' Jasper replied as he opened the door and nodded to signal to William Parron that he had finished his business with the king, so the astrologer may enter.

Parron swept into the room with an extravagant low bow which he maintained for far too long as Jasper shut the door behind him.

'Ah, Majesty, it is good to see you again,' he said, finally rising upright.

Henry couldn't help but like the man for all his dramatic unsubtlety.

'Your prophesy came true, Master Parron. You told me the bear shall remain in chains and all of my enemies would soon die.'

'Of course, Majesty, the stars are never wrong. They just need someone who can read them correctly,' the Piacenzan astrologer said, arrogantly gesturing at himself.

Henry admitted that Parron had reason to be so cocksure.

'Warwick is indeed still in chains and I have put down two rebellions during my progress to the north. All of my enemies have either been killed, captured or are about to submit to me and take an oath of allegiance.'

Parron nodded in smug self-satisfaction.

'All enemies except one,' Henry added.

The smugness instantly dropped from Parron's face leaving him with a look of consternation.

'I want to know what the stars foretell about the traitor Francis Lovell.'

'Majesty, in anticipation of your arrival I have already divined what the stars tell of the future of the realm, and it is good, neigh it is great!' Parron declared with a flamboyant sweep of his arms. 'The birth of your son in the autumn will herald a new era of peace. The few who dissent shall be cast over the seas where they will fester in hiding. A golden age shall ensue in which you will make England a rich and most powerful nation and the envy of all Europe. Your daughters will marry into the royal houses of Spain, France and Scotland, and beget a dynasty of kings who will all look up to Your Most Serene and Wise Highness as their founder, and your son Arthur will one day be as great as his namesake: a most wise and brave king who will lead his people on a crusade against the Turk. As for this Francis Lovell, he is not important enough to be written into the stars. He is a no-one, a non-entity, and certainly not worthy of Your Majesty's attention.'

Henry smiled at that and hoped that William Parron was right.

23

he Duke of Suffolk refused to help directly but still turned a blind eye to his wife's predilection for the Yorkist outlaw, Lovell. The Countess of Suffolk, Elizabeth de la Pole, was sister to the former kings Richard III and Edward IV. She was still a Plantagenet through and through and would just as soon take in and feed a Yorkist rebel as a stray cat, he thought. The wily old duke was not prepared to get involved in such politics. He knew the danger of it as his own father had been Henry VI's key advisor forty years ago, but finding himself in the middle of the power struggle between Lancaster and York, he had been attainted by parliament and sent into exile abroad, only for his ship to be intercepted mid-channel and the ex-duke beheaded. The story Duke John heard about his father was that the execution had taken place with an old rusted sword and it had taken six blows to remove his father's head, which was then left on a stake facing out to sea on Dover beach. No, he was better off not being involved with such politics or intrigue. If the king's men came calling, he would claim to be ignorant, blame it on his foolish wife, and promise to keep her on a tighter rein in future. He decided to leave his estates in East Anglia and go to his London townhouse for a week or two, where he would be publicly seen, and his hands and his conscience could be clear of the matter.

As soon as the duke and his entourage had set off for London, Elizabeth sent her maidservant to the barn to fetch Lovell out of hiding. She waited inside the house until the maidservant finally returned with a dishevelled Lord Lovell in tow.

'Francis!' she exclaimed as she hugged him tightly, noticing how much thinner he'd become since last time she'd seen him. 'It's been years and you look so thin!'

'It has been years, my lady, and I have been too busy trying to put a Yorkist king back on the throne to think about eating.'

Elizabeth chuckled at that. 'Then you shall eat now.'

She called the maid and gave her instructions.

'Sarah, prepare food for Lord Lovell and his servant.'

'Ah! Elizabeth, this is not my servant,' Francis said apologetically, bringing the boy out from behind him as the maid scurried away to complete her errand. 'I'm sorry, I should have introduced you properly. This is your nephew, Richard Plantagenet.'

Elizabeth stared wide eyed at the boy then unexpectedly grabbed him and hugged him tight. Then she released Richard from her tight embrace and held him by the shoulders as she looked him up and down.

'You are my brother Richard's son?'

'Yes,' Richard confirmed.

'I can see my brother in you. You have his eyes, and his look of quick-wittedness about you. You are a handsome lad, Richard. How old are you, sixteen, seventeen?'

'Seventeen, nearly eighteen,' he replied.

'You are older than John of Gloucester!' Elizabeth stated in surprise before suddenly turning to Francis. 'He does know about the others?' she checked.

'He knows,' Francis replied.

'And you know that sweet Katherine died last month too?'

'I'm sorry, I didn't know that. I would have liked to meet her,' Richard said with regret as he felt tears well up unexpectedly in his eyes. He tried to wipe them away casually without anyone noticing.

'Oh, I am sorry to break the news to you in such an unexpected way. I'm so sorry. She died in childbirth, the baby too. It is so sad. I'm truly very sorry, Richard,' Elizabeth said as she hugged him tight once more.

'What of my half-brother John?'

Elizabeth looked at Francis who just shrugged.

'We have been on the run or in hiding,' he told her. 'We have heard very little news of the outside world.'

'John was removed from his position as Captain of Calais soon after your father died,' Elizabeth explained to her nephew. 'Henry Tudor had him taken to the Tower in London where, as far as I know, he's still held.'

'Could we try to free him?' Richard asked Francis optimistically.

Francis let out a little laugh.

'History has shown that it is impossible to free anyone from the Tower without an army or an angry mob at your back, and we have neither.'

'So, what are we going to do?' Richard asked in frustration.

'We're going to enjoy the hospitality of your aunt and then we're going to board a ship to Flanders where another aunt of yours, Margaret, is the Dowager Duchess of Burgundy. With her help we'll raise an army and come back to finish the job we've started.

'Warwick or Lincoln?' Elizabeth asked him suddenly.

'What?' Francis replied, rather taken aback by her question.

'Who do you intend to make king, Warwick or my son?' Elizabeth calmly asked. 'Francis you were my brother's best friend and you've always been a loyal servant to him and the House of York. I have no doubt that whoever you intend to put on the throne it will be the right choice and you will have my support if it means ridding the country of Henry Tudor, but if you mean to put my son on the throne then I have a right to know.'

'Yes, my lady you do,' Francis agreed, 'but if truth be known I am not sure. The Earl of Warwick is held prisoner in the Tower and your son shows no inclination to take the throne even if it is handed to him.'

'Don't be so sure of that!' Elizabeth said knowingly. 'There are plans afoot that I haven't been made privy to, but do not be too hasty in your choices, Francis Lovell. Speak to my son and to Margaret in Burgundy, and they will tell you all you need to know. I will happily play messenger between you, as I already am between them.'

'What plans are afoot?' Francis pressed her.

'Now, didn't I just say that I'm not privy to them?'

'But you know something is happening so please tell me, what is it?'

'It is a plan that you'll have to speak to my son and sister about! Now stop pestering me about something I have already told you to speak to them about. I'll get you parchment and ink if you want to draft either of them a letter.'

Francis let out a sigh of exasperation knowing that he was beaten.

Richard liked his Aunt Elizabeth. She was affable and maternal but she had a steely core stronger than any woman, or indeed man, that he had ever known. He couldn't imagine anyone else getting away with speaking to Lord Lovell like that.

'I gather you've not heard about Sir Humphrey Stafford?' Elizabeth enquired.

'I know that he and Thomas were dragged at sword-point from Culham Abbey,' Francis told her.

'And the trial?'

'No, what happened?'

'Humphrey was found guilty and suffered a horrible death. He was taken to Tyburn and hanged, but taken down while still alive and then they castrated the poor man and disembowelled him. His tarred head stands on a pole on London Bridge and his quartered body has been sent to York, Worcester, Warwick and Hereford to be displayed.'

'A traitor's death. It is what awaits me if Tudor ever catches me,' Francis exclaimed.

Richard looked aghast.

'Don't worry, I have no plans for that to ever happen,' Francis grinned at him.

'Did Thomas suffer the same fate?' Francis asked as an afterthought.

'No, he was pardoned as it was decided that he was misled by his elder brother. He lost his estates though. A rather lucky escape if you ask me.'

'Lucky indeed!' Francis mused as the maid returned with food.

'Enough of such grizzly matters,' Elizabeth urged. 'Eat, get cleaned up, and then you can get some rest.'

'How long before we can find passage to Flanders?' Francis asked as he chewed on some cold roast chicken.

'There will be a ship in a week or so, so take the time to rest and hatch your plans.' Elizabeth cast Richard a mischievous smile then added, 'I will get you that parchment and ink. You'll be wanting to draft a few letters before you leave, I'm sure.'

*

King Henry entered the privy chamber at Sheen Palace where his counsellors had been urgently summoned. They stood and bowed as he entered and took his seat at the head of the great table. Bedford, Oxford, Stanley, Northumberland, Lincoln, Morton, Foxe, and other confidants of the king were in attendance.

Lincoln observed that the king had a look of simmering anger about him that matched his crimson and black doublet. Henry bid the lords to take their seats, which they did in silence. All eyes were on the king as they waited to find out why they had been summoned.

'The birth and baptism of my son and heir, Prince Arthur, heralds the dawning of a new age of peace, King Henry declared. 'The wars of the last thirty years are behind us. All rebellions against my most royal person have been crushed and the rebels have either been attainted by parliament, received traitors' deaths – their heads displayed for all to see, or have fled like scared rabbits. And yet my lords, I have grave news.' The latent anger now became apparent in King Henry's rising voice.

'Some malcontents are not satisfied that the realm is finally at peace, that the Houses of Lancaster and York are finally united, and that I have a son and heir to continue the Tudor bloodline into the next generation. No!' Henry shouted as he hammered his fist down on the table.

'Now I am informed of a web of conspiracies against me. I hear murmurs of risings in my counties of Devon and Cornwall, of Robert Stillington, Bishop of Bath and Wells, colluding with others to stir up a rebellion against me, and that my wife's own mother has been speaking with these traitors!'

An astonished gasp from several lords was audible in the chamber, which Henry ignored as he carried on talking.

'I have therefore issued a writ for the arrest of knights, Henry Bodrugan and John Beaumont for inciting rebellion in Devon and Cornwall, and tasked Sir Richard Edgecombe, Sherriff of Devon, with apprehending them. Robert Stillington has already fled and taken up hiding in Oxford, claiming benefit of clergy and the university's munificence to protect him. I have written to the chancellor of the university demanding that they release Stillington unto my care and authority.

'Also, my agents have discovered a plot in the north of my realm. Men disguised as merchants were in Hull to meet with Sir Thomas Mauleverer. They then moved on to York to meet with the Prior of Tynemouth Abbey. My agents inform me that these men have bags of gold and silver coin upon their persons; far too much for simple merchants.'

The king's description hit Lincoln like a hammer blow. These merchants were his men sent north to garner support for an uprising. Was he about to be implicated in the plot? Was he about to be arrested? Lincoln sat implacably, listening to the king as a dutiful counsellor should, yet inwardly he felt sick, his stomach churned, and his hands trembled.

'Of course, I have had Mauleverer and the prior questioned but so far they have given no useful information. Unfortunately, the merchants seem to have disappeared but I have men searching for them as we speak.'

King Henry glared at his herald-recorder to ensure that all the facts were being written down. The man scribbled his notes, trying to ensure he missed nothing of importance, while unaware that the king's gaze was upon him. Henry was prepared to wait until the herald finished writing before he continued. In the short silence he cast his gaze across the gathered lords and came to rest his eyes on the Earl of Lincoln, who gave him a half-smile. Henry reflected on how Lincoln, once King Richard's heir-presumptive, had not joined the Yorkshire rebellion as half-expected or partaken in any of the sedition or conspiracies that threatened his grip on the realm. Strangely enough, Henry thought to himself, Lincoln and Northumberland, two of King Richard's right-hand men, were now rocks that supported his regime.

Lincoln felt beads of perspiration form on his forehead as he saw the king stare at him and he couldn't help but avert his gaze. He hoped this gesture didn't make him look suspicious.

The herald looked up and Henry continued, speaking slowly so that the herald could write down verbatim every word that followed.

'Regarding my wife's mother, the Dowager Queen Elizabeth, née Woodville, widow of King Edward IV: I propose that she forfeit all of her estates, lands and possessions in favour of her daughter Elizabeth, and retire to the convent at Bermondsey, beside the Thames, where the good sisters will look after her. In return I will grant her an annuity of 400 marks. I ask for my learned counsellors' approval on this matter.'

The lords temporal and spiritual roared their approval. Many had a personal grudge against the king's mother-in-law for previous slights, and others hated her because she had risen from common stock to become the most powerful woman in the land, with her marriage in secret to King Edward IV. That she had abused her power did not ingratiate her to any of the lords assembled there that day.

'That is not all, my lords. There is a pretender to my throne; a boy, the son of an Oxford baker or some such tradesman, who claims to be the Earl of Warwick.'

A spontaneous bout of laughter rippled through the chamber.

'It is no laughing matter!' Henry admonished his counsellors. 'This imposter has gone to Ireland where the lords of the Pale are in collusion with the exiled traitor Lovell, and together they support this boy posing as the Earl of Warwick, even though I have the real earl in my care in the Tower!'

'Forgive me, Your Grace,' Lord Stanley said, 'but couldn't you just bring out the real earl and exhibit him to the populace to expose this boy in Ireland for the imposter that he is?'

'That, my lord Derby, is exactly what I have already decided to do,' the king declared. 'The boy Warwick is to be paraded through the streets of London and shown to the congregation of St Paul's. Bishop Morton, the Earl of Lincoln, the Lord Mayor, and other worthy and honest men who know him can publicly verify that he is the real earl.'

Morton and Lincoln both nodded their assent. Lincoln wiped away a trickle of sweat that ran into his right eye. He glanced upwards hoping that the king was not staring at him.

'I have also decided that it is wise for me to issue a proclamation declaring a general pardon to all former rebels and supporters of the Yorkist cause provided that they no longer conspire, spread sedition or ever take up arms against me again. Of course, there will be some exclusions from this pardon such as

Francis Lovell and a few diehard Yorkists who have fled abroad and continue to conspire against me. What do you, my counsellors, think of this?'

Shouts of, 'Hear him, hear him,' echoed around the chamber as the king's counsellors gave him their support. Lincoln joined in with the show of support for the king but thought to himself that it was only a matter of time before King Henry discovered that he was linked to the conspiracies that were being unearthed. When this Privy Council was over, he decided, he would depart, as far as anyone else was concerned, back to his estates in East Anglia but would at the very first opportunity board a ship to Flanders to join his Aunt Margaret and the Yorkist exiles with whom he'd been plotting.

*

The journey to Flanders was Richard's first time on a ship and it was the most exhilarating thing that he had ever experienced. He loved the smell of the sea that permeated his nostrils and the sense of pure freedom as he leaned over the side watching the ship cut through the white-crested waves. Francis laughed at him when he said that it was like taming and riding a giant sea creature. Francis had never seen anyone so excited by a sea journey. Apart from hardened sailors, most men he knew abhorred the sea and were frightened of it. He had seen men turn green and deathly white on board ships before, and seen men spew their guts up for days on end, until there was nothing left in them, and even then they would retch endlessly with the ship's movement and the churning of the waves. But not Richard. The boy was genuinely disappointed when they arrived in Antwerp and the sea leg of their journey was finally over.

From the busy port at Antwerp, it was less than a half day's ride to Mechelen and the court of Richard's aunt, the Dowager Duchess of Burgundy. King Richard's sister was a powerful and, from what Francis told him, a formidable woman. She had been married to the Duke of Burgundy, Charles the Bold, to seal an alliance between the English and Burgundians against the French. Duke Charles died fighting at the battle of Nancy in 1477 and his seven-year-old grandson was now the official ruler of Burgundy, although Duchess Margaret's stepson, Maximilian was regent. Margaret and Maximilian, King of the Romans, were useful and wealthy allies who could help fund an army and a fleet if they were ever going to sail back to England to challenge Henry Tudor, Lovell explained to Richard.

Richard expected Margaret to be a scary, sour-faced woman from what Francis had said of her, but when they arrived in Mechelen the woman who greeted them was very much like her older sister Elizabeth, Duchess of Suffolk. She wore a dress of dark plum-coloured velvet with ermine cuffs, and her hair was tied back under a very formal black, diamond-shaped headdress, lined with pearls. However, there was nothing formal about her. She was jovial and chatty, greeting them warmly, hugging both Francis and Richard, and demanding to know news of England and her family. Francis introduced Margaret to her nephew but to his surprise she already knew all about him and was expecting their arrival. Her sister Elizabeth, he discovered, had sent a messenger ahead of them.

After they had dined, attention turned to the important matter of ousting Henry Tudor and restoring the York line to the throne of England.

'It is difficult to know what to do,' Francis bemoaned when the question of replacing Tudor was raised. 'Warwick is a prisoner in the Tower and Lincoln has no interest in the matter.'

Margaret laughed. 'Oh Francis, you have been removed from court politics far too long. I will let you into a little secret.'

Richard recognised then the mischievous glint in her eye that he had seen in his Aunt Elizabeth.

'I have been in correspondence with my nephew, the Earl of Lincoln, for a long time now and I can tell you that he wants to see the end of Henry Tudor as much as any of us. He has been the spider in the centre of a web of intrigue these past months and he is the eyes and ears at the heart of Tudor's court. He is a member of the Privy Council and close to the king. The usurper trusts and confides in him despite knowing that King Richard named him as his heir.'

'What is this web of intrigue you speak of?' Francis asked.

Margaret's eyes sparkled and she gushed with enthusiasm as she told Francis and Richard the story.

'A priest from Oxford came to me almost a year ago and tried to convince me that a boy with him was the Earl of Warwick. He wanted payment for rescuing the boy! I would have had him thrown out on his ear except that the boy does bear a striking resemblance to my brother George when he was younger. Looks aside, the priest had clearly trained and educated the boy to try to pass off this deception but it was obvious that the boy knew nothing of courtly life. However, it gave me an idea. I have had the boy educated and trained here at Mechelen so that he is more like Earl Warwick than Earl Warwick himself!'

'To what purpose, Aunt?' Richard asked.

Margaret smiled at hearing the word Aunt and lovingly

stroked Richard's hair, which only made him flush with embarrassment.

'Well, dear nephew,' she replied as the rosy flush spread across Richard's cheeks, 'if we have *our* Warwick crowned king, we can rally the support of the lords who have supported the House of York in the past and I believe they, and the general populace, would flock to our side if this newly crowned King Edward landed in England to claim his throne. He is after all the last legitimate Plantagenet of the male line.'

'This is madness!' Lovell exclaimed.

'No Francis, it is already happening. My nephew John, Lincoln as you prefer to call him, has already garnered support across the land if we can get Edward crowned and land with an army at his back.'

Francis rubbed at his eyes and forehead, still trying to come to terms with what Margaret was proposing.

'This raises so many questions,' he said.

'Then ask them!' Margaret replied.

'Alright, where do you propose to have this boy crowned?'

'At Christchurch Cathedral in Dublin. He is already in Ireland with the priest, and Gerald Fitzgerald and the Irish lords and bishops have already accepted him as Edward Earl of Warwick. Fitzgerald has promised four and a half thousand Irish troops and my stepson, Maximilian, will fund two thousand more Swabian Landsknechts.'

'What if you win?'

Margaret looked confused by the question. 'What do you mean?' she asked.

'I mean, what happens if you win? Do you actually put this boy with no royal blood on the throne? Doesn't this make a mockery of all we stand for?'

'No! No, it doesn't,' Margaret replied, getting visibly angry with Francis. 'If we win, the real Earl Warwick will be released to take his place as king and the boy will come to live here in Mechelen, with a suitable annuity that will see him and the priest more than comfortable for the rest of their lives. That has already been agreed with the boy and priest.'

'And what if Henry has the real earl already in his captivity executed?' Francis continued to question.

'He can't, can he? He will have to display the real earl and claim that our earl is an imposter.'

'Which is true, so what happens when the identity of the real earl is verified?' Francis asked.

'By whom?' Margaret asked him before answering her own question. 'He has been locked away in the Tower for nearly two years and has rarely been out of confinement for two years before that. He is still only eleven or twelve at most. Most of the men who did know him as a seven or eight-year-old in Edward or Richard's reign are now perished. So who can truly verify that he is Warwick, and would they be believed anyway if another Warwick lands with an army at his back to claim the throne? Besides, I have people in London to spread rumours and counter rumours that the boy Tudor has in captivity is not the real earl.'

Francis laughed at that. Against his better judgement, he started to see sense in Margaret's plan. He knew it was risky and it seemed so complicated that there must be a flaw in there somewhere, but the problem was that he wanted it to happen so badly that he was beginning to be won over.

'Oh, this is all so confusing,' he cried. 'Why couldn't you just put Lincoln forward as the challenger to Henry Tudor if he is so willing?'

'Because the name de la Pole, a family that a hundred years ago were just wool merchants, does not carry the same weight and ability to rally men as the name Plantagenet. No matter that he was named heir by King Richard, or how unpopular Henry Tudor is becoming with his endless taxes and fines, men will follow Edward Plantagenet over John de la Pole every day of the week.'

Francis could not argue with that logic.

'It seems to me, Margaret, that you are the spider at the centre of this web of intrigue rather than the Earl of Lincoln,' Francis chided her.

Margaret smiled, pleased at the thought.

ing Henry was angry to the core. The Earl of Lincoln had left the Privy Council at Sheen, ostensibly to return to his estates in Suffolk. Instead, he had boarded a ship and fled to Flanders to the court of the Dowager Duchess of Burgundy and the other Yorkist rebels. Henry had found out, days later, of Lincoln's involvement in sending men posing as merchants to the north of England to garner support for a rebellion against him. Lincoln had funded these men with vast amounts of money to pay supporters to raise troops for the Yorkist cause. Henry's agents in Ireland also suggested that Lincoln was involved in the conspiracy with the boy who was impersonating the Earl of Warwick in Dublin. As more facts emerged about the boy, Henry sent his most trusted herald to interview the imposter in front of the Irish lords to discredit him. Unfortunately, the boy was able to answer every question posed and pass every test that the herald gave him, only strengthening his claim in the eyes of the lords of the Pale. Oh what a fool he'd been, Henry lamented, finally realising how organised Lincoln and the rebels were. Even parading the real earl in front of the people of London, and to the congregation and dignitaries gathered in St Paul's Cathedral had backfired, as it just fuelled rumours that the boy in Henry's captivity was an imposter.

After Lincoln's escape, Henry made a royal progress to East Anglia to shore up support in the counties where Lincoln held sway, and to monitor the Duke of Suffolk to ensure that he was not inclined to go over to his son Lincoln and the other rebels. While in East Anglia Henry ensured that men were recruited from nearby towns to man the coastlines of Norfolk, Suffolk and Essex, that beacons and fortifications were repaired, and ships built and victualled in readiness for an invasion of his eastern counties. A Yorkist-fuelled storm was coming but he did not know when or exactly where. The uncertainty was fraying his nerves and wearing him down. He suspected many of his lords of colluding with the rebels but despite his agents being spread far and wide, he had no proof to indict any of them. Nevertheless, when the Marquess of Dorset brought troops to East Anglia to join him, Henry had him arrested. Many of Henry's followers began to suspect that the tension of sitting on a throne coveted by others was too much for him and that his mind was beginning to unravel.

'If the Marquess of Dorset was as loyal as he claimed, then he would not object to being imprisoned for the duration of the rebellion,' Henry declared.

Thomas Grey, Marquess of Dorset, may be his brother-in-law, but after all, Henry had just deprived his mother, Elizabeth Woodville, of all her lands and possessions and sent her off to the convent at Bermondsey. It was getting harder and harder to know who to trust but Henry was taking no chances.

Once he was satisfied that East Anglia was prepared to face an invasion, Henry rode to Walsingham where he gave devotion at the ancient shrine of Our Lady of Walsingham, as had many kings before him. He prayed for victory in the forthcoming battle but also used the opportunity to show his men how pious a king he really was. His devotions over, Henry led his heavily armed entourage towards the Midlands, rapidly passing through Cambridge, Huntingdon and Northampton, until, on the eve of St George's Day he arrived in Coventry.

Mayor Thomas Bagott, John Hales the Bishop of Coventry, and the city's aldermen and Masters of the Guilds welcomed the king at the city gate and escorted him through the city walls, which were second in size and splendour only to those of London. People cheered as the procession wound its way along cobbled streets to St Mary's Priory in the centre of the city, but Henry was in no mood to receive their adulation. He quickly dismounted his horse at the half-timbered Guildhall of St Mary's. He walked into the courtyard, turning right to climb the staircase into the magnificent hall with its ornate oak-panelled ceiling with gilt and painted angels looking down on the earthly host.

Henry stood at the far end of the well-lit hall looking out of a window at the nearby Priory of St Mary, as the Dukes of Bedford and Suffolk, the Earl of Oxford, Viscount Lisle, and a host of lords and bishops crowded into the hall to await his instructions, along with the heralds who would record everything.

'My lords, we must ready ourselves for an invasion by the rebel Lovell and the former Earl Lincoln, who I shall have attainted by parliament as soon as this affair is over. The rebels may decide to attack from East Anglia, which I think is most probable, or they may divide their armies, which is why I have brought us to this central place so that we may quickly sally forth to defeat them, wherever they choose to land.

'Before I discuss with my lords temporal, the preparations for battle, I exhort my lords spiritual; the Archbishop of Canterbury, the Bishops of Winchester, Lincoln, Exeter, Ely, and Worcester, and the Prior of St Mary's here in this fair city, to go forth to declare the papal dispensations for my marriage from the pulpit and to curse with holy book, bell and candle, the rebels that threaten our beloved kingdom.'

*

Richard was now eighteen and had shot up in height and bulked out with muscle since he had left England for Mechelen three months earlier, especially since he had been training with Francis every day with sword, mace and axe. The sword was his preferred weapon. Francis had taught him how to wield and fight with it, and he had learnt quickly. He was not as skilful as knights who had been trained to be warriors since they were very young boys, but he was certainly proficient with the weapon. He was also not afraid to work hard, practising his sword strokes for hours on end, and challenging local squires to practice fights. Win or lose he would carry on until he was sweat-stained and exhausted.

Lincoln arrived in Mechelen two months after Francis and Richard did. John de la Pole had a very formal side to him and Richard did not warm to him as quickly as he had to Francis or to Lincoln's mother and aunt. Lincoln was pleasant enough but expected Richard to address him as 'my lord' even though Richard was his cousin and was permitted to call Viscount Lovell by his first name. Lincoln also chose to speak privately with Francis and his Aunt Margaret about their plans to defeat Henry Tudor, excluding Richard from these meetings. Richard decided to keep out of his way and chose instead to practice with the sword his Aunt Margaret had given him.

One afternoon as he swung and parried, going through the pattern of movements that had become a ritual, Richard noticed his Aunt Margaret standing looking forlornly at him. It was rare that she would come down to the practice yard and even rarer that she would look so sad. Behind her stood Francis and Lord Lincoln.

'I'm sorry Richard,' Margaret uttered as she approached him.

'Sorry for what?' Richard asked as he sheathed his sword.

'A messenger has brought sad news from London. Your brother John has died in the Tower, deprived of food by that bastard Tudor.'

Richard was surprised by the sudden vehemence in his aunt's voice.

She hugged him tightly and as she let go, she saw a tear run down Richard's cheek.

'I swear, Aunt, I will make him pay for this,' Richard promised.

'We will all make him pay,' Lincoln added.

Richard ignored him and continued to address his aunt. 'I never got to meet my sister or either of my brothers. Of my father's four children I am the only one left.'

'Dear God!' Lincoln loudly exclaimed.

The others turned to stare at him.

'It makes sense now,' he said.

'What does? What on earth are you babbling about?' Margaret asked her nephew.

Lincoln had the look of someone who had been told a prized secret.

'Well?' Margaret demanded.

'As we left Leicester on our way to fight Tudor, an old woman the king had stopped to speak to shouted after him. She said, "Your garden has been blessed with four white roses. Three survive, but two not much longer." I have never seen King Richard looked so stunned. I thought he was going to fall off of his horse but now I understand why. You are the fourth white rose. You are the remaining child.'

'And one we must protect,' Margaret declared as she looked scathingly at Lincoln.

'I'm sorry Richard, I meant no harm,' Lincoln said, placing a hand on his cousin's shoulder in a show of solidarity. 'You are as much a Plantagenet as any of my cousins and I am sorry for the way I have spoken to you since I arrived in Mechelen.'

Richard nodded his thanks and wiped a tear from his cheek.

'As you say, we will all make Tudor pay.'

Within a few days the time came to leave Mechelen and, although sad to leave his aunt behind, Richard relished the thought of being on a ship again. The Dowager Duchess gave him a parting gift the day before he left; a suit of armour especially made for him. A squire helped Richard put the armour on and he then practiced with his sword to see if the armour slowed him down, and he did not take it off until it was time to sleep. The next day, after a tearful farewell, Richard rode with Francis and Lincoln to Antwerp where a fleet was assembled, ready to take them to Ireland.

Richard marvelled at the Landsknechts on board in their colourful striped and slashed uniforms and floppy feathered hats. They were professional soldiers recruited in the southern German region of Swabia, as a standing army by Maximilian King of the Romans. He sent two thousand of them to join the expedition with their captain, a renowned soldier named Martin Schwartz. Richard was amused by their unusual accent and their strangely odd habit of wearing hose of different colours and patterns on each leg, but after a while the asymmetry began to grate on his senses. He wondered if they had sumptuary laws in their country that regulated the style of clothing, and the colour and material permitted to be worn by each level of society to maintain the distinction between them. He thought not, but when he asked, Francis confirmed that these soldiers were exempt from their country's sumptuary laws because they were regarded as some of the best organised and most feared soldiers in Europe. They were certainly the most colourfully flamboyant soldiers he had ever seen but he did wonder whether the enemy would view them as fearsome or just a laughing stock. They did, however, provide some light relief on an otherwise uneventful journey.

The skies were blue and the weather fair when they landed in Dublin at the beginning of May. Gerald Fitzgerald, Earl of Kildare and Lord Deputy of Ireland, welcomed Lords Lovell and Lincoln like they were old friends. The great black-bearded Irishman also gripped the hand of Martin Schwartz and for a moment they squeezed the life out of each other's hands trying to prove who was the toughest. Neither flinched and Richard feared that a brawl might ensue between the two men, so fierce were they.

'So, it is true,' Fitzgerald suddenly bellowed. 'You Landsknecht are as tough as Waterford whores and as strong as a soldier's fart in a laced up tent.'

Fitzgerald and the English and Irishmen around him burst into laughter but Schwartz was confused by the Irish earl's jape and looked to Lincoln and Lovell with a furrowed brow for some sort of explanation. Fitzgerald released his grip on the Landsknecht officer's hand and Francis patted the German on the back.

'Never mind, Martin. Just accept it as a compliment,' he advised Schwartz.

Schwartz gave out a half-hearted, belated laugh.

Just a few weeks later, on Ascension Day, Gerald Fitzgerald and his good friend Martin Schwartz proudly stood side by side amid the convocation of Christ Church Cathedral in Dublin. Around them were Lords Lincoln and Lovell, Thomas Fitzgerald of Laccagh who was the Earl of Kildare's brother and Lord Chancellor of Ireland, the mayor of Dublin, and a great number of English and Irish lords, knights, bishops and priors, come to watch the coronation of King Edward VI.

The Earl of Warwick's imposter was led in solemn procession along the aisle, preceded by the sword of state, to sit regally upon a chair of sumptuous purple silk and gilt wood before the altar. A sermon was preached by John Payne, Bishop of Meath, wherein Warwick's title to the crown was read out. A fully armoured knight on horseback rode into the cathedral and challenged anyone who doubted the right of the Earl of Warwick to be crowned king here in Dublin this day, to speak up and take him on in combat. Richard stared around the cathedral at the assembled lords, knights and colourful Landsknecht officers, expecting someone to speak out and accept the mounted knight's challenge. No one did, or at least no one dared to challenge the boy's right to be king if it meant fighting his champion.

After a long and solemn ceremony in which prayers were said, hymns sung, and the head of Earl Warwick anointed with holy oil, Walter Fitzsimons, Archbishop of Dublin finally placed a plain gold crown upon the boy's head and named him King Edward VI of England, Ireland and France, to huge acclaim from all gathered there. The new king was led outside by Archbishop Fitzsimons between a guard of honour made up of Lords Lincoln, Lovell, Kildare, his friend Schwartz and other notable English and Irish dignitaries. Once outside, the new king was lifted onto the shoulders of William Darcy, known as Great Darcy of Platten – a giant of an Irishman, who walked head and shoulders above the throng of Dubliners with the boy king held aloft so that they could see him, to the castle where a feast was being held in King Edward's honour.

*

King Henry stopped his conversation with the Duke of Bedford to read through a report just arrived, and urgently brought to him in his castle at Kenilworth. Jasper Tudor sat down while the king perused the report. Thomas Butler, the Irishman who delivered it from his kinsman, the Earl of Ormand, stood patiently before the king. Eventually Henry cast the report down on the table and sighed heavily.

'Kildare supported this? My own Lord Deputy of Ireland supported the crowning of a pretender? A boy of common birth no less!'

'Yes, Your Grace,' Butler confirmed.

He kept his eyes fixed firmly on the oak floorboards as he feared the ire of the Tudor king that he had heard so much about.

'Where did they get the regalia of state; the crown, the orb, the sceptre?' Henry asked.

'I don't know if they did use an orb and sceptre in the ceremony, Your Grace, but I know that they placed on the boy's head a simple gold crown taken from the statue of the Blessed Virgin Mary, kept in a church called by her name, near Dames Gate in the city.'

Henry laughed out loud.

'These Irish would crown an ape if they thought it would bring them power!' he scoffed.

Thomas Butler ignored the slight on his nation and its people.

'All Ireland supports this pretender?'

'No, Your Grace. The Bishop of Armagh was asked to officiate at the coronation but refused and fled to Waterford. The Butlers of Ormand refuse to recognise the pretender, as does the city of Waterford. My kinsman, Mayor John Butler, wrote on behalf of himself and the people of Waterford protesting against crowning the lad. It is in the report, Your Grace.'

Henry looked again at the report lying on the table before him. He picked it up and read to himself the words of Waterford's mayor to the Bishop of Dublin.

It is a great pity that ye are deceived by a false priest,
that this matter began, and that ye this child as a prince received,
a low born boy, a lad, an organ maker's son.

'And how was this message received in Dublin?' the king enquired.

'The Earl of Kildare ignored our pleas. He had the messengers sent from Waterford hung on Hoggen Green, in Dublin. He then held a parliament in the name of Edward VI at Drogheda where they confirmed the rights and titles of the boy king and instated Kildare as the pretender's lieutenant, tutor and protector. Kildare issued patents in the name of this King Edward and arranged to have coins minted bearing the boy's image. This parliament also issued Acts of Attainder against myself and my brother, William Butler. Kildare has seized our lands in the name of this false king.'

'Fear not, for you and your loyal kinsmen will have your lands returned and be well rewarded with further estates once these rebels are beaten,' the king assured Butler.

He then turned to his uncle.

'My lord Bedford, what say you that we take the army to Waterford to join the Earl of Ormond, and from there to Dublin to crush this pretender?'

'Dublin is well fortified but…'

Jasper Tudor looked up as Sir Reginald Bray knocked and entered the room, preventing him from finishing his reply to the king.

'Forgive me, Your Grace, but I have grave and urgent news,' Bray blurted out, clearly out of breath. 'A rebel fleet has landed near Furness in Lancashire with an army seven or eight thousand strong. Lincoln and Lovell are at its head along with the boy who claims your throne.'

'Dear Christ!' King Henry exclaimed as the colour suddenly drained from his face.

25

I t was a warm June day when the Yorkist fleet docked below the castle in the deep-water harbour of Piel Island. Men, armour, weapons, provisions and horses were unloaded and ferried across the short stretch of water to the mainland. Sir Thomas Broughton arrived with a further eight hundred men to join King Edward's army, as the last of the supplies were being loaded onto the horses. Francis was dearly pleased to see his old friend again and he rushed across the damp sand of the beach towards the broad, stocky man.

'You outwitted Tudor's horsemen then!' Thomas stated the obvious as he hugged Francis. 'I knew you would. It's damn good to see you again.'

'You too, Thomas,' Francis said, looking at the men who had come with Broughton to join his army.

There were many faces he recognised: John, Lord Scrope of Bolton, Thomas, Lord Scrope of Masham, Sir Thomas Pilkington, James Harrington, Thomas Harrington, John Broughton, Robert Percy of Knaresborough, Sir Robert Percy of Scotton and others. All loyal men who had supported King Richard and now, as far as they knew, came to support his nephew King Edward.

The newly arrived knights and their retainers all knelt and

lowered their heads in homage to their new king. The boy thanked them for their support and wished them God's good grace in the battle ahead. The English knights rose to their feet and gave their king a rousing cheer which seemed to please him greatly. Then the boy king told them to go about their business and stood happily chatting to Lord Lincoln and Thomas Fitzgerald.

'That's an interesting choice of attire,' Thomas Broughton said to Francis, nodding towards the Landsknechts with their colourful striped and slashed uniforms with large codpieces protruding over their genitals.

'They may look strange but they have a reputation for fighting like Kilkenny cats,' Francis said.

'Kilkenny cats?' Thomas asked inquisitively.

'Oh, just an Irish tale that Earl Kildare told me about two cats from Kilkenny who fought each other so fiercely that at the end of the fight there were only their two tails left.'

'Hmmm,' Broughton said, shrugging and not quite knowing what to make of the story. 'Which one is Earl Kildare?' he asked, looking across at the Irish contingent of knights and unarmoured kerns.'

'He has remained in Ireland to deal with Earl Ormand and his troublesome clan. He's sent his brother Thomas Fitzgerald in his stead,' Francis said, gesturing to the man talking to King Edward and Lincoln.

Lincoln saw Francis and Broughton look in his direction and excused himself from the king's presence.

'Thank you for joining us, Thomas,' Lincoln called as he approached.

He shook Broughton by the hand then spoke to both men.

'Everything is unloaded now so we need to get moving. If we

cross the Pennines and head towards Middleham and then on to York, we could be there in four days. If the men of Yorkshire join us in numbers and York opens its gates to us, we could soon have twelve or thirteen thousand men under my command; and then we could march south and hit Tudor before he knows what's happening.'

Francis noted that Lincoln said 'under *my* command' rather than under the king's command, and he wondered if Broughton had noticed too. Lincoln needed to take care he didn't arouse suspicion that the boy wasn't really who he purported to be.

Thirty minutes later the Yorkist army set off with King Edward leading it across the Lancashire countryside. Riding with him were Lincoln, Thomas Fitzgerald and the priest, Richard Symonds, who had first brought the boy to the attention of Margaret, Dowager Duchess of Burgundy. Behind them were Francis, Richard, Thomas Broughton and the other English knights all mounted on horseback, followed by Martin Schwartz's colourful Landsknechts who marched in neat formation with their eighteen-foot-long, thin wooden pikes with metal tips, held over their shoulder as they walked. Among their number were smaller groups armed either with ten foot long halberds, zweihander – long double-handed swords which they carried over their shoulder, or hackenbüchse, an odd-looking contraption that had a metal tube affixed to a wooden stock, which Martin Schwartz had said could fire a lead shot like a small hand-held cannon.

At the rear of the army which now numbered around seven and a half thousand, were the squires of the English knights, who protected the baggage train, and the Irish kerns: highly mobile troops armoured only in leather jerkins or quilted linen jacks stuffed with flax. They carried short feathered spears, three or four to a man, meant to be launched from a sling to give them greater range, and long handled axes and daggers. Many had long drooping moustaches and an odd hairstyle where the top, sides and rear of their head was shaved to a short stubble, but at the front they had a long fringe that covered their eyes. Many wore cloaks dyed yellow with moss, while half of them did not even wear shoes. This motley collection of warriors looked a very strange sight as they marched their way across the Pennines into Yorkshire.

They travelled via the towns of Middleham, which had been Richard III's royal home and where his only legitimate son, Prince Edward had been born; Masham, the home of Lord Scrope who had joined the army at Piel; and Ripon, where Francis had gathered his forces for the Yorkshire rising; and yet by the time they arrived at York less than five hundred additional men had joined their ranks. It was not the great swell of support that Lincoln had predicted. From Masham Lincoln sent a messenger ahead with a letter for Sir William Todd, Lord Mayor of York, requesting that he open the gates of the city to King Edward and his army. Todd politely declined and Lincoln, infuriated by this, decided to push on to York to force the issue.

King Edward's army halted before Bootham Bar, York's northern gate, from where the twin towers and spires of York Minster could be seen looming above the city walls. York's militia looked down on them from the walls and were no doubt also hidden inside the gate ready to repel any attack. For forty minutes Lord Lincoln tried to negotiate with the Lord Mayor and aldermen of York; thanking them for the city's constant loyalty to the House of York, pleading with them show the city's support for King Edward, nephew of their well-beloved King Richard; assuring them of his, King Edward, and their army's good intentions towards the city. He even pleaded that if the city would not open their gates, then at least allow loyal followers from within the city to come out to join them. All to no avail as the governing hierarchy of York feared the retribution of King Henry, should King Edward's army be defeated. Sir William Todd leaned over the city wall one last time and shouted down to the Earl of Lincoln.

'Myself, the aldermen, and the people of York wish King Edward no harm but we can in no way be seen to support him. Therefore, our decision is final, we will not open the city gates to His Grace.'

Lincoln was livid. He and the six English knights accompanying him turned their steeds and rode back to the army, encamped a short distance away.

'They won't let us in,' he angrily shouted at Francis as he returned. 'Call Schwartz and the others. We need to hold a council of war.'

'John, a scout has returned. There is more bad news,' Francis informed Lincoln. 'King Henry's northern army under the Earl of Northumberland is marching towards York. They are a day away at most.'

'Gather the others and we can discuss our options,' Lincoln said, undeterred.

A tent was hastily erected and Lords Lincoln, Lovell, Scrope of Masham and his relative Lord Scrope of Bolton, Sir Thomas Broughton, Martin Schwartz, and Thomas Fitzgerald all convened inside to talk. The boy king was not made privy to the talks.

'York will not open its gates and Henry Tudor's northern army is bearing down on us,' Lincoln stated quite bluntly. 'They will be here in less than a day.'

'How big is zis northern army?' Schwartz asked in his Swabian accent.

'Maybe five to six thousand, commanded by the Earl of Northumberland,' Lovell confirmed.

'Ve have eight thousand so ve should face zem, ja?'

'We don't want to get dragged into a protracted battle here,' Lincoln said. 'Henry has another army somewhere in the Midlands. If he brings them north, we could get trapped between the two. No, we need another option.'

'What if we forget about York and march south to face Tudor's army instead? If we defeat him then Edward is the only remaining king and it is over,' Thomas Fitzgerald suggested.

'But we would be marching with Northumberland's forces at our back. We would be harried the whole way south and when we get there, we would still be trapped between the two armies,' Lincoln explained.

'So, what choice does that leave us?' Fitzgerald asked.

'I have an idea,' Lovell said as a plan began to formulate in his mind. 'We use a small diversionary force to attack one of the main gates here at York. When Northumberland arrives, that force retreats north taking Northumberland's army after it. Meanwhile our main army will already be marching south.'

'It's an excellent plan, Francis,' Lincoln stated.

'It will have to be the English knights who attack the gates as they're the only ones with enough horses to keep ahead of Northumberland's army. My lords Scrope,' Lincoln said, looking at Masham and Bolton, 'you will both attack Bootham Bar while we take the rest of the army south.'

Both men nodded their consent.

'Excellent!' Lincoln exclaimed. 'Take what provisions you need, but travel light. If Northumberland looks like turning south again, harry him, make him chase you north. Do not allow him to turn south, make him follow you north even if you have to escape into Scotland. Do you understand?'

'Yes, my lord,' Masham and Bolton both responded at the same time.

'The rest of us will ready our men to retreat the way we came. Once out of sight of the walls we turn south and drive on into the Midlands. With luck we will divide Tudor's forces,' Lincoln smiled as he said it. 'God be with us all, my lords.'

King Edward's army pulled back from the large fortified northern gate of York, leaving a force of just two hundred men still visible to the city's defenders. The defenders on the wall would think that the main part of the army was waiting just out of view behind the horizon. Meanwhile Lord Scrope of Masham sent out scouts so that he could keep track of Northumberland's approaching army and be forewarned hours before they arrived. He could then launch the attack on Bootham Bar before escaping northwards. With a little luck Northumberland would pursue them thinking they were the tail end of the rebel army.

Once out of sight of the city, Lincoln turned the army southwest, marching to Tadcaster, then westwards to Bramham to join the old Roman Great North Road, which would lead them south all the way to London, unless they encountered Henry Tudor first. Before they reached the village of Bramham just before dusk, a scout brought news to the Earl of Lincoln.

'A force of around four hundred men on horseback wearing the livery of Lord Clifford have been tailing us for some time now. They are holding their distance at about a mile behind our rearguard but they are definitely following us, my lord.'

Lincoln dismissed the scout then turned to Lovell.

'I think it is too dangerous to leave this force behind us, regardless of its size. They could harry us from the rear as we travel south or even bypass us and ride ahead to join up with Tudor to inform him of our numbers and whereabouts at any time,' he said.

'Agreed,' Lovell stated. 'I think it is time to see what these Irish kerns are made of. If you take the army south along the Great North Road, I will take half the kerns and lie in wait for Clifford's men. I'll catch up with you where you set up camp for the night.'

'That won't be too long as the light is already beginning to fade,' Lincoln stated.

He clasped Lovell on the shoulder.

'Be careful, Francis, I can't afford to lose you,' he said.

'You won't,' Lovell replied with a big grin on his face.

As darkness surrounded them, and Lincoln forged on southwards, Francis Lovell, Richard Plantagenet, and two thousand kerns lay silent on the moor just outside the village of Bramham. It was a clear, cloudless night and a myriad of stars twinkled above them. The jingle of harnesses, clatter of hooves, and the breathing of horses could be heard approaching as Clifford's men passed through Bramham, out onto the track that led across the moor, and on to join the Great North Road. The kerns lay motionless in the tall heather beside the track, while Richard's heart pounded with nervousness and trepidation. His new suit of armour seemed constricting as he lay on his side in the soft earth and heather. He only hoped that he would be able to get up in it when the time came, and he prayed that all the hours of sword practice in Mechelen would now pay off. His stomach tightened as the sound of horses was almost upon them, and he felt hot and uncomfortable in his armour; a reaction to his nerves rather than the temperature of the night air.

Everyone remained still and silent as the first horses reached them. It seemed an eternity to Richard as horse after horse walked by on the track just a few feet away. He wondered if Francis had fallen asleep while they waited, and if Clifford's knights would slip by them into the night, but looking across he could see that Francis was awake and sharp, poised to attack. Francis' timing was perfect. Lord Clifford and the lead knights had not yet reached the kerns positioned furthest from Bramham, but the baggage train at the rear of Clifford's convoy had passed the kerns lying in the heather nearest the village. Clifford and all of his men were trapped between two lines of kerns when Francis leapt up, sword in hand, and gave an almighty cry to start the attack. Francis swung his sword at a mounted knight, taking him clean off his horse with one stroke, as waves of kerns rushed out from the tall heather to swamp the unsuspecting convoy. Kerns threw their short feathered spears from slingshots, bringing down horses with devastating effect from short range while others, screaming and bellowing an unholy din, raced in to swarm around fallen riders to hack at them with axe and long knife.

Richard leapt out of the heather, surprising himself with his agility, and lunged at the nearest rider. The knight's horse reared up, its two front hooves, kicking out at him as it had been trained to do in such a situation. This prevented Richard from getting near the knight but a kern leapt through the air from the opposite side of the track, hitting the knight from the side so that the pair tumbled onto the track. Before the knight had time to move a dozen kerns were upon him, hacking at his armour and stamping on him until one pushed a long dagger through his visor and thrust it several times into the knight's eyes until he wriggled no more.

A man on foot came at Richard with a sword and Richard reacted without thinking, as his endless hours of training had taught him. He sidestepped the man's blow and then chopped upwards, slicing along the man's arm and into his torso at the armpit. The man collapsed in a welter of blood. Richard turned to see Francis slash and take down another knight, and then it was over. The slaughter ended as quickly as it had begun. Richard and Francis looked along the line of the convoy to see kerns looting the baggage train, but of the four hundred men and knights they had ambushed, nearly all were dead or wounded.

Lord Clifford and around twenty knights narrowly escaped the massacre. They fought through the kerns that surrounded them to flee along the track to the far end of Bramham Moor, where they now sat astride their horses looking back at the scene of carnage as kerns skipped, danced and taunted them. The kerns threw their darts and challenged the English lord to come back and face them but Clifford and his knights stayed well out of range before finally turning and fleeing north. King Edward's invading army had claimed first blood against the forces of Henry Tudor.

*

The news was mixed and confusing. King Henry rubbed his left temple as he mulled over the reports that had been brought to him over the past two days. He knew the rebel army had marched across the north of England from Furness in Lancashire, through the Lakes of the north, across the Pennines and Yorkshire moors on the poorest of roads, to reach York in only four days; a marvellous feat, Henry acknowledged to himself. From this point on the reports he received were conflicting. Most messengers had brought news that York had closed its gates and refused to admit the rebels, but one report said that York had supplied the rebels with men and arms before sending them on their way. There was another report suggesting that the rebels had mounted an attack on Bootham Bar, the most northerly of York's fortified gates, but the attack had been repelled. According to this report the Earl of Northumberland brought his army to York's rescue and chased off the rebel army which he was now pursuing northwards. The latest report said that the rebel army had routed a force of four hundred men under Lord Clifford near Tadcaster which would suggest that Northumberland wasn't chasing the rebels north.

'I don't know what to make of all this,' the exacerbated king said to Jasper Tudor. 'Which reports are correct and which are misleading? Has the rebel army been pushed further north by Northumberland or has it moved south and defeated Clifford near Tadcaster? Or maybe the rebel army has divided in two, but that would be a mistake to divide such a small army, surely?

'I think,' Jasper explained, 'that it is impossible to be sure at this stage what is happening. My advice would be to assume the worst, hope for the best, but prepare for all eventualities. I would suggest that you immediately send an expeditionary force ahead to ascertain the true position, but we also march north with the army to engage with the rebels. We have six thousand men ready and waiting at Coventry and Lords Stanley and Strange have another five or six thousand. You could send a message for them to join us, Your Grace.'

'That is wise counsel, Uncle. Send a messenger to Lord Scales to tell him to take his men and ride north to find out where the enemy is. They are only to engage if they can be sure of victory, otherwise they just observe and send regular reports to keep me updated. I will request Lords Stanley and Strange meet us at Nottingham. From there we can push our united forces north and trap the rebels between us and Northumberland's forces. I will say goodbye to my mother, the Queen and Prince Arthur. I'll leave the bishop of Winchester to attend the queen while I'm gone,' he added as an afterthought.

'Ready the army, Jasper, it is time to go,' the king commanded with gusto.

From Coventry the royal army marched to Leicester and then on to Loughborough. In order to speed up the progress of the army King Henry issued a proclamation, read out by the heralds, first in Leicester and then in Loughborough the following day, which stated that the soldiers must dispense with the usual rag tag of camp followers, prostitutes and vagabonds. This proclamation was to be strictly enforced by the heralds and sergeants with severe consequences for any soldier who failed to follow it.

From Loughborough the royal army pushed on to Nottingham where the king waited for father and son, Lord Stanley and Lord Strange, to bring their forces to join him.

*

King Edward's army marched rapidly from Tadcaster, south along the Great North Road, until they passed through Doncaster and on to the outskirts of the great forest of Sherwood. It was here that Lincoln's vanguard of English knights encountered their first real resistance, in the shape of Tudor's advanced cavalry led by Edward Woodville, Lord Scales. The initial clash was short but brutal, leaving three dead on either side, but Lincoln's force drove Scales' knights back into the forest. For three days Scales' knights harried the vanguard of King Edward's army but the Irish kerns proved adept at fighting in the forest. They hunted in packs, quickly moving through the densely packed trees, outmanoeuvring and then isolating small groups of knights who were sent by Scales to harry and hold up Lincoln's forward lines. The kerns laid in wait and jumped from trees onto the unsuspecting knights. When they attacked, they were savage and ruthless, quickly cutting the straps to get a knight's helmet off so they could slash his throat, or holding him down and ramming their long knives into his visor slit, through his eyes and deep into his brain. Their hit-and-run tactics were extremely effective but even so, the fighting was not all one way. Groups of knights were able to hunt down small groups of kerns, where their armour and better quality weapons told against their unarmoured opponents. For three days Scales held back Lincoln's advance until he escaped the forest and retreated with his remaining knights to the safety of Nottingham Castle.

Upon hearing the news that King Edward's army was pushing south towards Newark-on-Trent, and the confirmation that Lincoln and Lovell had already annihilated Lord Clifford's force, inflicted heavy casualties and pushed back Lord Scales' cavalry, and outwitted Northumberland leaving him stranded in the north too far away to help, King Henry decided to leave his army stationed outside Nottingham for the night while he retreated further south for safety. Bishop Morton also commended his small band of soldiers to the care of the king and retreated out of harm's way.

News of Lord Scales' retreat and tales of fearsome Irish kerns with their strange garb and haircuts, who fought like forest demons, spread like wildfire through King Henry's camp. The sergeants were powerless to do anything as they watched hundreds of men desert in the night, fleeing across open fields never to be seen again. The news that the king was a coward and had retreated south rather than camp with his own army for the night did not help their cause, and there were too few sergeants to patrol the whole perimeter of the camp to stop more men fleeing into the darkness.

King Henry returned to the camp the following morning to make his devotions and to instruct his commanders to wait while he went off to locate Lord Stanley's force, which had still not joined them as expected. Henry worried about having to face a strong enemy of around eight or nine thousand men with just six thousand troops of his own. He desperately needed the Stanleys to join him and wondered if, as they had in his previous battle with King Richard, they were holding back their forces to see which side would prevail before joining the battle. He could not afford for that to happen so he set off with a small force to protect him, in search of the missing Stanleys. The king's absence again fuelled rumours and led to more desertions from the royal camp as night fell.

The following morning six thousand well-armoured soldiers and knights, under the command of Lords Strange and Stanley, joined the royal host outside Nottingham. Cheers resounded from the royal camp as the reinforcements joined their ranks, swelling their force to double its original size. King Henry was also pleased to see the young Earl of Shrewsbury and the giant knight Sir John Cheyne arrive shortly after, with even more men. Even though a few more men deserted the camp that night, the king was now ready to take on the pretender's army. The arrival of Lord Strange and Stanley came just at the right time as, on the same morning,

King Henry received news that the rebel army had crossed the Trent at Newark. He had no choice but to try to engage the pretender's force, so he led his army away from Nottingham, along the southern side of the River Trent for just over three miles, to halt at a village called Radcliffe. That night the two kings, Henry and Edward, camped just 8 miles apart, surrounded by their armies. The following day only one would be called king.

ing Henry awoke before first light. He had slept restlessly knowing that this day would bring a reckoning for himself or the pretender. He dressed and sent for Bishop Foxe to perform mass, after which his squire readied him for battle, encasing him in plate armour and ensuring all the straps were tight and steadfast. Henry chose not to address his troops before battle but to allow his individual commanders, Bedford, Oxford, Strange, Derby, Scales, Shrewsbury and Viscount Lisle to talk to their men to rally them. Henry already knew that gold and silver were a better incentive than words, and the soldiers knew that not only would they be paid but there would also be booty to claim when the battle was over.

The previous night King Henry sent soldiers into Radcliffe to find local men who knew the area well. Now he used these five men to lead his army towards the enemy forces near Newark. They marched in three columns, the Earl of Oxford leading the vanguard, King Henry with Jasper Tudor at his side leading the main body, and Lord Strange leading the rearguard. Just before nine o'clock in the morning they came upon the rebel army in full battle array, perched upon a gently sloping hill overlooking the ancient Roman Fosse Road. It irked Henry greatly that the rebels flew the royal standard of quartered lions and fleur-de-lis above their position. He gritted his teeth as he glared at the massed ranks below the royal standard trying to spot the figure of the pretender among them.

The rebel army was arranged in one battalion, with the most highly trained and proficient of their soldiers, Martin Schwartz's Landsknechts, in the front ranks. The wild-looking Irish kerns were positioned behind them, with the English knights joining the infantry on foot on the two flanks. The faux king, Edward, remained at the rear of the army, while Lord Lincoln took command. Behind the pretender's army was a steep slope leading down to the River Trent. It was a strong defensive position and the Earl of Lincoln had done well to scout it and have his army ready before the arrival of his own forces, Henry thought.

The Earl of Oxford, commanding King Henry's army, arrived at the base of the hill first with the vanguard and began to arrange them at the bottom of the slope parallel to Lincoln's force at the top of the hill around a third of a mile away. King Henry with Jasper Tudor and Lord Strange, were to bring the main battle and rearguard in behind to support Oxford's troops as needed during the battle, rather than deploying them in the more traditional method, of wings either side of Oxford's vanguard.

Lincoln stared down the hill at the army beginning to assemble below him. Francis Lovell and Martin Schwartz stood as able deputies and advisors beside him, and Richard stood with them. He was wearing the armour his aunt, the Dowager Duchess of Burgundy, had given him, which was a little worse for wear since the skirmish at Bramham Moor. Richard twiddled nervously with his father's Hopper ring that he had decided to place upon his finger rather than keep on a cord about his neck. He stopped fiddling with his ring and his hand unconsciously dropped to his sword hilt when he saw, in the far distance on the river plain, the figure of Henry Tudor escorted by a body of Yeoman of the Guard, beneath his royal standard, with the unmistakable banner of the red dragon on a green and white background fluttering beside it. The sight rekindled the hatred and anger that he had felt after the deaths of his father, Catesby and the Skelton brothers. Richard was no longer fearful; he was vengeful, and he wished for the battle to commence as soon as possible.

Lincoln had the look of a hawk staring down at a meadow from upon high, just waiting to swoop down on an unsuspecting mouse or vole.

'We could charge down there now and crush Oxford's vanguard before they've had a chance to deploy properly and before Tudor can reinforce them,' Lincoln suggested.

'I think it would be a bad idea to give up our position on this hill. We are strong here. They outnumber us so we shouldn't let them fight us on the plain where their numbers will tell. Keep our position, John, and make them fight uphill,' Francis argued logically.

'I can see your point but one decisive crushing blow now could end it quickly,' Lincoln said, still entertaining the idea of charging down the hill.

'What do you think?' Lincoln said, turning to Martin Schwartz.

'Yah, I agree, a quick decisive blow while zey are not ready,' he replied in his thick German accent.

'What if we do deal Oxford's vanguard a crushing blow? Tudor can still escape. What then? Do we have to do this all over again?' Francis asked.

Lincoln continued to watch Oxford's men arrive along the

narrow track and be directed into position behind the front rank below him.

'If Tudor flees then we march on to London. He then becomes the outcast and Warwick the king,' Lincoln stated matter-of-factly.

'Warwick is already the king!' Francis exclaimed.

'You know what I mean,' Lincoln replied, not wanting to state out loud the deception that Francis was touching upon.

'I have asked your counsel and Martin agrees; we must be decisive. Sound the horn. We are going to attack.'

'You plan to use the same tactic that failed King Richard?' Francis asked tersely.

Lincoln ignored that stinging barb and ordered the horn to be blown to sound the attack.

With one long note King Edward's army surged down the slope towards Oxford's vanguard that was still only five or six ranks deep. King Henry and his main battle were still over half a mile away and his rearguard even further.

Schwartz's Landsknechts were superbly organised and moved down the hill quickly. They kept their formation as they moved; pikemen in a line, four men deep, with arquebusiers spread between them armed with hand-cannon, and the men armed with halberds and zweihander: large two-handed swords that they carried down the hill resting on their shoulders as they ran behind the lines of pikemen. And behind them all a surging mass of frenzied Irish kerns bursting to be unleashed on the enemy.

The arquebusiers sprinted ahead of the pikemen, and then suddenly halted and aimed their hackenbüchse at the ranks of terrified men at the bottom of the slope. Some planted a metal fork into the soil to rest their gun on, others rested the stock of the hackenbüchse against their thigh or shoulder. As matchlocks ignited gunpowder, the weapons erupted in a cloud of white smoke, and a hail of lead shot tore into Oxford's front ranks. Men fell as the shot hit them, some dead on the ground, others writhing and screaming in pain. Others around them shouted in panic and a few turned and tried to flee into the ranks behind them but were pushed forward by more experienced soldiers who tried to steady the ranks before them to prevent a rout.

The arquebusiers, having discharged their shot, would take several minutes to reload their hackenbüchse again so they sank back into the ranks of pikemen and then dropped behind as the men with halberds and zweihander also ran past. With extraordinary skill and effort, as they reached the bottom of the hill, the pikemen lowered their eighteen-foot-long pikes in one coordinated movement and slammed into Oxford's already shaken vanguard. The pikes impaled scores of men and the impact of them as a whole knocked the vanguard backwards, so that even the most resolute veteran couldn't maintain his position against the bristling hedge of pikes that pushed forwards into their terrified ranks.

Oxford was quick to react. As he saw the first signs of movement down the hill, he ordered his archers quickly forward to fire volleys of arrows over the heads of his vanguard, whilst also urging his foot soldiers forward to shore up his partially formed vanguard. The steady flow of soldiers added extra ranks at the rear, preventing the total disintegration of the vanguard as Schwartz's pikes struck.

Arrows sailed over the heads of Oxford's vanguard and Schwartz's Landsknechts to fall on the mass of Irish kerns behind them. The unarmoured kerns fell in great numbers as volley after volley of arrows rained down upon them. They crouched behind small wooden shields that barely covered their heads and left the rest of their body exposed. Their flax-stuffed linen and hard leather jacks provided no protection against the iron-tipped wooden shafts that rained death, decimating their ranks.

Lincoln, Francis and Richard, along with other English knights and infantry, charged down the hill on foot, arriving at Oxford's faltering vanguard just behind the lethal rows of Schwartz's pikes. Arrows clattered like hailstones off plated armour, occasionally finding their mark and felling a knight or mailed soldier. Despite their exhilarated whoops of joy as they charged on foot and saw the ranks in front of them smash and destroy the front rank of Oxford's vanguard, the English did not get to join in with the action immediately as the pikemen continued to push forward. The first row held off Oxford's soldiers while the second and third rows stabbed their pikes into the faces, chests and legs of the men who opposed them. At first the eighteen-foot-long pikes caused terrible carnage among Oxford's terrified ranks, but eventually the Landsknechts began to tire from the exertion of holding their massive pikes.

The arrow storm ended as the two armies became compressed in hand-to-hand fighting. Men slipped on the blood, entrails and contents of spilt bowels that lay slick on the flat grassland at the foot of the slope, and proved easy prey once on the ground. Gaps opened up between the rows of tired pikemen, and Oxford's battle-hardened soldiers began to hack their way through and past the pikes. Eventually, as the pikemen retreated back through their own ranks to recover, and other foot soldiers stepped forward to take their place, the battle opened up into a melee at the foot of the hill with every man for himself.

As one pikeman in front of him was hacked down and several

others retreated past him, Richard found himself at the forefront of the battle, with Francis on his left and Sir Thomas Broughton on his right. Richard was faced by the mailed soldier who had already killed the pikeman that lay between them. The growling soldier stepped over the dead body and came at Richard with a sword, lunging forward at his throat. It was simple to parry the blow with his shield and chop down on the soldier's extended arm. The man screamed in pain as his bones shattered but the mail he was wearing prevented Richard's sword from taking the arm clean off. Richard smashed his shield into the man's face as he lurched forward screaming in pain, then finished him off with a blow to the head.

As the dead man slumped to the ground another soldier stepped into his place ready to take Richard on with shield and mace. Richard stepped forward, chopping his sword down but the soldier deftly raised his shield, deflecting the blow sideways while at the same time swinging his mace down towards Richard's head. Richard regained his balance and quickly raised his shield to deflect the incoming blow. The two men squared off again and continued to trade blow for blow as they sought to defeat each other. Richard's arm muscles ached and his lungs burned with the exertion. He needed to rest but his foe kept battering him and wouldn't give him time to. Richard had to defend himself and retaliate, hoping to wear the man down before he battered him into the ground. It seemed to Richard that he would trade blows until he was too exhausted to fight any longer and then he would die. It was as simple as that. He would be battered into submission and die at the foot of a hill just outside of Newark. He screamed with the exertion as he swung his sword at the soldier once more, determined that he would not die; and then out of nowhere a kern darted between them, below the level of their shields, and stabbed a fletched throwing dart into a chink in the mail at the back of the soldier's knee. The soldier let out an angry yell and crumpled, going down on one knee. Sir Thomas Broughton stepped in and ran the man through with his sword, then dragged Richard back letting other knights and soldiers take their place.

'Take a breather, son,' Broughton advised him through his raised visor. 'It's going to be a long hard fight so conserve your energy,' the veteran explained. 'When you start to ache or get tired take a step back and a man in the next rank will take your place. If you go all out you will tire and make yourself an easy target.'

'Thank you,' Richard said, red faced and gasping for breath as Francis joined them.

Francis raised his visor, leaned on his sword and breathed deeply. Two huge dents in his breastplate showed that he had been in the thick of the fighting.

'I told Lincoln this was a bad idea,' he gasped.

He surveyed the battlefield. After the damage caused by the initial charge, Oxford had managed to reinforce his vanguard. Although Tudor's main battle and rearguard held back they were regularly sending more troops forward to strengthen the vanguard as soldiers died or were wounded. It was a battle of attrition and whichever side held out the longest would win.

Schwartz's Landsknechts fought valiantly. His rested pikemen returned to the fray, this time with swords, to support the halberdiers who fought toe to toe with Oxford's soldiers. The Landsknecht with double-handed zweihander caused havoc amongst the enemy as they stepped in slashing through formations of halberds or into the massed ranks of soldiers to create an opening for fellow warriors to step into and exploit. The Irish kern were also causing losses amongst the enemy as they skipped and jumped, as nimble as dancers, slashing and stabbing their darts and long knives into open visors or gaps in armour, before retreating to safety behind the Landsknechts and English knights. But no matter how many of Oxford's vanguard they killed, Tudor had more to send forward to replace them.

Richard, Francis and Broughton stepped back into the fray and fought together, often retreating to catch their breath and rest weary limbs. Eventually the attritional nature of the battle took its toll. The Landsknechts were organised, fearless and impossible to break and the Irish kerns fought like madmen, killing far in excess of their own numbers; but eventually the kerns succumbed to Oxford's soldiers because of their lack of armour. An army that had started off as eight thousand strong was gradually whittled down over three hours until only around two thousand remained. Weight of numbers told and eventually Lincoln's forces began to waver as Oxford's soldiers exploited large holes to get in behind Lincoln's front ranks. Lincoln and his commanders continued to send men forward but as unarmoured kerns were cut down and fewer and fewer knights and Landsknechts were available, Francis could see that the end was inevitable. As the rebel ranks began to break and men began to flee, Richard knew his hopes and dreams went with them. He felt sickened as he realised the battle was lost. Then the rout began.

'Get back up the hill to the horses before they reach us,' Francis shouted as Oxford's soldiers swarmed through the broken front ranks and surrounded the small groups of English knights and German Landsknechts that fought on. Others surged forwards chasing the retreating soldiers up the hill. The remaining English foot soldiers, Landsknechts and kerns broke and ran in the direction from which they had come to the battlefield. King Henry, seeing the rebel line break ordered forward his cavalry to charge them down.

The English knights fleeing in terror discarded helmets, gauntlets and any other pieces of armour they could remove to lighten themselves and make it easier to ascend the slope to get to the top of the hill. Many were cut down from behind by the pursuing soldiers as they fled. One of Oxford's soldiers lunged and caught Lincoln in the heel with a halberd as he climbed the slope. Lincoln stumbled then got to his feet, but it was too late as his pursuers, the smell of blood and victory in their nostrils, stabbed and hacked until Lincoln was dead. Richard glanced back at his cousin, only to see Oxford's men swarming like ants around a dead insect, stripping the body bare as they plundered Lincoln of his high-quality armour. The sight of Lincoln and other English knights being caught and slaughtered spurred Richard on up the hill.

Breathless knights reached the summit and immediately mounted their horses. Their squires had fled as soon as they realised the battle was lost, but remarkably the boy king, Edward, and the priest, still sat on the grass at the summit of the hill as though they were oblivious to what was happening.

'Run for your lives, you fools!' Francis shouted at them as he mounted a horse and turned to gallop down the slope away from Oxford's men.

The priest just looked at him implacably and replied, 'God will see us safe, my lord.'

Francis did not have time to argue as Oxford's soldiers reached the summit and began to slaughter any knight who could not find and mount a horse quick enough to escape. Sir Thomas Broughton was caught with a sword blow to the back of his head as he prepared to mount a horse. His scalp and back of his skull were sliced clean off revealing the white matter of his brain as he slumped to the ground dead. A few knights, unable to find a horse but quick enough to escape their pursuers, jumped and tumbled uncontrollably down the steep-sided ridge at the rear of the hill, until they splashed into the depths of the River Trent below and drowned under the weight of their armour. Francis, along with Richard and a few dozen knights, managed to flee the slaughter on horseback down the slope, back towards the town of Newark.

Relief at their escape did not last long as they became caught up with the great exodus of men fleeing the battlefield. As their horses were slowed by the sheer volume of fleeing men and they were bumped and buffeted in the panicked melee, Richard realised that he had become separated from Francis. He halted and turned back to look for his friend only to see a Yorkist knight, unhelmeted and bleeding from a slit throat, hurtling towards him. Richard did not have time to react before the horse careered into him, knocking his own horse sideways so that he lost his balance and fell backwards to the ground to lie winded on his back. The dead Yorkist knight was thrown from the saddle and landed forcefully on top of Richard, squeezing the breath out of the former king's son with his sheer bulk and the weight of his armour.

Of the men escaping the battlefield, some chose to flee down a small ravine that led towards the river, but Lord Scales cavalry soon caught up with them and they were mercilessly butchered in that enclosed space. Scores tried to escape across the river near the foot of the hill but most of those drowned and were swept away by the current. The majority, whether on horse or foot, fled across the open plain towards the village of East Stoke, hoping to escape over the Trent at the shallow ford at Fiskerton or beyond to cross the river over the bridge at Newark. Most failed in their endeavour, being hunted down by horsemen and slaughtered in their hundreds.

After the battle King Henry ordered mass burial pits to be dug where most of the rebels had fallen on the plain outside East Stoke. He was disappointed to hear news that Earl Lincoln and the other rebel leaders had fallen fighting as he had hoped to gain some knowledge of how the rebellion had begun and who the conspirators were, besides those dead on the battlefield. The king, secure in his victory, issued a proclamation. All rebels were to be hunted down. Any English or Irish rebels found were to be hung, any German mercenaries were to be stripped of their money and possessions and sent on their way. Henry knew that most of these would die of starvation, lost in a foreign land with no way to get home but he had no compassion left for men who had tried to kill him and deprive him of his crown.

Jasper Tudor and the Earl of Oxford escorted the king across the battlefield where he was shown the bodies of Martin Schwartz, Thomas Fitzgerald – brother of Gerald, Earl Kildare, Sir Thomas Broughton, and John de la Pole – Earl of Lincoln and once heir to King Richard. King Henry allowed himself a brief smile. At the summit of the hill where the rebel banner had stood the king came face to face with the pretender.

The blond-haired boy smiled sweetly and bowed before King Henry.

He spoke with surprising calm and dignity. 'I am truly sorry for the trouble my likeness to the Earl of Warwick has caused, Your Grace.'

Henry wanted to hate the boy but found that he could not.

'What is your name?' he asked.

'My name is John, Your Grace,' the boy answered.

'A good English name, but not one that will go down in history. Can you turn a spit, boy?' the king asked him.

'Yes, Your Grace,' the boy replied.

'Then you shall work in my kitchens and be pleased that I have chosen to spare your life.'

The king looked at Richard Symonds standing beside the boy and then turned to his uncle.

'Take this priest and question him. I want to know all there is to know of this rebellion,' the king instructed Jasper Tudor.

Across the River Trent near Fiskerton, a lone rider, with battered and dented armour, sat astride his horse and watched as Tudor's men plundered the battlefield, stripping the dead of armour, collecting purses, jewellery, and any weapons of quality. He snorted in derision, turning and riding off before Tudor's horsemen, scouring the area for rebels, would find him.

Jenkin Burne was only a lowly foot soldier but like so many others that day he would earn a good living scavenging the battlefield and selling off good pieces of armour and weapons, or if he was really lucky, finding a purse of gold on a wealthy knight. His eyes widened with glee when he saw two dead knights slumped one on top of the other in the middle of a mass of common foot soldiers. He bounded across desperate to reach the bounty before anyone else saw it. He grinned and cackled to himself, a sound of pure delight, as he saw the richness and quality of the two suits of armour. They were dented but that was to be expected on the battlefield. It was nothing that a good smith couldn't hammer out. He unbuckled the straps on the first knight's armour, removing it piece by piece, and placing it in a pile on a blanket he had brought for the purpose. Helmet, gauntlets, breastplates, grieves and other valuable items were stripped away, and as a bonus the knight had a silver ring and a purse containing thirteen silver coins.

When Jenkin had finished, he rolled the body away and surveyed the second knight. A ring of bright, shining yellow gold set with a large ruby caught his eye. What a find! He wanted to shout with joy. That ring alone would make him a rich man. He could finally ditch that miserable wife of his and find himself a lady and a servant. He giggled to himself with sheer glee, then suddenly jumped up and withdrew his dagger as he heard others approaching behind him.

'Piss off, I found him,' he yelled as he spun around.

'I'm sorry, sire,' he immediately apologised as he recognised the dark-eyed man with greying hair at his temples as Sir Reginald Bray.

'Good pickings?' Bray asked him.

'Not too bad. Some armour and a few coins,' Jenkin said nervously, trying to play down the wonderful finds he'd discovered.

Bray stared down at the high-quality armour on the blanket and smiled to himself as he realised that the scavenger was worried he might take some of his bounty.

'Have a good day, soldier,' Bray said, turning his back on the man and walking away.

A groan from one of the bodies startled them both and Bray turned back as Jenkin leaned in to slash the man's throat. The knight raised a hand in a futile attempt to save his life, and it was then that Bray caught sight of the Hopper ring.

'Wait!' Bray shouted, rushing across to the knight who now

had Jenkin's knife poised against his throat, ready to slice.

'Wait,' Bray repeated as he stepped closer to look down on the knight.

He didn't recognise the man who was only about eighteen years old but he knew that he was a member of the Hopper fellowship.

'You may have the armour and whatever else you have already taken from the others but this man is my prisoner.'

'Err, what about the ring, sire? I'd already espied it before he awoke,' Jenkin said in expectation.

'The knight keeps it,' Bray said resolutely.

A look of deep disappointment crept across Jenkin's face as he bundled up the bounty in his blanket. He knew there was no point in arguing, so instead he huffed and tutted as he dragged it away across the bloody battlefield in search of more plunder.

Bray extended a hand to help the knight to his feet. Richard initially struggled as he'd been crushed beneath the weight of the dead knight. His ribcage and back throbbed and his legs were tingling with a sensation of stabbing and prickling as the blood rushed back into them to replace the numbness. He was in pain but at least he was alive.

He stood shakily and took a deep breath, clutching at his aching chest as he was finally able to suck in a lungful of air.

'Thank you,' he wheezed to the man who had just saved his life.

The man extended a hand of friendship and Richard noticed that he too wore a Hopper ring, identical to his own.

'Sir Reginald Bray, Knight of the Garter, doctor, architect, and financial minister to the king, at your service,' Bray introduced himself grandly, omitting to mention that he was also the king's spymaster.

'And you are?'

'Richard… Eastwell,' Richard replied after a momentary pause. He tentatively shook Bray's outstretched hand.

'Well Richard Eastwell,' Bray said, 'it seems that we have much to talk about.'

'Am I your prisoner? I have no wealth or family left if you intend to ransom me,' Richard stated bluntly.

'No, you are not a prisoner, you are a fellow knight.' Bray extended his hand to show Richard his own Hopper ring.

Richard glanced at it then smiled. Thank God, he was safe! He knew that he could soon flee to safety, maybe back to Eastwell, or his Aunt Elizabeth or even to his Aunt Margaret in Mechelen or… Then the realisation suddenly dawned upon him; he could not return to Eastwell and his previous life or flee abroad because he knew that those responsible for his father's death must pay, and now the most perfect opportunity had just presented itself to him.

He would listen to what Bray had to say. The man was the king's financial minister after all. Richard realised that could use this as an opportunity to get close to the heart of the Tudor regime. He would befriend Bray and in time wheedle his way into a position where he could maybe even get close to Henry Tudor himself. As the idea began to fully form in his mind, he looked Bray straight in the eye and smiled.

'Yes, Sir Reginald, it does indeed seem that we have much to talk about.'

The king's spymaster smiled kindly back at Richard, already having decided how this young knight could be of use to him.

*

It is strange to think, as I stare at the simple headstone beneath a yew tree in St. Mary's Church, that Richard of Eastwell was the son of King Richard. Yet it is true that he and I are of royal Plantagenet descent. But these are dangerous times, and it would be imprudent of me to speak of this other than in these pages. Was I foolish to have my father's true name recorded in the parish record and to trust that a gold coin would silence the priest? Maybe, but only time will tell.

I do know that my father never used his royal name to gain him favour or fortune in life. He did, however, use the Hopper ring that my grandfather had given to him. It enabled him to open new doors, to seek out, and to gain vengeance upon those men who had betrayed King Richard. The Hopper ring and the chance meeting with Sir Reginald Bray also opened up a whole new world of opportunity and courtly intrigue that my father revelled in. But that is a whole new tale, and one that I shall recount on future pages.

Historical Notes

There is a 1598 transcript of an original record in the parish register of St Mary's Church, Eastwell, Kent that states:

'Rychard Plantagenet was buryed on the 22 daye of December, anno ut supra. Ex registro de Eastwell, sub anno 1550.'

There has been much debate about who this Richard Plantagenet, buried in 1550 at Eastwell, was. A story first appeared in print in *Desiderata Curiosa Vol II* edited by Francis Peck in 1735, which suggested that Richard of Eastwell was the child of Richard III. It tells of an old bricklayer working in Eastwell for Sir Thomas Moyle who, when caught reading a book in Latin by his employer, confessed that he was taken as a child to meet Richard III the night before the Battle of Bosworth, and that the king told him that he was his father. Whatever the truth of the matter, it makes for a fascinating story. I have told Richard Plantagenet's story, weaving it into the actual events of 1485 to 1487.

William Catesby was executed in Leicester three days after the Battle of Bosworth. However, he was hanged not beheaded as I have it. His last words were not recorded but his will, written on the day of his execution, includes the line: 'My lords Stanley, Strange, and all that blood, help and pray for my soul, for ye have not for my body as I trusted in you.' I have used this as the basis for Catesby's last words before he was executed.

There is a myth that an old woman, or witch, or a blind man depending upon which version of the story is told, made a prophesy that where King Richard's spur struck Bow Bridge on the way out of Leicester, his head would strike on the way back. After the battle King Richard's corpse was slung over a horse which carried it back into Leicester and reputedly the horse was startled or strayed too close to the parapet and the dead king's head did indeed hit the same spot that his spur had struck on the way to battle. Bow Bridge still stands today although the medieval bridge has long been replaced by a more modern version. Another prophecy about King Richard that I grew up hearing was that he was forewarned that 'the moon would change twice on the day of the battle.' The significance is that as well as the normal passage of the moon in the night sky, Sir William Stanley, whose armorial device contains a crescent moon, changed sides in the battle and led the final charge which defeated King Richard at what is now known as the Battle of Bosworth.

My character William Herricke is fictitious but there was a Herrick family of goldsmiths recorded in London in the sixteenth century. William Herrick or Heyrick was sent to London in 1574 to be apprenticed to his elder brother Nicholas Herrick, a goldsmith in Cheapside. William later became principal jeweller to King James I in 1603, was knighted in 1605 and elected M.P. for Leicester on several occasions between 1601 and 1622.

The Yeoman of the Guard was first instituted in October 1485 as fifty archers to protect Henry VII at his coronation. This body of guards accompanied the king on his royal progress to the north in the spring of 1486. The city of York was never at risk of being besieged during the Lovell-Stafford rebellion of 1486. King Henry may have left London at the start of the royal progress with a small body of guards and around a thousand poorly armed retainers but that number swelled as many nobles, knights and landowners flocked to the king's side as they heard that he was in danger, before he even reached York. The Yorkshire rebellion crumbled in the face of the king's growing numbers, precipitated by his heralds having offered a pardon to all those who laid down their arms. However, I have set this scene with the king based at a panic stricken and rapidly emptying city of York to convey the sense of panic and fear that this rebellion would have initially caused. As the Tudor historian Polydore Vergil wrote: the king 'was struck with great fear' upon hearing of the rebellion.

John Alcock was Bishop of Worcester from 15 July 1476 until he was appointed bishop of Ely on 6 October 1486. He twice held the office of Lord Chancellor, once from June 1475 to September 1475, under Edward IV, and then again from October 1485 to March 1487 under Henry VII. He was one of several clerics who openly proposed that Henry Tudor should marry Elizabeth of York. Interestingly, he was also tutor to Richard III's nephew, Prince Edward, later Edward V, but continued to work closely with Richard III, after Edward V was declared illegitimate, even participating as a member of the English delegation that met the Scots at Nottingham Castle with King Richard. This suggests that either he did not believe that King Richard had ordered his nephew's murder or that he had no qualms about working alongside a murderer. I have deliberately left the fate of the 'Princes in the Tower' unanswered as that debate is not for this book.

The Garter feast at York is based on a description by the French historian Legrand d'Aussy, of a feast given in 1455 by the Count of Anjou. The main ingredient for marchepane (a medieval form of marzipan) was sugar. Legend has it that Alexander the Great first brought sugar cane back to Greece after his military exploits in India. However, it is generally accepted that sugar arrived in

Europe around 1100. It was a commodity that only the very wealthy could afford. In the Medieval period, Venice was the main importer and exporter of sugar in Europe. It arrived as raw cane sugar, imported from India, and was refined in Venice before being exported to the rest of Europe as a crystallised rock. A piece of this would have been chopped off and ground into a powder before being used as a sweetener for food and drink or as a medicine. Elizabeth I is notorious for her black teeth caused by brushing them with sugar!

While at Nottingham Castle on 3rd May 1486 Henry VII appointed the Duke of Bedford and the Earls of Oxford, Derby and Lincoln to 'enquire into treasons, felonies and conspiracies in Warwickshire and Worcestershire.' However, I have Jasper Tudor, Duke of Bedford, hunting down Francis Lovell in Yorkshire and Lancashire at this time.

I have condensed some of the events of February and March 1487 to help the narrative of the story to flow. Henry VII and his Privy Council did decide, at Sheen on 2nd February, upon the proclamation of a general pardon, the exhibition of the Earl of Warwick, and the forfeiture of Elizabeth Woodville's property in favour of Henry's wife, along with her banishment to the convent at Bermondsey. They also discussed the boy (later known as Lambert Simnel) who had gone to Ireland and was supported by the Irish lords as the Earl of Warwick. Also, Lincoln did sit through the meeting knowing that his role in the conspiracies against Henry was about to be exposed. However, the threat of risings in Devon and Cornwall, Bishop Stillington fleeing to Oxford, and Lincoln's men disguised as merchants, who were seen by Henry's spies with bags of gold and silver trying to garner support from men in the north of England, didn't happen until the following month. Lincoln left Sheen on 9th March 1487, ostensibly to visit his estates in East Anglia, but two days later he boarded a ship to Flanders to flee to his Aunt Margaret's court and join Francis Lovell in exile.

There is still debate about the identity of the boy pretender whose name comes down to us through history as Lambert Simnel. However, King Henry's herald-recorder initially wrote that his *'name was in dede John'*.

Francis Viscount Lovell's body was never found on the battlefield and his whereabouts after the Battle of Stoke remain unknown. However, on 19th June 1488, a year after the battle, James IV of Scotland issued safe conduct to him. There is no evidence to suggest that he was alive to accept it.

The fellowship of the Hopper ring is fictitious but if you look at the famous portrait of Richard III given to the National Portrait Gallery by James Thomson Gibson-Craig in 1862 you will see that the gold and ruby ring worn by the king on his right thumb does have an image within the ruby that appears to be a white face. A gold loyalty ring mounted with a black diamond, dating to the fourteenth century was discovered in 2002 on farmland at Manley Old Hall on the edge of Cheshire's Delamere Forest, which was a favourite royal hunting ground of Edward III. The ring was inscribed with the letter E three times, each one followed by a star. This and the ring in Richard III's portrait were the inspiration for the Hopper ring in my story.

Richard Plantagenet's story, and that of the fellowship of the Hopper ring, is to be continued.

Darren Harris, 2021

About The Author

Darren Harris lives with his partner Lisa and their children, in Leicester, where he grew up. He qualified as a History teacher in 2001, teaching at several city and county schools before becoming Head of History at a special needs school for eleven years. While Head of History he created a school museum so that students could learn about the past through handling historical artefacts and hearing the stories he told about these. He has a lifelong interest in history, researching many friends' family trees, and has researched his own family tree back to the fifteenth century. He is a founding member of his local heritage society and gives talks on matters of historical interests to local heritage and historical societies.

Printed in Great Britain
by Amazon

71249761R00210